Payback's a Witch

Payback's a Witch

LANA HARPER

JOVE
NEW YORK

A JOVE BOOK
Published by Berkley
An imprint of Penguin Random House LLC
penguinrandomhouse.com

Library of Congress Cataloging-in-Publication Data

Names: Harper, Lana, author.
Title: Payback's a witch / Lana Harper.
Description: First edition. | New York : Jove, 2021.
Identifiers: LCCN 2021016312 (print) | LCCN 2021016313 (ebook) |
ISBN 9780593336069 (trade paperback) | ISBN 9780593336076 (ebook)
Subjects: GSAFD: Love stories.
Classification: LCC PS3608.A7737 P39 2021 (print) |
LCC PS3608.A7737 (ebook) | DDC 813/.6—dc23
LC record available at https://lccn.loc.gov/2021016312
LC ebook record available at https://lccn.loc.gov/2021016313

First Edition: October 2021

Printed in the United States of America
1st Printing

Interior art: Starry frame © Tanya Antusenok / Shutterstock
Book design by Alison Cnockaert

For my mother, who took care of my baby so I could chase a dream.

1

The Prodigal Witch

AS SOON AS I crossed the town line, I could feel Thistle Grove on my skin.

That I was in my shitty beater Toyota made no difference; maybe the town could sense one of its daughters coming home, even after almost five years away. A swell of raw magic coursed into the car, until the air around me nearly shimmered with potential, bright and buzzy and headier than a champagne cocktail. As if Thistle Grove's own magical heart was pulsing eagerly toward me, welcoming me back. No hard feelings about my long absence, apparently.

Made one of us, I guess.

The onslaught of magic after my dry spell was so intoxicating that I hunched over the steering wheel, taking shallow breaths and wondering a little wildly whether you could overdose on magic after having gone cold turkey for so long. From the passenger seat,

Jasper cast me a glinting, concerned glance from beneath his silvery fringe and shoved a clumsy paw onto my thigh.

"I'm okay, bud," I murmured to him through a thick throat, reaching over to stroke his warm neck. "It's just . . . a whole lot, you know?"

That was the thing about growing up with magic. Until you left it behind for good, you had no idea how incredible it felt just to be around it.

And it wasn't only the air that seemed different. Through my spattered windshield, the night sky had changed, snapping into über-focus like a calibrated telescope. Above Hallows Hill, the unlikely little mountain the town huddled up against, a crescent moon hung like a freshly whetted sickle. *Waning crescent*, my witch brain whispered, already churning up the spells best cast in this phase. Its silhouette looked like it could carve glass, impossibly perfect and precise, the kind of moon you'd see in a dream. The constellations that surrounded it like a milky spill of jewels were arranged the same as on the other side of the town line but better somehow, more intentional, clear-cut and brilliant as a mosaic set with precious gems. So enticing, they made me want to pull the car over and tumble out, head hinged back and jaw agape, just to watch them glitter.

This fucking town. Always so damn extra.

With an effort, I resisted the temptation. But when the orchards that belonged to the Thorns appeared on my left, I gave in just enough to roll down my window.

The night air gusted against my face, smelling like an absolute of fall; woodsmoke and dying leaves and the faintest bracing hint of future snow. And right below that was the scent of Thistle Grove magic, which I've never come across anywhere else. Spicy and earthy, as if the lingering ghost of all the incense burned by three hundred years of witches had never quite blown away. A perpetual Halloween smell, the kind that gave you the good-creepy sort of tingles.

And fallen apples, of course. The Thorns' rows and rows of Galas, Honeycrisps, and Pink Ladies, sweet and cidery and indescribably like home.

It all made the part of me that used to adore this place—*oh, cut the shit, Emmy, the part of you that* still *does, the part that will never, ever stop*—throb like first-love heartache. My eyes welled hot with sudden tears, and I knuckled them clear more violently than necessary, angry with myself for sinking into nostalgia so readily.

Sensing my mood plummeting, Jasper gave an aggrieved snort, tossing his regally mustachioed snout at me.

"I know, I know," I groaned, dragging a hand over my face. "I promised not to get too in my feelings. I'm just tired, bud. From now on, it'll be all business till we can get out of here."

He huffed again, as if he knew me much too well to buy into my stoic crap. I might be back here only because Tradition Demands the Presence of the Harlow Scion, but nothing in Thistle Grove was ever that simple. Especially when it came to the heir of one of the founding families.

Ten minutes later, I pulled into my parents' oak-lined residential neighborhood, rattling onto their cobbled driveway. My chest clenched at the sight of my childhood home, fisting tight around my heart. It was a perfectly nice house, though not all that impressive as founding family demesnes go. The Blackmoores had their palatial Tintagel estate, the Thorns had Honeycake Orchards, and the Avramovs the rambling Victorian warren of a mansion they insisted on calling The Bitters, because they thrived on such old-world melodrama.

And we, the Harlows, had . . . lo, a house.

A stately three-story colonial almost as old as the town itself—though you wouldn't know it, to look at its magically weather-proofed exterior—Harlow House has never had a fancy name, thereby upholding the timeless Harlow legacy of being both the least pretentious and least relevant of the founding families. As always, a candle burned in every window; thirteen flames, for prosperity and protection. The flying owl weather vane spun idly in the night breeze, and the dreamcatcher windchimes hung by the front door clinked delicately against one another. A plume of smoke coiled from the brick chimney in a curlicued wisp before vanishing into the velvety dark above.

It looked like a storybook house belonging to your favorite no-nonsense witch—which, come to think of it, sounded like both my parents.

And it was all like I remembered, except that the thought of going inside made me feel painfully stripped of breath. There was an invisible moat of hurt surrounding my former home, years of unanswered questions. Restless water, teeming with the emotional equivalents of piranha and stinging jellyfish.

I couldn't do much about the hurt, and "because Gareth Black-moore ruined this town for me" still seemed like a shitty answer to the question all the others boiled down to, which was: *Emmy, why haven't you come home all this time?*

So I turned the car off and just sat with my head bowed, listening to the ticks of the engine settling and Jasper's low-grade whine, focusing on my breath. When I'd collected myself about as much as I was going to, I lurched out of the car on travel-stiff legs and let Jas out to baptize the quiet street, then hauled my battle-scarred suitcase and gigantic duffel bag out of the trunk. By the time he came loping back, I'd managed to wrestle everything up onto the columned porch with an admirable minimum of cursing.

I still had my key, but it seemed horribly rude and presumptuous to use it after a five-year absence, so I knocked instead. When the door swung open, I managed to flinch only a little, blinking at the warm light spilling from within.

"My darling," my mother said simply, stepping out to greet me. Her voice was characteristically composed, all British stiff upper lip, but her green eyes—my eyes—were suspiciously shiny. Glossed with the same stifled emotion that burst at my own seams.

"Mom," I half whispered, a lump rising in my throat.

It wasn't like we hadn't laid eyes on each other in five years, because this *was* the twenty-first century. Even a magical haven like Thistle Grove got decent reception and Wi-Fi most of the time, barring the odd magical tantrum disrupting coverage. But seeing her face on a screen wasn't the same, not even close. When I leaned forward to wrap her in a hug, it took all I had not to whimper at her familiar smell, lemon and wildflowers. Though we were nearly the same height, the years between twenty-six and six abruptly melted away. For just a moment, I was small again, and she was the mummy I used to call for in the night after a bad dream, who soothed me with her gentle hands and infinite catalog of lovely British-inflected lullabies.

Then the awkwardness seeped back in between us, like an icy trickle of rain sluicing past your collar. When I pulled away from her, clearing my throat, she bent to offer Jasper the back of her hand.

"A familiar, really?" she said, smiling up at me as he gave her a subdued sniff. "I confess, I'm a bit surprised."

"Ah, no, actually. Jas is just . . . your average cute pup," I said brightly, quelling a spurt of irritation that I somehow hadn't seen this coming. Only in Thistle Grove would your mother assume that your well-trained standard schnauzer must *obviously* be a familiar. "He usually has more pep to him, too, but he's a little wiped out. Actually, we both are, do you think we could . . . ?"

"Right, of course," she said hurriedly, reaching over to wrench my back-breaking duffel across the threshold before I could stop her. "You've both had a terribly long drive, haven't you? Let's get you settled."

Inside, the smell of home hit me like a sucker punch: lemongrass floor polish, tea leaves, the melting sweetness of beeswax candles. I abandoned my monster suitcase in the foyer, shedding my denim jacket and hooking it on the coat tree before trailing my mother to the darkened kitchen. Instead of switching on the overhead light, she flicked her hand at the clusters of pillar candles set on the table and granite countertop. Their flames sprang obediently to life, illuminating the cozy breakfast nook with its vase of peachy tulips, yellow curtains, and my old cat-shaped clock on the wall with its swinging pendulum tail. Lighting candles was a small, homey sort of magic, the kind even Harlows could easily do.

The kind I used to be able to do almost without thinking before I left.

But I hadn't been able to coax so much as a flicker from a candle for almost four years now, and the ease with which my mother did it sent a well-worn ache of loss rolling through my belly. That was why members of the founding families rarely ventured far from Thistle Grove; any amount of distance attenuated our magic. The longer you stayed away, the fewer spells you were able to manage, until your abilities eventually huffed out altogether the way mine have.

I still felt the pain of their absence like a phantom limb, a hollow throb of yearning that never really faded. Seeing even this tiny spurt of magic happen in front of me only reignited the craving.

But, I reminded myself firmly, this was part of the price I'd agreed to pay for my new life. My *real* life, with my real job, real college degree, and unfortunately extremely real assload of student debt. This was the trade-off that I chose—the loss of magic, in return for a life that I could mold into a shape that actually fit.

"You've missed dinner, I'm afraid," my mother said, leaning back against the counter and crossing her arms over her slim middle. I sank down into one of the wooden chairs by the breakfast table, Jasper sprawling out next to me on the travertine tiles, and made an apologetic face in response, as if I hadn't timed my arrival precisely to avoid an hour of mandatory social entrapment with my parents before I had a chance to decompress.

"And your dad's gone back to the shop for a few hours to get the ledgers in order," she added. "The Samhain bedlam seems to set in earlier each bloody year. We're swimming in tourists already, and you know what that does to your poor father's peace of mind."

"I can imagine," I said, wincing in sympathy. "Think of all the *strangers* he has to talk to, the utter horror of it all."

Thistle Grove kicked into high gear every spooky season, starting the beginning of October and sometimes lasting well into mid-November. It was a Halloween destination the rest of the year as well—though of course the tourists had no idea just how deep, and very real, the town's "mythical" magic ran—but quiet enough to be less of a nightmare for my introverted father.

"But if you're hungry, I could make you a sandwich?" my

mother offered, wilting a little when I shook my head. "A bit of tea, then? I could use a cup myself."

I'd been driving for hours, and would much rather take a steaming shower and dive directly into bed before facing any further scenes from the prodigal-daughter-returneth playbook. But she looked so hopeful at the prospect of sharing a cup of tea with me that I couldn't bring myself to say no.

"Tea would be wonderful, thanks," I relented. "And could I have some water for Jasper?"

"Of course. What a terribly polite fellow he's been, too." She squinted at him thoughtfully, cocking her head to the side. "Are you *quite* sure he isn't a familiar?"

"Stone-cold certain, Mom."

I watched as she moved purposefully around the kitchen, all deft hands and competence, her periwinkle cardigan swirling around her, glossy dark braid swishing over her shoulder. When she set my favorite old mug, oversized and painted with a gold foil dragonfly, in front of me, she tapped the side lightly with an index finger to cool it to the perfect temperature. It was a little Harlow party trick, a pretty lackluster one as affinities went. My mother, Cecily Fletcher Harlow, hadn't been born a Harlow, of course; but marrying into a founding family was kind of like marrying into royalty. Only instead of a lifetime of fascinators, anemic finger sandwiches, and wearing nude pantyhose in public, you got to become a witch yourself.

"So, darling," she began, wrapping long fingers around her own mug as she sat down across from me. "Tell me how you've been."

"Really good," I replied, relaxing a little as the rooibos steeped into my chest and loosened some of the underlying tightness. I'd forgotten how medicinal my mother's brews could be. "I, um, even got promoted a few weeks ago. I didn't want to mention anything until the ink was dry, but yeah. Officially creative director at Enchantify now."

"My goodness, that's wonderful!" She beamed at me, though I could see the slight tightening at the corners of her eyes as she registered that this was the belated first she'd heard of my good news. "Congratulations, sweet. What a coup for you."

"Great timing, too. Gave me some leverage for requesting such a long sabbatical."

"And such a treat for us, more than one whole month with you! To be frank, I rather doubted you'd be able to come at all."

I chewed on the inside of my cheek, a little taken aback by such uncharacteristic bluntness. We weren't usually like that with each other, the Harlows. Not insular elitists like the Blackmoores, chaotically codependent like the Avramovs, or nearly empathically linked like the Thorns. We preferred to give the difficult stuff a wide berth, leave each other abundant room to breathe.

Maybe too much room, sometimes.

"'And the Harlow scion shall serve as Gauntlet Arbiter,' remember?" I said with forced levity. "Kind of hard to duck a centuries-old magical obligation. Could I *really* have been sure I wouldn't have turned into a hedgehog for flouting ye ways of old?"

She chuckled, taking a sip. "Not-impossible-though-fairly-unlikely hedgehogification aside, the Grimoire doesn't forbid the next-eldest Harlow of the younger generation from taking your place. Delilah could certainly have stepped in for you."

"Oh, I just bet Delilah could have," I muttered under my breath, trying to stifle the reflexive eye roll my cousin's name reliably provoked.

"Don't be mean about your cousin, darling. She's only a bit . . . eager."

This was one of my mother's epic British understatements, as Delilah was both the eagerest of beavers and the ultimate Harlow stan. She was a year older than me, but unfortunately for her, she wasn't the firstborn of the Harlow main line—which automatically disqualified her from serving as Arbiter unless I stepped down.

Delilah's borderline obsession with our family history had always struck me as kind of hilarious, given the role the Harlows actually played in the founding of the town. Legend had it that a little over three hundred years ago, four witches were drawn to Hallows Hill, lured by the siren song of magical power that emanated from this place. To consecrate the founding of the town below, Caelia Blackmoore conjured a spectacular lightning storm, Margarita Avramov summoned spirits from beyond the veil to serve as witnesses, Alastair Thorn called down the birds from the sky as his congregation, and Elias Harlow drew forth his mighty quill and . . .

Took a bunch of notes.

Seriously, that was it. My esteemed ancestor participated in this magical event of unprecedented majesty and drama by writing it all down in the driest possible manner, diligently avoiding wit or flair lest a historical account actually *entertain* future readers, perish the thought. Making him more or less the equivalent of the accidentally purple-haired lady named Irma who jots down the talking points of every town council meeting ever.

To be fair, Elias was also responsible for the Grimoire, the spellbook that contained the four families' collected spells and the rules for the Gauntlet of the Grove, the tournament held every fifty years to determine which founding family got to preside over all things magical in Thistle Grove. According to the rules, the competition was intended for the rising generation, so that each new Victor started their reign in the prime of their life—which meant that the firstborn scions of each line, the heirs apparent, went up against one another, as long as they were older than eighteen.

The Harlows didn't even *compete*, being so magically stunted that we've historically overseen the proceedings instead. And as the Harlow heir and the other scions' peer, the Grimoire also demanded that I be the Arbiter, rather than my father.

Woot for tradition.

"Well, bully to Delilah," I replied a little sourly. "But, huzzah, here I am! So she still doesn't get to steal my thunder as Emmeline, scion to House Harlow, the magical admins of Thistle Grove."

My mother frowned at me over the rim of her mug. "If you're going to be so glib about it, darling, perhaps you really *should* have let her step in for you. You know respecting the spirit of the thing is terribly important to your father."

I leaned back into my chair, my insides churning. I *did* know that, thanks to the tragically heartfelt and impressively guilt-trip-ridden letter my father had sent me a few months ago. Even thinking about his swooping script across the grainy Tomes & Omens stationery made my stomach twist, with the particular flavor of angst reserved for disappointing daughters.

> *Dearest Scoot, I know you've chosen to make your life a different one—a separate one from us. But, please, consider coming back to the covenstead just this once, for tradition's sake. Consider*

*discharging this final obligation to your history and kin, to your
mother and myself, and I promise this is the last we'll ever speak
of duty.*

How could I have said no after that—especially to parents who
had always been so supportive of my choices, and my magicless life
in Chicago? A life they'd never understood, and one that so pointedly made no room for them?

"I know that," I said, not mentioning the letter, because there
was no way my mother would have let him send something so emotionally manipulative had she known about it. My parents were
basically the living embodiment of #relationshipgoals, and I had
no desire to stir the pot between them. "And the *spirit of the thing*
demands that it be me. And since the Blackmoores have won since
pretty much time's inception, it's not like I'll have all that much
arbitration to even do."

This was technically incorrect. The Thorns won once, back in
1921—but only because Evrain Blackmoore was such a roaring
drunk he lit both himself and the Avramov combatant on fire
while transforming a fishpond into a fountain of flaming
spiced rum.

See? Suck it, Delilah, I *did* know my Thistle Grove history.

My mother sighed softly and capitulated, rubbing her temples.
"I suppose that's true. And you'll have a few days to rest up before
the tournament opening on Wednesday. Acclimate a bit to being
back."

At the mention of rest, I tried to stifle a yawn and failed miserably, my jaw nearly unhinging from the force. "Sorry," I barely
managed through it. "I'm just beat."

My mother pushed back from the table and swiftly gathered

up our empty mugs, then set them in the sink. "No worries, sweet. I have the carriage house all ready for you," she told me over her shoulder as she rinsed them. "I thought, for a whole month, it would be nice for you to have your own space rather than a guest room in the house proper."

"That would be great," I said, my heart lifting at the prospect with genuine pleasure. I'd loved the carriage house as a kid, and spent most of my sleepovers with Linden Thorn sequestered out there, apart from my parents but never too far away for help if any was needed. The kind of distance they'd probably envisioned would carry over into my adulthood, instead of the two hundred miles of Illinois flatlands that now yawned between us, vast and intractable.

Together, we lugged my things out the back door and down the paved path that led through my mother's flower garden. The night bloomers stirred in their beds, swaying toward one another and tittering in high-pitched tones like gossiping fairies. Jasper trotted over to sniff a particularly lively evening primrose, leaping like a rabbit when it leaned over with a tinkling giggle to bop him on the nose.

It was a simple animating spell, though nothing like what a Thorn could have done with one. Flowers in a Thorn-animated garden might have distinct names and personalities and the power of speech, all the trappings of sentience. I knew because Linden Thorn, my best friend of over twenty years, once animated a cherry tree in the Honeycake Orchards for me as a birthday present. Cherry—so styled by yours truly, the world's most literal eight-year-old—whooped my ass at chess a solid four games out of five, and enjoyed regaling me with its gorgeous, uncanny dreams.

Sometimes I still really missed that tree.

We both dropped my luggage at the threshold with a pair of matching, extremely unladylike grunts, grinning at each other as she handed me a key.

"Your dad may very well sleep at the shop if the night gets away from him," she said, rolling her eyes fondly. "As they so often do. So don't rush to breakfast tomorrow on his account."

"I have brunch plans with Linden anyway." I'd messaged Lin a few weeks ago to let her know I'd be in town for the Gauntlet, and to see if she wanted to get together as soon as I was back. We were still close, mostly thanks to Lin's staunch commitment to keeping us abreast of each other's lives even from a distance, so I figured it was on me to swing our first real-life reunion in years. "But I'll stop by Tomes and Omens right after, if that works?"

"Of course it does," my mother said, leaning over to brush a kiss over my forehead. "Good night, my darling, and give me a shout if you need anything at all. It really is so *very* lovely to have you back."

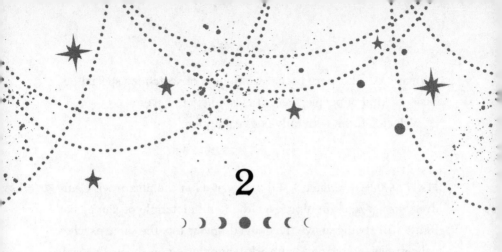

2

))) ● (((

The Shamrock Cauldron Fiasco

INSIDE, THE CARRIAGE house was an airy loft open to the rafters, complete with a kitchenette, a rustic little fireplace, and a queen bed positioned right beneath the skylight. It usually served as my mother's candle-dipping studio, but her creative clutter was nowhere in sight. Instead, every surface all but sparkled, and she had even left out a bowl of dimpled Sumo oranges, my favorite.

The effort she'd put into my homecoming made me yearn for a drink, in a way that might be considered a tad problematic if I allowed myself to dwell on it too long.

After I tucked the very last set of I-probably-won't-need-these-*BUT-WHAT-IF-I-DO* shoes away and slid my suitcase under the bed, I found that my exhaustion had morphed into the kind of maddeningly buzzy fatigue that I knew wouldn't let me sleep without some help. And the last thing I felt like doing was venturing back to the house in search of the kind of complicated liquor that my parents, who were both "two fingers of scotch for special occasions" kind of people, weren't even likely to have.

Which left me with only one real option.

HALF AN HOUR later, I slid onto a stool at the Shamrock Cauldron, my gaze skimming over the familiar tangle of jaunty bat lights still strung above the gouged-up bar top, the same psychedelic green and purple shamrocks shimmering on the walls. And, of course, Dead Frederick: the plastic skeleton in a leprechaun's top hat and Mardi Gras pearls who presided over the bar's back corner with, puzzlingly, a ukulele propped on his bony lap.

You really couldn't beat the Cauldron when it came to class.

The bar was off the beaten path enough to get only modest play with tourists, making it the perfect local haunt. Past nine on a Sunday night, it was almost empty, save for a solitary bachelorette with a bride-of-Frankenstein headpiece hanging askew on her disheveled hair, grimly sucking down a bright green cocktail by herself.

At least someone was having a worse time tonight than I was.

As I reached for the drinks menu, the bartender set down the tumbler he'd been wiping and leaned forward, squinting at me, before breaking into a broad smile.

"Hey . . . Emmy Harlow? Shit, is that you?"

I gave him a blank look, momentarily at a loss—then his adult face meshed with the memory of a younger face I hazily recognized from years of classes together. Same dark tousle of hair, same eyeliner around bright blue eyes; even the suspenders-over-a-blousy-shirt look felt familiar, though it was now rolled up over tattoo-sleeved forearms. Morty and I had been only passing acquaintances, but I discovered with a little shock that it felt sur-prisingly good to see him again, and better still to hear that he even remembered my name.

"In the flesh," I admitted, smiling back. "First night back, actu-ally. How've you been, Morty?"

"Can't complain. Pops retired a few years back and charged me with the keeping of this stellar joint." He waved at the Cauldron with an all-encompassing flourish. "Happy to report that our buf-falo enchiladas are now edible, and that the craft cocktail list has been, mercifully, revamped. Get you anything?"

I ran a finger down the new set of hideously schlocky-sounding Halloween drinks before reaching the classic cocktails. "Just an old-fashioned to start, please."

"Coming right up." He shot me another grin, wide and disarm-ing, as he reached for a shaker. "It'd be great to catch up once you settle in. Would love to hear what you've been up to in the city all these years."

It gave me an unexpected pang to hear that an old classmate not only cared to know what I'd been doing, but had even both-ered to find out where I went after I left. When he slid the cocktail in front of me, I downed half of it in three smoky-sweet, delicious mouthfuls, thinking that, just maybe, being back for a month might not be quite as bad as my worst fears.

Then the Cauldron door swung open, letting in a chill blast of autumnal air—and I heard *his* voice, followed by the unmistakable whipcrack of his laugh.

Gareth Blackmoore himself came tripping into the bar, his little brother, Gawain, and a welter of interchangeable Blackmoore cousins trailing in his wake, all of them obviously only a half step shy of being fully stumbledrunk.

"Are you fucking serious, universe?" I moaned to myself through clenched teeth, barely refraining from sinking my head into my hands.

And because I'd clearly committed unspeakable crimes against both kittens and human babies in a former life, Gareth shambled over to the bar top and dropped onto the seat right next to mine. His entourage filed in after him, still man-cackling and jostling each other as they commandeered the remainder of the bar.

"Heeeeeey," Gareth crooned at me, as if we ran into each other here on a regular basis, shooting me the lopsided grin that had once derailed my entire life. When he knuckled the sandy flop of hair off his forehead, my entire body clenched with mortification at his closeness, the devastating familiarity of a gesture I should have long since exorcised from my mind. "This seat taken?"

"It is, actually," I forced out, heart pounding painfully at the base of my throat. "Extremely taken."

"Really?" Gareth raised a bleary eyebrow and made a big production of scoping out the Cauldron's mostly deserted expanse. "Because I don't, like, see anyone else here."

"The thing is, it's *always* been taken. It has what one might call a long-standing tradition of not being free ever, so . . ."

He squinted at me, still giving me that slapdash smile, trying to determine if I might be screwing with him.

"Then why don't I just hold on to it until its *traditional* owner returns—that work for you?" he proposed, leaning over conspiratorially, so close I could smell the beer and rye mingled on his breath. "Like a compromise."

Shifting away from me in an alarming, full-body sway, he rapped his knuckles on the bar. When this failed to garner an immediate-enough response, he went ahead and snapped his fingers in Morty's general direction, like an Entitled Drunk Shithead caricature of himself. "Hey, man, a round of Don Julio Real for the crew!"

I gaped at Gareth, appalled that the reality of him was somehow managing to be worse than even my vilest recollections. "Did you . . . did you seriously just snap your fingers at an entire living human?"

"Oh, it's just *Morty*!" Gareth declared, spreading his arms wide in drunken bonhomie, abruptly enough to nearly elbow me in the face. "Morty's my old pal. Morty doesn't mind, right, my man?"

Morty, in fact, looked like he might choose violence tonight if Gareth said his name again in that heinously belittling tone. But he only nodded once, pressing his lips together until they paled, and turned to slide a silver-topped bottle off the highest shelf.

It was a cardinal rule in Thistle Grove, applying to the magicless and magicked communities alike: One simply did not fuck with a Blackmoore. Blackmoores were what passed for royalty in this town, and they did not take kindly to being fucked with.

I was something of an object lesson in this regard, given that literally fucking a Blackmoore had driven me into self-imposed exile nine years ago.

When I opened my mouth again to protest, Morty caught my eye and gave me a tiny shake of the head. *Not even worth it*, he mouthed at me as he poured tequila into six skull-shaped shot glasses, a thousand-yard stare he must reserve for just such distasteful occasions fixed on his face.

As Gareth lifted his shot and proposed some rambling toast to Camelot, the Blackmoores' crown jewel, his attention thankfully shifted away from me. I curled both hands around my tumbler in a death grip, as though it might anchor me from spinning so far out of control that I wheeled into the mesosphere and then outer space beyond, so propelled by rage and anxiety as to actually escape the earth's gravity well.

Just when I thought I might have gotten something approaching a grip, Gareth swung back to me. "So, anyway," he said, as though we had been having a mutually amiable chat before he was called away. "You in town for the weekend, or what? Don't feel like I've seen you in here before."

I stared at him, confusion warring with resentment at the fact that he'd gotten even more attractive with age. He was wearing a slightly rumpled pinstriped suit that fell elegantly across his broad shoulders, and his blond hair was expensively cut, swept away from the darker eyebrows and gas-flame blue eyes my seventeen-year-old self once found so inescapably compelling. And his face was a little leaner than I remembered, both jawline and brow heavier and more defined. Being nine years older, woe and alas, actually suited him.

His personality, on the other hand, was clearly still in dire need of an overhaul.

"Gareth Blackmoore, are you fucking with me right now?" I demanded. "You don't feel like you've *seen me in here before*'? What the hell is that, some pickup artistry bullshit? Because if so, that's a stunning new low even for you."

"Hey, easy now," he drawled, eyebrows lifting as he held up both palms. "Shit, I feel like we got off on, like, a real wrong foot. I'm Gareth, and—wait, but you already knew that, right? Hey, new girl, how come you know my name?"

As a slow grin began spreading over his face, I found myself struck with one of the most tragic revelations of my life. Gareth Blackmoore—my first love, my most humiliating and heart-

crushing breakup, and the reason I abandoned an entire life—
genuinely did not remember me.

Forget unspeakable crimes. I clearly straight up *ate* kittens and
babies in a previous life, until a pitchforked mob drove my mon-
strous self out of that town, too.

To be fair, it had been nearly nine years since we really saw
each other last, not counting the glimpses I'd caught of him back
when I still used to come to Thistle Grove for covenstead holidays.
My style had changed quite a bit since then. Instead of a wild, sun-
bleached tangle that nearly whisked my waist, my hair was dark
and sleek, cut in an asymmetrical bob that whispered by my chin.
Small tattoos were scattered across my forearms, and these days
I wouldn't be caught dead in one of the fluttery white-witch
dresses Gareth used to like so much on me.

But this man had been *inside* me many, many times. Our emotional history aside, shouldn't that alone have warranted at least a
flicker of recognition? I clearly had no trouble recognizing *him*.
Yet there was nothing in his eyes, beyond the generic glaze of a
drunk and horny male who wanted into my pants.

For a moment, I found myself struck speechless, so mortified I
wished I could sink into the earth while a tsunami simultaneously
closed over my head. Meanwhile, Morty's wide eyes flicked rapidly
between Gareth and me, like a spectator at the world's most miserable tennis match. He couldn't know exactly what was going down
here—the list of people privy to what had happened between us
was so short and sweet it didn't even include my parents—but he
must have been able to discern the gist.

"God*damn*," he muttered under his breath, his kind face dissolving into an expression of such sympathy that it abruptly tipped
my humiliation into rage.

As if on cue, the tumbler shattered to pieces in my hand.

"Oh, shit, your glass!" Gareth exclaimed, blue eyes flaring wide with genuine concern. For all his faults, he'd never been an *intentional* sadist. "Here, wait, let me help."

Without asking for permission, he slid his palm around my hand and its fistful of shards. A tingling sluice of magic coursed from his skin and into mine, turning the tumbler's shattered remains into an iridescent liquid, sinuous and glinting as quicksilver. It warbled and wavered in place before flowing back into its former, unbroken shape, crystallizing into solidity with a neat little snap.

That was what the Blackmoores did best—manipulating matter, turning one element into another with ease, breaking and unbreaking things at whim. The story was that they were descended from Morgan le Fay, King Arthur's legendary sorceress, as one could surmise from all their ridiculous Arthurian names. (Gareth had gotten off comparatively light in this respect, but the rest of them . . . not so much. Cases in point, his little brother, Gawain, and sister, Nineve.) They were staggeringly strong witches, hands down the most powerful of the families.

But even *they* weren't usually so brazen as to work magic in full view of a regular human like Morty—who was staring at us with a slightly haunted expression, mouth working as he tried to reconcile the laws of physics with the unquestionable reality of the restored glass in my hand.

While we were all taught to avoid spellcraft in public as a general rule, the Avramovs had also cast a glamour over the town centuries ago as a fail-safe, to prevent locals from looking too closely at any spells gone astray. I could see it working on Morty already, misting his eyes with uncertainty as it rewrote his memory like a document being revised.

Gareth must have mistaken my own shock for awestruck fascination, because he let his fingers linger suggestively on mine. "Cool trick, right?" He leaned a little closer, a sour gust of liquored breath wafting over me as he struggled to focus on my face. I wrinkled my nose, wondering how I'd ever found this living, breathing, swaying cliché attractive. "Got more where that came from. You want, we could get out of here, and I could show you some even cooler shit."

"Or *you* could get out of here," I suggested hotly, snatching back my hand. "Ideally, next time I blink, you'll already be gone."

He leaned back, brow knitting with bemusement as he rubbed the back of his neck. "*Or*, bear with me, I could stay and buy you another drink?" he offered, still failing to fully process the idea of rejection by a tourist who must *surely* be starstruck by an encounter with the storied Blackmoore heir.

"She already said no, man," Morty interjected. His face had cleared; he'd probably already forgotten the unbroken glass, or confabulated some story that lined up better with his understanding of the way the world usually worked. "And one 'no' is enough for a gentleman, am I right?"

A moment of bracing lucidity crossed Gareth's face, and his jaw tightened with a sudden, dangerous belligerence. He glared at Morty, and then me, lips pursing as he slid his tongue over his teeth. From what I remembered, while entitled, overindulged, and clueless about his own failings, Gareth wasn't an actual bully—at least, not when sober. But he *was* a Blackmoore, on top of being a tall and powerfully built drunk man with a crew of like-minded companions. I felt myself go a little jangly with adrenaline as I watched him pondering his options.

The tension gathered around us like an encroaching thunderhead—and then Gareth rolled his eyes elaborately, pushing back from the bar top with an exaggerated yawn.

"Sure is, Morty, my man," he said, pointedly turning his back to me and clapping his closest cousin on the shoulder. "Hey, y'all, it's getting a little stale in here. Let's go hit up the Avalon."

A chorus of *hell, yeah, man* and the like later, they'd all trampled out the door, leaving the atmosphere in the Cauldron almost palpably lightened by their absence. Morty and I sat in shell-shocked silence for a moment, regaining our bearings. Then Morty gave a full-body shudder as if to clear his head, and grimly poured us both a double shot of Grey Goose. I clinked my glass wryly against his, before tossing it back in a single swallow, hissing through my teeth.

"You okay over there, Emmy?" he asked, eyes warm with concern. "Can't say I'm a hundred percent on what just went down. But I did manage to make out that Gareth is still an industrial-strength asshole, color me stunned."

"I'll survive," I mumbled, sinking my forehead into my hands. "Thanks for stepping in before I did something actively dumb. Wait a second . . . did he even bother to pay for those shots?"

"He's got a tab," Morty replied, already assembling a fresh old-fashioned before I could ask for one. What a human treasure. "And frankly, I don't really give a shit as long as he's gone. Blackmoores always give me the crawlies, you know? Bunch of unnerving fuckers, rolling around here like they own the whole damn town. I mean, granted, they *do* own a ton of it. But they could really use a solid attitude adjustment about that whole deal."

"Cheers to that," I said with a bitter husk of a laugh, picking up my glass. This tumbler was identical to the one I'd broken, but now its solid heft felt somehow surprising. It was made from glass so heavy and dense that I couldn't imagine breaking it with my grip alone.

Which meant I must have done it with a spurt of instinctive magic.

Which meant my magic might already be coming back.

3

The Sexy Tundra Wolf

I WAS STILL MARVELING over the glass when a husky, amused voice broke into my thoughts.

"So, if I were to say hi, would you be inclined to break anything else? Or is that greeting *traditionally* reserved for Blackmoores?"

I jumped a little, head whipping to my right. Natalia Avramov now sat three chairs down from me, nestled in the shadowy corner at the very end of the bar, right next to Dead Fred. The Avramov scion lifted a hand in a greeting just short of a wave, in the pleasant and approachable manner of a person who has not just appeared out of thin air.

"Talia," she reminded me, tapping two fingers, polished a glossy midnight blue, against her collarbone. As if I could possibly have forgotten her.

Granted, Talia had been two years ahead of me in school, but she was also the heart-stopping kind of gorgeous that tends to stick with you. The entire Avramov clan was aggressively attractive, all soaring cheekbones and distinctive eyes and jawlines that could carve glass; like seductive villains that had climbed out of some dark fairy tale with briars still twisted in their hair. They claimed to be descended from Baba Yaga, the notorious Slavic witch hag—who must also have been a stone-cold fox in her youth, judging by the genetic wealth she'd conferred upon her line.

But even by Avramov standards, Talia was a showstopper. A shining sweep of inky hair, creamy skin with a subtle glow that I suspected did not derive from any K-Beauty mask, the kind of impossibly plush lips that gave you *notions*. And nearly translucent gray eyes, with a sooty ring around each pale iris that made her look like a tundra wolf. A really, really sexy tundra wolf, if this was, in fact, a thing.

She was watching me now with those unnervingly lovely eyes, a hint of amusement coloring her features. As if she knew exactly what kind of effect she had on people.

"Emmeline," I responded inanely, a little thrown off balance by the intensity of her gaze. "Uh, Emmy, I mean. Harlow."

"Oh, I know who you are, *Harlow*." She tipped her head to the side and smiled at me, a slow, lazy drawing back of those spectacular lips. Talia always did have a weapons-grade smile, along with a truly staggering amount of swagger. The sight of it made my knees feel a little giddy, even though I was already sitting down. Could a knee even *feel* giddy, I wondered.

Apparently, yes.

I cleared my throat and took a sip of my drink, just to give myself something more socially acceptable to do than stare at her while my knees swooned under the bar.

"Good thing someone does," I muttered, liquor searing down my throat. "Unlike certain other individuals."

She snorted a little, rolling her eyes. "I don't know that Gareth Blackmoore qualifies as an *individual*, per se, so much as an irredeemable asshat. Or dickwad. Choose your appendage or orifice at your leisure."

I sputtered a laugh. "Fair point. Though to play devil's advocate, at least I could see him when he walked in."

She swayed her head from side to side, like, *touché*. Then she picked up her drink and slid over the stools between us to sit next to me, with a languorous and long-limbed grace like some kind of sexy tai chi. From this close, I could smell her perfume, creamy sweetness with hints of sandalwood and cocoa. It was surprisingly decadent for someone with so much edge, and only gave me further notions.

"Deflection glamours are, admittedly, a bit rude," she said, sounding not even a little sorry. "But I wasn't in the mood for making nice with anyone tonight. And even I would have felt like a monster for shooting down the saddest bachelorette in all the world when she went looking for a shoulder to cry on."

I glanced over my own shoulder, to find that the bachelorette in question had abandoned her melted green mess of a cocktail, leaving behind only a wad of crumpled dollar bills pinned by a coaster.

"Ugh, do you think she left with the Blackmoores?" I asked with a shudder. "Because, wow, talk about choosing the wrong pool in which to drown your woes. I bet whichever one she winds up with doesn't even bother to buy her brunch tomorrow."

"In theory, I would agree. In practice?" Shrugging, she took a sip from the curly straw bobbing in her suspiciously tropical-looking drink, complete with an umbrella topper. "Haven't we all been there?"

I stared at her, my mouth dropping open. "And when you say 'we,' you would be referring to . . . ?"

"Myself," she said, lips rounding enticingly around her straw. "And, unless my emotional-carnage radar has gone totally awry, also you."

I watched as she took another serene sip of her unlikely drink, my mind whirling. Talia and *Gareth*? This . . . did not compute.

In high school, while I dated in equal opportunity fashion, Talia had almost exclusively pursued girls. And the prettiest ones at that, lithe cheerleaders and ruddy-cheeked soccer players and the pert vice president of the student council. All of them hopelessly smitten with her, and invariably crushed when she eventually lost interest and wandered away to her next pursuit. It wasn't that she was cruel so much as easily bored, and completely frank about her disinterest in inhabiting any relationship beyond a month or two. Getting your heart broken by Talia Avramov, one way or another, was basically a Thistle High queer girl rite of passage, one for which you could really blame only yourself. The fact that she'd never seemed to notice I even existed had been my particular bane.

And of the few guys I remembered among her conquests, none had been of Gareth's dick-swinging ilk.

"Trust me, I'm aware of the cognitive dissonance," she said dryly, as if she'd read my mind. But though divination was among the Avramovs' skills, they were much more into communing with the spirit world than prying into living people's thoughts. "It was not my finest hour. But I was coming out of a pretty terrible breakup, and he was around, and he can be, you know. Oddly charming when he's not too far up his own ass to make an effort."

"I do know," I said, mortified when my voice wavered a little. I set my jaw, absolutely refusing to cry over the memory of my own stupid, broken heart.

"So, it was because of him, then," Talia said softly, still watching me with that hyperfocused intensity. "Why you never really came back after high school."

"Partly, yeah. But it was . . . more complicated than that, too." I paused to toss back the dregs of my drink, taken aback by just how much I suddenly wanted her to understand what had really happened.

It wasn't like Talia and I had some profound and long-standing bond, beyond the shared history of all the Wheel of the Year holidays our families had celebrated together by Lady's Lake, the solstice and equinox circles blessed by moonlight. But neither of us had ever gone out of our way to seek each other out at those events, what with her being older and intimidatingly hot, and me too shy and self-contained to even consider initiating contact. At best, we'd been fellow celestial bodies whose orbits coincided at regular intervals.

But maybe it was that I felt half-drunk, along with battered and off-kilter from the collision with Gareth. Or maybe it was that Talia was unspeakably beautiful and smelled like a goddess and was watching me with those magnetic eyes, with the kind of concentrated attention that made me feel almost tipsier than the liquor. Whatever it was, I very badly *did* want to tell her. And for once, my pride didn't feel like a compelling enough reason not to throw caution to the winds.

"The thing is, it's presumably more complicated than someone who, say, hides under a glamour so they can canoodle with Dead Frederick while avoiding *living* human interaction would care to hear about," I added, giving myself a respectable out in the event that she was only being polite, though from what I remembered, decorum had never been her style.

Talia gave a low little laugh, a rich sound that sparked an actual physical reaction somewhere just below my navel, like iron striking flint.

"Let's say, just this once, I *might* be willing to set aside my comfortable misanthropy long enough to listen. I'll even throw in as many drinks as it takes to dull the pain. Sound like a plan?"

She raised an inviting dark eyebrow at me, drawing a silver-ringed hand through her hair and sweeping it over her other shoulder. With it out of the way, I could see her double helix piercing—a silver snake coiling around and through her ear—and the slim black choker snug around her long neck, set with the traditional Avramov garnet at the center. It made her look more like the person I remembered, the chaotic-neutral girl who smoked unfiltered cigarettes under the bleachers at recess and managed to make fingerless gloves look unironically cool.

The kind of girl who should definitely *not* be drinking a tourist-trap concoction with such evident relish.

"Technically, yes," I said, eyeballing her drink with more than a little trepidation. "Literally, I'm a little afraid of what you might consider a beverage suitable for this occasion. I mean, what *is* that travesty? A Sex on the Beach with Scorpion Bowl aspirations?"

She pressed a fingertip to her lips, her eyes flying wide with mock outrage. "Hush, child, before you utter something that cannot be unspoken. I'll have you know this is a Rainbow's End Gimlet, the finest of all Morty's creations. The homemade bitters really highlight the flavored vodkas, of which I believe there are at least three. It's delicious, and it *will* knock you straight on your ass."

I cocked my head, nodding slowly. "It's . . . shall we say, *interesting* to me that this is your drink of choice on a Sunday night."

"What can I say? I'm basically Russian. Random drunkenness is part of my life philosophy—and yours, starting now. Excuse me, sweet pea," Talia called out to Morty, who'd emerged from the back. He turned to give her a beaming smile several leagues away from the stoic courtesy he'd reserved for Gareth and the Blackmoore brood. Unlike them, she was clearly a genuinely welcome regular here. "Think you could curate a Shamrock flight for us?"

Morty popped her a crisp salute. "Nothing I'd rather do, lovebug."

While he set to mixing and pouring, Talia propped an elbow on the counter and cupped her chin, eyes drifting back to mine. "So, before we get into the heavy—what have you been up to all these years, Harlow? Living the normie dream, I take it?"

I winced a little at the slur that I had once slung around with similarly casual abandon, before it occurred to me that maybe this wasn't entirely cool. "Pretty much. Kicked things off with a comparative lit degree at the U of Chicago, with a minor in business."

"Figures." Another of those high-voltage smiles, a coy little tilt of the head. "Ever the high achiever. Weren't you valedictorian your year?"

I blinked, surprised that she'd remember, especially since she'd graduated two years before I did. "Uh, yeah, I was. Just one of those weirdos who loves to learn, I guess. For a while there, I thought maybe I even wanted to go into academia. But since I'm partial to the idea of paying off my student loans before I have grandkids, I wound up taking a job with a subscription box start-up a few years back."

She lifted her eyebrows, pitch-black and naturally dramatic, and gave me an admiring nod. "Oh, well played. Those are all the rage, right? What kind of goodies?"

"Well . . ." My cheeks heated a little, and I nibbled on the inside of my lower lip, wondering if I was just imagining the way her gaze briefly leapt down to my mouth. "It's called, uh, Enchantify. 'Magical treasures to indulge your inner witch.' Incense, chakra-cleansing bath bombs, fancy pendulums, that kind of thing. My job is coming up with the concepts, then sourcing the contents each month from local vendors."

"I . . . see." A suspicious hint of a smile flickered over her full lips. "And, if I may, what was September's theme?"

"It was Find Your Inner Goddess, actually," I admitted, my cheeks now fully aflame. The irony of a former witch peddling pseudo-magical artifacts was far from lost on me. "It included a truffle box that came with a hand-painted tarot deck and meditation crystals. So you could discover your inner goddess while fondling a chunk of sustainably sourced selenite and enjoying an artisanal nougat. As, you know, witches are wont to do."

"As I *myself* was planning on doing tonight, before I came here instead." Now she was grinning fully, rolling the stem of her glass between her fingers. But there was no sharp edge to her teasing, no malice to it at all. "So, what you're telling me is, you're a wannabe-witch enabler, is that about right?"

"More or less," I admitted. "It's about as far from real magic as you can get, but, false modesty aside, I pretty much kill at it. And it's a booming business. Can't throw a rock without hitting an Instagram witch these days."

Talia toyed with her straw, looking more pensive than mocking. "All jokes aside, that's a really smart take. I keep pitching Elena on adding an online presence to the Emporium, but she's such a pigheaded traditionalist. Claims it would 'dilute' the 'authenticity.'" She put both words in finger quotes, rolling her eyes. "As if you have to earn the right to shop there by physically showing up, like it's some kind of pagan pilgrimage instead of an upmarket Witch Walmart."

The Avramovs owned the Arcane Emporium on Hyssop Street, a sprawling megastore of all things occult, including magical tools and herbs, divination sessions, séances, and even an adjoining haunted house. I couldn't really imagine Talia's mother, Elena, the imposing Avramov matriarch, allowing the taint of anything so plebian as PayPal and Square and URLs to creep into her eldritch domain.

"Maybe she has a point," I said with a shrug. "I can't tell you how many 'magical artifacts' I've come across out there, but none of it's the real deal. There *must* be witches beyond Thistle Grove, but if any of them happen to be in Chicago, they're keeping well to themselves."

What I didn't tell her was just how oppressive living without magic could be, after having grown up with it running through you like a current, the absence of it a deep and relentless ache that sank its roots into the chambers of your heart like some encroaching weed. That part of the reason I wound up at Enchantify in the first place was that a (reasonably well-paid) excuse to seek out even instruments of fake magic satisfied some deep yearning inside me I couldn't otherwise seem to quell.

But I wanted her to know I was happy and thriving out there, regardless. Because I *was*, in a way I never could have been had I stayed here.

Talia nodded thoughtfully, her eyes a little distant. "And you've been away, what, almost ten years now?"

"Closer to nine."

"Must get pretty rough sometimes. I took a few years of finance classes at the university in Carbondale," she added, naming the closest decently sized town near Thistle Grove. "So I could keep the Emporium's books better—which is what I do these days, along with some of the fun touristy shit. I even thought about committing to a master's program, but I just fucking hated the way the magic fades out there. Being weak like that . . . I couldn't stand it, not for long."

"Eh, you get used to it," I said, which might have been one of the baldest lies I'd ever managed with a straight face. Though to be fair, compared to Talia, I'd been weak all my life. "And there are a lot of upsides, like actually good sushi and killer pierogies. And being valued for something besides your bloodline."

Talia flicked me a doubtful look, but before she could say anything, Morty deposited three flamboyantly garnished mini cocktails in front of each of us with a flourish.

"May I present Demonic Decadence, Pumpkin Pandemonium, and the Flirty Mermaid, for miladies' tasting pleasure."

"Speaking my language, sweet pea," Talia said, scooting her cocktails closer with both hands, like an animated dragon hoarding treasure. Morty flashed her a grin and a saucy wink, then ducked out back again.

"Where does one even begin, when all options inspire equal fear?" I pondered aloud, gaze shifting skeptically from the Flirty Mermaid's glitter-speckled surface to the Pumpkin Pandemonium's neon-orange froth.

"Don't be precious about your cocktails, Harlow."

"Not all of us were lucky enough to be born with a taste for liquefied gummy worms, *Avramov*."

She held up a commanding finger. "Not born with—*acquired*, through hard work and sacrifice."

When I burst out laughing, she gave me that wolf's grin again, her eyes narrowing above it. "Just suck it up and trust me, okay? Upon my honor, I promise you'll be pleasantly surprised."

She scooped up her Demonic Decadence, which came in an admittedly adorable coupe with a devil's tail wrapped around the stem.

"To *fucking* Gareth Blackmoore," she pronounced, lifting the glass toward me, "whose heart is darker than even his ancestral name. May he step into a puddle and ruin his uninspired and overpriced Italian footwear every day for the remainder of his life. Which will hopefully be as brutish and brief as the poets promise."

"To a toast that literally can't be improved upon," I agreed, clinking my plastic pumpkin to her coupe, then taking a devil-may-care swallow of my drink. It was richly creamy but not at all cloying, with notes of bourbon and maple bitters and only a hint of sweet pumpkin pie.

It was also so strong that I could feel a smolder catch in my belly, the heat radiating upward to my chest like smoke off a fresh-lit bonfire.

"Tasty, right?" Talia said smugly, catching my startled expression. "Told you. Morty's this town's best-kept secret. I mean, besides its generations of real-life witches."

"I'll allow that it tastes way less like a Chili's seasonal special than I feared."

"Aha!" She pointed at me with her cocktail toothpick, speared with a chocolate-dipped strawberry, before taking a nibble of its tip. A vivid sense impression popped into my drink-hazed brain of what kissing her might taste like—tart and fruity and candied sweet—before I hastily banished it. "So you admit that you've actually sampled a Chili's cocktail!"

"I *have* made the occasional late-night Chili's run in my misspent youth, yes, before I came to know better. It's called personal growth."

"Never heard of it."

I took a few more swigs, until my head felt like it was bobbing somewhere above my neck like a loosely tethered balloon. For a second, I had the vague and troubling realization that it had been a long time since I'd eaten much of anything, but I dismissed this as something I could worry about down the line.

"So," Talia prompted, nudging my shoulder with hers. "You were going to tell me about how Gareth drove you out of town."

"I was." I slammed the rest of the Pandemonium down for liquid courage, fiddling with the empty plastic pumpkin. "Though it wasn't quite *that* dramatic. We started dating end of my junior year. Right before his graduation, and school letting out for the summer. He insisted we keep it under wraps; too many Blackmoore haters in his business, was the alleged reason. Should have been my first red flag right there."

Thinking of that summer, the sweltering heat cut by the balmy breezes that swept down from Lady's Lake—like every other season, Thistle Grove summers were never less than flawless—resurrected a deep, dull pain, like prodding at a thick scar. That May, Gareth had started leaving magical-missive spells in my locker. A coin that turned into a hummingbird with a teensy note strapped to its needle of a leg, before the whole thing vanished in a puff. Origami stars that burst into miniature fireworks spelling out haiku composed just for me.

Hackneyed, juvenile spells that, at the time, seemed like the most charming and meaningful of romantic gestures.

Especially to seventeen-year-old Emmy Harlow, who in her wildest dreams would not have imagined that Gareth Blackmoore—scion of the most powerful magical family, captain of the basketball team, and swoon-worthiest male specimen at Thistle Grove High—might take an interest in her.

"Who *wouldn't* have been swept off their feet," Talia said cuttingly after I described it to her, but the edge in her voice wasn't meant for me.

"Right? It was all so profoundly ridiculous. But it meant so much that he noticed me." I stirred my drink absently, mouth twisting as I stared into the tiny whirlpool at the center. "You don't know what it was like growing up here as a Harlow, permanently on the lowest rung on the magical ladder. Knowing that you were born into mediocrity and never going to work your way up, no matter how hard you tried."

"Well, we're not as powerful as the Blackmoores, either," Talia pointed out. "No one is."

"Maybe not, but you're the next best thing," I countered. "Even the Thorns can do amazing shit, whereas the Harlows barely even have an affinity to speak of. But being with Gareth . . . it wasn't just about being in love with him. The really intoxicating thing was, if he could see something special in me, maybe it meant I really *was* more than just the Harlow girl. Like maybe I could still become *someone*, even if I stayed here."

And I had always been the kind of ambitious that demanded the culmination of becoming Someone. I craved the validation of high achievement, the sense of wielding control over your own life. The fulfillment you could find only through setting up lofty goals for yourself, then knocking them down one by one.

"Fuck," Talia said grimly, intuiting the trajectory of my sorry tale. "And then the bastard dumped you."

"That, he did. He said he needed to start thinking about his future, and he just 'couldn't see himself with a Harlow long-term.' I think he actually meant for it to be an easy letdown, like, 'It's not *you*, babe, it's your last name.'"

My face burned with remembered humiliation at the blithely casual way in which he'd delivered this gut-wrenching line. As if we hadn't spent every waking moment of that summer tangled together by the picturesque ponds that lined his family estate. As if he hadn't called me pet names, bought me a million little presents, even told me that he almost, nearly, all but loved me.

Apparently, when stacked up against the unfortunate accident of my birthright—or lack thereof—none of that mattered in the end.

"When I asked him who he *could* see himself with, he was all, 'I don't know, a normie heiress or something?'" My fists clenched in my lap at the memory of his bewildered expression. Unclear as to what sort of future partner might be on his level, while simultaneously certain that she would be superior to me. "Not me, in any event. That much he knew for sure."

Talia let out a humorless bark of laughter, looking so venomous on my behalf I could believe that a vengeful witch queen's blood ran through her veins.

"So, anyway," I said flatly, reaching for my Demonic Decadence, because I badly needed to be even drunker than I already was. It tasted like dark chocolate shavings and a warm dash of cayenne pepper, and under any other circumstances would have solved most of my problems. "I wasn't about to tell anyone what happened, because I'm pretty sure the embarrassment would have finished me off. And I *definitely* wasn't going to stay here after that."

Before Gareth, I was still envisioning a place, a future for myself in Thistle Grove. After Gareth, I realized that if I stayed, I would never amount to anything more than a Harlow. The inconsequential no one he already thought I was.

"So senior year, I took the SAT, applied to a bunch of colleges, and vowed to never come back here again. Or, alternatively, only to return once I was accomplished as fuck, enough to make Gareth eat crow for not choosing me," I finished. "As you saw, that backfired kind of spectacularly."

Talia stayed silent for a long moment, a muscle in her jaw ticking. Then she reached over and slipped her hand over mine, her smooth palm whispering over my skin.

"Let it be known that if I hadn't already decided that the Prince of Bastards should suffer a thousand hells," she said, with a surprising gentleness at odds with the biting words, "this would have been the exact moment I knew I wanted him to burn."

And just for a minute, as I savored the heat of her palm resting over my hand, Gareth Blackmoore was the last thing on my mind.

4

))) ● ((

Fried Cake and Revelations

HE NEXT MORNING, I woke up to my alarm with Jasper snuggled against my back like a snoring thermal blanket, and the kind of hangover that made you wish you'd died in your sleep.

I only half remembered Talia giving me a ride home, followed by a drunken stumble to the carriage house through the garden, and a vague interlude of lying down among the primroses and trying to coax them into talking to me. I was probably only alive at all because, as per my last reliable memory, Morty had served us tater tots and the new-and-improved enchiladas long after the kitchen had officially closed. Along with being largely responsible for my continued existence, the enchiladas *had* been delicious as promised.

I was much less pleased by what I remembered of my conversation with Talia.

In the sober light of day, cascading cruelly onto my head through the skylight directly above, I wondered what on earth had possessed me to engage in so much soul baring with her. Granted, there had been a *lot* of excellent booze—besides the Flirty Mermaid, which was truly beyond redemption—but still, it wasn't like me. Pride had always been one of my choice vices. And sober me would have liked at least the option of Talia Avramov, Sexy Tundra Wolf, not knowing exactly how decimated I had been by Gareth Fucking Blackmoore.

But talking to her had been . . . oddly fun. And had I imagined the flicker of something even more than fun, something alive and charged leaping between us as Talia's face swam close to mine, liquor-stung lips parted and pale eyes intent?

Sadly, a glance at my phone screen confirmed I didn't have time for further reflection on Talia's mouth or intentions. After a hot shower that only fractionally restored my will to live, I threw on my most hangover-friendly clothes, left the door cracked open for whenever Jas deigned to rouse himself, then drove over to Angelina's to meet Linden for brunch.

Inside, the diner appeared frozen in time, as if the black-and-white checkered floor and bottle-green booths had been preserved in amber, or some kind of extemporal spell. Velvety blues still strummed from the speakers, and the aroma of fried batter, powdered sugar, and bacon enveloped me like an olfactory hug. The diner was Monday-morning empty, and I quickly spotted Linden in a booth toward the back, waving me over. She stood to fold me into a tight, sweet pea–scented hug as we exchanged hellos.

"Okay, it's clearly been way too long since I had a proper Linden Thorn hug," I said into her hair, squeezing back hard. "I'd forgotten just how quality they were."

"And whose fault is that?" she teased, as we pulled apart to slide into the booth. "I've only been trying to lure you back for years."

"Fair point. Damn, it smells amazing in here," I half moaned, sagging against the crackling vinyl as I drew a deep breath. "Did it *always* smell this amazing?"

"The Harlow stomach still in full effect, I see," Lin said, amused by my rapture. That I could eat her under the table, despite her being the enviably taller and curvier of the two of us, was one of our longest-running jokes. "Fried cake for brunch was a good call. Though now I'm thinking maybe it also qualifies as first aid. Tore it up a little your first night back, I take it?"

"More or less," I admitted. "I stopped by the Cauldron and accidentally had a little too much fun. As one does. And here I thought the shower at least masked my transformation into hungover hag from beyond the grave."

She tilted her head solemnly from side to side, considering. "I mean, we're not talking Samara from *The Ring* or anything. But a touch deathly, yeah."

Lin, on the other hand, looked lovely. Though she wore her hair natural now, in a twist-out that just barely brushed her shoulders, her deep brown skin and huge doe eyes were exactly the same. She wore yards of ivy-patterned teal scarf over a slouchy eggshell sweaterdress, along with impossibly dainty, feather-shaped silver earrings; courtesy of her little sister, no doubt. Lark Thorn had been into designing jewelry even before I left.

"Might I offer my services?" she asked, holding up her hands and waggling her fingers playfully. Though all the families technically had access to the same healing spells in the Grimoire, the Thorns were the most skilled healers of the bunch, by far. The talent tied in somehow with their affinity for nature-based green magic, a lineage they could trace back to druids in Ireland.

"By all means, do give me the hands," I replied, leaning across the table toward her. "As much as I'd like to pretend I'm still the gritty party animal you remember from high school, my situation's actually pretty dire."

"Oh, yeah, the party animal who used to set her own Saturday night curfew so as to not 'waste' too much of her Sundays being hungover," she teased, pressing her fingertips to my temples.

"Establishing a sustainable work ethic is *important*, Linden."

Scoffing fondly, she closed her eyes and murmured a low incantation. A honeyed swirl of warmth spiraled through my head, vivid scrolls of amethyst and emerald green unspooling in the darkness behind my eyelids. Healing magic felt wonderful; comforting and somehow ineffably luxurious, like an aromatherapy massage complete with one of those gingerbread-scented pillows warm under your neck.

"Ugh, I can't quite get it all, sorry," she said when she drew back, grimacing and shaking out her hands, as if some of my hangover ick was physically adhering to her skin. Maybe it was; having never been strong enough to pull one off, I had no idea how healing spells worked in practice. "Unfortunately for you," she added, "Rowan's still better at this than I am."

I swiveled my head experimentally, relieved to find that the pounding ache had eased quite a bit, though I still felt sludgy and a little green around the gills.

"How *is* your brother?" Linden's twin and I hadn't been close, but I had fond memories of him as a quiet, wiry boy with an exceptionally sweet smile, doctoring sparrow fledglings with bent wings and smuggling barn kittens into his bedroom. "Still trying to heal every fallen bird and stray he can find?"

"Pretty much. He actually took over for our dad as barn vet last year."

Before she could continue, a baby-faced server raced over with a coffeepot and ice water, thirsty for a tip on a slow morning. A cursory glance at the menu confirmed that Angelina's offerings hadn't changed much since I was last here. After he took our order, I pulled the chilly glass closer and took a long sip, raising my eyebrows at Lin.

"Does that mean Aspen's officially retired?"

"Nah, he's just pulled back from daily operations a little. Calls it his semiretirement. He still oversees most of the orchard logistics with me, though, what with him being too damn obstinate to actually take it easy a day in his life. Mama and Lark are good, too, always asking after you."

I smiled at the thought of Linden's stately mother, Gabrielle, who'd basically been my third parent, and her exuberant little sister.

"And what about you?" I gave her a meaningful look. "The romance updates have grown alarmingly sparse of late. How am I supposed to keep my friendship card current without knowing who's attending to my bestie's carnal needs?"

Lin nibbled on the inside of her cheek, giving me an uncharacteristically restrained twitch of a smile. "Not that much to report, really. Just taking a little step back from dating, kind of a break. Focusing on myself instead, and prioritizing work."

I squinted at her, bemused. Linden was one of the most energetic daters I'd ever met, a devout believer in the idea that the pursuit of love was ultimately a numbers game, a lottery you were bound to win as long as you maximized your entries. The idea of her "taking a step back" from putting herself out there felt fundamentally wrong, as if the entire universe had gotten up on the wrong side of the bed.

"I find that . . . a little challenging to believe, Lins," I said, striving for tact. "Seeing as you've never taken a break from dating the entire time I've known you, which is your whole life. You were dating in the *third* grade—or must I remind you of Tommy Giacomo, of the Bieber hair and worm-collecting habit verging on life-ruining addiction?"

She laughed a little at that, still avoiding my eyes. "I did start pretty damn early, didn't I? Guess it was past time for burnout."

I examined her more closely as she busied herself with her water glass, drawing little doodles in the condensation. There was a new cloudiness to her, a watercolor wash of sadness I couldn't quite reconcile with the relentlessly upbeat sunrise of a person with whom I'd shared a childhood and young adulthood. It was true that our correspondence had felt a little flat over the past few months, but I'd ascribed it to an organic growing apart. The settling in of a natural and healthy distance, as our friendship evolved by necessity into something less intimate than one based on shared experiences.

But now that she sat across from me looking so unwontedly sad, the thought of willingly drifting away from her gave me a painful pang of loss. How many shimmering nights had I spent in the orchards with Lin, drunk on hard cider and heckling the tourists on the haunted hayride, picnicking in secluded nooks of the hedge maze that thorned up for anyone but us, feasting on her aunt Wisteria's orchard pie on hungover mornings after?

I had good friends in Chicago, of course, the kind who'd stay overnight at the hospital with you when your appendix nearly burst—and better yet, who didn't blink at sharing their Netflix and Hulu passwords. But none who had grown up with me, or done magic with me in the hushed heart of a town so enchanted it felt alive around you.

Then our food arrived, jostling aside all other concerns as my immediate priority. I cut into the fried cake with the side of my fork, my eyes sliding closed at the first perfect mouthful. Just as I reached for Lin's milkshake to steal a sip, a lanky, raven-haired form slid into the booth next to her.

"Morning, Harlow," Talia said, nudging a reluctant Linden until she scooted over to make room, and flicking me a smile that immediately drew heat to my cheeks. "Glad to see we can still count you among the living. I confess I had my doubts."

With her glossy black waves and radiant skin, a burgundy top baring her porcelain shoulders, she looked like she'd emerged from our night of drunken debauchery not only unscathed but somehow refreshed, as if she'd washed her face with morning dew like some kind of Slavic nymph. It made me wonder whether the rumor was true and Avramovs really had a crossroads deal with the devil going, to keep them good-looking at all costs.

"What the hell, Tal?" Linden groaned before I could respond, burying her face in her hands. "What are you doing here already? You were supposed to give me more time!"

"'Tal'?" I echoed slowly, shifting my gaze between them in growing confusion. In all the years our families had known one another, I couldn't remember these two exchanging more than perfunctory greetings. "You two are on a nickname-and-brunch-crashing basis now? That's . . . *curious.*"

"The thing is, Harlow, we have a proposition for you," Talia replied, draping her arms over the tabletop with her wrists crossed, like a lazing cat. "And pardon my early appearance, Lin, but I didn't fully trust you not to chicken out on telling her. So hex me."

Courtesy of my gutter-minded disposition, I found myself stuck on 'proposition.' Courtesy of years of friendship, Linden read my mind with a single look, rolling her eyes.

"Not *that* kind of proposition, Em, damn. Keep it in your pants."

"Wait, so this is some kind of collusion?" I narrowed my eyes at them, increasingly baffled. "You two not only use nicknames, but collude? What else have I missed? Has a new age dawned or something?"

The Avramovs and the Thorns did not, historically, get along. The Avramovs were a little too Sturm und Drang, practitioners of a darker shade of magic than the nature- and light-working Thorns were comfortable contemplating, though even the Avramov clan kept well away from the truly dangerous shit like hexes.

At least, as far as I was aware—though with Avramovs, who ever knew for sure.

"Not a new age, exactly," Talia said thoughtfully, cocking her head. "Although that would be cool. But the circle of witches scorned by Gareth Blackmoore is hereby complete."

"What the hell are you talking about, Talia?" I demanded. "I mean, yeah, you and I have both had unfortunate relations with Gareth, but Lin doesn't even . . ."

My voice trailed off as I considered the chill in Linden's recent communication, her withdrawn demeanor in person, the faint pall of sadness hanging over her.

"Linden Sharee Thorn," I said, a surge of raw pain welling up my throat. "Have you, *likewise*, had unfortunate relations with Gareth Blackmoore?"

Linden hid her face behind her hands, sighing so gustily I could actually hear it through her fingers. When she finally lowered them, she looked so sad and plaintively guilty that I almost felt bad for her.

Key word, *almost*.

"I'm sorry, Em, I really am," she mumbled, chewing on the inside of her cheek and avoiding my eyes. "It's not like I planned it! We'd been spending a lot of time together, trying to hammer out a deal for the Blackmoores to carry Honeycake cherry wine and brandy at Camelot. And it just kind of . . . happened, I guess?"

Camelot was the Blackmoore family's most lucrative holding, a massive indoor-outdoor Renn Faire housed in a full-blown castle on their property, where tourists could enjoy immersive theater, medieval jousting, a Cirque du Soleil–esque show that stealthily incorporated the Blackmoores' flashy magic, and several themed restaurants and bars.

It was also, in my opinion, the very soul of tackiness.

"And you'd been gone so long," Linden added, shoulders hunching, hopefully at the utter feebleness of this excuse. "I didn't think it would even matter to you that much if he and I wound up together."

"And you seriously believed that you might get a happy ever after with him, Lin?" I demanded, struggling to believe that even my relentless optimist of a best friend could be so astoundingly naïve. Or that she would do something like this to me. "Gareth Blackmoore, of all people? After the way he treated me?"

"He was a dumb asshole of a kid, yeah," she said, sucking her lower lip through her teeth. "And he hurt you horribly, I *know* that.

But he's an adult now, and okay, maybe it's still a weird and screwed-up thing for me to believe, but for a while it felt like we had a real connection. And I *swear* I didn't think you'd be that upset about it, not after all this time. If you ever even came back at all."

She was partly right; I had written Thistle Grove off as definitively as I could, had even begun resigning myself to the prospect of an eventual, inevitable drifting away from Linden herself. I didn't have any legitimate right to feel betrayed by her choice, not after the ones I'd made.

But it hurt anyway, with the visceral intensity of a full-fledged betrayal.

"We both thought it would be a good idea to keep it quiet, at least for a while," she continued. "Just give ourselves some space. You know how the families like to talk."

"And that way he could also continue fucking me on the side," Talia chimed in, very helpfully. Linden fisted a hand against her belly at the phrasing, her face scrunching up. "We were keeping our thing under wraps, too, since it was mostly casual. So you can see how this was all working out swimmingly for him—until my sister saw him with Lin, on a cozy dinner date in Carbondale. Bastard's lucky I managed to talk Isidora down, or he'd still have baby spiders hatching out of his ears."

"Gareth Blackmoore, two-timing my best friend and Talia Avramov," I murmured, pinching the bridge of my nose hard as I tried to wrap my head around the span of this mental abomination. "Wow, wow, wow."

"I don't know that I'd call it two-timing per se," Talia said, tapping a finger to her chin.

"I would," Linden said grimly.

"Of course *you* would, sunshine," Talia replied, giving Linden's arm a brisk rub. "He hurt you much worse than he hurt me. He and I were just having fun—though, yes, I was under the distinct impression that it was exclusive fun. Whereas you were in full-throttle love with the shithead."

"I was not in *love* with him!" Linden protested.

Talia waved away the semantics with an irritable swat. "Passionate and emotionally invested lust, then. Whatever you want to call it, you can't pretend he didn't break your heart."

Linden sucked in a shaky breath and pressed her lips together, then allowed herself a clipped nod. Another spike of pain lanced through me at the thought of my childhood best friend and my most detestable ex not only together, but involved enough that it had left Lin this gutted. Whatever had happened between them, it had clearly run much deeper than a fling.

"He tried to give me that 'so sorry, it didn't mean anything' crap, too," Linden added tightly. "As if that *ever* flies."

"I call bullshit, too. I have it on good authority that I'm an extremely meaningful lay," Talia quipped. But her eyes flashed with restrained anger, simmering close beneath her flippant facade; she was clearly still smarting from the heedless way Gareth had treated her.

"And then there's me, the one who kicked off Gareth's streak. We really are the coven of the scorned, aren't we?" I murmured, dragging a dismal hand down my face. "Maybe a new age *has* dawned—and it's terrible."

"Or maybe it has, and it's fucking fantastic," Talia countered, a dangerous smile playing on her lips, "because it's a time of come-uppance for cocky dipshits who think they're larger than life. Starting with Gareth Blackmoore, Prince of Bastards."

5

The Witches' Vengeance Pact

"SO, WHAT EXACTLY are you proposing?" I asked, taking a sip of lukewarm coffee to jolt my lagging brain back into life.

"Sweet revenge, of course," Talia replied, crossing her arms and leaning back against the booth. "When I found out what was up, I reached out to Lin to see if she was interested in some payback. Because obviously this level of abject fuckery could not be allowed to stand."

I glanced dubiously over at Linden, who'd never been much of an eye-for-an-eye person, preferring instead to trust karma with the meting out of just deserts in due time—only to find her nodding along with Talia, steely-eyed, her shoulders squared with unusual resolve. Gareth really had left scorched and salted earth behind him yet again. For a moment, I found myself marveling over the way he managed to continuously one-up himself when it came to reprehensible behavior, like a constant and perplexing self-own.

From a certain angle, that much skullduggery was almost impressive.

"First I thought, maybe Issa had a point," Talia continued, "and we could look into some suitable hexes. You know, a lifetime of erectile dysfunction, uncontrollable overgrowth of pubic hair, that type of shit. However, Angelcake McSparklepony over here would 'not be privy to causing harm.'"

She put this last in finger quotes, rolling her eyes, as if an aversion to causing harm indicated a moderately loathsome weakness of the temperament. Linden blinked beside her, mutely repeating *sparklepony* to herself.

"Sparklepony?" I asked, barely managing not to laugh.

"Like a unicorn, but worse," Talia replied with an exaggerated shudder. "Unwilling to impale even the deserving with one's head."

"First off, I am not a . . . a *sparklepony*," Linden said hotly, having regained the power of speech. "Forgive me for having a working moral compass, I know it must seem super weird to you. Second, stop acting like you're some kind of bad-bitch warlock. As I recall, you weren't down for any hexing, either."

"I'll allow that I'd prefer not to fuck with the powers of darkness if an alternative is readily available. And lucky for us, one is." She tipped her sleek head toward me, lazy grin glinting like a blade's edge. "Enter the final member of our vengeance coven."

"And I come into play how, exactly?" I said, a murky possibility looming out of my mental fog like an iceberg. "Might this have something to do with the Gauntlet of the Grove?"

"Indeed, it might. Because what could be a better punishment for Gareth than losing the Gauntlet to Rowan Thorn?" Talia bit her full lower lip through her sly smile, her gray eyes widening with anticipation. "Or, better yet, losing it to me?"

What with last night's emotional turbulence and the ensuing brownout, it had somehow entirely slipped my mind that while I arbitrated the Gauntlet, Gareth, Talia, and Linden's older-by-six-minutes twin brother would actually be duking it out against one another as the Blackmoore, Avramov, and Thorn scions, respectively.

"Assuming you could even pull something like that off—and given that the Blackmoores have been sweeping the Gauntlet since the town was founded, let's say I have some reservations," I started. "But even if I didn't, what would be the point? Do you sincerely believe that blocking Gareth from becoming Thistle Grove's *magical mayor* is going to cut him all that deep? He already has everything he could ever want. What's another title on top of all that?"

Talia cocked her head like a disgruntled raven, leveling an incredulous stare at me.

"Seriously, Harlow?" she demanded. "I know you've been out of the loop for a while, but even you must know that Victor of the Gauntlet is much more than an honorary title. It increases the winning family's magical power by magnitudes, even bends fortune to their favor. Not to mention the longevity perks. Gareth's grandmother Igraine won fifty years ago, and she still looks like a silver fox snack."

"Tal, *ew.*"

"What, Lin? It's true." Talia widened her eyes, looking downright delighted at Linden's appalled expression. "The dowager Blackmoore—aside from being an awful soul-dead harpy—is remarkably well-preserved for a woman pushing eighty."

"Moving right along," Linden said, giving a little shudder, "look what the Blackmoores have done with all the centuries they've

been winning. They're multimillionaires, and absurdly strong witches to boot."

"Exactly," I pointed out. "Which makes their winning almost a self-fulfilling prophecy."

"But that's the beauty of this plan," Talia insisted, raking a hand back through the shining fall of her hair, her eyes glittering with conviction. "What Lin and I want to do is team up against them. Something that's *never* been done before, not in more than three hundred years of Thistle Grove history."

I crossed my arms over my chest and leaned back against the wheezing upholstery, narrowing my eyes at her. "I *am* the Arbiter, remember? I assume that entails cracking down on any cheating-type shenanigans. And I'm not sure two houses teaming up against a third qualifies as playing by the rules."

"Just because it's never been done doesn't mean it's forbidden," Talia retorted, her lips curving with mischief. It was an extremely good look on her, much like most looks I'd seen so far.

"So says the morally ambiguous gray hat," Linden interjected. "Though in this case, I'm compelled to agree with her, Em. I've pored over the Gauntlet rules and the fine print, and there's just nothing in the Grimoire prohibiting alliances."

"We've done our research, Harlow," Talia pressed, leaning into my hesitation. "If it's the Thorns, the Avramovs, *and* the Harlows against the Blackmoores, we might have a real shot at this thing."

"You can't really count the Harlows in," I pointed out. "No matter how you're envisioning me playing into this scheme, the whole point of an Arbiter is impartiality."

"Sure, but that doesn't mean you can't be part of this," Talia argued. "For starters, your family's been keeping records of this town's magical history since its founding. There must be Gauntlet lore over at Tomes that you can dig into for us, if you're down for it. I'm not suggesting anything underhanded. Just . . . a study guide for the challenges, if you will. To help me and Rowan prepare."

"So your brother's in on this, too, then?" I asked, glancing at Linden.

"Of course," she replied steadily. "You know how it is with me and Rowan. He knows how . . . how I've been feeling. And he's been itching to turn the tables on Gareth since I told him what happened."

"How long *have* you two been cooking this up, anyway?" I demanded. "Actually, hold up—is that why you were at the Cauldron last night, Talia? To feel out whether I might be game?"

The idea of it bothered me in an indistinctly twinging way, hitting somewhere been embarrassment and hurt. If she'd been there only for strategy's sake, then that unexpected, glimmering spark between us couldn't have been anything more than a figment of my imagination.

"Believe it or not, that was a happy coincidence," Talia answered with a shrug, and I relaxed a little. "Courtesy of whatever elder gods look kindly upon me, I'm assuming. I've been toying with this idea since the summer, and Linden and I were planning on an alliance regardless. But with you on board? This would play out *perfect*."

I tilted my head from side to side, still not quite convinced, tapping my fingertips against my upper arms.

"What's the hesitation, Harlow?" Talia prodded, leaning over the table and fixing me with that disconcerting stare.

"Honestly? I'm not sure it's worth all this effort, just to keep Gareth Blackmoore from taking home yet another trophy, even a major one like this. I don't love the idea of being so focused on him." I thought back to last night, the effortless ease with which Gareth had unbroken my glass. "Especially if he's still likely to win no matter what."

Talia's gray eyes narrowed, gaze intensifying until I could almost feel its weight alighting on me like some tangible, predatory force. Something with talons, and a very wide wingspan.

"Listen," she said, interlacing her fingers on the table. "We all know Gareth's likely to get the win anyway. But just think . . . how fucking *satisfying* would it be to see him squirm, make him look bad in front of everyone? Can you imagine how much it would sting, getting his ass handed to him at even one challenge?"

"You do have a point there," I conceded.

"I sure as shit do, Harlow. That entitled dickhead has sailed through his whole life with a silver spoon in his mouth, getting exactly what he wanted at every turn. Including the three of us. So let's not let him have this, too."

I flicked between Lin's pained expression and Talia's stormy eyes, struggling to keep abreast of my own tumbling thoughts. Gareth had stripped the three of us of so much, stolen from us like a thief. My future in Thistle Grove, Linden's faith in love conquering all, Talia's . . .

Well, maybe he'd only dinged Talia's pride. But the Avramovs put a lot of stock in their pride, something I keenly understood, and the casually deceptive way he'd treated sleeping with her had clearly stuck in her craw.

"The thing is, I've already let Gareth shape my life more than I'd like," I said, trying to articulate what was really bothering me here. "And as much as the idea of bringing him down sounds fantastic, I came back here because it was important to my family that I uphold Gauntlet tradition. I didn't come back for that asshole, not in *any* shape or form."

Talia's eyes thawed at that, reminding me of the oddly gentle and earnest way she'd listened to me last night, the heat of her hand over mine.

"And I respect that, Harlow," she said. "I do. Consider, though, that this isn't *just* about him. It's also about the Blackmoores stacking the deck in their own favor for centuries."

"What do you mean?"

"Four families founded this town, not one. But they've been making Thistle Grove all about them, edging the rest of us out since they built that trashy monstrosity and called it a 'historical' attraction. And put yourself in a tourist's shoes—if you come here to get your Halloween fix, what do you spend your money on? A séance at the Emporium, or a whole fucking medieval castle with all the bells and whistles?"

"She's right, Em," Linden said somberly. "We've been feeling the pressure, too. The Blackmoores have their own pumpkin patch and sunflower farm out at Camelot now, too, even a whole jack-o'-lantern display every season."

I remembered Gareth bragging to his bros about the expansion of Camelot last night at the Cauldron, even raising a toast to the new additions. So this was what he'd been so proud of, stealing business from Talia and Lin. For all I knew, they were planning on opening a themed bookstore, too, and just hadn't gotten around to it yet; I wouldn't have put it past them.

"We've really had to tighten our belts this year," Linden went on. "That's why the liquor deal with them was so important in the first place."

Talia nodded, her face hardening until her delicate features looked chiseled from some unyielding stone. "Things continue the way they are, the Emporium only has another season or two before it goes under for good."

A sudden anger spun up in me, like an unforecasted hurricane, at the thought of the Blackmoores turning this enchanted jewel of a town into a cheesy spectacle engineered purely for their profit. There was so much more to Thistle Grove than the Blackmoores, just like Talia had said. Four witches founded Thistle Grove, and its power was meant to be shared equitably between their families—not hoarded by one family year after year, until they eclipsed the others into irrelevancy.

Maybe the founders would never have established the Gauntlet in the first place, had they known that *this* was what would come of it.

The wrongness of it whipped through me, along with a bitter tinge of regret that I'd let my connection to this place snuff out so thoroughly that I hadn't even known about any of this. I might have forged a new life away from Thistle Grove, but this was still the town that grew and made me. I owed it to my own family, as well as the Thorns and Avramovs, to help right its foundering balance.

And seeing Gareth Blackmoore, Prince of Bastards, take it on the chin surely wouldn't hurt.

"You know what, fuck it." I slammed my hands flat on the table, my fingers flexing. "I'm in, witches. Let's run amok."

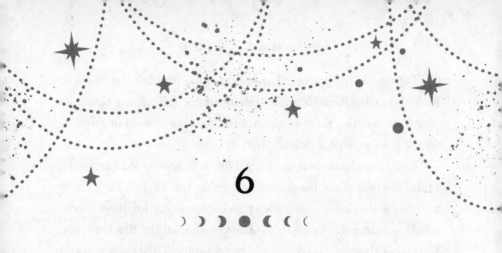

6

The Original Grimoire

As I swung open the heavy door to Tomes & Omens, a brass bell sang out above my head. I could feel the wisp of an identification spell it sent flitting through the shop's dust-laden air, spinning this way and that like a sprite until it darted off into the back room. Letting my father know who'd darkened the bookshop's door, so he could attend to or ignore the visitor at his leisure.

While I waited for him to emerge, I wandered between the bookshelves and glass cases, running my fingers over cracked spines and the magical novelty items displayed between them. Athames with sigil-inscribed hilts, carved figurines of gods and goddesses, stoppered jars filled with dried herbs and incense sticks. Everything I touched buzzed under my fingers with a prickly warning energy. A protection spell wreathed the entire space, my father's most ambitious magical undertaking; it surged in every object on display, ready to singe the greedy hands of any aspiring shoplifter or vandal who wandered inside with ill intent.

Good-natured as he was, James Harlow would never stand for one of his charges being hurt or misused.

And it worked the other way around, too. While most of the books in here were the sort you could find at any indie bookstore, my father was also a rare and antiquarian book seller, collecting magical treatises of every kind. Years ago, while I was dusting, I stumbled across a hoary copy of the *Necronomicon* on one of the back and topmost shelves; a single touch infected me with hideous nightmares for over a month. The protection spell also made sure you never left with anything you weren't equipped to handle.

"Everything like you remember, scoot?" my father's deep voice rumbled from behind me.

"Definitely smells the same," I answered, smiling as I turned to greet him. He still towered over me—I'd inherited my diminutive height from my mother's side, no question—bending down to draw me into a brief hug, my cheek rubbing against the coarse wool of his houndstooth vest. And he smelled the same, too, like cedar and strong coffee, mingled with the bitter tang of the old ink always lingering on his fingers. "Maybe dustier, if that's even possible. Couldn't bribe anyone else to keep the place up for you after I left, huh?"

"Wouldn't *trust* anyone but you with the job," he corrected with a wry grin as he pulled away, a network of lines creasing into his weathered cheeks. For a dyed-in-the-wool bookworm, the man who taught me to love books and play chess, my father played against type by being outdoorsy, too. I could barely remember a Saturday without him coaxing me awake with Darjeeling at dawn for some adventure, hiking on Hallows Hill or kayaking on the lake. "Always said I'd only ever have one apprentice."

"I bet Delilah's made a play or two for it, though," I quipped.

He acknowledged the joke with a somber nod of his curly dark head, much grayer at the temples than I remembered; a testament to the time I'd let pass between us. "Like I always said, scoot. No one but you."

He didn't mean for it to sting, I could tell from the tenderness in the brown eyes behind the beatnik frames he always wore. But I'd known since I was little that my father always meant for me to inherit this place, and to travel the world in little bursts just like he did, venturing from Thistle Grove only to trade in books rare and old as relics. That was how he and my mother had met; she was studying English and literature at Oxford when he visited to sell a first edition of some obscure masterpiece to the Bodleian collection. They came across each other at a local pub, and the rest was history.

It was hard to forget that I was basically the product of my parents' love affairs with books. And given how much I'd cared about this shop before I left—how much I'd considered it a certain part of my future—it was impossible not to feel that I'd let my father down with every single choice I'd made as an adult.

"It's good to have you back, is all," he said, on the wake of a long sigh. "Thanks for coming, scoot. I know you have another life to live out there. Means the world that you took the time."

"Wouldn't have missed it," I replied weakly, such a giant and awkward lie that my cheeks threatened to combust. I turned away from him a little, clearing my throat against the discomfort. "So, Mom said the Halloween crowd's kicked up already?"

"Oh, yes, it's been chaos for weeks now." He grimaced with distaste, rubbing the side of his narrow nose. "Feels a bit beyond the pale this year. It does occur to me that it could be the energy of the Gauntlet firing up. Might draw sensitives, maybe even dormant witches. It would certainly explain the uptick."

"But the Gauntlet doesn't even formally begin until Wednesday, I thought?"

My father cast me one of his rare smiles, wide and bright and startlingly rakish. It made him look more like a rogue wizard on the run from some Magical Establishment than a quiet, middle-aged proprietor of a store trafficking in *mostly* harmless books. Seeing it made me understand why my mother would have flung aside a whole life to forge a new one with him, on the other side of an entire ocean.

"Oh, it began as soon as you set foot within town lines, scoot—if not even before that, when you first agreed to come. Don't tell me you didn't feel Thistle Grove bidding the Gauntlet's Arbiter welcome when you arrived."

"So *that's* what that was," I said, thinking of the cresting swell of magic that had greeted me when I crossed town lines. "Nearly knocked me off the road."

A complicated expression drifted over my father's face. It was both speculative and knowing, tinged with something close to sadness. It vanished so quickly, like a suppressed memory, that I didn't even have a chance to ask what he was thinking before he moved on.

"I thought I could give you a little primer on the Gauntlet," he said more briskly, turning to head toward the back of the shop. "Run you through what everything will look like."

"Sounds like a plan. I could definitely use a brushup."

I followed him through the maze of stacks—my father had never believed in fostering any library-like semblance of order here, though the contents of the shop were flawlessly cataloged in his mind—to the spiral staircase in the back, wending vertiginously up to the bookstore's attic. This was where the most powerful books were safeguarded, along with all the records of the founding families and the town's magical history, which the Harlows have kept for centuries.

The attic swam with dust, too, maybe even more so than below, but it also smelled intoxicatingly of incense-sweet Thistle Grove magic. Some of the books themselves exhaled that distinctive scent, the fragrance seeping from their pages. Clear midday sun streamed through the dormer windows, and yet the light in here felt oddly golden, just like I remembered. Dreamy and sepia-toned, as if the magic had steeped into the molecules of the air and subtly changed their hue.

The Grimoire waited for us, set between two banker's lamps on the hulking pedestal desk that occupied the attic's left corner—and not the much more modest Harlow copy I'd grown up with, either. This edition of the Grimoire was massive and leather bound, with gilded lettering embossed on the age-weathered cover. And this version of the spellbook *sang* to me, in a distant whisper both dreamy and lilting, beckoning me over. It sounded like the ghost of some ethereal serenade, sung by sirens sprawled over ancient rocks; a gorgeous, faraway melody, enticing and just the slightest touch sinister.

Before I knew it, I'd crossed the room to place both palms flat on its cover.

Without warning, a gout of magic crashed over me like a breaking wave. It was akin to what I'd felt when entering the town, but magnified a thousandfold. The sensation literally took my breath away, roaring through me with untrammeled force, powerful and ravenous.

Weirder yet, I could feel my own dormant power surging within me in answer, rising up to meet it, uncoiling inside me like a dragon spreading its wings for flight. For a moment, it felt as if I was lifting into the air myself, my senses shooting out like tendrils to caress the sinuous boundaries of the town, as though I could feel Thistle Grove itself. As though I was *inside* it, in some much deeper way than just by physical presence alone.

All in all, it was way sexier than touching a dry and dusty tome should ever really be.

"Okay, wow," I managed through tingling lips, yanking my hands back. "That is, uh, *not* how I remember our copy of the Grimoire."

"I'm not surprised. This is the original, after all." My father spread his hands, grinning at my awe, though a trace of that complex look still lingered in his eyes. "The spellbook written by Elias Harlow himself. It's kept locked away by our family between Gauntlets, to foil any attempts at tampering or cheating. And you *are* the Arbiter now, scoot. It's been waiting for you to open it for many, many years."

I shuffled a half step away from the desk, leery of being reeled in again by that forceful undertow. "So what does that mean, really, being Arbiter? What am I going to need to do?"

My father took a seat at the desk, motioning me toward the other chair. "How much do you remember about the Gauntlet?"

"All the basic stuff. A spellcasting tournament of three challenges for the three competing houses," I said, ticking them off my fingers as I sat down a healthy distance from the desk, still wary of getting too close to this Grimoire. "Magical contests of strength, wit, and speed. Kind of drawing a blank beyond that, though. I don't recall reading much about the Arbiter's specific responsibilities."

It had been a very long time since I read the Harlow copy of the Grimoire from cover to cover. Back when we were in our early teens, Delilah and I had alternated weeks in checking it out from my dad at Tomes & Omens, all but wrestling each other to the ground over whose turn it was. As if the store was our personal library, and the Grimoire itself something that rightfully belonged to us even if it did have to be borrowed.

That nerdy little witch I used to be, immersed in my family's spellbook for hours and so in love with magic, felt like a distant, achy memory. Somebody I'd once known well, but hadn't seen in years.

"That's because that bit wouldn't have been in our family's copy of the Grimoire. The four others are almost exact facsimiles of this one, but the original isn't just a spellbook . . . part of it *is* a spell. You won't find this particular section in any of the others."

His eyes agleam with the zeal of a scholar on a roll, he cracked the heavy book open about three-quarters of the way through, sliding it toward me.

"'Incantations for the Gauntlet of the Grove,'" I read on the open page, in a flowing antiquated script full of flourishes and loops. Below the title, the rest of the page was blank. "But there's nothing here?"

"The challenges will appear only for the Arbiter, and only when it's time," he explained. "That way, the competing families couldn't possibly prepare for them in advance. On Wednesday night, you'll put on the Arbiter's mantle, and once its spell activates, the charm that declares the Gauntlet open will manifest for you. The mantle's spell also serves to magnify your senses—so you can see what plays out between the combatants during challenges, down to the smallest detail."

"Like superhero senses?" I made an appreciative moue, raising my eyebrows. "Sounds nifty."

"From what she's told me, your nana Caro certainly thought so, back when she arbitrated." His smile faded a little, and he fixed me with a semistern look, brows beetling together. "The magic will also force you to be impartial in your verdict—not that I'd expect any less of you, even if that weren't the case."

The idea of being a lightning rod for a current of magic as powerful as what I'd felt touching the Grimoire—maybe even *more* powerful—hollowed out my stomach with both excitement and a chilly curl of trepidation.

"So, okay, I play master of ceremonies," I said, striving for composure. "And then what happens?"

"The Avramovs will host the opening gala right afterward, as is traditional. After that, Lady's Lake will . . ."

My father's words receded into a background murmur as I wondered dreamily how Talia Avramov might dress for a gala hosted at her imposing family manse. Something formfitting but dramatically dark, I'd expect, against all that creamy skin. Maybe she'd wear her hair up for it, all the better to showcase the Avramov garnet against that absurdly long and slender neck. Maybe—

"Scoot?" I emerged from my reverie to find my father watching me with a touch of censure, one expectant eyebrow raised. "Have I lost you already?"

"No, no, sorry," I said, chastened. "Lady's Lake, you were saying?"

"Yes, next Saturday, in lieu of a Sabbat," he said, a touch impatiently. The families held witches' Sabbats every Saturday in October, I remembered, though it'd been a long time since I'd last been at one. "The lake is always the site of the opening challenge, whichever one falls first. Remember, it's the Grimoire that chooses the order in which combatants are tested for strength, speed, and wit. They won't know which it is until you tell them."

"And they're always different, the challenges?" I asked, taking care to keep only innocent curiosity on my face—though I was wondering how Talia and Rowan could practice for something completely unexpected, and how I could possibly be of any help without compromising the Arbiter's integrity. "Or does the Grimoire ever recycle them?"

My father's brow furrowed into a pensive frown. "They're new each time, as far as I know. But you could take a look at the records, if you're interested. You'll be adding to them yourself later on; part of the Arbiter's job is to document the challenges for posterity, once the Gauntlet is done."

"The Harlows always get stuck with the damn paperwork," I muttered, and my dad chuckled in response, shrugging a shoulder.

"There are much worse things than documenting this town's history, scoot. Being its voice, its quiet champion."

I gave him a flat *agree to disagree* look. He stifled a sigh, but let it go.

"Where were we . . . ah, the second challenge. That one will take place at the Thorn orchards, a week after the first," he went on. "And the final challenge is always held on Blackmoore grounds a week later—followed by the closing ball on Samhain Eve, also hosted by the Blackmoores at Tintagel, when the Victor is formally crowned."

"Of course, so they can enjoy their victory lap," I commented sourly. "So, three challenges, three combatants . . . what happens if there's a tie?"

"Well, it never *has* happened," he said, brows peaking at the prospect; my father had always managed to pack an impressive amount of emotion into his unruly eyebrows. "But in the very unlikely event that it does, the Grimoire will put forth a final tie-breaker challenge. And the Victor of that one will take home the wreath."

We probably wouldn't need to worry about that possibility this time around, either, if Gareth's effortless reconstruction of my glass was any indication of things to come. But from what I remembered of him, Rowan wasn't exactly a pushover—and given the general caliber of Avramovs' abilities, Talia might very well be a powerhouse herself. With the two of them working together, who knew how things might unfold?

"So, those are the broad strokes," my father said, flipping the Grimoire closed with the quasi-reverent care he reserved for books. "In the meantime, this Grimoire is at your disposal for the duration of the Gauntlet, should you need to refer to it for anything. I'd recommend reacquainting yourself with all the Gauntlet entries, to begin."

I reached for the Grimoire, steeling myself for another overwhelming magical assault. I didn't really want to touch it again at all, but at the very least, I'd want to read over the rules, make sure this version didn't contain any prohibition on an alliance between two houses. As if it sensed my apprehension, the spellbook sat circumspect under my touch, buzzing pleasantly against my skin but nothing more. I found its restraint oddly reassuring, giving me just a little hope that I wasn't in quite as far over my head as I suddenly felt.

Maybe arbitrating the Gauntlet in the town I thought I'd left behind for good, while I helped Linden and Talia scheme against Gareth Blackmoore, Prince of Bastards, would be manageable after all.

7

The Ring Effect

MY GOT-THIS ATTITUDE soldiered on until the night of the opening ceremony, before summarily abandoning me.

I stood in the vast and unruly garden behind The Bitters, the Avramovs' demesne, my high heels sinking into the soil beneath the overgrown grass. Wearing the pair of power Jimmy Choos I'd splurged on to celebrate my Enchantify promotion had probably been a bad call, but tonight I needed every shred of confidence I could muster. Deep night loomed above, the crescent moon glowing against it like some trickster's impish smile. Behind me, an ornate wrought iron fence, twined with ivy and topped with wickedly sharp finials, guarded against the thick woods that hulked behind The Bitters.

And in front of me, the three hundred or so members of the founding families stood robed and gathered, waiting for me to declare the Gauntlet begun.

Firelight from the scattered braziers painted their features with writhing lines of light and shadow, stripping even well-known faces of their familiarity. I couldn't even pick out my own mother, Nana Caro, or Delilah amid the hooded throng, much less Talia or Linden, though I knew they must all be here tonight; I'd forgotten just how many of us witches there were in this town.

I wasn't usually one for stage fright, but with the expectant weight of all their eyes on me, the sense of being scrutinized by a host of sinister strangers instead of people I'd grown up with, my heart pounded in sickening lurches, my knees going watery and weak.

"Ready, scoot?" my father murmured into my ear. He'd come to stand behind me, the heavily embroidered purple velvet of the Arbiter's mantle slung over his arm. The Grimoire sat waiting on the stone table in front of me, splayed open to the page of incantations, two fat pillar candles flickering on either side. The spellbook's pages stirred in the breeze, and I could feel the eager swell of its magic lapping against me like a rising tide.

Which meant it was almost time.

"Ready," I whispered back, licking my lips. Trepidation surged in my throat as he unfolded the mantle and shook it out, my stomach twisting with irrational qualms. What if it didn't work? What if the mantle felt the way my magic had guttered since I'd been gone, and rejected me as Arbiter? What if—

Then the fabric settled lightly over my shoulders—and its spell ignited, burning out every last trace of nerves.

A sudden wind kicked up around me, swirling around my feet. It built upon itself, gaining in intensity until the Grimoire's pages fluttered wildly in the gale like thrashing wings. A swell of magic thundered through me until I felt as though I were *expanding*, growing like the giant beanstalk in the tale, rushing up and up into the sky. Soon I loomed above the peaked roofs, turreted towers, and widow's walks of the Avramovs' manse, its wolf-and-serpent weather vanes whirling in the gusts of wind. I was somehow so tall that I could see Lady's Lake glimmering atop Hallows Hill to the west, could even spot the glowing storefronts and the milling streams of tourists coursing down Yarrow Street toward the east.

Whooooa, I marveled giddily to myself, high on the magical equivalent of heroin. The mantle's magic was immeasurably stronger than any spell I'd managed on my own before, and it felt nothing short of fucking *spectacular.*

Did not *expect the Galadriel-puts-on-the-Ring effect, but must admit it is absurdly cool.*

Amid the dizzying euphoria, I found that words had appeared on the page of incantations, emblazoned in a glowing script. And even though I *felt* miles high—and maybe even looked it in some way, judging by the stunned expressions in the crowd—the Grimoire was still exactly where it had been before, right within reach of my fingertips.

"Elder Igraine, matriarch of House Blackmoore," I boomed, in a knelling cadence that sounded like some behemoth orchestra playing my voice, "Victor of the sixth Gauntlet of the Grove. Your time now comes to cede the wreath."

A figure peeled away from the shadowy mass of people that seemed impossibly far below me. But I could see Gareth's grandmother perfectly well as she approached, the silver wreath perched on a chignon of ice-blond hair. She really did look no older than when I'd left Thistle Grove, and even then she'd seemed uncannily youthful, just as Talia had said; her skin porcelain pale and smooth, a stern cast to her patrician face.

She took off the wreath and set it on the table in front of the Grimoire, giving me a grudgingly respectful dip of the head. But I could see the challenge blaze to life in her pale blue eyes, the way her hand lingered on the circlet before she withdrew.

As if she was saying, *Don't get too attached, my girl. Me and mine will be having this back.*

Rebellion surged up in my throat, a revolt so hostile and potent it almost felt like it hadn't come entirely from me. *No, ma'am, you won't*, I thought back at her. *Not if I have any say in it.*

As Igraine rejoined the throng, I slid my fingers down the page, where more words had resolved. "I call now upon the combatants of the seventh Gauntlet of the Grove. Scions of Houses Blackmoore, Thorn, and Avramov . . . you may approach."

The three of them stepped out from the crowd's lip, moving to stand in front of me. Gareth wore a pair of titanium vambraces like some kind of modern knight errant, and flowing robes in the family's traditional onyx and gold. Allegedly the colors of Morgan le Fay herself, though it was beyond me how the Blackmoores might know the favorite colors of an Arthurian sorceress who'd lived a thousand years ago, if she'd ever lived at all. I guess they figured what the hell; not like there was anyone around to prove them wrong.

Gareth must have known that it would be me, but the sickening recognition on his face as the pieces fell fully into place—Arbiter Harlow, Emmeline Harlow, the "new" girl from the Shamrock Cauldron—was *immensely* satisfying all the same.

Next to Gareth, Rowan Thorn stood swathed in a druid's moss green and brown hooded cloak, holding a hazelwood staff in one strong hand, a tiny wren perched on its tip. He was much taller, broader across the shoulders, and even more handsome than I remembered, with his hair in waist-length locs and a sprinkling of freckles across the wide bridge of his nose. He shot me a closed-lipped smile, his hazel eyes warm as he tipped the tiniest of winks, as if to say, *It's on*.

And then there was Talia.

Her cowl was pushed back, hair twisted away from her face and piled on her head in a gleaming mass. Under a mulberry cape, she wore a bell-sleeved charcoal kirtle with a plunging neckline; the Avramov garnet winked in the hollow of her throat, above the silver corvid skull pendant that nestled against her cleavage. She was all strong jaw and winging cheekbones in the firelight, her eyes ghostly pale against the shadows that played across her face.

She looked like a daughter of Lilith, the kind of succubus you'd want creeping into your bedroom at the dark of the moon. And she smiled at me like a secret, the slightest curve to the corners of her mouth.

Even caught up in the mantle's heady magic, I couldn't make myself stop looking at her.

After a lengthy pause, Igraine Blackmoore stirred impatiently, clearing her throat from where she stood at the crowd's edge.

"Arbiter Harlow?" she called out, all but tapping her foot. "Perhaps you would like to carry on?"

I managed to peel my eyes from Talia, both annoyed and slightly abashed.

"I would *indeed*," I said snippily, and this time I sounded a little more like me than like the eldritch chorus of the Arbiter's voice. Bending back to the Grimoire, I searched for the next legible line. "Combatants, come, and pledge your intentions upon the wreath."

The three of them drew together seamlessly, almost as if they'd been expecting this; the other family Grimoires must have held their own Gauntlet instruction for their scions. Talia's hand landed on the wreath first, followed by Rowan's and Gareth's piled on top. All three of them paused for a count, and then called out in the same breath, "Upon my honor and my undying witch's soul, I intend victory for my House!"

As their voices died away, the wreath melted down into a burst of brilliant blue light, racing up the combatants' arms like a living flame before launching into the sky. High above us, it shaped the tripartite sigil that designated the Gauntlet, before fracturing into a fireworks display—a flower unfurling to reveal an armillary sphere, which deconstructed into orbs that cycled through the lunar phases before dispersing. Raining sparks down on the gathered families like a cascade of falling stars.

As everyone erupted into a tumultuous cheer, I felt the Grimoire pulse where my hand still rested against the page. I looked down and read the final phrase, my voice ringing out like a canon of church bells.

"As Harlow Arbiter and the voice of Thistle Grove, I declare this tournament begun!"

8

Because You Left

I<small>N THE</small> A<small>VRAMOVS'</small> grand ballroom, maroon velvet wallpaper clung to the walls, its tattered edges rippling in a faintly chilly breeze even though the room had no windows I could see. A gothic masterpiece of an iron chandelier, lit by real candles fat with strata of melted wax, swung ominously from the ceiling's embossed copper tiles. To top things off, a portrait of sloe-eyed Margarita Avramov hung above the red-veined gray marble fireplace, overseeing the proceedings with an air of vague contempt. The founder of House Avramov looked like she wouldn't mind making the Blackmoores eat some salty crow.

It all straddled the line between elegant and decrepit so seamlessly that the ballroom seemed custom-made to host your more vintage vampire ball. It looked like a room that should have a name, something classy yet sinister.

After I shed the mantle and the younger Avramov siblings

ushered everyone inside, my parents had downed a courtesy drink and shortly thereafter hightailed it out, crowded social gatherings having never been their scene. I would have loved to leave, too, but I refused to grant Gareth the luxury of forgetting that I was here. Talia and Linden must have been hidden within one of the knots of guests clustered along the walls, so I stood alone, increasingly aware of sidelong looks flung my way, ranging from the hostile to the merely curious.

I might not really be an interloper here, but after so many years away from Thistle Grove, maybe some of them felt that I no longer belonged. And maybe they were right—wasn't that what I'd intended, after all, by leaving without looking back?

When one of the tarnished silver trays bobbing through the air hovered to a stop in front of me, I gratefully snagged a goblet of red wine, a little unsettled by the magical aerodynamics of the thing. The tray seemed less enchanted, and more like some invisible server must be carrying it. It left me wondering whether I should say thank you just to be safe; maybe conjuring an entourage of spectral waiters was part of the Avramovs' uncanny repertoire. I made a mental note to ask Talia about it when I found her, a giddy thrill whorling around my stomach at the idea of seeing her again in that clinging dress, her hair up just like I'd hoped . . .

"Emmeline," a thin, familiar voice said behind me, banishing any further pleasant thoughts.

"Delilah," I said flatly, tossing back the remainder of my drink as I turned around to meet my cousin's prissy face.

True to form, Delilah wore our traditional dove gray and white family robes, the hems embellished with some subtle arcane embroidery that she'd probably added herself. Delilah had always gone hard on the "craft" in "witchcraft," mostly as an excuse to crochet or needlepoint to her introverted little heart's content. And because she was so very deeply extra about all that came with being a Harlow witch, speckled feathers—the tawny owl being part of our family crest—were woven into her hair, which was nut brown and curly and even longer than mine had been back in my Thistle Grove days.

"So, you're really back," she said, casting a disdainful eye over my own outfit; my precipitous heels, and a black lacework and chiffon Reiss dress that just skimmed my thighs. Given my witchy abdication, I couldn't quite bring myself to wear the family robes, which, in timeless Harlow tradition, were also criminally lacking in any sort of panache or style.

"Sure am," I said, in the same aggressively bland tones. "Gosh, nothing gets by you, Lilah. Although to be fair, I *was* just ten times my usual size, so, you know. Kind of hard to miss."

She licked her lips, flicking her big brown eyes to the side in just-barely-not-an-eye-roll. "And you're still planning on going through with it?" she asked, not quite managing to suppress the hope that flashed across her face. It was so painfully earnest that for a moment I felt a stab of guilt for what my being here took away from her. "Actually arbitrating the Gauntlet on Saturday?"

"Certainly seems that way."

"But *why*?" she demanded, and this time her frustration boiled over. "Why did you even bother to come at all, Emmy? You think our family's a joke, and everybody knows it. Why not leave it to someone who, I don't know, genuinely cares about our legacy? About our traditions?"

I glared up at her, irritated anew that she'd drawn her impressive height from my father's end of the gene pool, which made her tall enough that I'd always had to look up at her. It was hard to make a soft Bambi face like Lilah's seem naturally pinched, but I could attest she'd had a lifetime of practice at perfecting it.

"Because it's mine to do," I snapped. "I *am* the Harlow scion, no matter what you like to tell yourself these days. So I guess the better question is, why would you be so sure it should be you instead?"

"Because you left, Emmy," she shot back, the words coated with contempt. "And I stayed."

For a moment, we glowered at each other—Delilah stewing in lofty indignation while I ballooned with outrage; who the hell was my snotty cousin to judge my decisions when she didn't know the first thing about what had motivated them?

Before I could form a coherent reply, she stropped off in a whirl of robes, chin in the air, ducking away from an approaching Nana Caro's attempt to lay a hand on her shoulder. Our grandmother turned to watch her stomp away, her face uncharacteristically rueful; she'd clearly overheard most of what had been said.

She shook her silver-threaded head, sighing, then turned back to me and opened her arms. I drifted into them gratefully, leaning into her hearty squeeze, breathing in the unchanged scent of menthol cigarettes and Shalimar.

"My Emmy," she said, drawing back to grin at me, a fine web of lines creasing into the suedey skin around her lipsticked mouth. "A feast for the goddess-damned eyes. Welcome home, peep. This town sure has missed you."

"You look great, too, Nana," I said, smiling back. "And thanks for the welcome. I'm getting the distinct feeling it may not be a unanimous sentiment."

"Try not to be too hard on Lilah, would you?" she said, squeezing my shoulders. "She's . . . sensitive, that's all, and she's had to play second fiddle to you for a long time. Even while you were gone. Tough to fill shoes like yours, kid, even if she does always give it her all."

While I blinked at that, trying to process this unexpected insight, she gave me a little shake. "So, the mantle," she said, grin widening into something more conspiratorial. "What'd you think of your first shot at it?"

"Woooo, well, it was certainly something." I shook my head, struggling to translate the euphoria into words that would do it justice. "I mean, that *feeling*."

"Don't I know it," she said, a wistful gleam in her brown eyes. "What a frigging rush, right? Better than a stiff drink after the lay of your life. Fifty years later, and sometimes I still wake up missing it."

That was Nana Caro for you. Never one for mincing words, even when you kind of wished she would. "I wouldn't have put it *exactly* that way, but yeah, that sounds about right."

Despite their shared coloring—though Nana's stylishly mussed hair was even shorter than my father's curls, her eyes darkened with an expertly applied smoky shadow I could not have replicated given a lifetime of YouTube tutorials—sometimes I wondered how my restrained father could possibly have sprung from her exuberant genetic material. She'd been exactly like this since I could remember her: unapologetically foulmouthed, joyfully extroverted, and driven entirely by the beat of her own drum.

"Any sage words of advice before I really jump in on Saturday?" I asked her. "From my Gauntlet Yoda?"

She quirked her head like some bright-eyed bird, her mouth pursed in a thoughtful moue. "Well, you already know for yourself how intense the spell can feel . . . but let me tell ya, peep, you've only barely scratched the surface. During the competition itself, the mantle's influence can get . . . let's say, a little more aggressive. It's a tough old spell, one of the strongest we've got. So don't bother trying to fight it when it gets revved up."

Just a *tad* bit anxiety inducing for a control freak such as myself, but okay, I could try to roll with that.

"Go with the flow, got it," I said, mustering a smile. "Not my natural inclination, but I'll see what I can do. Anything else?"

"Like I said, just make sure not to overthink it. See how it goes this Saturday—and after that, you know where to find me if you need me." She pulled me close, forehead against mine, her eyes twinkling. "And don't forget to enjoy yourself, got it?"

"Loud and clear, Nana."

I smiled after her as she wafted away—likely in search of a vesper martini, given that my nana was basically the low-key witch version of James Bond. Just as I considered my own empty glass, a serving tray scooted my way; *damn*, this ghost service was on point. This time, after I deposited my goblet on it and snatched up another drink, I did give the tray a slightly self-conscious nod of thanks.

I was lifting the wine to my lips when Gareth appeared in front of me like some unfortunate ghost of asshole heartthrobs past, ridiculous vambraces agleam.

Goddess, *why me.*

"Gareth," I said, taking a giant swallow to fortify myself. "Greetings."

"Hey, Emmy. Been a long time, huh?" Gareth rubbed the back of his neck, attempting a wan version of his low-rent Chris Pine smile. "It's, uh, good to see you."

"Would that I could say the same. Super cool vambraces, though! Wilt there be a joust later? Or were you planning on getting into it with some time-traveling Anglo-Saxon invaders?"

He held up an arm and fisted his hand, turning it back and forth until the slick black metal caught the light in an aggressive glint. "They're a little cheeseball, I get it. But part of the traditional Blackmoore regalia."

I stared at him, dumbfounded, shaking my head as if I hadn't heard him right. "I'm sorry, what? There's no fucking way a bespoke titanium vambrace is part of *anyone's* traditional regalia."

"So maybe they're a little stylized," he said with a shrug. "But you have to admit, still pretty sick."

"I assure you that I one hundred percent do not have to admit that."

"Agree to disagree about the vambraces, that's cool." He nodded to himself, then paused. "You look really great, Em. Very different, but great."

"*Do* I, Gareth?" I demanded, slugging back another swallow. My better judgment insisted that I should really save myself the angst and walk away, but instead I found that I was downright itching for a confrontation. Maybe a trace of that fierce mantle magic still spiraled through my veins. "Or do I look more like, 'Hey girl, you must be new here, how long are you in town?'"

He at least had the good grace to wince at that, dragging a hand down his face.

"So that's how it's gonna be, then, okay. I was hoping we could make, like, a gentleman's agreement to pretend that never happened."

I scoffed, amazed he thought I might be inclined to let him off that easy. "Pretty sure neither of us is a gentleman. So, yeah, this is most definitely how it's gonna be."

"Look, Emmy, I really am sorry about that," he attempted, trying out another tack. "I was having . . . kind of a shitty night. The four-Jäger-shots-too-many kind. By the time we made it to the Cauldron, I wasn't exactly seeing twenty-twenty. It was dark, I didn't expect to see you there, and I just . . . I didn't recognize you for a minute. It happens."

Of course he still drank Jäger. All his pricey suits and adult bone structure aside, an overgrown frat boy still squatted inside that artfully tousled head.

"It happens to dipshits, maybe. And as I recall, you were toasting to Camelot's expansion, so it couldn't have been all *that* terrible of a night," I pointed out. "So I'm going to need you to try that again."

He looked on the verge of saying something, then shook his head instead, a mutinous flare of anger streaking across his face.

"Are you seriously not going to just chill a little, Emmy, even after an honest apology?" he demanded, knuckling back his hair, wincing a little as the vambrace thumped against his forehead. "I know we have history, but come on. Cut me a break. You must see what an awkward position I'm in, here, with you as Arbiter. Caught totally wrongfooted."

I stared at him, my blood boiling as it always did at being exhorted to *just chill*, even more so at the fact that he was somehow managing to perceive himself as any kind of victim here.

"Oh, is my being back—and back with some clout—really just the worst for you? Are you even aware of how extensively you fucked me up back in the day?" It went against my dignity, and all my rules of self-preservation, to admit this to him, but I was now aflame with righteous fury. There was no turning back. "How worthless you made me feel? This is what they mean about actions having consequences, Gareth. What you did, it wasn't the type of shit that conveniently fades away."

"Listen, I know I handled it badly back then." He huffed a surprisingly wry laugh, shaking his head. "Handling shit badly tends to be my thing, okay? But fuck, it's been ten *years*. We were *kids*. What else do you even want me to say?"

"It's been less than nine years, actually. During which time you managed to screw—*and* screw over—my best friend," I fired back. "Not to mention Talia Avramov. Bold move on that one, by the way. I sure as hell wouldn't have crossed an Avramov. Hope you have a spare vambrace for your balls."

Gareth paled at that, then closed his eyes and sucked in a breath. Talia was right; watching him squirm really was profoundly gratifying.

"You *know* about all that? I thought for sure Lin wouldn't have . . ."

I held up a hand. "Don't you dare say her name to me."

He opened his mouth, working his jaw from side to side. "Shit. Wow, *fuck*. Okay, first, it's not how it sounds. I know that's the standard line, but in this case it happens to be true. Lin and I . . . I really didn't mean to hurt her, Emmy. The thing with Talia—"

Talia appeared beside me, like some gorgeous demon summoned up by name alone. She smiled at me, setting a gloved hand on my shoulder; I could feel the smolder of her palm even through the lace. Then she shifted her attention to Gareth, her smile growing wider and more lupine until it was closer to a baring of the teeth.

"Blackmoore," she said, in a deceptively pleasant purr. "Don't you and those overgrown cock rings around your arms have somewhere else to be?"

I couldn't help it. I burst out laughing, even more delighted when Gareth's appalled gaze ricocheted between me, Talia's face, and Talia's hand on my shoulder with mounting horror.

"Are you . . ." he began, mouth opening and closing like a landed fish. "Are you two . . . ?"

His obvious terror at the prospect of me and Talia as an item gave me a sly twist of an idea. I turned to Talia and smiled into her face, then slid my hand over hers where it still rested on my shoulder.

"About to share a dance?" I finished for him innocently, threading my fingers through Talia's and lifting our joined hands above my head to give myself a little twirl. "Why, yes, we are. So if you'll excuse us . . ."

Talia caught on quick, mischief lighting in her eyes. Snaring her lower lip through her teeth, she gave me one of her obliterating smiles, then tugged me against her until her free arm slid around my waist. Her perfume drifted over me like a delicious mist, and from this close, she seemed even taller. If I leaned forward just a little, my mouth would press right up against the tantalizing spot where her neck and shoulder met.

I was a little shocked by how badly I wanted to taste her skin.

"But you can't *do* that!" Gareth protested, his cheeks mottling as his gaze pinballed wildly between the two of us. "You're a combatant, Talia! And she's, she's the Arbiter!"

"The Arbiter whose mantle enforces impartiality," I reminded him. "And I don't remember any prohibitions on . . . *dancing* with a Gauntlet combatant. So what's your issue?"

"But, but, *still*," he sputtered. "What if it, I don't know, affects the magic somehow? Skews your calls? That's just—"

"Unethical?" I suggested, voice rimed with frost. "Unfair? Just plain wrong? Wouldn't those be more *your* areas of expertise?"

He wilted under the ice in my gaze, still fumbling for a response. Without sparing another glance for him, I turned on my heel and struck off toward the dance floor with Talia in tow.

9

The Color of Impure Thoughts

THIS EARLY IN the evening—though by non-witch time, it was already well after eleven—Talia and I had the dance floor nearly to ourselves. Haunting minor-key sonatas wafted around us as I let her draw me close, and spin us into a lazy, swaying dance. She was one of those aggravating (yet irresistible) people who looked even better up close; skin seemingly poreless, eyeliner perfectly winged, deep plum gloss lending her lips an edible sheen.

Or maybe it was just a gloss like any other, and me who wanted to bite her.

"Well, *that* was delightful," she crowed, her wolf's eyes sparkling. "I feel almost faint with glee."

I felt myself flush hot, elated by her admiration. "I just thought making him sweat a little could come in handy for you and Rowan on Saturday. Throw Gareth off his game for once."

She let out a low whistle, lifting an approving eyebrow. "Downright diabolical. I really didn't think you had it in you, Harlow. Would have figured classic psychological warfare to be out-of-bounds for such a good girl."

"It's just like chess; there's cheating, and then there's outwitting your opponent," I replied with a one-shoulder shrug. "One is dishonorable and vile. The other? Just good strategy."

"The honor of a Girl Scout, and the twisted mind of a Targaryen." Talia shuddered in mock ecstasy, grinning. "I'm perilously close to liking you, Harlow."

"How close, though? Close enough to consider using my first name?"

She leaned in, dipping her head until our cheeks nearly brushed. Her warm breath fanned out against my ear, sending a flurry of goose bumps racing down my neck.

"Let's just say I'm trying to pace myself."

The music segued into something a little more up-tempo, closer to a macabre version of a waltz. Now that I thought about it, the eerie strains of song purling around the ballroom sounded live, but I hadn't seen a single musician all night.

"What's the deal with your invisible help?" I asked Talia. "The trays, the music . . . How does it work?"

"Family secret," she whispered, tipping a conspiratorial wink. "I *could* tell you, but then *strigoi* would claw their way through the floor and drag you down to the nether realms."

"Naturally." I pursed my lips in thought, cocking my head. "So, probably better not, then."

"I mean, it's up to you." She pulled a face. "But I hear this is *not* the time of year for excursions into hell."

"So, does it feel like all the elders are staring at us?" I asked her as we whisked by a cluster of Thorns that included Linden's parents, Aspen and Gabrielle. Aspen was technically the patriarch of the family, being a Thorn by blood, but Gabrielle had become its de facto head, being the stronger witch despite having come into her magic by marriage. It was one of those mysterious quirks that just happened sometimes, yet another Thistle Grove phenomenon no one had ever properly explained.

Gabrielle looked beautiful tonight, candlelight playing over her dark skin as if the years had parted around her like water streaming around a stone, without carving any lasting mark. A swarm of moths fluttered around her, alighting on her long box braids; she was the only witch I knew whose magic attracted an entourage. Her liquid dark eyes moved over me and Talia with a speculative cast, but she lifted a hand in greeting and smiled at me as warmly as when I used to spend half my life over at her orchards, getting into mischief with her daughter. As if my long absence had changed nothing between us.

A few people over, copper-haired Elena Avramov stared at us with much sharper curiosity as we whirled past, her feline eyes narrowing.

"I do believe your mother just gave me the old evil eye," I added. "Approximately how long do I have to live?"

"Oh, I doubt it. That's not so much her thing, these days."

I eyed her askance. "You know, I can never tell when you're joking about bad magic and when I should be scared."

"Probably safest to always assume I'm serious." Her eyes glittered with sly humor. "And of course they're all looking at us. Gives them something to gossip about over their sherries."

"I don't think middle-aged people *necessarily* gravitate toward sherry."

"Elena does. It's a disgrace. These days she even skips her customary Stoli aperitif."

"Because there was a time when your mother *did* slam predinner vodka shots as, like, a matter of course?"

She gave me an odd look, as if I was questioning some basic tenet of a universally accepted life philosophy.

"Right, I remember, you're basically Russian," I said with a crisp nod. "Speaking of parents—I haven't gotten a chance to dive into the Gauntlet records at Tomes yet for you and Rowan. But it's on the agenda."

"I don't think we're going to need an assist for the first challenge, anyway." Her lips tugged into that sly marauder's grin I found so enticing. "Gareth won't be anticipating an alliance. And knowing how spineless he is under all that bluster, I bet he'll still be rattled by tonight."

I leaned in closer to brush her cheek with mine. "Then we should probably give him something to *really* think about, right?"

"You don't have to ask me twice, Harlow."

As the music reached a crescendo, Talia grazed her hand down to the small of my back, sweeping me into a more structured dance. My heels were high enough that normally I'd have had to focus on my footwork—but following her felt effortless, a rhythm that didn't require conscious thought. When she lowered me into a slow dip, smiling into my eyes, it blew my mind a bit to remember high-school Talia. Gorgeous and unattainable as some feral goddess, the kind that might turn into a fox and dash away into the dark if you ever crept too close.

Or fuck your brains out by a sacred lakeside, depending on the night.

Having her so close to me felt like some forbidden pleasure, the kind that kept crossroads demons in the business of buying souls. It was almost as unlikely as the idea that, in this town I so badly wanted to leave behind, I might actually be enjoying myself tonight.

"Penny for your thoughts," she whispered into my ear as she drew me back up.

I started a little, caught out. "What if I'm not thinking anything?"

"Oh, I doubt that very much." I couldn't see her face, but I could hear the smile in her voice. "For starters, your cheeks are the exact color of impure thoughts."

"Fine," I relented. "I *was* thinking about you. And how Baby Emmy would never have believed she'd be dancing with the hottest girl at Thistle Grove High. Especially not under her ancestor's gimlet eye, in her family's gorgeous, if somewhat creepy, ballroom."

"It's called the Mandrake Salon."

"Of course it is. How exceedingly Avramov."

She chuckled at that, tossing her head to clear a stray tendril creeping into her eyes.

"Next time, I'll have to show you the Wormwood Suite. It is, I assure you, *peak* Avramov."

"Who says there'll be a next time?"

"Your cheeks do, Harlow." She slid her fingers down the shorter side of my bob before tucking it behind my ear. "And so do I."

The way she held my gaze made my heart speed up, until I could feel it beating at the base of my throat like a pair of tiny wings. So it was real, then, the magnetic pull I'd been afraid I was imagining. The spark that seemed to shiver in the air between us like something electrified.

"And for the record, back in high school, *you* were the one who never even looked at me," she added.

"That's because I was *scared* of you. I knew this girl who dated you for maybe three weeks our sophomore year, then built an entire Talia shrine after you broke up with her. We're talking disturbingly elaborate. I think you probably ruined her for life."

She burst out laughing, giving me another bitten-lip smile. "Fair enough. Baby Talia might have been a bad decision, once upon a time . . ."

An abrupt sadness blew across her face like a wayward breeze; her eyes went a little distant, as if she was unspooling some painful memory.

When she focused on me again, I caught a hint of vulnerability I would never have expected to see, not in someone like Talia Avramov.

"But maybe . . . maybe I've learned a thing or two since then," she said, eyes shifting between mine. "Maybe I'm not such a bad decision anymore."

Before I could think of what to say to that, Linden came tripping over to us, lips aquiver, tears glistening in her eyes.

"Gareth, he wanted to talk . . . and I just . . . I . . ." was as far as she got before dissolving into a muffled sob, hiding her face in her hands.

I stepped out of Talia's arms, giving her a regretful look as I reached for Lin.

"You need doughnuts and coffee from Emilio's," I finished, tugging her close, just like I'd done any of the countless times I'd comforted her after a bad breakup. She nodded miserably against my shoulder, letting me take her weight, and for a moment it was like

I'd never left, like everything between us had been perfectly preserved.

Just waiting for me to slip back into the Emmy-shaped space I'd left behind.

"I got you," I told Linden, looping an arm around her waist, trying to stifle my unease at how natural all this felt. "Talia, do you want to come, too?"

She shook her head hastily, wrinkling her nose a little.

"Oh, no, I don't think so. This . . . type of thing isn't really my scene." She chewed on the inside of her lip, then patted Linden's shoulder so gingerly I nearly laughed, as if emotional distress might have turned Lin into spun glass. "But be sure to ply her with lots of sugar for me. I've heard that helps."

"On it," I promised. "So, I'll see you soon?"

She nodded, tipping me a glimmering wink over her shoulder as she turned away, fluttering one hand in a coy little wave.

Trust Talia Avramov to make even "goodbye" feel taboo, more a tantalizing promise than a farewell.

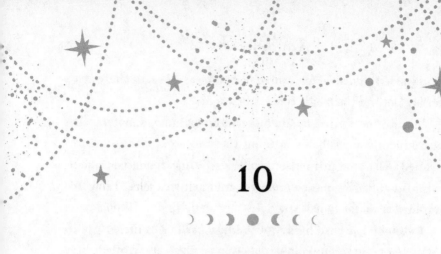

10

Upon My Mark!

HE MIDDAY SUN wavered on the surface of the lake like a
sunken coin, caught in the reflected ring of trees that circled
the water's edge. Bright sprays of purple clustered all along the
banks, the Scottish thistle that grew wild and abundant up here
lending the town below its name.

I'd forgotten how tiny the town looked from here, as if you stood
much higher than the 512 feet listed in the tourist guidebooks as the
official height of Hallows Hill. It was another of those quirks of
Thistle Grove—a lake vaster than it had any right to be, atop a hill
that measured much smaller than it felt. It almost made sense, given
that Lady's Lake was Thistle Grove's enchanted heart, the central
font from which magic gushed like a geyser before flowing throughout the town. Theories abounded as to what made it so special;
maybe a sorceress of untold power drowned here millennia ago, or
some minor goddess claimed it for her own. Or the veil between this

world and the next had torn somewhere far beneath the water's surface, letting the magic come coursing in.

The lake was too deep to properly plumb—and even if it hadn't been, there was probably nothing there to see. So the story remained that some lady, at some unknown time, rendered it magical through some unknown means. And just for kicks, threw in a whole mess of fancy fish you didn't normally find in Illinois.

I stood on the south end of the lake, with Thistle Grove directly to my back. The combatants were arrayed at the other three cardinal points, an audience of family members clustered behind them at the tree line to cheer them on. They stood too far away for me to make out their faces—which was too bad, given how badly I was itching for a glimpse of Talia, whom I hadn't seen since the night of the opening three days ago. Poor Linden's mini breakdown had only devolved after we left The Bitters, and I'd ended up sleeping over at her place to make sure she was okay. She'd been too drunk and distraught to make much coherent sense, so I just sat with her instead, washing down Emilio's famous day-old dozen with boxed white wine and letting her cry against me. I'd woken up back-to-back with her, with crumbs and frosting sticky in my hair, feeling more at peace than I had in years. There was something uniquely magical about sleeping cozied up with a best friend, a primal sense of safety and contentment that couldn't really be explained.

It had just been really, really nice to be with her again.

Just as the sun arced into noon overhead, a faint blue glow began to radiate from within the Grimoire where it sat on a portable pedestal in front of me. This time I'd chosen to stand alone, feeling confident enough to shrug into the Arbiter's mantle myself.

Scratch that, not just confident. Downright eager, practically aching to immerse myself in that heady exhilaration again.

As soon as the mantle settled over my shoulders, there came that sense of surging growth, followed by a giddy head rush as each of my senses kaleidoscoped into dazzling life. I expanded until my head all but brushed the canopy of creamy clouds, until I could see all the way to the clear horizon; past the web of streets, orderly orchards, and rolling woods of Thistle Grove, past even the fields of crops that spread out far beyond.

A strange, deep conviction sang through me, almost like a summons. *You were born for this.*

When I looked back down at the Grimoire, words had coalesced into my first prompt.

> Vying scions from the families three, eager to don
> the Victor's Wreath,
> You must hurry, and hasten, and demonstrate your
> speed!
> By west and south and east and north,
> Hie thee bring the flower forth!

So it would be speed first, then, I thought, a thrill corkscrewing through my belly as the Grimoire's glow melted from blue to a delicate rosy gold. The light spun up into filaments, spooling into a ball that hovered just above the pages. Petals peeled off and unfurled from its center, forming a gilded flower, a filigreed rose made of softly pulsing light. Then it zoomed straight up like the prettiest-ever UFO, glow intensifying as it lifted, its radiance eliciting a chorus of gasps from combatants and spectators alike.

It was making a show, I understood, ensuring that everyone could see that it was meant to be the prize.

Then the rose sailed off toward the water, juddering to a stop a few feet above the middle of the lake. Under my hand, the Grimoire hummed; I looked down to see more words materialized below.

"Combatants!" I called out in my titaness's voice. "Prepare to fly upon my mark!"

With my enhanced Arbiter's vision, I could see Gareth to my left, his jaw squared and tense, lifting his stupid vambraces up in readiness. To my right, Rowan Thorn's grip tightened on his ceremonial staff, his face setting into a mask of intent concentration.

And directly across the lake from me, a ferocious shieldmaiden's grin split Talia's face, and the Avramov garnet at the pulse of her throat began to glow like a bloody little star.

Then, as the Grimoire instructed me to do, I clapped my hands three times. *BOOM, BOOM, BOOM*, each a deafening peal, like three rolls of thunder crashing across the lake. So loud that whoever heard this below in Thistle Grove would pause to consider the blueness of the sky, momentarily bewildered, wondering how and where lightning might be splitting such a perfect day.

Say what else you would about him, Gareth was *fast*. At my final clap, he streaked toward the water's edge in a blur, his gold-trimmed robe swirling around his feet, long stride eating up ground. Just before his booted foot landed on the water, a chunk of ice came rising from the lake like the prow of some frozen shipwreck. He landed on it without missing a beat, barreling ahead at full force. With each stride the water yielded more and yet more filmy ice, huge milky swathes of it, so unmoving under his weight it was as though he was conjuring whole glaciers underfoot.

As more of it reared up into view, I could see that its shape resembled a clever suspension bridge, as if he were summoning up some Atlantean wreck from the lake's invisible depths.

I couldn't even fathom how much raw magic that must take.

To the right, Rowan tossed aside his staff and took a running dive into the lake, sliding gracefully under the surface without so much as a splash. I winced on his behalf, imagining how cold that water likely was already, though it would get a good deal more frigid closer to month's end. Then his head breached the surface, which churned around him like some primordial cauldron, sluicing and twisting in wildly unexpected ways. It looked almost like it was *torqueing* around his body, propelling him forward like some sentient current tasked only with driving his momentum.

When I looked more closely, I could see that it wasn't just water abetting his progress. Silvery bodies flashed around him, of all shapes and sizes, sunlight sparking off their scales. A massive school of fish, maybe the entirety of the aquatic life of the lake, busily swam him toward the center.

Linden was *so* going to give him Aquaman shit until the end of his days.

And directly across from me, Talia had also begun her ascent.

With the garnet at her throat glowing like some otherworldly beacon, a fog began to gather around her. It was an eerie, unnatural mist, ashen and somehow unctuous, writhing in a way that made it seem disturbingly alive. It wrapped itself around Talia in questing tendrils, then lifted her from the ground and propelled her into the sky.

Caught up in its tangle, she drifted toward the middle of the lake like a dark comet, a sooty smear trailing in her wake.

My mouth dropped open as I watched her wing her way toward the center like a wraith; I'd never seen anything remotely like this spell. Whatever dark Avramov magic this was, there was no denying that it was both entirely fucking cool and hot as hell.

The problem was that Gareth was still outpacing both of them.

He was already so much closer to the golden rose than either Talia or Rowan that he felt comfortable enough to slow his sprint to a more leisurely jog, dimples clefting his cheeks as he readied a triumphant smile. He even went so far as to pop off a snarky salute to Talia, whose answering glower from amid her cloud of darkness would have turned a wiser man to stone.

Then a curtain of water and flopping airborne fish came cascading over his head.

"What the *fuck*," I heard him splutter, dashing water from his eyes. "What—"

Another deluge broke over him before he could finish, plastering his hair right back over his eyes. A fish, iridescent and tropical-looking, wriggled under his flared collar and disappeared into the folds beneath, squirming around under his robe while Gareth flailed and shrieked, batting at his front.

Even from within the mantle's magic, I couldn't suppress a delighted chortle—which emerged as such a loud and malevolent *BAHAHAAA* that I clapped my hand over my mouth, gritting my teeth.

Must remember to never do that again.

But the next time Rowan showered him, Gareth was prepared.

Flinging one hand up, he froze the water before it could crash over his head, hardening it into an icicle-dripping arch. It was all good fun, he must be figuring, a trace of smugness seeping back into his face as he skidded under the arch and dredged up yet more bridge for himself up ahead. After all, combatants were traditionally allowed to mess with one another during the challenges—if they could afford to lose the time while battling their own way toward victory.

Except, as Rowan sent another tidal wave cresting over Gareth's icy bridge—a towering wall of water full of thrashing purple squid, along with an actual fucking stingray most definitely *not* native to Illinois—it was clear he wasn't even pretending to make for the middle anymore. Instead, he bobbed in place, wet brow furrowed with concentration, funneling all his energy into thwarting Gareth by battering him with wave upon relentless wave. It was all Gareth could do to keep freezing them, one after the next, before one inevitably swept him right off his feet.

So that was what they had planned for today, I realized with mounting delight. Rowan was taking this one for the team, throwing all his strength into helping his alliance partner secure her win.

I witnessed the precise moment the same understanding darkened Gareth's face. This was not a contingency for which he was prepared. He turned to fling me a wild look, throwing up his arms like a soccer player at a lagging referee, as if to say, *Were you planning on doing your fucking job today?!*

When I spread my hands placidly—*no foul play here*—he actually snarled, punching at the air in sheer frustration before wheeling back around to his task.

Then he rushed headlong with all his might, darting under arch after arch of ice, skidding to a stop every few feet to fling a freezing spell at each fresh wave. But even with renewed commitment, I could see him starting to flag; the next wave that Rowan hurled at him just didn't quite take, drooling over Gareth's head and shoulders in a sort of swampy slush. It infuriated him so much that he overdid his next try—expending so much energy on the water that it set too hard, bursting into an explosive shrapnel of icy shards.

One of them grazed Gareth's cheek, drawing a bright, beaded line of blood—just as Talia drifted to a stop in front of the gilded rose, her features aglow with its soft light. Her hair swirling like black seaweed around her face, she reached for the flower with cupped hands.

As soon as she touched it, it dissolved into a blinding flash that flared once, twice, three times before dying away. The Grimoire gave an answering pulse beneath my palm. I looked down to read its proclamation, my booming Arbiter's voice thundering with an elation that was very much my own.

"By west and east and south and north, a scion has brought the flower forth! First victory goes to House Avramov!"

Then chaos broke loose across the mountaintop.

11

On Rolling Like a Demigoddess

To my Arbiter-augmented hearing, the sudden ruckus hit a lot like noise torture.

Even with my hands clapped over my ears, I could hear every cacophonous nuance as the three scions returned to their respective camps. Milling Thorn confusion, Avramov revelry (were they *really* cheering in some other, rough-and-tumble language while dark swirls broke above them like macabre fireworks, or did Avramov joy just naturally sound that sharp?), and sheer Blackmoore outrage.

And then Igraine Blackmoore portaled furiously across the lake.

I'd never seen anyone use a portal spell before, so maybe it always looked a little aggro, but there was an element of extravagant rage to her display that couldn't really be mistaken for anything else. It took her all of three steps to reach me. With my enhanced Arbiter's vision, I saw her disappear into a prismatic cocoon like a pearly rainbow spun around her—appear at the apex above the lake, where Talia had hovered moments ago—disappear into another whirl of fractured light—and then reappear right in front of me, glaring bloody murder up into my face.

"What is the meaning of this, Arbiter Harlow?" the Blackmoore matriarch demanded, each word vibrating with outrage. "You say nothing, as the Thorns and Avramovs behave in lawless collusion? You make no pronouncement, even as my grandson has been *bled*?"

There was something off-putting about such antiquated syntax coming from that youthful face, though at least some of it was probably just affectation. Her features looked as though they'd been carved from ice, but her eyes were nearly incandescent, glowing cobalt blue with wrath. Though the family resemblance was there, I'd never seen an expression remotely as intimidating on Gareth's face. Gareth might've been convinced of his own importance, but his grandmother took it to such a different level she made him seem like some paragon of humility and restraint.

To be fair, what she'd just done *was* a massive flex. Portal magic was big-time stuff, an enormous exertion of power and will; the magical equivalent of some glitzy and dangerous move like a triple axel, the kind that ended in a trophy or a shit ton of broken bones. Except that it wasn't just air, but both space and time being spun around you, dimensions wound like wool around the spindle of the witch's body.

The seemingly effortless way Igraine Blackmoore had done it made it feel like an unspoken threat.

"Oh, come on, your grandson has a *scratch*," I retorted, drawing myself up to my full, colossal height, the mantle's gravitas lending my tone an outsized disdain. "And the Thorns and Avramovs haven't run afoul of any rules. You saw the Grimoire's acknowledgment yourself when the Avramov scion touched the token. According to the rules, the victory stands."

Her regal eyebrows soared, scaling her forehead. Another inch of aggrieved contempt, and they'd be congregating right up there with her widow's peak.

"Haven't run afoul?" she spat. "My understanding is that this is a *competition*, Arbiter Harlow—which presupposes the combatants acting in their own interests. Not aiding and abetting each other to their mutual opponent's detriment."

"One, that isn't strictly true. Two, maybe you should attend to the Grimoire more closely, Elder Blackmoore," I replied, falling into the Arbiter's authoritative cadences even without the Grimoire's prompting. I'd always hated when people got in my face, and this time, it wasn't just me pissed off on my own account. I could feel how much bristling exception the mantle's magic took to Igraine's accusations and overbearing attitude. It hissed and sparked inside me like a cat at peak aggression—if the cat were the size of a small mountain, and maybe also part dragon a few lines up the family tree. "You won't find any prohibition on teamwork within its pages."

"She's right, Igraine," Gabrielle Thorn said from somewhere beyond my hermetic eyelock with the Blackmoore matriarch. "This whole thing might be a little unconventional, but Rowan and Talia haven't done anything wrong. The Thorns are considering it a fair-earned win."

I looked away from Igraine to find that the other elders had arrived. Gabrielle and Aspen had reached us already, Elena Avramov and my own parents close on their heels. Gabrielle met my gaze with dark, collected eyes, and though she wasn't quite smiling, I sensed a low-key approval there, even something like pride.

It didn't really surprise me; Linden's mother was exactly the kind of person who'd be proud of her son for the sort of symbolic sacrifice he'd just made for Talia, even if it had cost his own family their shot at this challenge.

"Is that so?" Igraine replied, pointedly transferring her gaze to Aspen. "Tell me, are *you* as convinced as your wife, Elder Thorn? Or do you also wonder why your son has taken leave of his senses to partner with the Avramov?"

"I'll thank you not to drag our son's faculties into this, Igraine," Aspen said through a tight jaw. The terse courtesy had a pronounced tinge of "keep my kid's name out of your mouth," an even more implicit "bitch" hovering just beyond. I knew Linden's father as an easygoing man with a ready smile, freckled and hazel-eyed like his son, always quick to lend advice or a hand. But his close-cropped black hair was flecked with gray now, the lines around his full, wide mouth more pronounced, and he clearly had a much shorter rope for bullshit.

"Just because this outcome doesn't sit well with you is no call for rudeness," he bit off. "I've got nothing else to add. Gabrielle's made our position clear."

"Rudeness?!" Igraine gasped, clutching a fist to her chest like some umbrage-stricken Karen. "I am not being *rude*, Aspen, but rather *appalled* at this travesty. This transgression against the very spirit of what the founders intended for this contest."

"Spending much time chatting up Caelia these days, are we?" Elena Avramov asked, tossing a sheet of hammered-copper hair over one shoulder. She wasn't literally inspecting her crimson nails, but the semibored detachment on her face suggested that she was buffing them on the inside. There was an indolent ease to her every movement, Big Witch Energy that somehow read like a provocation. "I had no idea you'd taken a new interest in necromancy, how fun and unexpected! You should have said, I would've joined you. Next time I'll bring the vol-au-vents and the scarab blood."

The Blackmoore matriarch cast her a withering glare. "*Unlike some*, I don't need to drag our ancestress from her rest, as if she were some common demon, just to know what she would have wanted."

Elena rolled her eyes, a tiny, skyward flick. "So a purely self-serving interpretation, then. I would've expected sour grapes to be beneath you, Igraine, after all these years of winning. Isn't *rising above it all* the vaunted Blackmoore way?"

"Not when my grandson has been cheated of his rightful victory!"

"Cheated?" The blasé act dropped in an instant, fire lighting in Elena's shimmery eyes. They were a pale jade green ringed dramatically with darker color. Black wisps began to rise off her hands, curling and smoking around her fingers, the same eldritch *stuff* that had propelled Talia's ascent over the lake. "Are you suggesting that my daughter didn't fairly earn this victory for her House?"

"This isn't a victory, it's a goddess-damned farce!" Igraine spat, gaze trawling around for more victims until it snagged on my father, who stood next to my mother a good few feet away from the fray. "Ah, James, there you are—our voice of reason! As our record keeper, what is *your* opinion on the matter?"

"My daughter is the Harlow Arbiter, not me," my father said, in a tone so frosty you could all but hear the icicles suspended from each word. "Which makes my opinion irrelevant. You should be turning to her for the final say, in respect of and accordance with the Gauntlet rules."

Even through the mantle magic's buffering effect, a vast relief expanded inside me at this implicit approval of my determination. I hadn't realized just how nervous I'd been that when push came to shove, my father wouldn't back my call. Or worse, that he'd be disappointed in me yet again, in a new and different way.

Igraine stood quiet for a moment, pale lips pinched, nodding slowly to herself. Nothing moved except the slight wafting of her robes in the breeze. The stillness felt somehow more ominous than her bluster had been, with an underhanded, plotty feel to it that I didn't like at all.

When she turned to look up at me, her elegant face was keen with scorn.

"Perhaps I have been considering this wrong, and the collusion isn't the trouble here. Perhaps *you* are the trouble, Arbiter Harlow. Tell me, how can we know that you are acting in good faith?" Her eyes sharpened with malice. "And that your verdict is not based on something . . . more personal?"

I hadn't thought Igraine even knew about Gareth and me, any more than Gareth's parents, Lyonesse and Merritt, had. As the Harlow girl, I'd been so far beneath Igraine's notice before I left Thistle Grove that I couldn't remember a single interaction with her. And let's not forget that I'd been Gareth's dirty little secret that whole summer by his own design; she had no reason to know we'd ever been involved.

Unless he'd gone sniveling to Grammy about how mean and unfair this whole setup was, playing the victim yet again.

The fury that rose up in me in response felt like some arcane summoning.

It grew like a conjured spirit gaining scope and mass; my own complicated anger at Gareth, magnified and enhanced by the mantle magic's own wrath at such a blatant show of disrespect. Apparently the spell had some degree of awareness, a semisentience I could feel, brushing up against my own consciousness.

And the Arbiter in me stone-cold *loathed* Igraine's trifling shit.

The banner of azure sky above us abruptly turned into a cauldron of roiling lead. Livid clouds appeared from out of nowhere, rushing and boiling until they'd blotted out the last bright swatch of blue. The day turned if not quite eclipse dark, then pretty damn close, enough to dampen birdsong and ambient insect buzz, the scent of ozone tanging in the air. Hey, at least this part would make sense to whoever might have been wondering about the random thunder rolling from the hill.

Except I was the sudden storm.

In the unnatural darkness, Igraine Blackmoore quaked a little at my feet, real uncertainty scrolled over her face. Seeing her thrown off balance sent a bolt of tingling satisfaction from the crown of my head down to my toes.

How do you like me now, *you sanctimonious bitch?*

"HOW . . . DARE . . . YOU!" I thundered, unsure if I was picking the words or if the magic was feeding them to me. "DO YOU PRESUME TO QUESTION THE MANTLE'S AUTHORITY, VESTED IN EMMELINE OF HOUSE HARLOW BY THE FOUR WHO MADE THIS HAVEN FOR YOU?"

She swallowed so hard I could hear the clicking gulp in her throat. "No, Arbiter, I—"

I cut her off with a slice of the hand. "YOU WILL ADDRESS ME AS YOUR EMINENCE."

That part was just me, but the magic didn't seem to mind.

"Your . . . Eminence," Igraine said through clenched teeth, as if she had a suspicion that this command wasn't entirely above-board. "I am only *wondering* if there might be something more at play here. Something at odds with the original intent behind the Gauntlet's rules."

"I AM THE ARBITER, THE FOUNDERS' ENDURING WILL MADE FLESH. AND IT IS *I* WHO WILL SPEAK TO *YOU* OF THEIR INTENT."

Now it was purely the spell being channeled through my mouth, with me along only for the ride. My delivery took on an unfamiliar timbre with each word, a chorus of voices emerging from me as if I were possessed. An imperious feminine tone that must have belonged to Caelia Blackmoore, Alastair Thorn's low masculine thrum, Margarita Avramov's foreboding purr, Elias Harlow's mild-mannered authority.

I'd become their echo, a temporary vessel for what shadow still remained of them.

I felt a moment of pure panic at being swept up by something so powerful and alien, along with a visceral urge to reassert myself as the driver of this ride—and then I remembered my nana's advice not to fight or overthink the mantle's spell.

With a deep breath, followed by a long exhale, I relaxed as fully as I could, relinquishing control. For once, simply letting go.

Then something else came surging beneath the mantle's spell, that same sense of unfurling I'd felt when I first touched the original Grimoire. An encompassing awareness that spanned from the lake rippling behind me, down to where a dragonfly had skimmed it with its grazing feet; to the slapping of shoe soles over the cobbles on Hyssop Street, where a little girl scrambled back to her parents, rattled by the darkened sky; to the smoke feathering from the chimneys of hearths that had stoked their fires for the season; to the shivering of leaves in the strange woods behind The Bitters, caterpillars clinging like commas to their tips. And much, much more; more than I was capable of registering.

For a moment, I was Thistle Grove, and the town itself was me.

Having so much magic pounding through me should have been terrifying, but it wasn't. Now that I'd chosen to let it run its course, it was *gorgeous*, revitalizing, like jumping into a lake after a decade of thirst, and sucking all that sweet water down your parched and aching throat.

And there was a poignancy to it, too, the bittersweet knowledge that this magic was only borrowed. For a moment, the thought of letting go of this, of the withdrawal that would set in once I returned to my small, real life, nearly bowled me over with anticipatory anguish.

Then the mantle's magic doubled down, drawing my focus to a single point—bending Igraine to my and the mantle's commingled will.

I folded at the waist until I loomed closely over her, my giantess's face bearing down into hers. "Elder Blackmoore, are we understood?" I asked her in a more restrained tone, closer to a small avalanche than rolling thunder.

She struggled, lips twitching, the feeling of being outclassed clearly both new and distasteful to her. When she hesitated too long for the mantle's liking, a bolt of lightning came streaking down from the churn of clouds overhead and leapt into my hands. It danced around them like a sparking web of electricity, warm and gently tingly, like touching one of those Van de Graaff orbs that made your hair stand on end.

It all fed very nicely into any superiority complex I might have been storing in the basement of my psyche. *You know what? I could kinda get used to this.*

"Are . . . we . . . understood?" I repeated, with slow and silky emphasis, twitching my fingers until sparks rained from them.

"We are, Your Eminence," she managed, dipping into something between a curtsey and a bow. Like she'd reluctantly remembered that I hailed from royalty, or maybe one of the more obscure pantheons. "Though I did not intend any disrespect, House Blackmoore offers you apologies. Let us set aside this . . . unfortunate misunderstanding, and move forward in good faith."

Okay, I could *really* get used to rolling like a demigoddess.

"Apology accepted," I said, straightening. The tame lightning in my hands died down as though it had been grounded through my feet. Above, the welter of clouds fled to the horizon in a surging rush, like a time-lapse photograph of a retreating storm. "Once more, and for all to hear—first victory goes to House Avramov!"

This time, the resultant clamor was purely one of joy, pierced by a high, triumphant whoop I suspected belonged to Talia. When I looked across the lake to where her camp stood, I found her hovering above the Avramovs, still suspended in a cloud of that dark matter, like ink and raven feathers airily commingled.

Even enrobed by the mantle's heady magic, the smile she flung my way, grateful and victorious and somehow semiferal, made me more exhilarated than I would have thought possible.

12

The Witch Woods

"Listen, I did not sign up for this mess," Rowan Thorn groused. The wine bottles he and Linden were bringing to the Avramovs' bonfire clinked together in the apple-picking tote that swung from one of his hands. A luminous sphere of witchlight hovered over his other palm, lighting a path through the thick forest behind The Bitters. "Comrades in collusion? Here for it. But tell you what, fam, I do *not* need to be in these woods tonight, with those trees looking like they want to suck my soul out through my nose."

"Quit being such a wuss," Linden told her twin, easily keeping pace with him thanks to her long legs. Her illumination spell took a different form—a cloud of shimmering radiance that seemed to emanate from her skin, as though it was dusted by bioluminescent plankton. It was beautiful, and made her look like the most literal version of a land mermaid. "We promised Tal we'd come celebrate with her. And they're just *trees*, which, need I remind you, happen to be our thing?"

"*Our* thing is nature. This?" He motioned at the sinister loom of woods around us. "This is some haunted-ass Avramov shit."

"But I thought you liked Talia!" I protested, lagging behind a little due to the fact that I was depending on a plain old Maglite, and the darkness of the Witch Woods seemed to actively resist more mundane forms of light.

"Talia's alright. The rest of that family, though, could sure stand some type of intervention." Rowan rolled his shoulders, casting his eyes uneasily over the warped boughs hanging above us. "Especially if this is their party joint."

He was right about that part; the Witch Woods were spectacularly creepy. Their official name was Heritage Forest, but I'd never heard a local call them that, for good reason. I, an actual witch, had spent the entire time we'd been walking peering nervously over my shoulder, the little hairs on my neck prickling like antennae. Overhead, the canopy knitted together so tightly it blotted out both moonlight and Thistle Grove's glittering ice-chip stars. Tendrils of mist crept low over the ground, clinging to the root balls of the hulking trees. Wisps of it snaked up to coil around the branches of the ancient evergreens that towered here and there, as if it drifted up and down according to its own whim.

Which tracked, given that I was pretty sure this mist was made of ghosts.

Though the woods were technically public property, they were often treated as an informal Avramov holding, since nearly no one else dared venture into them. I'd snuck in a time or two in high school on a dare, like any self-respecting local teen, but I'd never wandered this far in, and certainly not at night. The darkness had a living feel to it, a slithery sense of motion at the corners of your eyes. As though *things* were constantly slipping in and out of sight at the edges of your vision.

The kinds of things that had no intention of hanging in any congenial way.

"You're not wrong," I told Rowan, wedging my flashlight under my arm so I could unscrew the bottle of Tanqueray I was bringing as my contribution—Talia *surely* wouldn't mind if it was already open, right?—and take a swig. The herbal taste twanged in my mouth and burned comfortingly down my throat. Instant ghost re-pellant, or at least the mental equivalent. "I'm also not loving it here."

"The good news is, we're almost there," Linden said, fishing her phone out of her pocket and squinting at the bluish glare. "Tal said to hang a left at the, quote, 'sycamore that looks like a hell-mouth.'"

"Amazing," I said under my breath, half tripping as my toe caught a hidden root. "What could be better."

"Horrible, yet helpful!" Lin replied sunnily. Gareth's downfall, and my cutting Igraine down to size, had done wonders in boost-ing her spirits. "There it is right there, I think."

I took another bracing swig as we rounded the corner, averting my eyes from the twisted burls of the sycamore's trunk as we passed by. Talia had nailed it with that description; the thing was supremely Guillermo del Toro–looking, even by Witch Woods standards.

The glade that lay just beyond it came from a very different cinematic genre.

Without the obscuring loom of trees, the clearing ahead seemed to almost glow beneath the pour of moonlight and sugary spill of stars. At the center, a flame roared in a copper brazier on an elevated stand, spitting a shower of hissing sparks. It was less your average low-key bonfire, and more a standard-bearing flame of Olympic proportions; the Avramovs clearly had no qualms about leaning hard into Talia's triumph.

The air smelled of both magic and real incense, musky, amber-scented gusts of it wafting from the central flame. Wooden furniture lay strewn around; a bunch of claw-foot tables, loveseats with scrolled wood backs, and velvet-upholstered chaises. There were even several four-poster beds for lounging, piled high with pillows and draped with brocaded canopies that fluttered in the cold breeze. Weirdly, the baroque furnishings didn't look at all out of place. If anything, the effect was of a dark fae bacchanal, like we'd stepped through a ring of stones and into the beginnings of some chill yet luxurious fairy hang.

"Haunted. Ass. Shit," Rowan muttered under his breath.

"Maybe pull back on the curmudgeonry a skooch, Row," Linden said, thumping him on the shoulder. "We're their guests, remember? And I think it's kind of charming."

As we approached the ceremonial brazier, moving through clusters of Avramov revelers, Talia unfolded from one of the loveseats and came bounding toward us, goblet in hand.

Despite the night chill, bare feet peeped from beneath the lacy hem of her black maxi dress. Her eye makeup was a little smeared, lips dark with wine, strands tumbling loose from the slapdash knot on top of her head. She looked half-unraveled and still triumphant, like she'd maybe taken a victory nap right before rolling out of bed to come celebrate.

Her mussed perfection bypassed all my defense mechanisms and went straight to my head, like a shot of mainlined adrenaline.

"*Privyet*, friends!" she called out—so apparently they *did* sometimes speak Russian—performing a sort of curtsey-in-motion as she swept toward us. It was graceful despite the deliberate silliness, even as she grimaced at the bit of wine that sloshed over the goblet's rim. "Welcome to the Wood!"

She kissed Linden on the cheek in mock European greeting, then Rowan, and then me. I could feel the heated imprint of her lips as they brushed over my skin, and she lingered over the kiss for a moment, long enough for me to notice. My stomach swooped, then engulfed itself in sparks as she drew back, giving me a tiny, private smile that didn't include Rowan or Lin.

Whatever was happening here, I was definitely, entirely screwed.

"*Privyet*, for real?" Rowan was saying with a grin. "Wow, y'all really stay milking that Slavic heritage shit. Your family's been here for, what, a solid three hundred years just like the rest of us? I think *hello* or possibly even *what's good* would suffice."

"The language of the motherland dwells in our blood, Rowan Thorn, my coconspirator," Talia proclaimed, lifting her chin. "And who am I to deny its call?"

"Yeah, you just think it sounds hardcore," Linden teased. "Tell me you know more than like three words."

Talia flicked one shoulder in a shrug. "I'm practically fluent for all the tourists can tell. It's all a matter of perspective. I also prefer to approach my vodka as an homage to the ancestors."

"Well, *that's* a handy take," I said, hefting my bottle of Tanqueray in salute. "Congratulations, by the way! I haven't even had a real chance to say that yet."

The families had dispersed soon after my confrontation with Igraine, scattering swiftly to the winds. I'd gone straight home from Hallows Hill, wrung out by the mantle magic, and collapsed into what was intended to be a power nap—waking up a disoriented six hours later to a group text with Talia and Linden about coming here tonight.

"Thank you, Arbiter Harlow," she said, adding a playful little twist to my title. "You were pretty legendary yourself."

"Seconded," Rowan said. "I mean, I'm the one who lost. But it was still worth it to see you acquaint that corny jackass and his gram with some grade A humiliation."

"This all calls for a proper toast," Talia announced. "Shall we?"

With the three of us in tow, she swept off toward a table stacked with bottles of liquor and decanters of red wine, deepened to almost black by moonlight. There were delectable-looking snacks too: silver dishes of chocolate truffles sprinkled with salt, trays of sliced cheese and grapes, whole rounds of fancily braided bread. It all had a decadent Persephone aesthetic that I personally felt inclined to steer clear of, just in case.

Haunted-ass shit aside, Rowan clearly had no such reservations, already making himself a plate while Talia poured wine for all of us.

"What, sis?" he mumbled in response to Linden's pointed side-eye; apparently she'd caught the same vibe as I had from the food. "I practically conjured a tsunami earlier, I'm freaking starving. I'll take my damn chances."

"It's not poisoned, if that's what you're worried about," Talia assured him, pressing goblets into our hands. I set my gin down on the table, feeling slightly self-conscious about double-fisting this early on. "We didn't invite any enemies tonight. And we made sure not to let Adriana near it, just in case. My baby sister's sense of humor is still a little . . . unreliable."

Rowan stopped midchew. "Define unreliable."

"Oh, it's fine, I promise," Talia said, waving her free hand breezily. "That whole shapeshifting hex thing Addie had going for a while was mostly just a phase. These days she's a way less terrifying child, overall."

Rowan swallowed hard and shook his head, eyes closed. "Damn. Even your *babies* are messed up."

"We like to inhabit a space of . . . creative anarchy, that's all," Talia said, unoffended. "It works for us. Now, since I'm hosting, anyone else care to propose the toast?"

"To not letting Blackmoore bastards keep us down!" Linden cheered, pumping a fist.

"*Or,* how about . . . 'to double double, toil and trouble, when plotters scheme and cauldrons bubble'?" I suggested. "A little spicy, a little derivative, what do we think?"

Talia let out a low, appreciative whistle. "Okay, yeah, *that's* the energy we want."

Linden looped her arm through mine as we all lifted our glasses and clinked them together, catching one another's eyes as we repeated my silly yet somehow perfect toast. Under the sluice of moonlight and the stars' keen twinkle, in this clearing that smelled of dying leaves, magic, and burning firewood, I felt such a warm rush of belonging that my eyes prickled with sudden tears. Something like homesickness struck next, a premonitory sense of the yearning I'd feel when I was ensconced back in my little one-bedroom in Bucktown, so very far away from home.

Cut this shit out, I chided myself, struggling to get a grip. *You love your life, and this is* not *your home—not anymore. This is just reunion nostalgia set on high, that's all. You'll get over it.*

Blinking the tears back, I took a deeper swallow of the wine to chase away the doldrums. It tasted as dark and rich as it looked, like some exotic vintage harvested under a full moon, imported from some otherworldly realm.

"This is delicious," I told Talia. "What is it? It tastes really special."

"Oh, this?" She peered at her goblet, shrugging. "It's just Seven Deadly Zins, I think? You'd have to ask Issa. She's the one who hit up the liquor store and Whole Foods for the spread."

I burst out laughing, feeling fully ridiculous. "Seriously? And here I was, like an entire fool, thinking it tasted like it hailed from some fairy terroir."

"That's because you have the secret soul of a poet, Harlow," she said, with a curling half smile, her pale eyes glittering against the dark. "Even if you try to hide it."

What was it about looking at her, I wondered as I held her gaze, that felt so enticing, so halfway to forbidden? Was it the extraordinary wolf gray of her irises, the intensity with which she looked at me, or maybe the thing her eyebrows did to the shape of her eyes?

Whatever it was, once we locked gazes, I could never seem to pry myself away.

Just then, one of the younger Avramov siblings came loping up to Talia, slung both arms around her neck, and smacked a kiss on her cheek.

"Hey, *sestra*," she said, tipping her temple against Talia's. "I thought I smelled fresh blood."

From what I remembered, Isidora Avramov was a few years younger than me, maybe twenty-three or twenty-four, and looked much more like their mother than Talia did. The same pale green eyes and a darker shade of Elena's auburn hair, her fair skin spangled with overlapping freckles like a robin's egg. Along with the

Avramov garnet, a cluster of bone pendants carved with runes hung above the leather and brocade of her jacketed steampunk corset, which she wore over a pair of chicly shabby velvet pants. In contrast, her nearly-makeup-free face was startlingly fresh and peachy. It made the entire look feel like a street style that deserved its own name. Strawberries-and-cream punk? Cinnamon witch burlesque?

Whatever she called it, it really worked for her.

"Try not to eat my guests, Issa," Talia said, with a fond eye roll. "They're friends, not food."

"I'm not able to make any such promises at this time." She smiled at me, a sweet and open grin, very endearing and not particularly indicative of cannibalistic bloodthirst. "Emmy, right? Hey, awesome to finally meet you. You know, outside of your chthonic-goddess form—which, by the way, is totally slamming. *Super* smitey."

"Um, thanks?"

Her eyes, still dancing with amusement, strayed to Linden, and she gave a pert salute. "I see you, too, Thorn. Must have been epic, watching that messy motherfucker go down like that. I thought I was gonna pee my pants when that squid clocked him in his shitty face."

"A certain amount of petty thrill *may* have been involved," Linden admitted, as I remembered that Isidora had been the one to suss out Gareth's cheating in the first place.

Issa's eyes shifted to Rowan, who'd just rejoined our group after wandering away to add more to his plate. In an instant, all the warmth fled from her face, leaving her affect so cold and implacable that she seemed almost like a different person. As her fingers drifted up to graze one of her pendants, the occult accoutrements suddenly took on a more ominous mien. She looked like she'd stepped from one of those tales in which the arrogant young noble doesn't pay proper respect to an impoverished crone, who later turns out to be a powerful, grudge-keeping (and usually foxy) sorceress.

"Rowan Thorn," she said, making his name sound like a two-word hex.

"Isidora," he replied, in a wary tone. "Hello. Thanks for, uh, having us."

"You didn't say *he'd* be coming, Talia," Issa said as if he hadn't spoken, imbuing the single pronoun with an impressive amount of contempt.

"You knew we were working together," Talia replied through an exasperated sigh. "Expecting him tonight wasn't exactly a leap. Besides, I didn't think it was still quite *this* much of a deal."

"Well, it is," Issa said, continuing to glare balefully at Rowan. "And it will *continue* to be."

"Well, okay!" Rowan said, eyebrows shooting up as he began to back away. A solid move, given that the younger Avramov was radiating such hostility it all but rippled the air around her like heat distortion. "This has been . . . *fun*, but I think I'll be calling it a night. Lin, did you wanna stay with Emmy, or—"

"Nope!" Linden replied, so hastily I turned to her, wondering what she could be picking up through her empathic bond with Rowan that would give her such a deer-in-the-headlights look. "I mean, Em, if that's okay with you? I don't want to leave Rowan to walk home by himself."

"Um, sure, if you really don't want to stay," I said, increasingly baffled.

"I'll make sure Emmy gets home safe," Talia assured her. "Thanks for coming. Sorry you have to leave so soon."

"No worries!" Linden called over her shoulder as she raced after her brother, who was already beating a speedy retreat toward the woods, his tied-back locs swinging against his broad back with each long stride. "Em, come by the orchard tomorrow for lunch?"

"I'll be there," I called back, as they disappeared into the darkness of the overgrowth beyond the clearing's light, vanishing from one step to the next as though the woods had swallowed them whole.

13

No, No, the Ghosts Live in the Trees

WHAT WAS *THAT* all about?" I asked Talia as we wandered toward one of the pillowed divans near the brazier. Isidora had stalked away in a huff to rejoin the party, and now waves of nervous excitement lapped at my belly; I hadn't expected any time alone with Talia tonight.

"I don't really know what happened there," she said, sitting down with one fine-boned foot tucked under her as I followed suit. Her ankle was tiny, dainty as a doe's, and I had a momentary image of lacing my fingers around its span before I dragged my attention back to what she was saying.

"Issa's been ultra tight-lipped about the whole thing, which isn't like her. But I do know they weren't involved or anything like that. I think they just worked together for a while a few years back, and it ended badly, somehow? And Issa's probably blowing it out of proportion, as is her general wont." Talia shook her head with fond exasperation. "When it comes to keeping grudges, Iss makes me look like a Disney princess."

"Well, *that's* a terrifying thought. Though less so than your baby sister with the alleged hexing fetish. Is that even true, or were you just screwing with Rowan?"

Talia chuckled, a honey-dipped rasp of a laugh that reverberated down my spine. "I *may* have been exaggerating slightly for Thorn's benefit. He's just such an easy mark, you know? Who could blame me?"

I gave her a look. "So does she or doesn't she turn people into naked mole rats for fun?"

"Now there's a visual. Definitely don't float that idea within Addie's earshot."

When I didn't lessen my stare, she relented. "Okay, for real. No, she's never successfully mole-ratted anyone. But one of the lesser Blackmoore brood rubbed her wrong her freshman year in high school, and she tried to curse the little turd bucket into a blobfish—which was no more than he probably deserved. Fortunately Issa caught her and cast a counterspell before Addie could land us all in deep shit, casting hexes as an unsupervised minor."

For all of Talia's playful talk of hexes, dark magic of that ilk was severely frowned upon by Thistle Grove's magical judiciary—especially with Igraine Blackmoore at its head. Even the littlest witches knew not to so much as play pretend at it.

"So in the end he just looked kind of *gooey* for a while," she finished, grinning fondly at the memory. "Glisteny, but in a really terrible way, like week-old pierogies. Don't rat us out, by the way. Somehow I doubt Igraine would buy into a statute of limitations in this particular case."

"Your secret's safe with me," I assured her, snickering into my wine. "*Gooey*. Wow, that sounds foul."

"Oh, it was most foul," Talia said, her smile widening. "Then Addie started a rumor that it was actually some kind of rare and highly contagious skin STD. So she got hers in the end, the clever kid."

"So I was right to think of you as chaotic neutral, back in high school," I said, taking a sip of wine. "And I get that sense from Issa and your mother, too. Very 'I am woman, hear me scare the living fucking daylights out of you.'"

"I do make it my life's work to be a nasty woman." She chuckled again, her pewter irises reflecting the fire's flicker. "Though Issa and Addie, and honestly even Micah, are way more like our mother than I am. At least in some respects."

"How do you figure that?"

"Well, you can't accuse Elena of being anything but freewheeling, in pretty much every way you can think of. We all have different dads, you know. She's never let anyone stick around for long enough to threaten becoming a real partner, much less a co-parent. More power to her, for the whole self-partnered thing. But I can't say I understand it."

"So that's not what you want?" I said carefully, unsure what it was I even wanted to hear. It wasn't like I had any intention of staying here beyond the month, of starting something serious with anyone who made their home in Thistle Grove. The crackle of attraction, the spark blooming between us . . . that was just temporary and unexpected fun, a delightful reprieve from all the bullshit and baggage that came with being back here. And Talia must know that, too, given how upfront I'd been about my feelings on this town.

So why did it matter to me now, to know what she might be looking for?

"No," Talia said, angling her head to catch my eyes. My breath snagged at the directness of her tone, the conviction in it. The utter lack of ambivalence. "Not anymore. Being that self-sufficient . . . that's how you drive away the people that matter. The people that you *want* to stay."

"Is that what happened before Gareth?" I asked softly. When her face shuttered like a portcullis slamming closed, I backtracked in such a hurry I nearly tripped over myself. "I'm sorry, I—I didn't mean to overstep. You said at the Cauldron that you got your heart broken, I just wondered if . . ."

"It's okay, Harlow. It was a fair question." She rubbed her lips together, scraping wine stain from them with her teeth. "But I don't want to talk about Jess tonight. I'm not saying never, just, not tonight. Not when we're supposed to be celebrating."

"No, I get it, really," I assured her, relieved I hadn't irretrievably spoiled the mood. "Speaking of celebrations, what's the deal with having one in these creeper woods? I assume it hasn't escaped you that they're kind of a raging horror show."

"Oh, they're not so bad." She gazed out toward the awful trees, her eyes softening with something like affection, like she had a soft spot for them. "More misunderstood than anything."

At my quizzical look, she stood, in a clean flourish of a movement like a single stroke of calligraphy dashed confidently onto canvas.

"Let me show you," she said, holding out a hand. "It'll be easier to understand if you're with me."

"I'm not sure how much more I need to understand about the

Witch Woods, really," I said, balking at the notion. "I feel like I got a plenty good sense of them on the way over here."

"Just trust me, Harlow," she insisted, in a satiny timbre I'd have been hard-pressed not to follow into one of the more moderately blistering circles of hell, much less just an eerie forest. "It's worth it, I promise. And have I led you astray thus far?"

"Let's be real, you haven't had *that* many opportunities."

She just watched me steadily, dark eyebrows raised. I hesitated for a moment longer, before deciding that, hey, at least I'd be plunging back into the woods more or less *with* one of the creatures that went bump in the night. Shit, that had to count for something.

When I laid my hand over hers, Talia tugged me up easily, leaving her fingers threaded through mine as we started toward the tree line. She paused by one of the tables to snag a hurricane lantern, with a freestanding flame that had been bespelled to glow an unearthly celadon green. Her skin was smooth and improbably warm against my own chilled palm, and the heat of it seemed to seep into my bloodstream. It made me think of what the rest of her might feel like, pressed hot against the rest of me, with nothing between us except the gossamer brush of peeled-back sheets.

When we stepped from the clearing's light and back into the woods, any further sexy thoughts died a swift death. There was a new tension to the predatory hush; an attention larger and more ponderous, as if the forest's own regard had fallen over us like an all-seeing shadow, or some yellowed Eye of Sauron strobing in our direction like a searchlight. As if to confirm my instincts, the rolling mist seemed to inch our way, and Talia's garnet began to shed a warning glow.

"What's happening?" I half squeaked, in higher-pitched tones than was probably cool, my skin bunching into goose bumps. "Dude, I do not like or appreciate this, I really, truly do not—"

"Try to stay calm, Harlow." Her hand tightened reassuringly on mine. "Nothing's wrong. It's just . . . the forest saying hello to me, let's say. It can feel a little scary, but it's just a greeting, that's all."

While I tried not to breathe like a hyperventilating rabbit— apparently I aligned much more closely with the Thorns than I'd thought, when it came to a strong preference for warm and sparkly breeds of magic—Talia led me over to a massive oak, its trunk knotted into such mournful burls that it looked like it was sprouting eyes just so it could weep.

She bent to set the lantern down, then tugged off the fringed shawl draped across her shoulders and spread it over the damp ground. Then she lowered herself cross-legged amid the oak's leviathan roots, gesturing me down across from her until we sat knee to knee. With a soft sigh, she pressed a palm against the peeling bark.

"The veil is very thin here," she said quietly, her eyelids dropping to half-mast as she focused on something beyond my perception. "Even if you don't make a study of the liminal boundary like we do, you can probably feel that much instinctively. And places where the veil is sheer . . . they belong to us."

"How do they belong to you?" I asked, echoing her hushed tone. I knew that of the families, it was the Avramovs who dealt most easily with the spirit world, but it wasn't like they were known for being chattily forthcoming about their affinity. If anything, most of them were notoriously secretive, shrouding themselves in very deliberate—and occasionally insufferable—mystery.

"Something about us naturally attracts the other side," she

said. "We're extra alive, somehow. Bright in spirit, I guess you could say, very cheesily. It makes the denizens of the other side drawn to us—almost like our presence thins the veil wherever we happen to be."

I considered this; the idea of Avramovs as paranormal lightning rods felt somehow viscerally right. "You're like ghost magnets."

Her lips quirked with repressed amusement. "If you want me to take back what I said earlier about your poet's soul, then sure. But if you're into less banal metaphors, we're closer to beacons, or lighthouses. The dead can see us more clearly from beyond the veil than they can see other living; a moth-to-a-flame type of deal. It's part of our magic—the part that also lets us manipulate ectoplasm."

That much I did remember from Baby Emmy's eager perusal of the Grimoire, though I'd never understood it in any meaningful way. "So, you work with spirit stuff, basically. I take it that's what you used as your suspension medium at the lake today?"

"That's right. It's a pretty cool material, naturally malleable and versatile." She wrinkled her nose a little. "Once you get over the inescapable ick factor, that is. It is *not* the nicest texture imaginable. Like some raunchy mix of spiderweb and eel skin. From what our oldest accounts say, not even Yaga completely loved working with it."

"Intriguing, yet also gross," I said, making a face. "So if ghosts are inclined to flock to you, how do you keep from being haunted? Or even possessed?"

"Well, we do have a fair amount of activity at The Bitters, which can't really be helped." She touched the jewel suspended above the hollow of her throat, still aglow. "That's where our garnets come in. The living and the dead can't—or shouldn't—mix too much, and the same goes for working with ectoplasm. The garnet fixes us here, stabilizes our living energy like an anchor. Makes sure we don't risk our own essence when fraternizing with the other side."

"And that's why it's glowing now?" I asked, a little anxiously. "Because you're, uh, *fraternizing* as we speak?"

She nodded, still trailing her fingers over the jewel's facets. "There are shades in the Witch Woods, what you might call active ghosts. And they're very eager to latch on to anything alive."

"I *knew* it!" I hissed, flinging a panicked look at the whirlpool of mist curdling around the edges of our makeshift picnic blanket. "That's what the mist is made of, right? Ghosts?"

"No, no, the ghosts live in the *trees*," she said, waving my concern away.

"Talia. In no way is that *better.*"

"Maybe not, but it's true," she said, with a little shrug. "They slip through the tears in the veil, and then they affix to the brightest life they can find—which, here, happens to be the wood itself. Sometimes they stay for a long time, even centuries. Long enough for their inhabitation to distort the tree's shape."

I shuddered a little, twitching my wrap tighter around me. "Honestly, that sounds like it super blows for the tree."

She patted the oak's hideous trunk, smiling at it as if at an old friend. "I don't think they mind so much. Unlike a person, an inhabitation doesn't drive the tree insane. And the lodged shades are anchored, less restless. No real danger to anyone who wanders into the woods."

"What is it that the shades want, anyway?" I asked, trying to understand why she seemed so sympathetic to them.

She drew her lower lip through her teeth, considering. "To be alive again, mostly. Which is a tall order, but understandable; I think we can all agree that being dead and restless sucks the big one. Barring a do-over, I think they just want to be seen by someone. To be touched. You know, pretty much the same things everyone wants, even while alive."

She leaned closer to the tree, stroking the trunk in a slow, deliberate way, like you'd pet a skittish horse or some other leery animal. As if beckoned by her touch, a dark vapor began rising from the bark.

It sifted through the tree's rough skin, coalescing into ferny fronds of ectoplasm; glistening, gelatinous, inkily alive. Once freed, it curled and roiled, churning itself into a roughly humanoid silhouette. Something that insinuated a feminine shape, with the suggestion of overlong and thinned-out limbs, and a smoky curlicue like a plume of hair. It had no discernible features, save for two eyelike patches of deeper darkness in the smudge that passed for its face. In the green-skewed light of our lantern, it looked like some baleful specter conjured up by Maleficent.

When the apparition bent toward us, I thought my heart might leap out of my mouth and go tearing off into the undergrowth. The only thing that kept my shit remotely together was the utter lack of fear on Talia's face as she looked up at the shade.

"Hey, sweet pea," Talia crooned to it, her voice low and even as she reached up to cup the general vicinity of the thing's cheek. "How've you been, hmm?"

It leaned into her palm like a cat, issuing a series of faint keening sounds that made all my hair stand on end. Talia merely smiled in response, as if this was the equivalent of a pleasant and normal exchange.

"Of course, whenever I can," she said to it. "I know it's been a minute this time, but I'd never come through without saying hello."

"What is that, Talia?" I said softly, almost afraid to speak. "Or, who?"

The shade twitched toward me at the sound of my voice, before turning pointedly back to Talia, as if it had decided it couldn't care less that I was also there. I felt, perversely, kind of hurt.

"A girl, who died a long time ago," Talia replied, without taking her eyes off the shade, her fingers combing through its plume of ghostly hair. "In childbirth, maybe, or from some disease antibiotics would have knocked out in a week. Old-timey bullshit of that nature, probably. I don't know any of the details, it's all too faded. But I know she went down kicking, and she's still too stubborn to consider crossing over fully. Gotta respect that kind of grit."

Based on what her spirit was making the tree look like, I thought it might be time to entertain other options—but hey, that was just me.

"Good night, sweet pea," Talia said, lowering her hand. "Back to bed. And see you again soon."

The shade gave a distinctly skeptical wail, cocking its head at her.

"Soon, I swear," Talia said, laughing. "Upon my witch's soul."

The shade bobbed once in acknowledgment, then turned away and drifted toward the tree, losing cohesion slowly until it dissipated altogether, sucking back into the bark.

"Well, that was horrifying," I breathed with a half laugh. "And extremely rad. I had no idea you could talk to ghosts like that."

"That's who we were, before Margarita came here," she said,

turning to me, her face still dreamy from her communion with the shade, her eyes aglitter with that ineffable tenderness. "Speakers to the dead. Necromancers, if you want to get technical about it. It's much more diluted now, no longer our main thing. But most of us can still do it to some degree."

"You didn't seem afraid of it—her, I mean—at all."

She shrugged one shoulder, a delicate, birdlike flick. The rustling canopy above us parted just enough to let the moon pick out a single stripe of shine in her inky hair. "I wasn't. When I'm talking to one of them, I can feel an echo of who they were in life. It's . . . intimate. A little bit like love."

"Then they're lucky to have you love them," I said without thinking, a blush igniting in my cheeks as soon as the words were out.

Talia's silvery eyes widened, lips parting. Then she smiled at me, slow and lush, reaching up to brush away a strand of hair the breeze had strung across her mouth. The atmosphere between us altered in a breath, as if the barometric pressure had dropped precipitously, turning charged and unpredictable like a coming storm.

She shifted her weight toward me a little, one light hand settling on my knee. "Harlow," she said, her voice throatier than I'd heard it before, "would this be way too weird a time to kiss you?"

I shook my head, not trusting myself to speak. A dazzling smile streaked across her lips like a lightning bolt. Then she closed the space between us, her mouth settling over mine.

Heat ignited in my belly, fanning out and spreading toward my thighs. She kept the kiss light, only grazing my lips with hers, fingers stroking underneath my chin and trailing toward my throat. Her lips were a softness beyond soft, plush and smooth and tasting of lipstick and red wine. That bewitching perfume crept into my lungs with every unsteady inhale hissing through my nose. It made me feel giddy and undone, so drunk with want I all but forgot where we were. For all I cared, we could have been in one of those outer rings of hell I'd have followed her into just as readily.

If anything, the whisper of the leaves and the unyielding dark beyond the lantern's strange light only added to the thrill, whetted it more keen.

Me and Talia Avramov, like some rare magic I could never have foreseen, even if I had her scrying gift.

I laced my fingers around her wrist, running my other hand up the length of her neck before burying it into her upswept hair. My palm cupping her nape, I pulled her closer, drawing her deeper into the kiss. Her lips parted, tongue warm and velvety against mine, searing like a fever and delicately deft. I drew her lower lip through my teeth like I'd seen her do so many times herself, nibbling until I could feel the gentle give beneath.

When she gave a hitching sigh against my mouth, I lost any of my remaining cool.

I slid my hands to her waist and pulled her onto my lap. She gasped against my mouth as she shifted to straddle me, her dress pooling around my legs, arms winding around my neck. The position put the curve between her throat and shoulder, that delicious spot I'd been coveting since the gala at The Bitters, directly in front of my lips.

And it wasn't like I was running high on restraint.

I leaned forward and kissed that enticing curve with parted lips, skimming my tongue over it. Her skin smelled like confectioner's sugar but tasted just a little salty, and I couldn't help myself. I bit her exactly like I'd wanted to, deeper than a nibble but not hard enough to hurt. She arched her back a little, shuddering, arms tightening around my neck. So this was the kind of thing that gave her tingles, very good to know.

I did it again, an open-mouthed kiss that ended with teeth, and this time her exhale crept a little closer to a moan.

I really, *really* wanted to make her moan in full.

"Harlow," Talia said breathlessly, drawing back a little. Her pale eyes were heavy lidded and unfocused, lips beautifully bee-stung. I reared up to steal another small kiss before she went on. "Not that I don't cosign this—very fucking enthusiastically, in case there's any confusion—but we need to stop."

"Why?" I asked, in a half-strangled tone that suggested I might die of such deprivation.

She jerked her head toward the dark beyond the lantern. "Because we're attracting an audience."

I followed her gaze, ice spilling like hoarfrost over my skin. "Oh. Oh, *shit.*"

Shades surrounded us, at least three deep in every direction, like the creepiest ever gathering of voyeurs. They hovered midair like untethered shadows, surveying us with those craters of not-quite-eyes that had taken on an even deeper darkness, like light-sucking vortices.

"Okay, so, this seems very bad," I whispered to Talia through a suddenly dry throat.

"Well, it's not the *best*, but it'll be fine," she said, unwinding her arms from my neck and shimmying fleetly off my lap. She kept her voice even-keeled and mellifluous, like some kind of hostage negotiator, which made me only more nervous; it was clearly for the shades' benefit rather than mine. "We were just acting a little too alive for comfort. Shades are drawn to sex, and uh, sex-type activities. Unbelievably dumb of me not to have thought of that before."

"My bad, I guess," I said, even though, all things considered, I still wasn't all that sorry about the part before the ghosts.

"Hardly," she replied, shooting me a wicked smile before she turned back to the shades. She lifted her hands in front of her blazing garnet, arranging her fingers in a complex fretwork. I could feel the crackle of fresh spell forming, brewing between her palms. Then she began a low chant that corresponded to the twitches of her fingers—as though she was modulating the working crafted by her hands and voice, like some invisible instrument. Like she was charming spirits rather than snakes.

At this show of power, I felt the resurrection of that old, familiar envy I'd tried so hard to kill and bury all these years. To unwind and extricate from my sense of worth.

Whatever she was doing, a Harlow witch could never do. Not even the Harlow Arbiter.

The shades clung stubbornly to their spots for a few moments longer, bobbing in place like eerie buoys suspended in an invisible sea. Then they began to slowly, reluctantly disperse, wafting back to their trees or simply vanishing where they hovered, slipping back through the veil and into the bleak beyond.

"So, listen, I know this was my idea of fun and all," Talia said when they were gone, the garnet's fierce glow subsiding and her hands sinking into her lap, "but next time? Maybe we skip the peeping ghosts and grab dinner instead."

14

Of Orchards, Jagbags, and Best Friends

AND THEN YOU stone-cold made out with her, in Ye Woods of Gloom and Devastation, in front of all the ghoulies and everything?" Linden marveled, looking awestruck. "Girl, that's metal."

I nodded, taking a sip of mulled apple cider. "I never thought I'd hear myself say this, but it was actually kind of weirdly romantic. Not my usual jam, as you know. But apparently with the right kind of motivation, I can hang with a little horror in my hookups."

"*So* thirsty," Lin teased, shaking her head with mock censure.

"If you search deep inside yourself, I think you'll find you mean *adaptable*."

Linden and I sat in the Honeycake sunflower field with Jasper sprawled next to our flannel blanket, leggy yellow blossoms swaying high above our heads. Someone—Lark, probably, this felt like her offbeat brand of humor—had animated the sunflowers to break into an occasional angelic-sounding chorus of emo cult classics, the kind of angsty-white-boy music Linden had always unironically loved. The spell must have been keyed to the presence of magic, to ensure the flowers didn't burst into song when tourists ventured into the field.

The field was currently regaling us with an a cappella version of some 3 Doors Down song, the sunflowers' yolky heads bopping to the beat beneath a sky full of feathered clouds that looked like natural contrails.

I'd forgotten how much Linden's family orchard felt like a modern take on the Elysian fields. It was almost annoyingly wonderful, a little like an admonition. As if Honeycake itself was asking me, *What kind of fool would ever want to leave all this behind?*

"Rowan's never gonna believe this," Linden said, shaking her head. "If I'm allowed to tell him, that is. That forest is like his big-man kryptonite. I practically had to hold his hand on the way back, especially after Isidora socked him with the whim-whams."

"What's the story there, anyway? Talia claimed ignorance, and seemed legit about it."

Linden tugged on one of her twists, pulling it taut. "I also have no idea, for once. Total systems shutdown when I asked about it on the way home."

"Seriously? I thought you two were constitutionally incapable of keeping stuff like that from each other."

"Yeah, we're not huge on secrets, but it's been known to happen. And when it does, 'no prying' is the rule." She shuddered, making a face. "Tell you what, though, their energy was super bad, it was coming off Rowan like static electricity. That chick freaks him out almost as much as the Witch Woods—which, *please* say I can tell him you got to first base there and everything." Her eyes shone at the prospect of her twin's impending mortification. "He's gonna be so embarrassed for himself."

I grinned, shaking my head. "Sure, go ahead. Always happy to help with your weird sibling rites of torment."

When I arrived at the orchard earlier that afternoon, I'd come through Honeycake Cottage first, in hopes of catching up with the rest of Linden's family. Though the twins and Lark had their own places in town, the whole gang tended to congregate at their parents' charming English Tudor home; basically a gorgeous hobbit hole writ very large, its half-timbered stone facade and mullioned windows still familiarly festooned with clinging ivy.

But Aspen and Rowan were at the barn supervising a difficult foaling, which Lark had tagged along to watch for reasons I'd never understand. Witnessing the gooshy miracle of horsey life once, back when Linden and I were twelve, had left me all set for the rest of time. At least Gabrielle had been around to greet me with one of her famous hugs, vanilla and shea butter scented and impossibly soft, like being embraced by a particularly gracious queen. A swarm of butterflies fluttered around her today; a few had deigned to alight on my head as an extension of her greeting, their little feet a ticklish caress.

Gabrielle Thorn really made other people's hellos look weak.

"It's so good to see you again, Emmeline," she'd said warmly, drawing back to cup my face between her hands and run her thumbs down my cheeks. It would have been phenomenally awkward to be face-snugged by anyone else, but Gabrielle was such a wellspring of affection that even I, a Harlow with the chilly soul of a British solicitor when it came to most PDA, couldn't help but be taken in.

"You too, Gabrielle." She'd only ever been "Gabrielle" or "ma'am" to me, never anyone's Gabs or Gabby. And she'd always called me by my full name, too; "own who you are" was one of the Thorn matriarch's big things. "Feels like it's been forever."

"That's because you've been gone from your family much too long," she'd said, setting her hands on my shoulders so she could push me back a little and search my eyes. "But we'll take that up another time. Now about this harebrained scheme my children have roped you into . . . not that I'm against it, in my heart of hearts, if it means the Blackmoores finally pay their damn dues. But you're in a unique position here, sweetheart, caught in the middle the way you are. You *sure* that's alright with you?"

"It's fine with me," I assured her, moved by her concern. "And, credit where it's due, it's my understanding that this was more Talia Avramov's harebrained scheme to start."

"I swear, I don't know whether to be terrified of that girl or proud of her," Gabrielle said, pursing her lips. "But I do know for a fact that I'm proud of *you*. You Harlows have a lot riding on your shoulders when this time rolls around. And the way you handled yourself yesterday . . . that took guts, Emmeline, mantle aside. A lot of that was you alone—and that part deserves nothing but respect. From all of us."

I'd blinked back tears, so overwhelmed I hadn't known what to say.

Later, as Linden and I traipsed toward the sunflower field with a thermos of cider and a picnic basket, I still felt a little tearful over the exchange. Growing up, Gabrielle had been like another mother, and that I still had some measure of her respect was no small thing. It slotted an extra lens of nostalgic wonder over the orchards' sights, not that they needed any help to stun. The pumpkin patch, with its curling vines and plump gourds, many bespelled to grow in whimsical shapes even when uncarved, felt both achingly familiar and devastatingly unique. Portraits of the founders so lifelike they looked like they might speak, sugar skulls dancing with hidden flames, a pumpkin orrery with a rotating sun, moon, and stars . . .

I'd never seen anything like them in the city—and probably never would for the rest of my life after I left for good.

Farther into the orchard, the trees seemed hung with blownglass replicas of fruit, glossy apples in a rainbow of blushing hues. The air was bright and sweet, suffused with a perfect ratio of sun to chill. It was all the kind of extravagant display that made Thistle Grove seem more like an autumnal snow globe than a real place; an unlikely perfection that made for a very rude awakening once you did the unthinkable and moved away.

"Everything okay, Em?" Linden asked, sounding a little worried. "You're making kind of a distressing face."

"It's just such a perfect day," I said, tilting my head to squint into the saturated sunshine, unable to keep a little wistfulness from my voice. "Chicago in the fall . . . let's just say it's not often like this."

I'd spent my first Chicago fall crying inconsolably every other day, depressed to the bone by the dreary wetness of so much of the season, the inescapable torment of the icy wind that blew off the lake like a curse. I'd gotten used to the temperamental weather since, and found lots about the city to love, but this reminder of what I'd been missing all these years shook me a little, all the same.

Fortunately, BLTs, fresh-baked cider doughnuts, and strawberry shortcake went a long way toward bolstering my spirits. Even Linden seemed content as we ripped the pastry into bites, more like her irrepressible old self.

"So what happens now?" she asked, dipping a finger in whipped cream and feeding it to Jasper, who thumped his tail and gazed at her with newly adoring eyes. My mustachioed prince had a very fickle heart when it came to food. "Are you two gonna go steady, whatever that even translates to in Avramov? Like, maybe she'll give you her pet snake or something instead of a varsity jacket?"

"Varsity jackets as a love language, wow. I had no idea you were inhabiting such a 1950s state of mind. And I . . . don't know what happens next?" I spread my hands. "There was some talk of getting sushi soon before she drove me home, so I'm hopeful we ended on a *To Be Continued* note."

A memory of Talia straddling my lap blazed through my mind like a comet; the press of her thighs against mine, the fevered heat of her mouth, the huskiness of that almost moan.

No lie, I was *dying* for a sequel.

"But if you do end up seeing more of her . . ." Linden said, her face suddenly serious. "What then? I mean, you *are* planning on being in and out, right? No lingering detours up ahead?"

"Well, yeah," I said, unsure what she was driving at. "But I figured, that doesn't mean we can't have fun while I'm here. We're both consenting adults, right? And she knows I'm not trying to stay."

Linden nodded, but in a wary way. "She might know, yeah. But she still might not *know* know, Em."

I stared at her, eyebrows raised. "I have no idea what you're talking about, Linden Thorn, except that it's giving me flashbacks to *like*-liking people in middle school."

She gnawed on the inside of her cheek, absently stroking Jasper's head. "How much has Talia told you about Jessica?"

I thought of Talia's face when I'd brought her ex up last night, the portcullis slamming closed. "Not much beyond the name, really. And that it ended badly right before she and Gareth had their thing."

Linden winced at the mention of his name. "The thing about Talia is, she puts up a front like no other, right? But she's actually pretty delicate. Really soft on the inside. And while I don't know the details, either, the thing with Jessica screwed her up pretty good, and then . . ." She sighed, steeling herself. "And then Gareth's two-timing sure didn't help. Which means if she's willing to go out on a limb for you—"

"Because, again, we're adults, and it's *fun*—"

"It still means she must like you, Em," she interrupted, holding up a hand. "Or is at least considering taking a chance again. Maybe she can't help it, because she's Talia and an Avramov and therefore innately impulsive. It doesn't make her feelings your responsibility, because like you said, adults. But it *does* mean you should at least be cognizant of where she's coming from."

I considered Talia's own mentions of pacing herself—as if flinging herself into things headlong might be a pattern with her.

"I don't know," I said finally. "I like her, too, Lin. But I've only been back, what, a week—and it was *one* kiss, you know? I don't feel like I have to worry about ramifications yet."

"Fair enough. Just wanted you to be clear on what you were getting into."

Linden gave me a small smile, her luminous eyes crinkling sweetly at the corners, the same knowing way she'd looked at me when we were six, and ten, and seventeen.

"I know how you are, Em, don't forget," she said gently. "You don't fall hard or fast like I do, you take your time about it. And then if someone beats you to catching feelings, it freaks you the hell out. Makes you feel guilty, and resentful that you're suddenly stuck managing all their emotions, all that inconvenient mess."

She pulled heaps of wind-tossed hair back from her face, sighing. "So please don't think I'm only watching Tal's back here, because I'm not. I just . . . I also don't want *you* to be the one who winds up feeling bad."

I blinked, a little taken aback by how seen I suddenly felt, as if I really had managed to forget just how well Linden knew me. While this depiction didn't make me sound particularly considerate or kind, it was true. Ever since Gareth, I did have a tendency to hold myself back. Maybe that heartbreak had been formative, somehow; or maybe it was just how I was made. Either way, I'd wound up feeling terrible more than once, when someone declared their love long before I'd begun to even consider the possibility of falling.

I was rational, careful, scrupulously sparing with my feelings when it came to lovers.

But Talia . . . "Careful" was miles away from how she made me feel. Galaxies away.

"I appreciate you looking out for me like that," I said, reaching out to cover Linden's sun-warmed hand with mine and give her a little squeeze. "And what about you? How are you doing?"

She contemplated her pastry thoughtfully before taking another bite. "Well, I'm not crying into *these* doughnuts. So that's gotta be considered progress, right?"

I chuckled, torn between amusement and sympathy at the memory of Lin slumping against me, alternating between sobbing, stuffing her face with Emilio's day-old dozen, and taking tear-gurgled swigs of boxed wine.

"You didn't actually tell me what happened at the gala," I said, "to prompt the carb rampage."

"You mean what happened while you and Talia were all wrapped up in each other, doing the Morticia and Gomez tango?" she said dryly. "No shade, I know it was for Gareth's benefit, *mostly*. And you guys looked hot together. It just made me feel all sorry for myself, thinking about when I went salsa dancing with him in Carbondale, and—"

"Gareth can *salsa dance* now?" I said through a fake gag, my soul shriveling at the idea. "Ugh."

"He actually has surprising rhythm for someone saddled with so much prep," she said, shrugging. "It was one of the things that . . . you know what, no, I'm not upsetting myself by dwelling on the stuff I liked when we were together. Anyway, I was in my feelings about missing him, and he apparently smelled my weakness like some kind of sociopathic shark. So when he came by to talk to me, I didn't say no like I should've. Instead I let him tell me all the reasons why cheating was the most terrible mistake, we were so good together, I was the very *best* thing before he fucked it all up, let's be in sweet love again, and so forth."

I stared at her, aghast. "He really thinks you're going to get back together? After what he did?"

She shook her head in bemused wonder. "I guess he thinks he's redeemable? Or that he deserves to be? For what it's worth, I don't think he's lying about missing me, or about wishing he were less of a fuckup. But it doesn't matter that it's true. I could *never* trust him again after what he did. It ruined everything, forever. And this nonstop trying to woo me back, or whatever he thinks he's doing . . . all it does is upset me."

I gritted my teeth, familiar anger churning in my belly. "So that wasn't the first time he's tried?"

"I wish." She scoffed through her lips, a frustrated *pffft*. "No, after I blocked him on every possible form of social media, and my phone obviously, he started ambushing me all over town, just trying to get me to talk. But I don't *want* to talk to him. I want to get over it, move on, feel better. And he just . . . he won't even let me do that."

"You deserve to be able to do that," I said, giving her another squeeze. "Just like *he* deserves everything we do to keep him from winning, and then some."

"And for what his family's doing to the orchards, too," Linden said darkly, shaking her head. "You should see their fancy new outdoor setup over at Camelot, Em. Maybe it's not personal to them, just more tourist money. Diversifying their assets or whatever. But Honeycake is special, anyone can feel it. How could they—how could *anyone*—put a perfect place like this at risk?"

Caught up in righteous outrage on Linden's behalf, I'd almost forgotten that piece of things. On a Halloween-month weekend like this one, the orchard should have been slammed with a steady stream of visitors, bouncing along on the hayride that became charmingly "haunted" after dark, rambling their way through the hedge maze, wandering through the tidy rows of trees with lumpy totes slung over their shoulders, apples rolling in their wake. But instead I'd seen only a thin trickle of tourists the whole time we'd been here.

And given how teeming the town was with visitors, there should have been more than enough to go around—had things not become so rigged in the Blackmoores' favor.

"That just makes me hate that jagbag even more," I said, jaw tight. "Him and his whole shitty family."

Linden let out a surprised little burst of laughter. "That *what*?"

"Jagbag, it's a Chicago thing. I think it's a slightly more couth version of jackass, or maybe jerkoff? I just like how it sounds."

"Jagbag," she repeated, trying it on. "Yeah, you know, I like it for him, too. It fits."

We lapsed into companionable silence as the sunflowers bobbed above us, their heads rippling as a brisker edge of wind scythed through the field. I tugged my fisherman's sweater tighter over my shoulders with a cozy shiver, enjoying both the spun wool and the chill.

"I've missed this, Lins," I said, tilting my head back to squint up at the sun. "Just talking with you. And all the dumb stuff we used to pull together, thinking we were such hot shit. Remember when we went swimming in the water tower à la the Ya-Ya Sisterhood, like that was *ever* gonna end well?"

"And then our hard cider buzz wore off, and we both remembered how we felt about heights. Poor Rowan had to come grow us a rescue vine." She breathed out a laugh, shaking her head. "We were so ridiculous."

"But in the best way, right? I really have missed us, Lin. I've missed you."

"Have you?" Linden said, in such a quietly wounded tone that my head snapped up, my heart suddenly tripping over itself. "Because I've tried so hard, Em, *so hard* to keep us together. To keep us friends. And sometimes it seems like you want that, too, and I feel like I still have you, like we're still us. But then other times . . ." She shook her head, the corners of her mouth drawing down. "You feel so far away. Like if we never saw each other again, you might be totally okay with it."

I stayed silent for a moment, a burst of pain blooming in my chest like a sharp-edged star, so gutted I didn't even know where to begin. I'd had no idea Linden felt this way.

Or maybe it was more that I'd thought she and I were on the same page, when it came to slowly letting each other go.

"I'm sorry," I whispered finally. "Lin, really, I . . ."

"You know, I honestly didn't think you were ever coming back," she cut me off, tears thick in her voice. "That's why the thing with Gareth even stood a chance. I'd never have looked at him twice, otherwise, but I thought you were over Thistle Grove for good. Done with this place, done with . . . with me. And that blows, Emmy. It . . . it truly *fucking* blows, on top of everything else, to feel like my best friend in the world had disappeared on me."

At that, she started crying in earnest, fat tears sliding in hitching trails down her face.

I'd heard Linden curse with her whole chest like that maybe two other times in my life, and only when driven to the most emotional extremes. Hearing it, and seeing those terrible tears, made me feel like my heart was cracking open like a geode. Breaking down a hidden fault line into two hunks of saw-toothed stone. It made me feel not just ashamed, but like I was even worse than Gareth, somehow, in my own special, garbage way.

While I spun in place like a broken compass needle, Jasper whined, nosing Linden's knee. She set a palm on his head, hiding her face behind her other hand as she cried.

My standard schnauzer was apparently a better person than

me, a dismal truth that just about summed up this entire mess I'd made.

"Lin," I started, helplessly. She shook her head, her spine tense as a drawn bow and shoulders quivering as she cried into her palm.

So I did the only thing I knew to do, the only thing I'd ever done when something threatened to drive a wedge between us. Even though this time, the wedge was me.

I reached for her.

For a moment, she held herself apart like I'd been afraid she would, and I felt a yawning fear at the possibility that I'd lost her, like standing at the edge of a precipice with miles of empty air gaping below my toes. It had been so foolish of me, so short-sighted and selfish and borderline cruel, to think that just because I'd excised this town from my heart, I could live without her, too. How could I have thought that, when Linden Thorn was such an essential part of me, the two of us braided into each other like trees grafted together when they were only saplings?

How could I ever have considered cutting myself away from her?

After what felt like an eternity, she finally relaxed enough to hug me back. Still tentative and wary, but with a quavering sigh that sounded like coming home after a long and draining day.

I could barely contain the relief that galloped through me as I held her. There was still a chance to fix this, then. A slim chance, even a vanishing one, but still too precious to let slip through my fingers.

I was *not* fucking this up again.

"I love you so much, Linden Sharee Thorn," I whispered into her hair, feeling wildly lucky, fortunate beyond belief, that my best friend was so generous. "Forever. I can't even imagine myself without you. I'm never, ever going to disappear on you again, I promise. And Lins, for what it's worth . . . I'm so sorry that I suck."

"You *do*," she said, so vehemently that both of us cracked up, laughing against each other. "But seeing as we'll always have the water tower . . . I guess I'll accept a do-over."

15

The Candle

I WENT TO BED early that night; I was meeting Talia and Linden for Gauntlet lore research at Tomes first thing. But I lay wide awake for hours, unable to stop mulling over my afternoon with Lin. Though she and I hadn't exactly reconciled, the tension between us had broken like oppressive heat extinguished by a long-overdue downpour—leaving behind a relief so heady it felt a little like new love.

I had my best friend back, and this time I wasn't ever letting go.

When I did finally manage to drift off, I wasn't sure what drove me from sleep. But as I came swimming up to the surface, my breath short and heart hammering, I reached out reflexively toward the candle on my nightstand and sent out a little tongue of magic to light it. The flame caught easily, without hesitation.

As the last of the sleep cleared and my heart settled down, I reached for the candle, unable to believe it. But the flame flickered lively between my hands, showing no signs of winking out. Happiness stole over me as I considered it, warm and sweet as melted butterscotch.

I had done this. I had made this little spell, entirely on my own.

Unlike the huge enchantment of the mantle, with its other-worldly feel—a magic that felt so indisputably other—this small spell was *mine*. And, as I tested my control over the flame, stretching it up and down like a fiery thread of taffy before winding it around my finger, I found that my control was consistent again. Maybe even fractionally stronger than it had been before I left. Even when I let the flame die out, I could feel the magic still surging inside me, glittery and buoyant, effervescently alive.

As though it had never left me at all.

I held the candle for a long while after that, cupped between my hands, so deeply happy I couldn't go back to sleep.

Happier, if I was willing to be honest with myself, than I'd been in years.

16

Big City, Little Orphan Witch

I F NOT PARTICULARLY helpful to the cause, the Arbiters' records of the Gauntlets turned out to be of unexpectedly top-notch entertainment value.

"I'm pleased to report that Arbiter Savannah Harlow was a deadass comedian," Talia said, still chortling as she flipped closed one of the slim tomes, sleeved in crackled caramel leather, that I'd dug up early that morning in the Gauntlet-designated section of the Harlow archive. "Get your affairs in order, Harlow. Savannah's out to kill."

I held out my hands as she lobbed the volume at me from where she lay sprawled on the ancient corduroy couch, worn down to its nap, tucked into one of the attic's corners.

"I want to see, too!" Linden exclaimed, abandoning the records she'd been reading and trotting up behind me to peer over my shoulder. "Wow, is that a—a stick figure with gigantic balls?"

"It's perfection, is what it is," I said gleefully, cracking up as I leafed through pages of flowing copperplate script—in sharp contrast to margins doodled with strutting stick figures, all featuring comical expressions and equally funny distinguishing marks, illustrating the one Gauntlet in which the Blackmoores had lost to the Thorns.

"She calls Evrain Blackmoore 'the prancing ballsack' every time she refers to him, but then strikes it through—*very* neatly, of course, so you can still read it just fine—and ultra-courteously replaces it with his actual name." Talia grinned, her eyes sparkling with admiration for my irreverent ancestress. "You know, for propriety's sake. She must have *despised* him."

"Doesn't take a stretch of the imagination to picture what he must've been like. She, on the other hand . . ." I said, feeling genuine fondness for my grandmother several greats removed. "Clearly a legend."

Talia, Linden, and I had been in the Tomes attic for hours, breathing in the magic-suffused air and reading by the dreamy, consistently late-afternoon light that slanted through its windows no matter the actual time of day. Since Mondays tended to be quiet, my father had taken one of his rare days off and flipped the shop's sign to closed, so there was no one around to disturb us. Rowan had declined to join our research session, trusting Lin to fill him in later on anything we turned up; allegedly he was busy with work, but I had a suspicion his absence had more to do with a desire to avoid being in close quarters with even a friendly Avramov.

It suited me just fine, given how upbeat I was feeling, so hopeful and optimistic I would have resented anything killing my vibe. I could feel the cleared fresh air between Lin and me, breezy and open as new spring; room in which she and I could find each other again. And I kept thinking back to last night, to the candle and my bespelled little flame. Every so often I'd test it, surging a little magic into my fingertips, letting the heat build inside my hands like tangible potential.

And each time it held steady, ready to realize my will, excitement glimmering inside me like a horde of fireflies trapped in my chest. There was no question that after years without it, my magic was fully, reliably back.

I was a real witch again.

Then there was Talia, the willowy length of her stretched across the dumpy old couch like some sexy sylph wandered out of myth, her shining hair flowing over its arm. We'd been trading heated little glances all afternoon like passed notes. Every time I looked over, I'd find her already looking back at me, a hidden smile tugging at her pillowy lips.

Taken together, it was all extremely fucking distracting in the best of ways, and the reason I couldn't bring myself to be bummed by how little of use we'd managed to dig up.

"Shouldn't these be, like, a little less crass?" Linden wondered, still engrossed in Savannah's lurid artistry. "I mean, not that I'm gonna shed any tears over the Blackmoores' maligned dignity or anything. But I always thought Harlows were supposed to be, you know. All bookish and dispassionate."

"I can't decide if I feel attacked, or like you haven't even met me," I said, though I was also taken aback by the, shall we say, *lighthearted* approach some of my ancestors had taken to chronicling the Gauntlets. Many of the records read nothing like the bloodless academic drone that I remembered hating in parts of the Grimoire; apparently not all Harlows were cut from Elias's cloth.

It gave me a weird feeling, acknowledging their humanity that way. Like they weren't all the severe, humorless, hidebound monoliths I always imagined when I thought about the line of forebears that wound into my past.

As if maybe I hadn't considered how much room being a Thistle Grove Harlow left for individuality.

"I guess she figured, who was ever going to read these anyway, particularly while she was still alive?" I continued.

"Or she was such a cast-iron badass she just didn't give a fuck," Talia offered from the couch.

"Also possible. Besides the comedic gold, did you find anything else?"

Talia swung her legs to the floor, sitting up to dangle her forearms between her thighs.

"Nope. Except that the combatants had to wrestle a whole-ass hydra for the strength challenge the time Savannah arbitrated, and then pry the token out of its mouth."

She said the last a little wistfully, as if racing Rowan and Gareth across the lake severely paled in coolness compared to squaring up against a sea monster conjuration.

That she hadn't stumbled across anything more useful wasn't all that surprising; the upshot of our research was that the governing spell that manifested the Gauntlet challenges was wildly inventive and unpredictable. And speed seemed to be of the essence in any challenge, not just the eponymous one, with the combatants always racing against one another to complete their given task.

But that was where the similarities ended. Sometimes the scions competed to reach the same challenge token first, like Talia, Rowan, and Gareth had done at the lake with the gilded rose.

Other times, the spell devised completely different, parallel courses with no overlap. The combatants might need to be underwater, underground, or airborne; facing down toothy creatures or cataclysmic weather or mind-bogglingly bizarre terrain. There'd even been a strength challenge in which the ground turned into a quicksand of salted caramel, forcing the combatants to dive deep into the gooey mass to retrieve the token and then somehow extricate themselves. The Arbiter that time, Nathaniel Harlow, had waxed poetic over how mouthwatering that challenge had smelled.

(At that point, seduced by the idea of diveable dessert, I'd gone on a snack run to the Wicked Sweet Dessert Shoppe across the street and bought us all way too much fudge.)

"I guess there wouldn't be much point if any of this were predictable," I said, pinching the bridge of my nose. "Still, annoying."

"So, do I tell Rowan to stick to the original plan?" Linden asked. "You'll waylay Gareth this time, Tal, and let Rowan shoot his shot?"

"He'll be expecting it this time, but yeah. Even without the element of surprise I still think it's our best bet—as long as we don't wind up with parallel tracks, in which case we're likely to be screwed," Talia added, lacing her hands behind her head and blowing through her lips. "That is, *unless* you two sweet summer children change your minds about the scrying mirror."

Talia had already floated the idea of peeking into the future for a glimpse of the next challenge, so she and Rowan could prep more specifically for it, to Linden's and my vehement double veto.

"It's way too close to cheating," I said again, with a brisk shake of the head. "Like, indistinguishably close. Even if I were willing to go along with it, which I'm not, the mantle would almost certainly object. Rule Twelve specifically forbids the use of any magical prescience to a combatant's advantage."

"But what if I *accidentally* had a prophetic dream—" Talia argued, widening her eyes and spreading her hands in a show of hilariously unconvincing innocence.

"Talia, *no*," Lin and I said in unison, cutting her off.

"No prophetic dreams, accidental or otherwise," I warned Talia, holding up a finger. "Swear on your witch's soul."

"Fine, fine," Talia groused as she stood from the couch and wandered toward the window, its pour of sepia light gilding her face. "I swear upon my stupid soul, my word is my bond, et cetera, *ugh*. Goddess forbid I be allowed to do anything *actually* helpful."

"So if we're all agreed, I guess I'll head out," Linden said, ignoring Talia's grousing as she gathered up her vegan leather purse and looped her teal infinity scarf around her neck. "I promised my mom I'd double-check the orchard invoices this afternoon, if I had time. See you two this weekend? And give me a shout if any emergency scheming needs to go down in the meantime."

With a quick smile and wave over her shoulder, she disappeared through the door, footsteps clattering down the spiral staircase. Without Linden in the room, the air between us seemed to grow both heavier and lighter all at once, like some kind of quantum paradox, as the molecules between us jostled to accommodate the sudden spike in tension.

"You doing anything right now, Harlow?" Talia asked, turning from the window to look at me.

"Nope," I said, striving for a casual tone, even though my heart had seemingly switched places with a rabid hummingbird. "What did you have in mind?"

"Grab a quick coffee with me? I have some Emporium financials to run through when I get home, and . . ." She melted into a yawn, tipping back her head to expose the long line of her throat and stretching her arms high, with the languor of a rousing cat. How did she even *yawn* hotly—that shit wasn't right. "This attic is like Rip Van Winkle land. I need some caffeine mainlined stat, and I'd rather not drink alone."

Spending too much time in the Tomes attic *did* exert a dreamy effect, all that dense, bookish magic swirling in the air like some soporific mist. I'd taken more naps on the worn couch than I could count, back when I spent my summers working in the shop below, whatever book I'd been absorbed in splayed out on my chest, bleeding its magic right into my heart. The old cushions probably still held the contours of my body, a lingering imprint of the hours I'd spent here.

"Lucky for you, I, too, am the kind of fiend who can pound caffeine this late in the afternoon," I said, reaching for my pashmina wrap as Talia shrugged on the bomber jacket slung across the back of the couch and headed for the door. "Though I'll have to warn you, Chicago's kind of spoiled me for coffee. So I can't promise not to be a bean snob."

"Precious about her cocktails, precious about her coffee beans . . ." Talia paused to shake her head slowly, in mock reproach. "Is this what the big city does to impressionable young witches? Where does it end?"

"Oh, no, Avramov, you are *not* gonna shame me for having standards. Not today."

She swung open the door for me, leaning in close as I reached her, a waft of her creamy perfume drifting over me. The nearness of her, the sudden heat that sparked between us, sent such a potent surge of thrill through my stomach that I caught my breath.

"In that case, I'll let you in on a little Thistle Grove secret, Harlow," she murmured close to my ear, her voice taking on a hushed, serious tone. "Try not to pass out, but . . . we even have *nitro cold brew* now."

I WAS STILL giggling under my breath as we stepped out onto the cobbles of Yarrow Street, the picturesque pedestrian main drag that wound through the heart of the town. Storefronts lined both sides, awnings fluttering prettily in the wafting, cinnamon- and apple-scented breeze; so Golden's, the bakery that sold melt-in-your-mouth croissants and mulled Honeycake cider, was still in operation. Along with the Wicked Sweet Dessert Shoppe, the Moon and Scythe tavern a few blocks down, and the little sandwich place on one of the side streets, it had been one of the few decent lunch spots within walking distance of Tomes.

But as we walked, I spotted a handful of new venues alongside the kitschy-witch offerings I remembered all too well. We passed the town's elegant witch history museum, a gorgeous art deco movie theater that specialized in horror movies, the Bespelled soap and candle store, the tchotchke-peddling souvenir shops— but also a funky pizzeria called Cryptid Pizza, its spookiness clearly tongue-in-cheek, then an artisanal gelateria, even what looked like an upscaleish gastropub. Tourists milled around us, darting in and out of the bustling storefronts with tissue-papered bags in hand and bespoke witch hats perched on their heads, their kids bedecked in adorable Halloween paraphernalia.

"See that place, Whistler's Fireside?" Talia said, pointing at the gastropub. "They have steak tartare sometimes, can you even believe it? With *real* quail eggs and black garlic aioli, just totally wild. If you close your eyes, you can pretend you're not even here."

"Okay, you can stop now."

Talia abruptly veered left, shouldering open a heavy, industrial-looking door that swung into a hip little coffee shop; all exposed brick walls and rough wooden planks, vintage Edison bulbs hanging over the distressed beechwood counter, the air sweet with sawdust and the rich cloy of espresso beans. The kind of third wave coffee shop that put as much cultish stock by their equitably sourced offerings as they did by their décor. In other words, the kind of place that checked off all my boxes—and that I'd never have expected to see in Thistle Grove.

I scanned the beverages listed on the blackboard behind the counter, delighted and semishocked to see a variety of Dark Matter blends.

"They carry my favorite coffee!" I squealed, so thrilled I actually clasped a hand to my heart, as if I'd spotted a long-lost friend. "My Chicago go-to! I can't believe it's made it all the way out here. I officially stand corrected."

"Let's not make any grand pronouncements just yet," Talia cautioned, holding up a finger, "before you determine whether these yokel baristas actually know their way around a French press. One *never* knows."

At her direction, I wandered over to one of the tables while she ordered our drinks, pulling out my phone to skim through my work email as I waited. Even though I was technically on sabbatical, my duties split between my colleagues—nice people whom I mostly liked, and the kind of rare coworkers who genuinely didn't seem to mind more than a month of picking up my slack—with my work bestie, Naomi, acting as lead, I was still copied on all the emails to keep an eye out for any fires.

"All quiet on the Box o' Witches front?" Talia asked, reading the screen over my shoulder as she bent to deposit a massive steaming mug in front of me.

"*Too* quiet," I complained, pouting. I drew the mug close as she sat down, inhaling a sweet mix of foamed almond milk, cinnamon, cocoa, espresso, and a spicy touch of cayenne. I was usually more of a purist when it came to coffee, but the Black Magic blend had sounded too enticing to resist, even if the name was a touch on the nose. "They haven't even had so much as a minor catastrophe yet. How am I supposed to feel needed?"

"Give it time," Talia advised. "You've only been gone just over a week. Surely the dire straits will be upon them soon."

"And to be fair, I did leave my colleague who's covering for me a novella of instructions. So all she has to do is keep the fires hot with the vendors, brainstorm some new concepts, keep on top of the printer, wrangle the interns, and execute the rest of my monthly checklist, and she should be fine."

Talia nodded, resting her elbows on the table and interlacing her hands. "So how long is this checklist, and will Temporary You be allowed to sleep?"

I waved my hand at the notion. "No time for such frivolities when you're bringing magic to the masses. She can nap when I get back."

"You really do love that job, don't you? You get all . . ." She pondered the right word, resting her chin on her laced hands and surveying me with those frozen-pond eyes. I struggled not to squirm under the discerning keenness of her gaze, the way it made me want to blush. "*Agleam* when you talk about it. Dewy-eyed."

"Well, it's my thing, right?" I spread my hands, shrugging a little. "My life, really. It feels so truly weird to be here, instead of heading in to work every day. Almost as strange as it feels to be quasi-living with my parents again. Tell you what, I was not prepared for the wealth of awkward silences."

Talia took a sip of her espresso, which she drank so black and bitter even I'd have considered it a punishment. Apparently, when it came to coffee, the same girl who liked her cocktails mega fruity and with extra cherries took sweetness as some kind of personal affront.

"I can't even begin to imagine," she said, shaking her head in puzzled wonder. "How strange it must be, not being comfortable around your own. What Elena and my siblings are to me, even all the aunts and uncles and cousins . . . they're not just family, they're my home. They're *me*."

"Yes, well," I said a little tightly. "We can't all be Avramovs, blissfully living in each other's pockets. And I might not have family in Chicago, but I *do* have a wonderful network, plenty of friends who always show up for me. It's not like, *Big City, Little Orphan Witch*, the famed tearjerker musical."

"But still, doesn't it get lonely sometimes?" she pressed. "I mean, friends are good, sure. But blood is blood. There's no substitute."

Despite myself, I thought of having tea with my mother in the mornings since I'd been back, the quiet oasis of those moments, and how much I'd missed my father's flashes of droll humor, the gentle fun he poked at the tourists' expense.

"I make it work," I said, trying to force my shoulders to unhunch, telling myself I had no reason to feel defensive about this. "And I like my space. I'm not sure I could ever do things the way you all do, living on top of each other in The Bitters."

"Oh, we're hardly on top of each other. It *is* just the five of us, plus whichever handful of relatives happen to be staying for a stint. And that crumbling old pile is so huge that we could each commandeer a wing for ourselves, play at being broke British peerage, never even see each other if we didn't want to. Trust me, there's plenty of space . . . and plenty of privacy."

She smirked a little at that, the devilish glint in her eyes drawing sudden heat to my belly as the memory of our kiss in the woods flared hot, an invisible flame hovering in the air between us.

"But at the end of the day, we just like being in arm's reach of each other," she finished with a shrug. "It means dinners together, impromptu dress-up cocktail parties, all manner of fun shit at random hours. Always someone around to grab if you need a partner for a tricky spell."

"To each their own, then," I said, taking a swallow of my drink and setting my mug down to signal the subject closed. "So what's the deal with all the new stores on Yarrow? I know the Emporium and the orchards are struggling to keep up with Camelot, but they don't seem to be hurting for business at all."

"Many of them are affiliated with the Blackmoores, in one way or another," she replied, mouth twisting into a bitter moue. "Tenants, or merchants carrying their products. The ones that aren't . . . well, I don't think the same rules apply to normie vendors. Thistle Grove magic doesn't seem to care about them as much, so I'd assume they sink or swim on their own merits."

"So it's just the other families getting screwed over," I said grimly. "What a bullshit take. By both the Blackmoores *and* the magic, to be frank."

"Except for you," Talia said pensively, toying with the ends of her hair. "Tomes hasn't suffered any, has it? Or is it that your parents play their cards that close, and I just haven't heard about it?"

"You know, they haven't mentioned anything like that at all," I said, frowning a little; the discrepancy hadn't really occurred to me. I'd just figured the Blackmoores hadn't yet bothered to try elbowing in on our humbler domain. "If anything, my dad has seemed a little overwhelmed with the tourist influx. I don't think he'd even mind if things were a little quieter, and I doubt he'd feel that way if they weren't doing reasonably well."

"Maybe it's that Tomes isn't such a direct competitor," Talia mused, tapping a fingernail against her lower lip. "Your family does books, not witchy attractions. It's not exactly a destination, at least not the way we are."

"Yeah, maybe. Or possibly it's because we're traditionally Arbiters, not even competing in the Gauntlet? So the magic itself doesn't even consider us in play?"

"Could be." Talia glanced down at the silver watch on her wrist, all dainty loops and filigree. Of course she'd be one to go all vintage analog, in glaring contrast to the rose-gold smartwatch snug on my own wrist. "Listen, I have to run—but hey, would you be free Thursday night, around seven? I haven't forgotten that I promised you sushi."

"My dance card's wiiiide open," I said, heart leaping into a shameless frenzy at the notion of an entire undisturbed night with her. "Were you thinking Carbondale, or is decent sushi within town lines another development I've missed?"

"As it happens, there's a new place right here in town, opened last year. Very decent, bordering on cool." A taunting flash of a smile, followed by a quirked eyebrow. "Not quite Michelin starred, but I think you might be surprised by how much you won't hate it."

"Hey, after how wrong I was about the coffee, I have zero legs to stand on," I said, holding up my hands. "Happy to go anywhere you want to take me."

"Careful how you phrase things, Harlow," she said as she pushed back from the table with a scrape of her chair, the flicker of a smile widening into something simmering and slow. "I'm a wicked Avramov, remember? And that sounds suspiciously like a dare."

17

Petals Caught in Amber

I COULDN'T DECIDE WHAT to wear.

It was ridiculous, especially given that I'd been mentally rehearsing for this date for the last two days. And in typical Emmy fashion, I'd overpacked so extensively for my Thistle Grove stay that I might as well have shipped my entire wardrobe here; I was swimming in options. Yet given the level of overthinking involved, you'd have thought I was solving a logarithm for the meaning of life, instead of picking an outfit for a date with someone I'd already made out with in a haunted forest. Dressing for a more conventional night out should have been a breeze.

But my clothes weren't the problem, I finally realized. That I was nervous—high-school-crush, first-date, clammy-hands nervous—was the problem. I didn't normally get pre-date jitters at all, but with Talia, there was always that sense of tempting danger that I couldn't quite put my finger on, the potential for some hazardous derailing of my path. A loss of the painstaking control I'd cultivated for so many years.

And while the night at the woods and our coffee date had just kind of happened on their own, this was different; this was *premeditated*. This was me and Talia, drinks and dinner, the entire night unwinding before us like a dark, enticing trail.

Leading into some unknown forest maybe even deeper than the Witch Woods.

"Oh, *do* get a fucking grip, Harlow," I muttered to myself, as I wriggled into yet another pair of pants. "You're getting sushi, not eloping with her into the underworld."

By the time I made it to Arami, I'd managed to more or less contain my nerves. I had to admit, the space *was* stylish—fitted with concrete blocks, gleaming chrome, and stark industrial finishes, a graffiti-inspired mural of a female samurai painted behind the pipes that snaked across the ceiling. Not a hint of Halloween to be seen anywhere in the edgily upscale decor.

I found Talia waiting for me at the bar, votives floating in lotus-shaped glass bowls all along its length.

"There you are," she said, smiling as I slid in next to her, her eyes feathering admiringly over me. After all my excessive agonizing, the faux snakeskin booties, metallic-finish moto leggings, and midnight blue blouse patterned with moody, abstract dahlias had clearly been the right choice—along with a sassy pop of hot-pink gloss to seal the deal. "And in such fine fettle. You clean up nice, Harlow."

"Likewise, Avramov." Her heavy waves were pinned up again, and the silky halter top she wore, looped around her neck by a dainty black chain rather than fabric, was the color of pomegranates. For all that I'd been convincing myself that she wasn't about to seduce me into the nether realms, in the flickering spill of candlelight she was porcelain pale and raven haired as any of the underworld's sultrier denizens.

"Our table's not ready yet." She ran a black-tipped finger up the stem of her martini glass before nudging it toward me. "Sake and prickly pear martini, if you want to try. Not Morty caliber, but still pretty good. And not even a *hint* of liquefied gummy worm, so no worries there."

"Wow, solid callback," I said, sputtering with laughter over my sip. "I'm duly impressed."

"I do always try my very best," she deadpanned. I could feel her eyes tracing my profile as I ordered the same cocktail, the heat of her gaze almost tangible. "So, don't keep me hanging. Does this place pass muster, or shall we drink and ditch?"

"Obviously I can't be definitive before the food. But I'll concede that so far, it beats most of my Chicago haunts—you know, the places I can actually afford to go," I admitted. "My real favorites are in the fifteen-dollar-cocktail range. *Not* the path toward quashing student debt."

"*Fifteen*, for a cocktail?" Talia shook her head in disbelief, reminding me that she'd never ventured far enough from Thistle Grove to encounter shockingly overpriced beverages. "Could that possibly be worth it?"

"Unfortunately, sometimes, yes."

I told her about some of my favorites: Violet Hour in Wicker Park, with its gauzily curtained rooms and cocktails bordering on alchemy; the historic Pub at the U of Chicago, with its impossibly ornate wooden paneling, which you could enter only with a card-carrying member and which looked like somewhere elitist wizards went to fetch themselves hot toddies; the narrow Parisian-themed bar on Division, with the velvet wallpaper, where they sometimes did magic burlesque shows.

"But my very favorite is Beatnik on the River," I finished. "It's this Moroccan-inspired place on the Riverwalk. You sit right out on the water, with all these plants and pretty carpets and art deco chandeliers dripping crystals right above your head. You get to sip cocktails out of coconuts and watch the death-wish kayakers and pontoons go by on the river. Maybe place bets on how likely they are to get capsized by one of the architecture cruises that absolutely do not give a fuck."

She raised a considering eyebrow. "Now that you put it that way, the sick thrill of it all just *might* be worth the money."

"Maybe you'll come out sometime, for a few days," I suggested, trying to keep the question casual, though the thought of Talia in Chicago stirred up a fresh swarm of butterflies in my belly. "I could show you around."

"Maybe," she said, looking doubtful. "I'm not sure I could handle it—even a long stint in Carbondale is a stretch for me. And all the way out to Chicago, that far north? You know how fast the magic fades once you get beyond town lines."

"Even for just a few days, though?" I pressed. "It took months and months before I couldn't do spellwork at all anymore."

"Not worth it," she said, shaking her head. "Even a few days of being that weak just isn't for me. Then what if something went wrong, and for some reason it never came back in full?" She shuddered bodily at the idea of such a loss. "Hard, hard pass."

I sipped my drink past the sudden lump in my throat, momentarily saddened by how much she would miss because she couldn't stand to let go of magic, and therefore of Thistle Grove, even for that long. But then again, I thought, recalling the gorgeously macabre spell she'd woven in the woods to dispel the shades—the sheer dark elegance of her magic—maybe I was the one whose priorities were out of whack.

"Then you'll have to take my word for it on Beatnik. It's eclectic in the best way . . . a little like this place." I looked around at the thoughtful installations, bemused. "This doesn't even *feel* like Thistle Grove. I mean, a solid coffee shop is one thing, but an actually tasteful dining establishment? Where are the inevitable bats? Why isn't it called, I don't know, Booo-nagi or something?"

She chuckled at that, shaking her head. "You've been gone a long time, Harlow. Like you saw on Yarrow the other day, it's not like Thistle Grove's been stuck in stasis since you left. Things change, new places open . . . If you'd just let your guard down the tiniest bit, maybe you'd find this place has a lot more to offer than what you might remember."

I held up a hand, taking a healthy swig of the martini. "Let's not go *that* far, just because I happen to enjoy a good transitional aesthetic."

A host arrived to lead us to our table, where I tucked myself into the banquette while Talia took the chair across from me. By the time we'd ordered and our appetizers had arrived, we were well into our second round of drinks; I was feeling warm and glittery and a lot more relaxed, any lingering jitters swept away by the martinis and Talia's equally intoxicating presence.

"My dilemma now is, how do I even admit how good this is without you gloating about it forever," I said, taking another savory bite of tuna tataki, "thereby ruining my enjoyment? *Quite* the quandary."

"If it makes you feel safer, I've been known, upon rare occasion, to be Jessica Lange gracious about being right." She dipped her petal-pink sashimi in soy sauce, then nibbled at it in a way that abruptly catapulted raw fish to the unlikely top of my "most erotic foods" list. "And my favorite sushi happens to be the kind I make fresh at home. So until you've had mine for comparison, I can't completely trust your judgment."

"Wait a minute." I stared at her with narrowed eyes, brandishing a chopstick at her. "*You* make sushi? You *cook*?"

She watched me, amused, candlelight dancing in her frosty irises. "I don't know that rolling maki qualifies as cooking. But I do like to actually cook with heat, too. And bake, even. Why, Harlow, are you surprised by my tremendous domestic prowess?"

I made jazzy exploding fingers on either side of my temples. "More like mind blown. Tell me more."

"Well, for your information, I enjoy doing all kinds of"—her voice deepened, turning deliberately husky as she leaned forward, holding my gaze—"homey shit. In fact, I've been told my chocolate babka is the dessert equivalent of tantric sex."

I burst out laughing, though a small, snotty part of me wondered if it was the notorious Jessica who had told her that. "Makes one of us, I guess. I keep trying out meal subscription boxes to get into cooking, but that particular skill set just does not seem to take. I'll lie about it if you ever tell anyone, but I've managed to burn rice at least three times in the past few months. Like smoke-alarm-and-pissed-off-neighbors burnt."

Her inky eyebrows soared. "I was going to give you the benefit of the doubt, but damn. That's tragic."

I swirled the prickly pear sediment in my glass. "I just don't have the patience for it. Like, what's the point of slaving over beef bourguignonne or whatever, when all your hard work is just going to get *eaten*? Hours of labor, and then poof, it's gone?"

"That *is* generally how food works, yes."

"I get that, but still. Feels like such a waste of effort."

She flicked one gleaming bare shoulder in a shrug. "For me, it's the satisfaction of it. You've fed someone, made them happy and comfortable for at least a little while. Taken care of them in a way that they could feel. Granted, there's a way bigger payoff if you're cooking for at least two—all that effort for just yourself *is* kind of a drag."

I took the last sip of my cocktail, trying to process this new information. I'd never have pegged the Talia Avramov I remembered, self-contained, lovely, and elusive as a ghost flower, as such a nurturer and caretaker. But then again, this novel perspective fit better with the Talia I'd seen in the Witch Woods, the necromancer witch who'd spoken to a lonely shade with such tenderness. The Avramov who couldn't quite understand the appeal of her own family's unfettered lifestyle.

Maybe, I remembered her saying at the gala, *I'm not such a bad decision anymore.*

And maybe, just like the Thistle Grove I thought I knew, the aloof and heedless Talia I'd held in my memory since high school, like a petal caught in amber, was a reflection of someone who hadn't really existed for years.

Somehow the complexity made her only that much more intriguing, an unexpected conundrum I badly wanted to unpack.

"What can I say," she said, reading my mind with one skimmed look over my face. "Frilly aprons by day, ectoplasm by night . . . truly, I contain multitudes. Your turn, Harlow. What don't I know about you that I should?"

"Hmm," I considered, as our main course maki arrived. "Obviously you know I really like to read. But! I'm also pretty into ice- and roller-skating. I was even part of a roller derby league for a while last year, before work got too intense for all that time off elevating ankles and icing my various bruises."

"No shit," she marveled, a lip-biting smile curving her lips. "Emmeline Harlow, elbow-throwing spitfire on wheels. You're right. Would not have guessed."

"Make that Electra Hex," I said, twirling one of my chopsticks with a dramatic flourish, "formerly of the Mass Marauders."

"'Though she be but little, she is fierce,'" she quoted, arching a playful eyebrow. "And don't tell me that one's overused, because I know—and in this case, don't care."

"I wasn't going to say that. The rest of that quote doesn't get as much love, but I like the whole thing. 'Oh, when she's angry, she is keen and shrewd! She was a vixen when she went to school.' *Such* Shakespearean sass." I grinned down at my sushi. "I always thought it might make a cool tattoo."

"On you, it would."

I canted my head, surveying the milky canvas of her shoulders and arms, my mind straying helplessly to the remembered salt-and-confectioners'-sugar flavor of her skin. "Speaking of ink, do you have any? Seems like it would be your thing."

A complicated expression slid over her face like a passing cloud as she glanced down at her plate. "I've meant to do it, a time or two," she said, quicksilver eyes flicking back up at me, both wary and vulnerable. "But it hasn't quite panned out yet, for . . . various reasons."

"You realize being cryptic about it is only going to make me want to dig deeper."

"In that case . . ." Her gaze swept over the collection of tattoos on the insides of my forearms, darkening with interest. "I'll make you a deal."

Reaching slowly across the table, she grazed a fingertip over the line of designs that ran vertically above the veins of my wrist. I felt her touch, the warm pad of her finger and the sharp edge of her nail, like a blooming tingle spiraling through my body. Coursing down my arm and into my torso, dipping into my belly and coming to coil hot between my thighs, as if she'd skimmed her finger directly along the raw skein of nerves that tangled under my skin.

"If you tell me what all of yours mean," she said, as I caught my breath, her voice low and honey glazed. "Then I'll return the favor."

"You're on." I cocked my head, feeling a little tipsy and a lot bold, her touch still lingering on my skin. "Do you . . . maybe want to come over? For a nightcap, and tales of tattoos good and ill?"

She considered me for a moment, anticipation leaping into those pale wolf's eyes. "You know what, Harlow? I think that sounds exactly like what I want to do."

18

Things Told in Confidence

MY MOTHER'S GARDEN felt different with Talia beside me; more intimate, wilder in its magic. A wedge of waxing moon surveilled us as we walked along the pavers, a secretive face set in three-quarters profile against a curtain of damask dark. The primroses went oddly quiet when we walked by them, then broke into racing whispers like a rumor passed behind hands. And a wind had spun up, smelling not just of cold and fall but of proper Halloween, the way it only ever smelled in Thistle Grove—like restive spirits, and the darker, deeper magic of things teetering on the brink of death. It felt, for the first time, like Samhain was nearly upon us.

That smoky smell made me want to spend the whole night outside, standing under that watchful moon with my mouth wide open, breathing it all in. I suddenly felt like I couldn't ever inhale enough of it, even if the night somehow stretched on for centuries.

"Cute," Talia remarked, startling me out of my reverie as she skimmed her hand over a primrose that had angled itself to follow her like some cheeky little spy. The flower froze under her touch, then recoiled vehemently away, quivering with indignation. "Who's the animator?"

"My mother. They're usually a lot more whimsically charming than this," I added, feeling weirdly like I had to apologize for the flowers' chilly reception. "And less . . . salty."

"No big deal. Animated plants never really vibe with me." She shrugged, unfazed. "I don't take it personally; it's that Avramovs feel anathema to them. It freaks them out to feel the veil thinning so close to them when one of us is around, life being antithetical to death and all that. Or at least, that's what Linden thinks, and she'd be the expert."

"A bummer, but I guess that does make sense."

I unlocked the door and let us both in, bracing myself for the wallop of love that Jasper delivered whenever we were reunited; whether I'd been gone for five hours or five minutes had no bearing on his level of enthusiasm. True to form, he came galumphing over, nearly tripping over himself as his claws scrabbled on the wooden floor, before colliding with my legs in a rapturous frenzy.

"Easy, bud, easy," I managed through helpless laughter as he leapt up to lick my face. "Talia, meet Jasper, my mustachioed prince. And don't worry if he's standoffish at first, he can be a little . . ."

I trailed off as Jasper thumped back onto the floor, snuffled at Talia's hand, and then proceeded to throw himself at her feet, rolling onto his back as she knelt to rub his exposed belly. He received the scratches with such over-the-top ecstasy it made me a little miffed; my prince was supposed to be a one-woman dog at heart. And she hadn't even given him treats.

". . . leery with strangers," I finished, jaw agape. "Okay, what the hell? He *never* does that right off the bat."

"An Avramov perk, this time," she said with a half shrug, looking up at me through a loop of shining hair that had slid across her face. "Dogs *do* like us. Yaga was pretty tight with forest wildlife, according to our lore, so maybe that's part of it. The wolf connection."

She gave Jas a final scratch, then smoothly found her feet, without the rattle of clicking joints that would've issued from my own roller-derby-weathered knees. Jasper lay where she'd left him for a minute, thumping his tail hopefully, before giving up the dream and trundling off to his bed beside the hearth with a dispirited huff.

Shaking my head at his treachery, I dropped my key into the owl-shaped bowl on the table by the door, then lit all the candles in the room with a flick of the hand, showing off a little for Talia's benefit.

"Harlow!" she cried, wheeling around to grin at me as the room lit with a muted glow, looking genuinely delighted on my behalf. "Look at you, back at the witching! Seems like congratulations are in order."

"I can't take much credit. It just came rushing back the other night on its own, out of nowhere," I said with a shrug as I headed toward the kitchenette, playing down my own bone-deep thrill at being magical again. "I must be reacclimating. Can I get you a drink? Your choices are . . ." I cracked open the mini fridge and peered inside, as though I had any actual doubt as to its limited contents. "White wine in a can, or rosé in a can. And I'm not sorry about any part of this situation."

"I'll take the white, and no shade here. Canned wine is abjectly underrated."

"I'm glad we can agree on the things that really matter."

While Talia prowled the perimeter of the room like a cat pacing out new territory, I grabbed two cans of Dark Horse from the mini fridge and a pockmarked Sumo orange from the fruit bowl. Talia joined me as I moved to the couch by the picture window and tossed her one of the cans, sinking down next to me in a cloud of sweet perfume.

"*Nazdravye*," she said, popping her can and clinking it against mine.

"You are far beyond ridiculous."

"So says Electra Hex, she of the atrocities committed against defenseless grains."

I gasped through laughter, clutching a fist to my heart. "Low blow, Avramov. Things told in *confidence*."

"Oh, don't worry," she assured me, "I plan to only ever mock you about it when there's no one else around to hear."

"And they say Avramovs aren't considerate."

I dug into the orange with my nails, peeling the rind in gratifyingly long curls, the sharp sweetness of citrus filling the room like a genie freed from a bottle. I tugged the two lobes apart with a neat *snick* and offered one to her, trying not to stare at her lips as she peeled off a section and lifted it to her mouth.

But she caught me looking; I could tell from the deliberate way she ate, lingering over each piece and sucking her fingers clean.

She chased the orange with another sip of wine, then set the can on the coffee table. "Speaking of confidences," she said, beckoning imperiously toward my arm. "I was told there'd be more."

"So *demanding*." I scooted closer to her with my feet tucked under me, until my knees brushed hers. Being so close to her made me feel dizzyingly present, hyperaware and oversensitized, as if the whole of my skin had woken up after a long sleep. My heart kicked up into overdrive, thrumming against my ribs. No one knew what all my tattoos meant; not my closest friends in Chicago, not even Lin. I'd been hoarding them like a treasure trove of secrets I carried around hidden in plain sight. And I was about to share them with Talia, whom I'd technically known my whole life but *really* only known for the last two weeks.

Trying to muster up some courage, I rolled up my sleeve and draped my arm across her lap. She ringed one warm hand around my wrist, keeping it in place, and lazily circled the first tattoo with a fingertip. "Let's start with this one. The arrow."

I cleared my throat, taking a sip of wine with my free hand. "That was the fall after the . . . you know, the summer that shall not be named. November, I think, so I would've just turned eighteen. It was when I decided I was getting the fuck out of Dodge for good."

Talia traced the arrow, a tiny, pensive furrow forming between her dark brows. "So that's what it means? That you were set on leaving?"

"I could have gotten more creative than an arrow, I guess, but I wanted something really simple. Something that I could look at and just think, 'Fly away.'" I bit the inside of my lip, remembering how teen me had felt in the chair at Black Cat Ink, Thistle Grove's one and only tattoo parlor at the time. The buoyant hope for a different future, the sea of sadness churning just beneath. "I was still kind of a mess, but it felt amazing to wrest back control like that, to decide something so big for myself. I remember I felt like such a total badass."

A faint smile ghosted over Talia's lips. Then she lifted my hand to her mouth and pressed a butterfly-light kiss to the arrow, like a token of thanks.

"And this one?"

I let out a little sigh as she traced the outline of a stylized phoenix, thrown more off-balance by that tiny kiss than I should have been. "That's, uh, the U of Chicago mascot. Phil the Phoenix. I got that my sophomore year, once I started feeling like I really belonged there. Like I'd made a good choice."

"Because you weren't sure before?"

I laughed through my nose. "Oh, not even close. I was *miserable* my freshman year. I missed home so badly and second-guessed everything, especially once my magic went. I barely had any friends, and I'm sure I drove the few I had nuts with the constant, high-key angst. Especially since it wasn't like I could tell them what my problem even was."

I swallowed hard, remembering. "But I was way too stubborn to call it quits, and then, at some point, everything just . . . clicked. I woke up and realized I could be happy there; that I *was* happy, for the most part. That it was the right place for me to be. A stepping-stone to the rest of my life."

Talia brought my wrist to her mouth again, and this time the kiss was a little longer, a touch sweeter. When she slid her finger up to the next tattoo—a tiny pair of scissors snipping off a curling loop of thread—it was like a silent question. Like she didn't want to derail me by speaking out loud.

"That was when I decided to finally cut my hair." A swell of pain grew in my throat at the memory; the hanks of golden-brown and chestnut and honey-blond littering the floor around the salon chair like discarded pelts. "I used to love my hair. It was ridiculously long, and I'd do all this silly shit with it. Lots of little braids, sometimes with talismans or crystals from Tomes and Omens woven in—kind of like the way my cousin Delilah wears hers these days, that copycat. I always wanted it to be *maximum* witchy." I shrugged, self-deprecating. "Overcompensation, I guess. If I wasn't ever going to be much of a witch, hey, at least my hair could look the part!"

Talia half smiled at that, a corner of her mouth curling. "I remember. It was past your waist, and so many different colors, but you could tell it hadn't ever been dyed. Really beautiful. Like summer going on fall."

I started at that, surprised. "You . . . really? You thought that?"

"I did." Now she smiled fully, her eyes warming. "I also thought it made you look like a little lioness."

I swallowed past the coarse lump in my throat, a dart of pain zinging through me for my long-lost hair. As if my sleek haircut wasn't the most high-maintenance thing about my appearance; as if I didn't make a conscious choice every single month to touch up the color and keep it trimmed, to blow-dry and flatiron it relentlessly to keep it styled this way. All that effort was deliberate, a statement in itself—that I wasn't *ever* turning back, taking so much as a half step toward who I used to be.

Sometimes I dreamed that it had grown back overnight, and I'd wake up feeling unutterably sad. But in my waking hours I'd never let myself consider growing it out again.

"I'd never even really had it cut before, just trimmed a bit. It was like . . ." I lapsed for a moment, trying to articulate my motivations. "Like I was staking out a claim for the person I wanted to be, without magic. And that person definitely didn't have Witch Barbie hair."

"You did *not* have Witch Barbie hair, Harlow. It was much classier than that."

"Maybe, but you get the idea." I took a deep breath, let it out in a shaky whoosh. "Anyway, you'd think a dramatic haircut like that would have been enough of a statement on its own, but it felt . . . bigger than just hair. Like another turning point. Maybe my hair wouldn't always be short, but even if it wasn't . . . I didn't want to ever forget that I'd made that decision for myself."

Talia's lips parted. Then she thought better of whatever she'd been on the verge of saying, and simply lifted my wrist back to her mouth. I could feel the warm rush of her exhale against my skin as she lingered over the kiss, and the banked heat inside me whipped up again, fanned by her breath.

Between sips of wine, she continued working her way up my arm; through the tattoos that marked my graduation, my decision to work at Enchantify instead of getting a master's, the key to the first apartment I rented alone, a series of promotions. All the cornerstones I'd laid down for the foundations of Chicago Emmy, building over the ground that Emmeline Constance of the Thistle Grove Harlows had once occupied.

Talia sealed each confidence with a scorching kiss, my skin under her lips growing increasingly sensitive as she neared the elbow crease. I didn't think I'd ever felt this particular mix before, this heady commingling of vulnerability and desire. I hadn't *close* to felt it with Anders from a few months back, or even Chrissy before him, though she'd been promising before work got in the way.

But being around Talia felt so *vivid*, so radiant and jewel toned. It made everyone else I'd ever been with seem to pale, to fade into unremarkable pastels.

My breath came shorter and more ragged with each incrementally more lingering kiss, until I started to suspect we might not make it to the end of my little narrative.

"And this one?" she coaxed, rubbing her thumb over the prickly purple blossom tattooed right below my elbow. I'd lost all pretense of maintaining my distance and was halfway onto her lap, as if the space between us had been magnetized. Her face hovered invitingly close, all hypnotic eyes and citrus-stung lips. The little indent above her upper lip was chiseled into a perfect diamond shape I was dying to kiss. All I could smell was oranges and the sweetness of her perfume, like a scented beckoning.

"Come on, Harlow, a deal's a deal. Tell me what this one means."

"The thistle, um . . ." I closed my eyes, struggling to rein in the *very* insistent clamoring of my loins enough to think. "It's recent. I got it end of August, when I decided to come home for the Gauntlet. I wasn't going to, at first, it felt too close to backsliding. But then I thought, no—that was the wrong way to look at it. I owed it to my parents to make one last appearance, do right by them. And if I could make it back here and then back out again, then that would be proof."

"Proof of what?" she asked, her voice so husky it was almost a rasp.

"Proof," I tried, though my heart felt like it had ballooned against the hollow of my throat. She was right there, so fucking *close*. Her hand so hot, her thighs pressing up against my leg in the most maddeningly intimate way. "That this place was out of my system. Out of my blood for good."

Her eyes latched on to mine, compelling as the Samhain night beyond the window. "And is it?"

"Oh, Talia," I whispered, with something close to anguish. "I don't know anymore."

Then I leaned in to kiss her.

Her lips parted immediately under my mouth, tongue sweeping against mine, silken and sweet with oranges. She slid both hands around my waist and tugged me fully onto her lap, running her palms up my back and then burying them in my hair, tugging my head down to deepen the kiss.

I cupped her face, trailing my fingers over her cheekbones and the sharp line of her jaw, whispering them down her neck and the jut of her collarbone beneath the chain links of her halter top. She wasn't wearing a bra, and under the slick fabric her breasts were warm and heavy in my hands, nipples standing out hard when I brushed my thumbs back and forth over them.

"Fuck, Emmy," she murmured against my mouth in a little groan.

"Did you . . . did you just say my *name*?" I asked, so startled that I pulled back a little, an electric thrill singeing through me at the way those two syllables sounded. Like no one before her had ever gotten my name quite right.

"Emmy," she said again, now with a teasing twist, smiling as she tightened her grip on my hair. I let my head fall back, gasping as she kissed the spot right under my jaw. It sent a coursing rush of tingles down my side, set a second pulse to beating between my thighs. I squirmed against her, helpless with want, as she trailed kisses all the way down my throat.

"Emmy," she said again, against my skin. "Do you like to hear me say it?"

"I fucking *love* it," I said, so strained with need I barely sounded like myself. Her fingers drifted down to my blouse's hem, and I lifted my arms to let her pull it over my head.

Then her mouth was everywhere, leaving smoldering trails across my breasts where they swelled over my demi-cup; a frothy wisp of black and silver lace that I'd put on earlier tonight, hoping she would see it.

She ran her tongue over the space between my breasts, one hand skimming down my ribs and waist before grasping my hip, the other tangling in my hair, keeping my head pulled back. I'd been dreaming of ways to make her moan, but instead it was me who couldn't stop making noise. When she peeled one cup of my bra down just enough to draw my nipple into her mouth, her tongue flicking over it, I groaned low and deep, winding my arm around her neck.

I wanted her so badly it hurt, a delicious, twisting ache between my thighs.

"Don't stop," I moaned as she pulled my hair a little harder, arching my neck. "Don't—"

Someone knocked on the door, three light raps.

"Motherfucker," Talia said through her teeth, pressing her cheek against my chest. "You have got to be shitting me."

I froze on her lap, resting my chin on top of her head.

"Don't move," I whispered. "Maybe she'll just go away."

"Who the fuck would it even be this late?"

"My mom, probably. That sounds like how she knocks."

Another knock came as if on cue, so light and questing it didn't even wake Jas by the hearth. My mother, a lifelong night owl, had likely seen the flicker of candlelight through my windows and surmised that I also wasn't asleep. And bless her heart, she had no reason to think I might be having *this* kind of company.

The knock came again, but more wanly this time. After a long moment of strained silence, I could hear the receding slap of her slippers on the pavers as she headed back toward the house.

With a whooshing sigh, I shimmied off Talia's lap, slumping against the loveseat with arms crossed over my middle, the pilled chenille of the cushions cold and scratchy against my bare back.

"So," Talia said conversationally, turning to look at me from where her head rested against the loveseat's back, "should we have invited her in, do you think?"

I burst out laughing, flinging my forearms over my face. *"Stop."*

"I mean, it would have been the polite thing to do. We're all adults here, and there's plenty more oranges, and I feel extremely confident you have more canned wine—"

I groaned into my arms. "I hate you, Avramov. I really, truly hate you."

"I have it on the *best* kind of authority that you don't, Harlow."

So we were back on last-name terms, then; even though I'd started it, I wasn't sure how I felt about that. The atmosphere had certainly shifted between us, that crackling tension momentarily fizzled out, blanketed by awkwardness.

"But I do think . . ." Talia peeled my arms off my face enough to let me see the amused glint of her eyes, the color slowly subsiding in her cheeks, "it may be time for me to clear out."

"I'm afraid so," I said, my own cheeks still ablaze. "My mom could take it upon herself to come back and check on me again. Make sure I don't burn the house down, sleeping with the candles lit. Safety first!"

"Kind of what I figured." She got up, flashing me that lupine smile. As I tugged my blouse back over my head, still throbbing with unslaked desire, she gathered up her things and moved to the door. "Harlow . . . thanks for tonight. I'd say I had fun, but that doesn't quite cover it."

I smiled despite myself. "I know exactly what you mean. And, uh, me too."

"Well, okay, then." She flicked me a parting smile over her shoulder. "See you soon."

Once she was gone, half of me deflated at her absence, while the rest of me flooded with something like relief. Telling her about my tattoos had laid me bare, in a way I would normally never tolerate with someone so new. And now that my head was beginning to clear, all I could hear was the damning echo of what I'd said to her when she asked how I felt about Thistle Grove.

After all these years away, all that single-minded effort to banish this town from my soul, and the best I could muster was still a flimsy *I don't know*. At least I had enough wits about me to recognize that some of that uncertainty had to do with Talia Avramov herself.

And it wasn't until I was in bed, the carriage house colder and darker without her there, that I realized Talia had never even held up her end of the deal.

I still didn't know why she had no tattoos of her own.

19

Anomalous Artifacts

I WOKE UP WISHING Talia was there.

As I stumbled from bed to let Jasper out, I inspected the feeling, turning it around in my mind like some anomalous artifact I'd stumbled across by accident, analyzing it from every perplexing angle. I wasn't one to long for company in my own space; quiet mornings in my own bed, with a book in hand and the ambient noise of Jasper's whistling snores, tended to be my happy place.

But this morning I felt listless, even a little sad. Worse than that, it was almost like I *missed* her. Even replaying some of last night's choicer moments didn't help put me in a better mood.

I was still ruminating as I stepped out into the chilly morning, in schlumpy sweatpants with a cardigan slung over my shoulders to ward off the cold. I had no Gauntlet-related plans today, so I was hoping to catch up on work email after I scrounged up breakfast at the main house. Outside, the day was overcast, all heaped-up drifts of leaden cloud. Mist clung to the garden in little clumps, wreathing damply around my ankles as I stepped onto the pavers. I'd missed it last night in the dark, swept up by Talia and the magic in the air, but my mother had apparently found the time to decorate. Dad would have missed the spooky season altogether if it weren't for the tourists and Samhain Eve itself to tip him off, but my mom caught the bug *hard* each year. Crooked tombstones protruded from between her flowers like an infestation—"By the pricking of my thumbs, something wicked this way comes!," "Here Lies Beryl E. Dedd"—and there were jack-o'-lanterns everywhere, along with a blood-spattered ghoul clawing itself out of the ground between the rose bushes. She'd even looped fake spiderweb all over the garden, whole yards of it, and the sequined dewdrops caught in its strands glittered with incongruous prettiness.

"What do you think, darling? Have I done the season justice this year?"

I looked up to see my mother on the ancient porch swing on the back deck, snug in a cozy bathrobe and fleece slippers, a mug of something steaming in her hand. It was almost eleven, but my mom was a big fan of stretching her mornings as far as they could go.

Smiling, I picked my way between the perky morning glories and swaying stargazers to the porch, settling beside her to the whining protest of the springs. Fortunately for everyone involved, I didn't detect any awkwardness in her smile as she scooted over to make room; she must not have heard anything untoward last night.

Thank the goddess for small mercies.

"I think it's safe to say you've outdone yourself," I assured her. "That ghoul guy? Outstanding work."

"Thank you," she said, with real satisfaction. "Macabre little bugger, isn't he?"

"Totally grotesque," I agreed. "I wish I had half your gift with this type of stuff. If *I'd* made him, he'd be less living nightmare, more sad stick figure."

For all my witchy blood, unlike my mother and Delilah, I couldn't craft my way out of a literal paper bag. And my poor mom, who'd borne witness to countless pasta elbow and papier-mâché disasters over the years, was well aware of my tragic limitations.

"I don't know," she mused, eyeing me askance. "There's a certain innate horror to the idea of *anything* you might contrive to make by hand."

I laughed, my teeth chattering as the wind picked up. She glanced over, immediately all maternal concern. "Are you chilly, love? Would you like a cup of something warm?"

"I would," I said, starting to rise. "But I can just get it myself—"

"No, no, you stay put," she said firmly, pressing me back down. "Let me get it for you. Please. I wanted a refill anyway. Tea or cappuccino?"

I settled back down, stifling a multilayered sigh. I couldn't deny her the extra mothering after how long it'd been since she'd last had a chance to do it. But it made me feel like three different kinds of asshole to let her cater to me like this.

"A cappuccino sounds amazing," I relented, wrapping my arms around myself. "Thanks."

Ten minutes later, we were sipping side by side, watching a pair of inquisitive crows that had come to roost on the ghoul's scraggy head.

"How are you feeling about arbitrating again tomorrow?" she

asked me, cupping both hands around her mug. "Ready for another go?"

"I am a little nervous, after last time," I admitted. "Feels like anything could happen."

"I would be, too, in your shoes, I'm sure." She flicked me a meaningful glance from the corner of her eye. "And have you lot cooked up anything dastardly-yet-not-quite-prohibited this time around? Not that you've any obligation to clue me in, of course. But it would be rather nice to know what your father and I might expect."

I licked my lips, staring down at my lap. "And when you say 'cooked up' . . ."

My mother rolled her eyes, reaching over to pat me briskly on the thigh. "Come now, my love, give your old mum a little credit. The one thing I can't quite grasp is the *why* of it. It must be about just deserts for you, of course, after what that Blackmoore git did to you back in school. But what of your accomplices? You and Linden have always been close, but surely it would take more than just the prospect of righting old wrongs against you to get the Avramov girl on board."

She paused at my dumbfounded stare, patting me on the leg again, like, *Welcome to the conversation.* One of the crows twitched its head at us, cawing starkly and fixing us with a beady eye, as though it took a special interest in fraught family affairs. I tried to remember what two crows meant as an omen; something transformative and good, from what I recalled. Which, nuts to *that.*

"You . . . *knew*?" I managed, feeling like the tectonic plates of reality were being reshuffled under my feet. "About Gareth? Gareth and me?"

"Not the particulars, obviously. But that something had happened between the two of you, something rather significant? Of course I did, how could I not?" She gave a wry laugh into her mug, muffled by the china. "You managed to slip his name into conversation what, several hundred times over dinner that summer, all twinkly eyes and innocence. I'm not *so* decrepit I can't still recognize the telltale signs of the hopelessly enamored, you know."

I sat with that for a moment, stomach bunched up like a dirty rag, utterly at sea.

"But you never said anything," I finally said. "You never mentioned him, after, you never—"

She shot me a severe look, tinged with hurt and accusation. "Because you didn't choose to tell me about him, my darling, and you were old enough that it wasn't right to pry. But it changed you, didn't it? *He* changed you. Damaged you, somehow. You were happy here with us, before. And then . . ."

She shook her head, and I realized with yet more noxious twisting of my gut that she was struggling for composure. My mother was not, by definition, a crier; the opposite, if anything, more of a stalwart stoic, devoted to her dignity and the nearly sacred concept of bucking up. But there was no mistaking the glistening in her eyes, the trembling corners of her lips.

As rarely as I'd seen it growing up, I still knew what my mother looked like when she was doing her very utmost not to cry.

"And then you could scarcely wait to get away from here," she whispered, reaching up to dash angrily at her eyes with her knuckles. I recognized the gesture, the irritable impatience with her own emotions, as yet another thing I'd inherited from her. "Away from us. I thought you simply needed space, at first, that nagging at you would only make it worse. But if I'd had any idea that you wouldn't come back to us . . ."

"You could have visited," I whispered, though I knew even as I said it that it was not just a miserable cop-out, but a flat-out lie.

She turned to look at me head-on, wet green eyes glittering like peridot, lifting one hand to rest it against my cheek.

"You know we'd never have done that," she said, with a terrible, quiet kindness. "Not when you made it so clear that you didn't want us there. Your father and I . . . No matter how terribly we missed you, we'd never have wanted to foist ourselves on you if the feeling wasn't mutual."

I bit my lip, swimming in sticky shame. It was true. They *would* have come, had I ever invited them with any real sincerity. But I couldn't have withstood it, their presence in Chicago, their magic radiant and inescapable when mine was dark and guttered and echoing as a long-empty house. They would have reminded me too much of what I'd given up, of what I missed down to my bones every single day I stayed away.

No matter that it was me who'd willingly left it all behind.

"I did miss you, Mom," I whispered, hanging my head, so beset by misery my body felt like lead. Talia had struck much closer to home than she might have thought that afternoon in the coffee shop, when she wondered how I managed on my own, so far from family. And she hadn't even known just how often and hard I'd pushed them away from me. "Of course I did. I should have invited you for real. I should've . . ."

"And *we* should have come even if you didn't. We should have, because discretion be damned, Emmeline Constance, you're my *daughter*," she said, overbright eyes shifting between mine, the corners of her mouth quivering. "My first and only, my absolute beloved. I should never have just let things sit and fester in the first place, I should have *asked* you before it was far too late . . ."

Her voice broke, and she subsided with a shaky sigh, turning away from me and closing her eyes. I hugged myself hard, wondering how many more people I loved were going to cry in the near future because of me. I'd been so caught up in my own pain, in the reasons for my flight from Thistle Grove, that I'd given shamefully little thought to the scars my departure must have carved into the ones I'd left behind.

My horoscope app had *not* seen fit to warn me of this incoming emotional reckoning—one star.

"It wasn't your fault, Mom," I said, low, my own voice wavering. I reached out blindly, without looking at her, fumbling for her hand. "None of it was. I'm the one who pushed you away whenever you tried to come close. And you're right, Gareth *did* damage me. Maybe . . . maybe more, and worse, than I ever even gave him credit for."

"Will you tell me now, love?" she said, so plaintively my heart quaked for her. "What happened to you back then? Why you thought you couldn't stay?"

My insides felt like they were constricting, like a snake had snuck down my throat and coiled around my rib cage, a slow and awful suffocation. This kind of vulnerability between us felt uniquely terrifying, completely uncharted terrain. I loved both my parents, but we had never been the kind of family that delved into one another's feelings deep enough to really hash things out. When it came right down to it, I just didn't know how to talk to her this way.

But I *did* know that I wanted to try.

"Of course I will. I should have told you back then, too," I said, stumbling my way forward like I had the first fucking idea how to do this. "Or anytime since. Not knowing how to say it to you . . . that's a shitty reason not to give it a shot."

"It doesn't matter, my love," she said. Her hand tightened on mine, and just like that, the buckling pressure in my chest began to taper, until I thought I could remember how to breathe again. "As long as you're letting me in now."

20

Now That's What You Call an Apple Corps

As WAS TRADITIONAL, the next challenge took place by twilight.

The skies above the Honeycake Orchards had gone the colors of bruised fruit; tiers of peach and apricot and indigo seamed with lines of molten gold, streaks from the slipping sun as it ducked behind Hallows Hill. I stood in the broad concourse in front of the Welcome Center barn, before it forked off into dirt roads that led toward the orchard's attractions. The central spot where tourists would've flocked for doughnuts, cider, and ride tickets on a normal day.

Except that this was anything but a normal day. Talia, Rowan, and Gareth stood at attention before me in their ceremonial garb—Gareth with a suspicious glower and darting eyes, comically out of place on his cookie-cutter Abercrombie face. At my back swarmed an expectant mass of founding family members, gathered to watch. The pervasive hum of tension felt almost electric, like tangible potential hovering in the air, some creation magic with a sparking power of its own to manifest.

It felt, like I'd said to my mother just yesterday, like *anything* could happen.

The Grimoire pulsed once from its pedestal before me, giving me a gentle nudge. Then it cracked itself open, pages whipping back and forth before they settled, glowing words inscribing themselves on the blank parchment as if drawn by an invisible, fiery quill:

> Though the blood of magic may course through your
>   ancestral tree,
> True power is not given but won—and never won for
>   free.
> When monsters made of magic threaten to take their
>   toll,
> You must shew the strength you bear, by striking
>   swift and bold!

I thought, not for the first time, that whichever of the founders was responsible for the poetry bits of the spell hadn't exactly been a lyrical gangster. That "shew" especially smacked of trying just a *wee* bit too hard; my money was therefore on Gramps Elias.

Just as my tolling words trailed off, three sinuous streaks of light ribboned from the Grimoire and wrapped themselves around the combatants like radiant ropes. In an instant, all three flickered out of sight, reappearing in the very next breath—Rowan at the entrance to the sunflower field, Talia out by the pumpkin patch, and Gareth just in front of the first row of apple trees.

As soon as they appeared, the luminous ropes unwound from them and coiled into gilded flowers, each whizzing off to the far side of its respective arena to hover in wait.

Even from half a mile away, I could see Talia grit her teeth, mouthing *fuck* to herself as she realized that the Grimoire had indeed thrown the dreaded wrench in our plans—they'd been assigned to parallel tracks. It would be next to impossible for Talia to duck out of her challenge, race all the way to the apple trees on the other end of the orchard, and derail Gareth in time to help Rowan secure a win.

Though I could see, by the determined cast of her jaw that I was coming to recognize, that she was going to do her damnedest to get there anyway.

Then the pumpkin patch began to stir.

Both the uncarved gourds and the bespelled fantasia of jack-o'-lanterns suddenly lifted off the ground, trailing vines. As if spun up by some fastidious tornado, they began to whirl slowly toward the center of the patch. Talia watched, slack-jawed with awe, as they rotated around one another like a solar system in miniature, before some invisible force sucked them in toward the center like a black hole.

Snapping them together into a shambling pumpkin monstrosity raining disturbed soil—a construct woven together with vines, topped by the same colossal sugar skull I'd noticed when I was last here with Lin.

The pumpkin gargantuan took two stumping steps forward, bending until it was face-to-face with Talia, sprite flames flickering in each of its ghastly hollow eyes. Then it issued a roar so bone-rattlingly loud it made me flinch even from my safe distance away.

In contrast, Talia endured the howling—so forceful it actually blew back her hair, and I could only imagine how pumpkin-monster breath might smell—with such a languid lack of affect that it was like gourd-based beasts got up in her face every other Tuesday. Then she held out a splayed hand and, like a squid shooting off ink, squirted a sticky mess of ectoplasm like a decaying spiderweb directly into its face.

The roar cut cleanly off, the beast swinging its blinded head from side to side. Talia wheeled around and took off toward the apple orchard—where Gareth was facing down what looked like a heinously ugly apple tree Ent.

The orchard had knit its own amalgam, a giant woven from warped trunk, bristling branch, and strategically placed clusters of fruit and leaves. Gnashing its serrated jaws, it lashed out at Gareth as he approached, snapping branches out at him like cracking whips. Gareth deflected a few blows with his vambraces—it made me grind my teeth to see those dumbshit things come in legitimately useful—and those he couldn't fend off, he attacked with transmutation spells. Branches that should have struck him senseless turned to harmless wisps of steam, confetti, or what looked like bright ribbons of shredded silk.

Though I logically knew he wasn't doing any of this for the sole purpose of annoying me, there was something inherently obnoxious about his display. Trust a Blackmoore to make a melee with Evil Johnny Appleseed look like a two-bit magic show, as if it took next to no power at all to manipulate molecules this way.

Meanwhile, Rowan was engaging in his own careful dance with a sunflower giantess.

The sunflowers Linden and I had picnicked beneath had braided themselves into a towering floral scarecrow, with, intriguingly, a feminine shape. Unlike the other two constructs, she was somehow almost pretty, with a spill of petaled yellow hair that flared around her like a corona, the green fronds and leaves that wove her body nipping in at the waist. Her eyes were huge, black, and compounded as a fly's, made of the spiraling seeds that formed sunflower centers. Each time Rowan feinted in either direction, she twitched to block him, moving with an eerie shutter-clicking speed that felt like too many frames per second to fully process.

As I looked back to gauge Talia's progress, Rowan had just begun conjuring crabgrass and giant foxtails from the ground to fling out like a weedy net, trying to trap her in place while he raced for the glowing token she guarded behind her back.

Back at the patch, Talia hadn't had much success. Though she'd managed to mute its howling and blind the topmost head, the pumpkin fiend clearly had plenty of other eyes at its disposal. As she raced toward the apple orchard, it shot off vines like lassos, curling them around Talia's ankles and yanking her feet out from under her. She fell *hard*, the kind of bone-crunching tumble only properly described as eating shit. My breath caught at how viciously her chin struck the ground, blood trickling from her lip where she'd bitten herself.

But then she lifted up on her forearms, giving her head a shake to clear it, sheer murder blazing up in her eyes. Teeth bared, she reached down to wrench off the vines; I couldn't quite tell what spell she'd used, but from the way they fell off her like corn silk, she must have somehow turned her grip razor sharp.

Then she staggered up to her feet and stalked toward the pumpkin fiend like one of the Furies, actually *growling* under her breath.

It was, Gauntlet matters aside, almost intolerably hot to watch.

The fiend charged her like a frenzied bull, swinging its arms. But then the air around the pumpkin patch began to shimmer, going silvery and somehow *thin*. I could see the strain of intense focus carve Talia's features even finer, her garnet blazing to crimson life as she lifted her hands and cupped them toward the sky. There was an abrupt shift to the air that felt strangely sepulchral; a cold breath blown over your shoulder in an empty crypt, a chilly finger drawn slowly down your spine.

Then shapes began to coalesce, the tattered and translucent gray of ghost ship sails, all around the pumpkin fiend. A keening whine emanated from them, building into an eldritch wail.

I realized that Talia was deliberately thinning the veil all around her—turning the patch into more of an in-between place like the Witch Woods, sliding it closer to her own domain.

As more and more phantoms appeared, circling the pumpkin fiend in a sinister swarm, it became clear that Talia couldn't just talk to ghosts, but also command them. They swooped and darted around the pumpkin fiend like rabid bats, until it had no attention to spare for anything beyond their blitz attacks. And insubstantial as they looked, the shades were clearly far from harmless; I could see gouges appearing in the fiend's bright orange skin, scrapes and ragged pits where the shades were taking whole chunks out of it.

Talia was whipping up their rage, turning them into poltergeists.

When the fiend began to howl in pain, Talia took advantage of its distraction. She spun herself into a woolly black cloud of ectoplasm, rose into the air, and began hurtling toward the apple orchard like a meteor. I'd had no idea she could move that fast; with a spurt of hope, rising awe, and an (uncool) hint of proprietary pride, I realized that she must be even stronger than I'd thought.

Which was good, because a glance at the apple orchard confirmed that time was rapidly running out for her and Rowan.

Gareth had made impressive headway against Evil Johnny Appleseed (the pun center of my brain kept insisting that the thing should really be called an Apple Corps) by aiming transmutation spells at its various grafted limbs. He'd even managed to turn one of its arms into a slab of solid stone that it couldn't really lift; it was listing heavily to the right, dragging the dead weight around as it struggled to fend him off. They were almost all the way to the other end of the orchard, where the Gauntlet token twinkled from just behind the monster's trunk, only a few feet away from Gareth's reach.

To his left, Rowan was still struggling with the sunflower giantess. Though he'd made it more than halfway across the field, she was tearing through his snares almost as quickly as he conjured them—while strafing him with a stream of sunflower seeds, forcing him to constantly expend energy shielding himself.

"Rowan!" Talia shrieked at him as she streaked by overhead. "You don't have time to fuck around! Go, go, *GO!"*

With a grim nod, he fell to one knee, a hand flung out to keep his bindweed shield erected while he clenched the other into a fist, drawing it down toward his chest.

The twilit sky darkened deeper just above the field, clotting into a maelstrom of whirring wings. A patchwork flock of birds, pigeons and swallows and ospreys and ravens, gathered overhead like a shrilling cyclone—then descended on the giantess in a pecking, cawing mass. But even as Talia plummeted toward the apple orchard, it was already too late.

With a massive burst of power that leached his face dead white, sweat slicking back his hair, Gareth called down a lightning storm.

The entire apple orchard filled with flickers of jagged light, like a million flashbulbs going off at once. I hissed in pain, shading my eyes as the glare threatened to scorch my enhanced Arbiter's vision into a burning haze. But I could still see well enough to spot the bolt of lightning that struck Evil Johnny Appleseed right down its center, cleaving it into two charred logs that toppled over to either side.

Just as Talia landed behind him with one knee to the floor, Gareth leapt over the split wood to snag the Gauntlet token out of the air. The light melted into his hands, enveloping his entire silhouette with a golden glow—and the words of acknowledgment fought their way out of my mouth.

"Second victory goes to House Blackmoore!"

21

This Will Always Be the Place

"So *THAT WAS* a cluster," Talia said into her arms.

The four of us were at the Shamrock Cauldron for an impromptu pity party the Monday after the challenge. Talia was downing drinks with grim efficiency, at a rate impressive even for her. Yet even facedown on the bar with her head pillowed on her forearms, she didn't seem to be getting much drunker, as if her misery was somehow absorbing all that alcohol like a hollow limb. Compared to her, Rowan, Linden, and I were taking it relatively easy—though once he gathered that our collective funk was Gareth related, Morty had made sure to keep all our glasses full.

"You really tried, though," Linden attempted, taking a stab at comforting. "Seriously, you both damn near crushed it. That's gotta be worth *something*."

Talia lifted her head long enough to stare at Linden with slit-eyed affront before dropping it back down.

"You know what Yoda said about trying," she said, muffled. "It's for fucking losers."

"Okay, so, he did maybe say something like that," Lin admitted, her brow wrinkling. "But I don't think he meant it . . . *exactly* that way."

"Weak, sis." Rowan shrugged, tipping back his Dos Equis. "Let's be real, that mess was not our finest hour."

I stayed quiet, toying with the lime slice floating in my drink. Though all of us were despondent over this setback, I felt inordinately glum; not just overcast, but like it was maybe hailing in my soul. Some of it might have been just mantle withdrawal, but I was wallowing in existential angst much stickier and deeper than I'd experienced in years.

It made even Dead Fred look somehow dourer than usual, more "Abandon All Hope" than the cheerfully macabre YOLO vibe he usually exuded.

Why did I even *care* this much that Gareth would probably bring home the win, I wondered, holding the bobbing citrus slice under the surface with a fingertip. We'd known from the start that this was the likeliest outcome, and Talia and Rowan had even managed to get a little egg on Gareth's face; more than we might have hoped for when we made the pact. And once this was all over, I'd disappear, headed safely back to my real life—and all of this would become just another unwelcome memory of Thistle Grove, lodged in my brain like a burr before it desiccated and fell away.

So why did that thought make me feel not better, but immeasurably worse?

"I'm really sorry, man," Talia was saying to Rowan. "I know I owed you this challenge. If I'd only gotten to him faster—"

Rowan shook his head, reaching over to grip her shoulder and give her a little shake. "Nah, you did what you could . . . I took too long. If I'd just managed to get Sunflower Stacy pinned down for even a hot minute . . ."

"At least you guys had the chance to do something," I groused. "My only actual job was to pronounce Gareth the Victor, blech."

"You know what, you don't get to have it the worst," Linden countered. "All *I* got to do was sit on the sidelines and watch that . . . that *jagbag* win."

At that we all lapsed into a dismal silence, heavy as graveyard dirt.

"So, what now?" Talia said, after a few minutes of communal languishing. "We *cannot* let this be the death of the pact. Especially since we're agreed, right, that it's not just about us anymore?"

I thought of the Thorns' semideserted orchard, and how vibrant it had been even the last time I came to town for a visit, about four years ago. And though I hadn't stopped by the Avramovs' Emporium, I was sure the sight of it emptied out and quiet—compared to the lively bustle I remembered, the town destination it made of Hyssop Street—would be no less disheartening.

Talia was right. This *was* bigger than three scorned witches and their private scores to settle. It may have started out that way, but it had grown into something larger by several scales of magnitude; something the rough size and shape of Thistle Grove itself.

"You know what," Linden mused, "maybe that's it. It's *not* just about us. The Blackmoores have had the run of this town too long, and we all know it. So maybe it's time we roped in the elders for real."

Talia cocked her head, intrigued. "What are you saying, sunshine?"

"I'm saying we really lay it out for them," Linden said, gaining steam, a trace of new excitement shading her voice. "What we're trying to do, and exactly why we're doing it. Obviously they must know the broad strokes by now—but not the particulars. So we bring them into the huddle, ask their advice. You know how the elders all love to play the sage."

"Hey, that's not a bad idea," Talia said, her face brightening. "They might have tricks up their sleeves, geezer shit we won't have thought of ourselves. I'll sit down with Elena, put our heads together. She's been dying for a chance to stick it to Igraine anyway."

"And I'll tackle Mama," Rowan said to Lin, shrugging elaborately when she narrowed her eyes at him. "What, sis, it only makes sense. I'm her favorite kid, it's my whole thing."

Linden stared at him, shaking her head. "You are *not* Mama's favorite, Rowan, that is delusional."

"I am, though. But it's cool, really, it's no big deal. You can just talk to Dad like you always do anyway."

Talia and I smiled at each other over their bickering. She reached under the bar to thread her fingers lightly through mine, my skin sparking to life at her touch like tinder. Apparently my abrupt-onset depression wasn't so complete that it could muffle even this, the fire that flared between us so reliably.

"How stoked are you to be an only child right now?" she asked, a corner of her mouth tugging up. "I can't imagine growing up all soft like that. Never even having to compete for resources."

"To be fair, being an only child isn't going to help me this time," I said, trying to focus on her instead of the soft way her thumb was grazing the inside of my wrist. "I won't be talking to my parents. My dad's too honor forward to participate in something like this, even if it isn't technically against the rules. And the two of them always close ranks, so trying my mom won't be any use."

"So who *will* you be talking to, then?"

"My nana Caro," I said, giving her hand a little squeeze. "My favorite grandparent. And the one who was Arbiter before me."

NANA CARO HAD the demanding social calendar of a *Bridgerton* debutante, which meant I hadn't seen her for so much as a brunch since the gala at The Bitters. I didn't take it personally; my grandmother had always been that way. Exuberantly loving with her grandchildren—a consummate confidante, and reliable smuggler of snack contraband—but also protective of the space she'd carved out for herself. It was her way, I guessed, of keeping her life hers, and I'd always respected her for marking out those boundaries.

But when I'd called to ask for her help, there must have been something extra in my voice, some granddaughter equivalent of a bat signal. She'd invited me for tea and sympathy the very same day.

"How are you bearing up, peep?" she asked, surveying me closely as I sipped a blistering cup of Mexican hot chocolate, which I should have known better than to accept. Despite the silly Harlow affinity for drinks at perfect temperatures, anything warm Nana served stayed dragon-breath scalding until it was gone—presumably because that was just the way *she* liked it.

"You're looking a little peaky," she added, flashing a quick smile to soften any sting. "The mantle doesn't take it easy on anyone, but from where I'm sitting, you've had an even more exciting go of it than usual."

"I think it *is* starting to wear on me," I admitted. "I'm getting a little frayed around the edges, if that makes sense. More sensitive than I usually am, verging on morose? Very weird, not like me at all."

"I know just what you mean," she said, leaning across the coffee table to pat my knee. "Even for an adrenaline junkie like me, it got a bit much as it wore on. And I had your gramps to see me through the rougher patches. Steady as stone, that man was. Could weather just about anything."

Though he hadn't been born a Harlow, my grandfather Sebastian had been much closer to what I considered our classic family disposition: reserved, self-sufficient, with a pained distaste for any type of drama. But they'd had a love affair for the ages before he died, so there must have been *something* under all that deceptively still water. Or maybe it was the whole opposites attract thing, who knew.

For some reason that made me think of Talia; the twisty paradox of her, like some captivating Gordian knot I was still struggling to comprehend. The ferocious girl who growled at pumpkin fiends as she stalked her way into battle, and also baked babkas to show people she loved how much she cared. The girl who embraced darkness, tended and cared for the phantoms that lived within it, while shedding such a scintillating light that it was damn near impossible to look away from her.

"Penny for your thoughts," Nana Caro said, one microbladed eyebrow arched. "I'd bet my bottom dollar it's not just the mantle making you look so fraught."

"No," I admitted, with a gusting sigh. "There's . . . someone. It's really new, still, but it's making my whole situation, you know. Another layer of complicated."

"*Ah.*" She nodded, setting down her cup. "That's another thing they don't tell you about the mantle spell. It tends to clarify things, makes you sink more into yourself. And sometimes that can be a dicey proposition. Say, if you're already at some kind of cross-roads."

I nodded a little shakily, beset by expanding tightness in my throat, the salty smart of tears. Striving for some chill, I took a breath and looked around my grandmother's eclectic apartment. A cauldron hung in the granite fireplace and one of my mother's handmade besom brooms was laid across the lintel, juxtaposed against modern furniture, framed prints of Yayoi Kusama installations Nana had likely seen in person, and a hanging spiral of Turk-ish mosaic lamps she'd probably bought at an actual souk. Unlike most founding family members, Nana traveled every year—taking adventure cruises with friends, jetting off on solo excursions, and generally being the type of person who may or may not be on a hot air balloon above a vineyard at any given time.

Nana might have been a Thistle Grove witch, but she'd never let magic define her life to the exclusion of everything else; an-other thing I deeply admired about her.

"What is it, peep?" she said more gently, abandoning her sofa chair to come perch beside me on the staunchly Scandinavian couch. "I know you said you needed advice, but it can't be the *Gauntlet* you're crying over—you've always had better sense. So, what is this really about?"

"You're right . . . it's not the Gauntlet, not really. Or even the person I mentioned." I'd come here specifically to get her take on how we might best Gareth in the final round, but suddenly that felt very far beside the point. And while a lot of this was about Talia—probably more than I wanted to admit—the chain reaction she and the mantle's spell were catalyzing had even more to do with me. "It's me, Nana. *I'm* the problem. I've done all this work to get to where I am, and now . . . it's like I'm flailing. Like I'm not sure about anything, anymore. About who I am, what I want for myself. Where I even want to be."

I told her how I'd taken to going on long midday walks to savor the fall weather; wandering in and out of the familiar tourist traps on Yarrow Street, getting lunch at Golden's or the new sandwich place with the incredible falafel wraps. Dipping into the funky coffee shop Talia had taken me to, exploring the new galleries, jewelry stores, and boutiques that had sprung up in my absence. I'd even picnicked by myself next to Lady's Lake, in sunshine so pure it felt medicinal, and taken a book and a hot chocolate to the town cemetery like I'd once loved to do, whiling away an entire afternoon.

Slowly falling back under Thistle Grove's spell without even putting up a fight.

Nana listened to me with an open stillness, the same way she had when I was twelve and broke an artifact at Tomes that I shouldn't have been touching in the first place. Back then she'd snuck into the shop with me and fixed it with a simple restoration charm, and kept my secret ever since; my dad had never been any the wiser about the whole thing.

This time around, I didn't think a spell was likely to do the trick.

Tears welled again, and I angrily dug the heels of my hands into my eyes. "Ugh, *damn* it, and then this! I haven't cried this much in my whole life, and now it's constant low-grade waterworks. Just absolutely horrible."

"Sometimes it all needs to come out." She patted my leg again, gave it a little squeeze. "Just think of it as venting built-up steam. It's good for the pipes."

I gave a wet little laugh, then took a shuddering breath. When I spoke again, I was fractionally calmer, at least enough to articulate my thoughts.

"It's just that, I thought I never wanted to come back here," I said, gears of pain turning in my chest like some rusting clockwork mechanism. "I thought I was done with Thistle Grove magic, with the way this place pigeonholes you into being only who you were born by blood. And it feels good to achieve things in Chicago, things that are interesting and impressive and *substantial*. I'm making a real life for myself, out there. I'm becoming *someone*."

"Oh, honey, you were always someone," Nana said with ultimate pragmatism, reaching out to finger a lock of my hair. "That what this is about, too? Don't get me wrong, I was never one for the hassle of too much hair myself. And it suits you. But I do wonder if *you* really like it quite this short."

Anyone else would've gotten reamed out for asking me a question of that ilk—*but don't you ever* miss *your pretty long hair*—but I knew what she was driving at. I bit my lip, feeling almost shamefully caught out. "What do you mean?"

She gave me a forthright look, like, *cut the crap, kid.* "When you were little, you screamed blue murder when poor Cecily went after you for so much as a trim. And even when you were older, you looked like a frigging *Tangled* cosplay half the time. More hair than girl."

Did I want to know how my grandmother knew about Disney movies and what cosplay even was, I wondered. Probably I did not.

"And then you leave town," she continued, "chop it all off, and never look back? That's a goddess-damned declaration, Emmeline. A rebellion. Or maybe even some kind of penance only you can understand."

I sat, feeling desperately unmoored, wondering whether it was possible that I'd misunderstood my own intentions. That my haircut wasn't just a celebration of a new identity, but also some obscure form of punishment; for the weakness I'd shown after Gareth, maybe, my willingness to take the easy road by running away instead of building myself back up, and for the way I'd treated those I'd left behind. I could tell myself all I wanted that I'd been just a kid doing the best she could, that I hadn't meant to hurt anyone, that I hadn't even really known how much they were hurting.

But maybe that had never quite cut it, not for the inner judge and jury that presided over my own conscience.

"But trust me, I hear you," she went on. "I know how this place can conspire to make you feel small, if you didn't happen to pop out with the right last name. And you're like me that way, peep. We weren't built to live small, neither one of us."

"But it's still so nice here," I admitted, closing my eyes at the sheer relief of saying it out loud after thinking it in secret for so long. "Just, incomparable. The smell of the magic, the way the air here buzzes. The night sky and the fall weather and the sheer stupid *perfection* of it all. It shouldn't even exist, but it does, it's *real*, and I've been lying to myself for years about how much I missed it. And it still . . ." I took a deep breath, girding myself for the worst part. "Even after all this time, it still feels like home."

There was something apocalyptic about this admission, like I'd opened the Pandora's box I'd kept buried in the cellar of my heart, along with all the other pale and withered truths I didn't want to exhume. As if it couldn't be unsaid or undone, now that I'd let it come swirling out.

"And you still love it," Nana finished for me. "You love Thistle

Grove, and you love our magic—even if we Harlows did get the raw end of the deal, in the grand scheme of things. Bitch of a thing, but the way it is."

I burbled a sad little laugh at that. "Definitely a bitch."

"The thing is, you've been trying to outrun this place for nearly a decade, peep—but maybe it's time to admit that you can't. Because like it or not, you're a Thistle Grove witch, and a Harlow to boot. This town is in your blood, in a way you might not even understand just yet."

"But you travel all the time," I said, almost accusatory. "You're always going somewhere else."

"But I come back, peep," she said, with infinite gentleness. "Every damn time. And I wouldn't have it any other way."

When I shook my head, turning away, she put a light finger under my chin, turning my face back toward hers.

"Because that's what it means to be a Harlow, my Emmy. Thistle Grove is where we become who we are. Which means that no matter where you turn, where you visit or escape to, this will always be the place that calls you back."

22

You Beastly Child

TALIA'S BEDROOM WAS not what I expected.

I'd arrived at The Bitters at half past eleven for the séance Talia and I had planned. Over the past few days, we'd all come up empty on practicable suggestions from our respective elders. The Thorns had chosen to stay out of our scheming altogether, and once I'd calmed down enough to give Nana Caro the scoop about the pact, she hadn't had any secret battle magics up her sleeve, besides the sheer ferocity with which she approved of our intentions; as far as she was concerned, the Blackmoores had had it coming for a long, long time.

So unless you wanted to count Elena Avramov's philosophical musings about what *really* constituted a curse—which Linden and I were not willing to do—we were back to square one.

Then inspiration struck, and Talia had the notion to summon Margarita Avramov's spirit for help.

"And the best part is, it *won't* be cheating," Talia had said when we met to talk it over at Angelina's Diner the day before, her eyes shining with that brash eagerness I was coming to recognize as her default state. "I won't ask her anything about what's going to happen, which is the biggest faux pas, right? I'll just politely request any . . . *thoughts and comments* she might have on the Gauntlet. Leave it nice and open-ended, let the Dread Lady take it from there. I mean, she cowrote the rules, she'll know what's out of bounds."

"Welp, that's a no from me, buds!" Lin said, slapping her palms onto the table. "Count me right out. Any ancestor that goes by "Dread Lady" is one ancestor I do not need to meet."

I considered the idea, arms crossed over my chest.

"I don't *think* it violates any of the Gauntlet rules," I said, with cautious interest. I was still so rattled by the revelations that had come to light at Nana Caro's that even planning a risky-ish endeavor felt like a nice change of mental scenery. "I mean, we'll be playing in the gray, like you said, but it's not like soliciting advice is prohibited. If we're careful about our wording, I think we should be in the clear."

And though I wasn't about to say so, I couldn't deny a certain level of personal fascination. I'd never witnessed a true Avramov séance, which they kept locked down to members of their close-knit clan, and those who were willing to pay steeply for the privilege. And the thought of seeing Talia in her element, like she'd been that night in the Witch Woods, held its own glimmering appeal.

"Fuck yes!" Talia had hissed, pounding a fist onto the table. "You and me, then, Harlow. It's gonna be bomb."

Now that I was here, I wasn't sure what I'd even thought her bedroom would be like. A macabre chic aesthetic, maybe, heavy on skulls, melted candles, and flocked wallpaper in the obligatory shades of black and red. Possibly a snake or two. Instead, Talia's suite was elegant and pretty, not a reptile in sight, and smelled distractingly like a distillation of her perfume. The bed was huge—which did actually track with my expectations—with a spindrift mass of pillows and comforters, and a button-tufted velvet headboard in a lovely shade of teal. A stunning chandelier hung above it from the coffered ceiling, like a more bafflingly intricate version of those birdcage lighting fixtures you saw at Restoration Hardware and knew you could never afford.

Talia smiled when she saw me craning my neck to admire it. "Micah made that for me," she said, naming her little brother, the second-to-youngest Avramov. "*Without* magic, imagine that. Kid is surprisingly good with his hands."

I wandered over to admire one of the haunting watercolors that hung on the gray walls. They were all of nightscapes, a fine balance between dark and bright; deep dusk edged with the ruffles of aurora borealis, or shimmering spills of galaxies like cosmic treasure chests. Each was lightly infused with magic, just enough to stir the stars into a slow, hypnotic sea of motion. Leaning in for a closer look, I could just make out Talia's name in the corner in a jagged scrawl.

"You painted these?" I asked, glancing at her over my shoulder with eyebrows raised. "How many secret talents do you even *have?*"

"I'm trying to parcel them out slow, for maximum effect," she said, leaning against the wall with one foot up, a smirk tugging at her mouth. "But now does feel like the time to tell you I can also whistle like a fucking nightingale."

"See, that's just not fair," I complained. "No one person needs baking *and* painting *and* whistling, not to mention necromancy. Really gilding the lily over there."

"What can I say?" She gestured showily at herself. "I'm extraordinarily well rounded."

We lapsed into a silence that quickly grew velvety and dense, both of us intensely aware of the proximity of Talia's foamy bed. Or at least *one* of us was intensely aware of it; images from our interrupted night seared through my brain like a meteor shower.

Talia cleared her throat and looked away, a smile twitching at her lips. "Speaking of necromancy, it's almost time. We need to pull the trigger at seven minutes past midnight."

"That's . . . specific," I said, trying to wrest my head back in the game. "The witching hour, I get, but why the seven minutes after?"

"Secrets of the trade, Harlow. You know how it goes. I could tell you, but then . . ." She clawed her hands, miming monsters bursting through soil. *"Strigoi."*

Rolling my eyes, I followed Talia to an ornate floor-length mirror hanging on one of the walls, clearly not part of her chosen decor. The glass was so heavily foxed it looked hazed with smoke, and two needle-tipped spires rose up on either side of the gold frame. The rest of it was worked into a flower-and-ivy trellis, wolves' faces and coiling snakes peering from behind dainty lilies and leaves.

"The Avramov scrying mirror," she said, a hint of pride in her voice. "All of us get to use it, but as the scion, it's my heirloom to keep. It's been in the family for almost five hundred years."

"Holy shit," I marveled, shaking my head. "Half a millennium. I don't think the Harlow family tree even goes that far back."

We sank down in front of the mirror to sit with crossed legs, me following Talia's lead. There was a makeshift altar set up at the mirrors' base, a heavy wooden serving tray holding an assortment of curiosities. Seven red candles and a scattering of crystals: blue lace agate, white quartz, and amethyst. A tarnished silver samovar, and two teacups of china so thin they looked like they might snap if you breathed on them wrong. A slice of black forest cake topped with cherries and chocolate shavings, next to a bowl of fresh-cut hellebore heads.

"I don't see any scarab blood," I said as I cataloged the items, remembering what Elena Avramov had said to Igraine after the first challenge.

Talia snorted. "That was just Elena being a dick. A summoning actually requires talismans of invitation, things Margarita liked when she was alive. And amplifiers, to cast the summoning net wide beyond the veil."

"Cool," I breathed, my pulse picking up. This was exactly the type of witchcraft I'd longed to do when I was younger, the elaborate kind a Harlow had no hope in seven hells of pulling off. And I was about to see it up close and personal.

"Anything else I should know before we start?" I asked. "Any matters of protocol?"

Talia flashed me a brief smile, her face already sharpening with concentration. "It's more of an organic flow, you'll see. Just let me do most of the talking for us, and we should be all set."

Then she snapped her fingers, and the seven candles flared to life.

I held my breath as she chanted in a low whisper, her hands moving in front of her in that deft way I'd seen in the Witch Woods—like she was weaving some invisible cat's cradle almost faster than I could follow. Her eyes were spectral in the candlelight, their slate gray cool and fathomless. The candlelight limned the line of her profile as if it'd been drawn in one long swoop, and I couldn't have dreamed of looking away from her.

Then she picked up a fork from the tray, slicing off a bite of the cake to feed me, then one for herself. Talia had probably baked it from scratch; magic was always much stronger when you made its component parts by hand. If she had, she was an even better pastry chef than she'd let on. I closed my eyes as the chocolate, sour cherry, and sweet cream melted on my tongue, wishing the spell called for more than just one bite.

Next, she poured from the samovar into the teacups, handing one to me. We toasted solemnly—and very carefully, with only the most delicate of clinks—eyes latched on to each other's. When Talia threw the contents back, I did the same—only to sputter, coughing so hard I almost gagged, as something that tasted like Everclear laced with cyanide singed its acrid way down my throat.

"That's . . . *not* tea," I choked out, eyes watering.

"Of course it's not," Talia said, candlelight licking at the corners of her widening smile. "You don't call the Dread Lady with just *tea*. It's medovukha, Margarita's favorite. And this samovar belonged to her."

Then the crystals began to glimmer in succession, as if a current was running through them, the candle flames trembling as if whipped by a stiff wind. The mirror's smoky surface began to roil like ink blooming in water, swimming with strange shapes like Rorschach blots.

And then it cleared all at once, revealing the spirit of departed founder Margarita Avramov.

Her black hair floated around her head like seaweed fronds caught by the tide, her sloe eyes shifting between colors, from lustrous black to blue to an impossible green, and finally a catlike yellow. Though I'd already seen her portrait downstairs, in person she looked more like Talia, but not in any uncanny way. They shared the same cheekbones, seven-minutes-past-midnight hair, and long, elegant column of a neck. And there was something familiarly combative about her resting expression.

But her image flickered as if under a strobe light, shuddering between the beautiful apparition and something different and much worse. Every so often, black filaments seemed to fissure her face and neck; like a starburst fracture in a broken mirror, or decaying veins rising to the surface of pale skin.

It was, as Lin would have said if she were here, *extremely* metal. Anyone who thought that summoning Bloody Mary sounded like a party would've had a real rager with Dread Lady Avramov.

"What do you want *now*, you beastly child?" the founder said to Talia. I could tell she wasn't speaking English, but the bespelled mirror had a Babel Fish effect; I had no trouble understanding every word. Her voice echoed as if it came from the bottom of a well, but even through the distortion, affection laced her tone. "And it not even your birthday for nearly another turn. Whatever it is had better be good indeed, Natalia."

"Tonight I seek not your blessing but your counsel, Dread Lady," Talia said formally, dipping her head. "Many thanks for answering my call."

I flicked her a look from the corner of my eye. "Wait, you two know each other already?" I muttered under my breath. "You didn't mention that part."

"The Avramov scion gets a happy birthday apparition from the Dread Lady each year," she whispered back. "It's tradition."

"Right." I looked back at the spectral woman, her face flickering between porcelain and fissured black. "So festive."

Margarita Avramov turned her head to look at me, mercurial eyes narrowing as she took me in. There *was* something dread about her regard, a fearsome sense of power and enormity. As though she could quash me with a single thought, even from whatever unfathomable realm she now inhabited. I struggled to maintain respectful eye contact with her, in favor of a sudden urge to run shrieking from the room.

But instead of annihilating me on a whim, her lips curved in a fond smile.

"A pretty little Harlow, come to see me!" she exclaimed, tilting her head. "Oh, what a treat. You have the look of Elias about that pointy little chin, you know, quite unmistakable; I hope you pay your respects to him when you can. Dreadful bore that the man was in life, our little Grove would still have been nothing without his hand at work."

Talia and I exchanged puzzled looks. I had no clue what Margarita was talking about, and Talia clearly didn't, either.

"I'll . . . be sure to light a candle for him on Samhain, founder Avramov," I said. When her gaze lingered on me, darkening, I hastily corrected myself. "Ah, Dread Lady, I meant."

Mollified, she nodded once, then shifted that piercing gaze back to Talia.

"Darling Natalia, you know I run short of patience by temperament," she said, a brittle edge to her tone. "Speak your piece, before I lose the precious little that I have."

"The final Gauntlet obstacle awaits us," Talia said. "And though the Blackmoore scion is . . . regrettably proficient, House Avramov has partnered with House Thorn to thwart him—and we still have a fighting chance. We were hoping for any words of wisdom from you, any advice you might be willing to share."

"I see," Margarita said, her eyes sparking pale yellow with new interest. "An unexpected partnership, how enterprising of you. And now you test the Gauntlet's rules for give, trace their edges for frayed threads that you might pull to your advantage."

"Something like that," Talia admitted, tilting her head side to side, unabashed.

"While your initiative appeals, I'm afraid the four of us *did* promise not to meddle once we shuffled off this mortal coil." She sighed, a little ruefully. "Caelia and I might have been . . . more flexible, perhaps, had it been only up to us. But Alastair and Elias, well. Always so insistent about keeping a balanced scale."

She pursed her pale lips, looking put upon. "Bless their hearts, ever preoccupied with fairness. So terminally dull. No wonder I was the last of us to go; I shouldn't wonder if those two perished first of the sheer frightful boredom of so much integrity."

I almost laughed, before it occurred to me that she might mistake that for disrespect. I had just about negative interest in seeing the Dread Lady's pissed-off face.

"But the Blackmoores have been winning for centuries . . . that's hardly fair. And is giving your advice *really* meddling?" Talia pressed. "We've already asked the living elders for their counsel. Is it so wrong to ask the same of you?"

"You do make strong points, Natalia," Margarita said, another flash of approval glinting green in her eyes. "Why don't I just take a little peek—purely for my *own* edification, of course, as is perfectly permissible . . ."

Her big eyes went distant, then clouded over, as if rimed by a thin skin of ice. Then her eyebrows lifted, and genuine surprise flitted over her unearthly face.

"My, my, how very curious," she said, more to herself than us. "The both of you! I would not have thought it *done*, and yet . . ."

The frost cleared, and she focused on us again, a smug little smile playing on her lips. "You don't need my help after all, Natalia," she said. "You've already got the way of it, you clever child. Simply forge onward *together*, just as you have begun."

She clasped her hands in front of her, fingers intertwined, giving us a meaningful nod above them, her eyes bright with a wicked mischief that looked just like Talia's.

"Farewell for now, my beastly girl," she said, breaking into a smile that was suddenly crowded with too many sharp teeth. "And do be *sure* to bring those Blackmoore bastards merry hell."

23

Like Starlit Oceans, or Alien Skies

TALIA AND I sat on the window seat with the window flung wide open between us, still buzzed from the intense flood of endorphins the necromantic magic had left behind when it receded. And the taste of the medovukha had grown on me, as we passed Margarita's samovar back and forth between us like a flask, taking little sips of liquid lightning.

Having now met Margarita in the spectral flesh, I felt reasonably sure she would approve of this repurposing.

"Well, this is . . . strange," I said to Talia, lolling my head back and forth against the wall as the world lurched around me, leaving a shimmering wash of psychedelic tracers in its wake. "Strange, but also nice?"

"Just let it happen," Talia advised, smiling lazily up at the ceiling. "It'll be like this for a little while before it fades. If you don't fight it, there'll be less of a crash at the end."

I took a deep breath, letting myself sink deeper into the swimmy sensation. "Duly noted."

"So what did you think of her? Her Fearsomeness, that is. The Dread Laaaaady."

I snorted a laugh. "She was actually surprisingly charming. I mean, also horrifying, obviously. But in a very compelling way."

"You should have told her you thought so. She'd have loved hearing that."

"Yeah, pass," I said, shuddering at the thought. "She also felt like she could think me out of existence if I rubbed her the wrong way."

"Except she's apparently all about you Harlows," Talia pointed out. "Which, no offense, came a bit out of left field."

"None taken." I looked out of the window, where the ripening moon hung above the Witch Woods, so fat and close it seemed like a magician's trick, like you could pluck it like a dime from the sky with a simple sleight of hand. "No idea what that was about, either. It's not like Avramovs and Harlows have some storied history of friendship or anything."

"And what did you make of the last part?" Talia laced her hands together with exaggerated import. "That whole wink-wink nudge-nudge *together* business. She was practically playing charades with us by the end."

I closed my eyes and thought back to the founder's cryptic eyes and her joined hands, her fingers so significantly intertwined. *Forge onward, together,* echoing in my mind on loop.

And then, assisted by the pleasant, free-associative drift of the séance afterglow, I had a sudden flash of seemingly unrelated memory—Talia's hand skimming over my mother's animated primroses as they recoiled from her. Then Talia's remembered words, when she explained why this would be.

Avramovs feel anathema to them. Or at least, that's what Linden thinks, and she'd be the expert.

"You know what," I said slowly, still making the connections as I spoke, my brain leaping from thought to thought like a toad traversing lily pads. "I'm not *sure* this is what she meant, but . . . it does give me an idea."

"Oooh." Talia lifted a languid eyebrow, leaning forward. "Do tell."

"So, Thorn and Avramov magics are fundamentally incompatible, right? They do green magic, life-and-light stuff; you do necromancy, death-based spells. Kind of . . . anathema to each other. Like what you told me in my mom's garden, the way you described why animated plants don't react well to your presence."

Talia nodded slowly, her gaze shifting back and forth somewhere above my shoulder as she ran this through her mind. "Okay, with you so far."

"So what if you and Rowan combined your raw magics, braided them together?" I barreled on, flushing with sudden excitement as the notion unfolded in my mind, gained breadth and clarity. "I'm thinking they'd cancel each other out into something like . . . like a nullifying field. So if Gareth starts gaining on you too closely, *boom*—you two spring a trap around him, keep him from advancing any farther."

"So it would be like antimatter, almost," Talia said, breathless, her eyes lighting with appreciation and that familiar, feral thrill. "Or antimagic. Harlow, that's a stroke of genius. I mean, batshit too, and dangerous as fuck; just think how insanely unstable a medium we're talking here! Nothing like that's ever been done before, I don't think. But also, yeah . . . just, *wildly* genius."

"I really think it might work, if the two of you are game," I said, glowing with the compliment. "I know it's risky, and asking a lot. But at this point, we go big or go home, right?"

"And risky or not, there's no chance in hell we're not going to at least try it, now that you've thought of it. I'll run it by Rowan, but after the way Gareth dunked on us last time, I think he'll be more than down." She lifted the samovar to me in toast, taking a swig and then offering it to me. "Cheers, Harlow. All may not yet be lost."

I took the samovar and toasted her back, feeling almost giddy with renewed hope. Then we sat quiet for a minute, both lost in separate thought, the silent dark pooling around us like slow waters. The Bitters grounds were perfectly still, broken only by the faint calls of night birds, the shrill chirrups of daredevil bats swooping around the mansion's many turrets and towers.

Then Talia turned from the window to look at me like some lovely harlequin, half her face submerged in shadow, the other half limned by the moon, each feature flung into cameo relief. Her pale eyes glittered like something out of a Billie Eilish song; a starlit ocean, or the sky above some frozen alien world, much colder than ours but maybe even prettier.

"Smells like rain out there," she said, tipping her temple toward the window.

"It's going to rain very soon," I replied without thinking. "It already is, over by Hallows Hill."

She cocked her head, giving me a questioning look. "And how would you know that?"

I frowned, wondering how the hell I *did* know. More than know, I *felt* it, with just the tiniest bit of effort; the surface of Lady's Lake trembling as each droplet struck the water, the quivering of the needles and leaves of the surrounding trees as their branches shook under the chilly onslaught, even the clammy saturation of the soil itself. Even stranger, there was nothing at all odd or out of place about this extracorporeal sensation; it felt like a natural extension of my own senses, as commonplace as if I were feeling my own skin and hair drenched during a storm.

"Must be leftover mantle magic, I guess," I said, releasing the feeling. It faded just as effortlessly as I'd summoned it up.

"Pretty weird, Emmy," Talia replied in lilting singsong, lingering over the syllables.

"*Definitely* weird, Talia," I sang back at her, my heart bucking at hearing my first name on her lips again.

So here we were once more, circling each other. And no matter what it did to my fragile peace of mind, how it compounded my already-complicated turmoil, I found I couldn't even imagine wishing myself anywhere besides this close to her.

"Emmy," she repeated, shifting a little in her seat, gaze never leaving mine. "You look beautiful by moonlight, Emmy Harlow."

"Only you could deliver such a cheesy line," I said, pretending like I hadn't just been thinking along the same lines myself, "and make it sound like grade A game."

"That's because I completely mean it."

She leaned forward, eyes intent, reaching out to delicately trace the outlines of my face. Running her fingertips over the arches of my eyebrows, the space between my eyes; then the long swoop of my nose, philtrum, and Cupid's bow. And then finally my mouth, her fingers drifting to cup my chin as her thumb grazed over my lower lip.

"You, Emmeline Harlow," she said, eyes locked on mine, "are so extremely fucking beautiful it hurts my soul."

"So are you, Natalia Avramov," I said, half sighing, tipping my head forward to close my lips around her thumb and draw it into my mouth.

She gave a sharp gasp, her eyes dropping heavy lidded. "Emmy," she said again, in that rasping whisper I liked so much, rock candy rough and just as sweet.

Things happened very quickly after that, in a tumbling cascade I could barely follow even as I was a pretty integral part of it.

Suddenly we were standing by the window all tangled up together, tugging each other's shirts over our heads. I could feel myself shimmer with heat everywhere Talia touched me, as if she was leaving glowing handprints like some neon rave paint on my skin. Together we half stumbled, half tripped toward the bed in a clumsy dance, awkwardly yanking off shoes and pants as we went, kissing like we would have rather swallowed each other whole.

Every so often we'd pull back a little and pause, hands still tangled in the other's hair, to just look, and marvel, and grin dizzyingly at each other, that this was really, finally happening.

"Damn, I feel like I could *eat* you," I exhaled into the curve of her neck, sliding my hands down the long line of her spine to the neat tuck of her waist.

"Then what, exactly, are you waiting for?" she whispered back into my hair, a smile curled like a secret into her voice.

When we fell onto the bed together, Talia's seafoam sheets were just as soft as I'd expected—though nothing in comparison to the searing softness that was her skin.

I traced the smooth outline of her with my hands and mouth, my lips on her instep, ankle, and then the tender back of her knee, all the way up to the silken inside of her thighs. I nipped at her lightly before biting harder, sinking my teeth in just deep enough to draw out those moans I'd been dying to hear from her for so long.

Then she was on top of me, with the scented tangle of her hair hanging around us, holding my face cupped between both hands as she kissed me hard and deep.

"Emmy Harlow," she whispered against my lips. "I want to do *everything* to you."

Then her mouth was a blaze down my neck and breasts, teasing out a moan low in my throat when she drew each nipple into her mouth. She trailed a scalding path over my belly, tracing circles around my hips with her tongue and lips, biting down on the thin, sensitive skin pinned taut over the bone. I twitched helplessly against her, caught by the tidal undertow of sensation, until it was all I could do not to outright beg her for more.

"Say it to me, Emmy," she demanded between kisses, husky and low, as if she knew just how wild she was driving me. "Ask for it."

"Please," I said, when I thought maybe I'd implode from the gravity of all that pulsing want. "Talia, just . . . *please.*"

Then her mouth was between my legs, parting me down the center; her hair sliding against my thighs, and everything inside me surging up to meet her.

I arched my back like a bow, not even caring how I sounded, stars swirling against the darkness behind my closed eyes. I said her name so many times that I lost count.

Talia, Talia, please, Talia.

Then it began to rain outside, just like I'd known it would.

It fell first in a soft, pervasive shush, cattails rustling against one another in high wind; then a loud, cascading downpour, rattling like marbles onto the roof above our heads. The room filled with the smell of rain and gusting cold, but the two of us were such an inferno that the creeping chill felt like a balm. We were pure heat together, a building blaze with no known boundaries. A tangled locus of lips and hands, driving each other wild over and over again.

A fire that felt like madness, like it might never be put out.

24

What You Do Best

I JUST REMEMBERED," I said, trailing my fingers idly down Talia's back. She lay pillowed on my chest, my chin tucked against her crown, her head rising and falling with each of my breaths. "You never told me why you don't have any tattoos."

"Seriously, Emmy?" Her laugh feathered over my chest. "*That's* what you want to talk about right now?"

"Just humor me." It was so nice to keep hearing my name from her, even now that we weren't caught up in the moment. It felt like gaining ground, like I'd won something precious that was finally mine to keep. "I have a feeling it's something I'd want to know."

She sighed, pouting against my skin, drawing runelike patterns into my lower belly. "But you're going to make fun of me."

"After you made me come, what, sixty-five thousand times? I could never. It's like you fucked the sass right out of me."

"When you put it *that* way . . ." She laughed a little, and then I heard her swallow in the dark. "Okay, I guess it is only fair. The thing is, I want to wait for matching tattoos. You know, with a partner. So we can have . . . something indelible, something that matters in a special way. Something that I'd never done on my own before."

"Let me get this straight," I said, biting down on the inside of my cheek to keep a straight face. "You want to be an ink virgin, because you're saving yourself for your first time with that extra special someone?"

"Oh, fuck *you*," she said, struggling against me as if to get up. I held her tight, locked against me until she lapsed back onto my chest, laughing despite herself.

"Wait a minute, now I'm processing the implications. Does this make me an ink slut? Dermally promiscuous?"

"You *promised* you wouldn't make fun!"

"That was before I knew you were such a closet romantic," I teased, tugging her up until we were nose to nose, her head nested on the pillow next to mine. "Now all bets are off."

"It's not like I go to such great lengths to hide it," she said, and I sensed from the wary shift in her tone that we'd somehow wandered back into serious territory. "Is that a problem for you?"

"Of course it's not," I said, nuzzling her nose. "Why would it ever be?"

"Because it has been before."

I drew back a little, enough to see the liquid glimmer of her eyes in the dark. "What do you mean?" I said, more carefully. "And I'm really not teasing now, I swear. I just want to know—if you want to tell me."

She hesitated, tucking a hand under her cheek like a little girl. "I really don't want to fuck this up by talking about exes."

"You're not going to," I assured her. "I don't get jealous of people who came before me, if that's what you're worried about. That's not one of my things."

"Okay, then. If you're sure." She took a deep breath, as if steeling herself. "Her name was Jess—but you already know that. She was a theater student, in Chicago, actually. That's where she was from."

"Oh," I said, a little surprised. "I don't know why I assumed she was a local."

"No, she was just passing through. Taking some time off from her master's in drama to make money—working at Camelot, of all the dumb things. Apparently they can afford to pay their professional cosplay performers really well over there, and she'd signed on for a season of playing Nimue in one of their cornball dinner musicals at the Avalon."

The Avalon was an upscaleish restaurant, marooned on an artificial island in the middle of the manmade lake that adjoined Castle Camelot's moat—yet another ridiculous outgrowth of the Blackmoore empire. Her participation in it seemed like a terrible reason to hate Jessica right off the bat, yet here we were. I'd already decided I basically couldn't stand her.

"So, girl meets witch, tale as old as time," I said instead. "With you so far. And then?"

"And then things got serious, fast. I broke the witchy news to her, she met my whole family, even joined in for a few Sabbats. And she took it all in stride, for someone who hadn't grown up with any of it." She smiled a little, shifting against the pillow. "That part . . . that part was really nice."

Despite my assurances, the lingering echo of fondness in her voice needled under my skin a little. Shit, I was only human, and

I didn't *really* want to hear just how intensely super rad Jessica had been.

"But then it started getting to her," she went on. "What it really meant, being committed to me, rooted to this place the way I am—and I'd made it clear I only wanted it to be serious with her. Jess was big on traveling, exploring . . . you know, globetrotting adventures, lots of perky sun salutes on mountain peaks. That type of #wanderingsoul #traveljunkie shit."

"And you didn't want to go with her," I said, quiet.

"Not so much didn't want to, as couldn't," she replied, a little defensively. "I'm the Avramov scion, a Thistle Grove witch. I can't just *leave* like that. And you know how I feel about being far from here."

"I do," I said, noncommittal, remembering my own dismay at her reluctance to even consider a visit to Chicago.

She blew out a long, unsteady breath, shifting in place. "It made her so frustrated with me. And by then she'd spent time with the rest of my family, too, gotten to know them. And the way she saw it, Avramovs were inherently problematic—not exactly a foolproof bet for long-lasting romantic partnerships. And if she was going to give up the world for me, I'd better be damn well worth a sacrifice like that."

The bitterness in her voice made me ache for her, even as I very reluctantly understood just a slice of how Jess had felt. Talia *was* an intimidating prospect, if you took her only skin-deep, all that beauty and brashness and semi-feral witchcraft wrapped in one very enticing and willful package. Not to mention her family's decidedly gray-scale magic (and morality), their emphasis on individual freedom above all else.

Though someone who had really loved her should have known

better than to leave her at that, instead of looking past the trap-pings and down to the tender core.

"In the end, she decided I wasn't worth the risk," Talia finished stiffly. "So the summer season ended, and so did we. She broke things off right before she left. Cue heartbreak, disillusion, devas-tation, and the like."

"I'm sorry," I said, tipping my forehead against hers. "That must have been so hard on you. And then Gareth's hot garbage, on top of all that? I can't imagine."

"It was all some fresh hell," she agreed, but then the tension in her face softened a touch. "So I guess you can see why I had to at least pretend to pace myself with you."

"Well, I for one am glad we managed to move past pretend-ing," I said, grazing a kiss over her forehead.

"Have we, though?" she said, wariness creeping back into her tone. "Because, what happens now?"

"What do you mean?" I asked, almost wincing as soon as the words were out, for how much they sounded like I was purposely playing dumb.

"You *know* what, Emmy," she said, a little impatiently, sitting up and pulling her knees to her chest, resting her chin on them. "There's only one more challenge left to go. And then what hap-pens with you and me, once the Gauntlet's over? I can't be the only one of us who's considered that this—whatever this is becoming—has a built-in expiration date."

"No," I said, drawing myself up against the headboard. "I mean, you're right. Of course it's crossed my mind. I do have to go home when this is all over, back to work. But we've both known that all along."

"Maybe, yeah." She licked her lips, eyes searching my face. "But

I was starting to hope you might . . . change your mind, consider sticking around a little longer. Extend your sabbatical for a while or work remotely, something like that."

"I can't just *do* that, Talia," I said, more sharply than I'd intended—because here it was, the glinting trip wire, exactly where Linden had warned me it would be. "That's not how real life works. Or a real job."

"Why not? From what you've told me, it sounds like a lot of what you do, you could do just as well from here."

"And why am I the one who has to be flexible?" I countered. "If we wanted to give this a real shot, we could . . . split time, maybe, try a long-distance thing? Chicago's not the moon, you know. There's no *legitimate* reason you couldn't come to me, too."

"No legitimate reason." She recoiled, mouth dropping open, as though I'd slapped her. "Wow, I can't fucking believe this. It's like Groundhog Day, Jess all over again. I knew, I *knew* this was how it would go this time around, too."

I felt a familiar panic mounting inside me, at the thought that I was solely responsible for her distress, that this sudden and precipitous unraveling was somehow all on me.

"Did you know?" I retorted, scooting away from her, the space between us chilling like an advancing cold front. "Then why did you even let this happen in the first place? It's not like I was the one chasing you all by myself. At least that's not how I remember it."

"I let it happen because I *like* you, Emmy!" she burst out, throwing up her hands. "And I could easily see myself much *more* than liking you, if we gave this a real chance."

"And how are we supposed to do that," I said, feeling leaden, suddenly hopeless, "if you're going to act like some kind of cursed princess, doomed never to wander so much as a foot away from here?"

"Oh, so *I'm* being unreasonable, now?" She yanked herself off the bed, winding sheets around her, the glitter of her eyes stark against the gloom. "How about *you*? You love it here, you're fucking dying to stay, anyone with eyes can see that. But you refuse to admit it, and why? Just because some ripe asshole broke your heart a decade ago, made you feel like you'd never matter if you stayed. Have you even considered that it might be time to decide what you want for yourself?"

"You have no clue what you're talking about." I shot out of bed myself, scavenging the floor for my clothes, stewing with anger while my stomach ached with how quickly the fragile, spun-sugar thing between us was disintegrating, eroding further with every acid-washed moment.

"Or were you planning to spend your whole life running away from here," Talia persisted, "letting Teenage Shithead Gareth dictate who you are?"

"That is not what I'm doing," I said through clenched teeth, biting back tears. "I'm the *opposite* of doing that. I'm making my own path."

"Are you?" Talia challenged, arms crossed over her breasts, looking just as furious and annihilated as I felt. "Because chasing change the way you've been doing since you left . . . sometimes that's just another way of burying your head in the sand. Of hiding from what you actually want, and think that you shouldn't have."

"Look, I really can't handle this tonight, Talia," I said wearily, stepping into my shoes. "I'm exhausted. I just . . . I need to go."

"Of course you do," she retorted, scathing, though I could see the telltale glisten of silvery tear tracks on her cheeks. "Is anything else even on the menu, besides the Emmy Harlow special?"

"And what the hell is *that* supposed to mean?" I snapped, already on my way to the door.

"What do you think it means?" Even in the dark, I could see the pain scrolled over her face. "That running the fuck away is what you do best."

25

When Even Magic Fails Us

"Is it remotely possible that she's right?" Linden asked, setting down her chopsticks.

I looked at her over the wreckage of Chinese food cartons from Pearl Dragon that littered the coffee table between us, most of which I'd demolished myself, in a frenzy of eating my many conflicting feelings. We were at Linden's place, so I could fill her in on what Talia and I had come up with for the next challenge; even with things between us in such abject disarray, I was assuming neither of us was willing to give up on the pact.

But we'd covered that part fast, and once Lin realized how supremely not okay I was, the evening had devolved into tears, wine, and an epic comfort food binge.

"About what?" I asked her, still a little tearful, though I was now too full of egg roll to muster up another proper cry. I'd also literally cried myself to sleep the previous night, not to mention having sloppy-sobbed all over Linden earlier, so the well was close to plumb dry anyway. "My apparent affinity for running the fuck away?"

"Not that part," Lind said, making a sympathetic face. "Sounds to me like she just said that because her feelings were so hurt, and she wanted to hurt you back."

"You don't know that. It's possible she *also* meant it. Both things could be true, and with my luck, probably are." I took a slug straight from the bottle of pinot grigio I'd appropriated as my own, wincing at the sour tang of the warm wine. "Shit, maybe she's even right."

"No one ever means the nastier stuff they say when their dander's up, Em," Lin said gently. "Not even an Avramov. And definitely not Talia."

"What is it you think she's right about, then?" I eyed another fortune cookie, an ominous rumble from my guts bringing me up short before I could reach for it. I should have known better than to self-soothe with so much MSG, but dire times called for drastic measures.

Linden worked her jaw from side to side, clearly strategizing the most tactful path toward what she wanted to say.

"*Do* you really want to go back to Chicago, Em?" she said. "I've noticed it, too, how happy you seem to be here whenever your guard's down. It's like you have to remind yourself on the regular that you hate Thistle Grove with fiery passion, or else the real truth comes bubbling out—which is that you kind of adore this town. Maybe even more than some of us lifers do."

"I never said I *hated* it," I protested. "I mean, how could I, how could anyone? It's ridiculously beautiful, the weather's amazing, the sky is the literal definition of #needsnofilter. Shit, the whole town even smells like a Yankee Candle Halloween special. The other day I flat-out admitted to my nana that I *do* love and miss it here, pretty much all the time."

Linden raised her eyebrows. "Is this the game where you make my points for me? If so, I'm into it."

"But it was never really the town itself that I hated," I clarified. "It was living inside the suffocating little box that Thistle Grove Harlows get stuck with. You know that, Lins."

"So do you still think it's worth it, now that you have a bigger, Chicago-shaped box?" she persisted. Leave it to Lin to (lovingly) chisel away at inconvenient truths. "Has it been worth giving up magic and this town and all your people in it, for getting to be the person that being there lets you be?"

I suppressed the reflexive urge to leap in defense of my chosen life, and took a minute to genuinely consider the question instead.

"Well, there's a lot about the city that I love," I said slowly. "The Riverwalk, the museums, the endless restaurants. The random pop-ups and breweries, the fancy bars and the best kind of shithole dives. Jackson Park and the 606 and the lakefront walkways. So many choices, for everything. You could live there forever, and still never feel like you've seen and done it all."

"I wasn't asking you to channel the Chicago bureau of tourism, Em. Though you should consider hooking them up with your résumé."

"But those things matter," I argued. "They're what make up a life. I *like* being surrounded by all that potential. And more meaningfully, I really like my job—plus, I'm extremely good at it, which I know you'll recognize as something that's always been important to me."

All this was true. Silly as the Enchantify boxes were when compared to the visceral intensity of real Thistle Grove magic, I

cared about scoring the coolest stuff for them every month, culti-
vating relationships with the vendors I'd found worthwhile. There
was even satisfaction to be found in watching the beautiful unbox-
ing videos made by the representatives we partnered with. As dis-
tracted as I'd been by the Gauntlet and Talia, and even with all
the work stuff I'd managed to get done on the sly, I'd still missed
having my job be the biggest part of my day.

"But do you have to be on location to do it? Is everyone re-
quired to commute in person to Enchantify HQ?"

She reached up to stroke the corkscrew Albuca that was swaying its swizzled shoots above her head, poking at her hair like a
playful toddler. Like most of her apartment, the picture window
behind her was lined with lush potted plants, every spare inch
hosting the kind of exotic, persnickety flora that would've made
me break out into a cold sweat at the prospect of keeping them
alive. The entire place was rigged for their optimal happiness,
from pink-shifted LEDs feeding them just the right spectra of
light, to the dewy warmth Lin maintained throughout the sea-
sons, all in addition to lavishing them with magic and love.

If you asked me, for something that (usually) didn't even talk
back to you, plants had way too little chill.

"Or could you actually do what Talia suggested, and work remotely some of the time?" she went on.

"I assume it's not impossible," I said, trying to suppress the
treacherous flutter of excitement that brushed against my belly at
the thought. Apparently my gut, at least, was not fundamentally
against this idea. "Some of the staff do live out of state. No one in
a position like mine—but I've been there for nearly five years now,
almost from the start. I wouldn't know for sure unless I asked, but
I think they're pretty invested in keeping me on deck. So they

might go for it, as long as I was still willing to spend as much time in the city as necessary."

"Which of course you would be," Lin pointed out, deadpan. "So as to not miss too many random pop-ups."

I snickered, throwing a fortune cookie at her. She snatched it easily out of the air, courtesy of all those years on the softball team, then calmly unwrapped it and snapped it in two, sliding the fortune out. "You are such an asshole, Thorn."

"Just keeping it real for you, city slicker." She grinned, popping half the cookie into her mouth. "Someone clearly has to. But seriously, like you said—that stuff matters to you. So why not consider figuring out a way to have what you like best of both worlds?"

"Because I don't know if I even want them both," I said, sobering. "I really don't, Lins. Yeah, maybe I wouldn't be *just* the Harlow girl anymore if I moved back here, but you can't deny this town's magical community is fundamentally caste-based. Living here, you can't get away from all that mess. And it still kills me that my magic isn't stronger, and I'd have to live with *that* every day, too."

"But then there's the rather large problem of the girl," she pointed out. "Hate to break it to you, but if Talia's not willing to come to you, I'm pretty sure you're not going to find another of her in Chicago."

"No," I said dully, dragging my hands over my face. "I think there may only be one of her. Full stop."

"You're really falling for her, aren't you?" Linden said, with such a wealth of gentle sympathy that my throat went tight again. "And *way* ahead of schedule, too."

"Right? With most anyone else, the only thing I'd be sure of by now would be the chemistry." I gave a brittle half laugh, fiddling with my fingers. "And instead, the idea of not seeing her again—of not ever knowing what we could have been—truly makes me want to hurl."

"Sounds like you're in a right pickle, my bud," Lin said. "I wish I could make it better for you."

"You sure we can't at least try the hands?" I wheedled. "This is *kind* of like a really bad hangover . . ."

"Unfortunately, the hands are pretty useless when it comes to matters of the heart," Lin replied, with a rueful smile. "Trust me, both Rowan and I have tried all sorts of charms to that effect. Turns out it's true what they say, about how nothing quite does the trick like time. Although, TBH, vengeance pacts also do seem to help."

"Leave it to magic to let you down when you need it most." I slumped back against the sofa chair, heaving an exaggerated sigh. "Guess I'll just be doomed and wretched. Is that what the fortune says?"

"Let us see." She unrolled the paper then looked up at me, shooting me a conspiratorial grin. "'When Pearl Dragon and cheap wine and even magic have all failed us . . . there will *always* be *Buffy* marathons.'"

"It does not say that."

She shrugged, toggling her phone into remote control mode. "Nah, it says that your business will prosper. But as your forever bestie, you can't tell me I don't get to take at least a little poetic license."

26

Sly Cantrips and Tricky Spells

PLACES FROM THE past are usually much smaller than you remember when you return to them years later, shocked that they'd ever managed to command so much space in your brain at all.

This was *not* the case with Castle Camelot.

The keep loomed against the night, so broad and imposing it could have served as a real fortress, the black-and-gold Blackmoore pennants strung from its corner towers snapping in the wind. The whole thing looked like a middle-school "elements of a medieval castle" diagram come to life in all its cheese-bucket glory, complete with ramparts, a drawbridge, and a parapet walk, along with lots of other intimidating bits for which I'd never learned the proper names. Floodlights set at its base illuminated the rough-hewn facade—as if it was some painstakingly preserved historical monument, instead of a construction built circa 1998—

flinging bars of green, blue, and pink onto the stone, their reflections caught by the rippling black water in the moat.

Now that I was here, I'd expected to feel some twinge of Gareth-related pain, from any remnants of teen Emmy that might still have been haunting my subconscious. But Gareth and I had spent more time together roaming the grounds of his family's Tintagel estate, several miles down the road, than here—and it turned out all I felt was pissed. The castle had clearly been added to extensively since my day, as the Blackmoores churned the profits from their mini empire right back into expanding it.

It made me even more furious with them, this irrefutable proof of how they were flourishing as they turned the screws on the other families.

And I was more than a little preoccupied with Talia, whom I hadn't seen since that night at The Bitters, two days ago. Now she stood in front of me, flinty-eyed and meticulously composed, with Gareth and Rowan flanking her, waiting for the challenge to begin. I'd thought about texting her dozens of times—okay, it was more like in the hundreds—in the past few days. But what was I going to say to her to bridge the rift? What was I supposed to offer to get us back to where we'd been, when I still wasn't sure what I even wanted for myself, much less for us?

Tonight, I thought grimly even through the mantle's euphoric glow, was *really* going to blow.

In front of me, blazing words materialized on the Grimoire's open page. With an effort, I shuttled my emotions as far to the side as they would go, letting the Arbiter rise to the fore.

> As you draw closer to the wreath, consider ye its weight and fit;

To become its rightful bearer, you must now
   demonstrate your wit.
Have you bent to the wisdom of your elders, to each
   sly cantrip and tricky spell?
Consider them query and answer both, and they shall
   serve you well.

I puzzled over the words even as I pronounced them with the Arbiter's booming authority, the customary light flaring from the Grimoire and knitting itself into a token at the final, dying echo of my voice. We all waited with held breath to see which way it would flit; the Blackmoores' holdings were huge, swathes of acreage extending in three cardinal directions from where we stood. Castle Camelot and all its attractions were only the beginning to their vast private estate.

But the token zoomed off toward the drawbridge without hesitation, the keep's towering double doors creaking open of their own accord to let it flit through.

Which meant Castle Camelot itself would be tonight's playing ground.

The combatants wasted no time; they raced off toward the drawbridge at a sprint, Rowan taking the lead. As I recalled, he'd run track in high school all four years just like Lin, and he still had a solid stride. Behind me, the crowd of spectators shifted impatiently, clearly wanting to follow, even as the doors slammed closed once Talia disappeared across the threshold. I flung my arms out in a barricade, following the mantle magic's prompt.

"No one else shall pass," I boomed, "until a victory is called."

After a moment of disgruntled protest that they'd be denied admittance to the final, and arguably most exciting, challenge, I heard the rustling of robes and low chant of incantations, as those who knew how—and happened to have the proper equipment at hand—summoned up scrying charms to let them spy beyond the walls.

One had apparently been built into the mantle magic's spell; as I instinctively closed my eyes, I found I could extend my sight beyond my body, my awareness whizzing out in front of me like some kind of incorporeal drone.

For a precariously queasy minute, this disembodied vision made me feel like I might hurl, and I hunched over a little, taking a few deep breaths that sounded like the rushing of a gale.

Keep it together, Harlow. No one wants to see a giant puke.

Then the disorientation passed—and I plunged through the closed doors just in time to see the combatants enter a gigantic admitting room that was probably called a Great Hall, or Ye Kingly Foyer; the place where tourists were first funneled to take pictures with the members of the "court" before continuing on their way to the shopping, food, and shows.

There, they came to a skidding halt, as a massive, clanking suit of armor stepped out to block their way. The Gauntlet token paused right behind it, glimmering above one of its shoulders like a taunt.

"Shoots from stone," the suit of armor demanded in a metallic wheeze, spreading its arms expectantly.

The combatants exchanged looks with one another, clearly baffled by what it wanted from them. Gareth decided to play it tricky and feinted to one side, presumably to see if maybe that's what the Grimoire had meant by wit. Juking sideways in a flash, the empty knight hauled off and whacked Gareth upside the head—hard enough for the clank of impact to ricochet all around the hall, apparently more for effect than to inflict any actual damage. Gareth took a stumbling step back, rubbing petulantly at his head, looking more annoyed than hurt.

"Shoots . . . from . . . *stone*," the suit said again, more belabored this time, as if it was coaching not particularly bright children.

"Shoots from stone," Rowan repeated to himself, face clearing, and I could see the glinting moment the penny dropped. "Shoots from stone, wait . . . The Verdant Awakening Charm! That's it, right? That's what you want?"

The suit tipped its head to the side encouragingly, then whistled the lilting notes of a melody, naggingly familiar. For some reason, it reminded me of the last line of the challenge. *Consider them query and answer both . . .*

"What the fuck?" Gareth muttered beside Rowan. "I still don't get it."

Rowan stood in confusion for a moment, then let out a whooping laugh, slapping his thighs. "Wow, *really*? Okay, I guess, why not. *What is* the Verdant Awakening Charm?"

"Grimoire *Jeopardy!*" Talia exclaimed, as she got it, too. "It's playing magical *Jeopardy!* with us!"

But the answering question wasn't enough by itself, I realized, as the suit of armor gestured at Rowan again; it wanted him to cast the actual spell. This challenge was about testing the combatants' knowledge and recollection of the Grimoire, but also their proficiency at casting the spells themselves.

And of course it would have been Rowan who remembered this one first; it was a green spell, falling squarely in the Thorn domain. But the Thorns also made a habit of studying the Grimoire's hundreds of spells more extensively than most Avramovs and Blackmoores ever bothered to do. The two stronger families could usually realize their magical intent by brute force, without bothering with specificity and finesse.

Unlike them, the Thorns tended to do their homework, and here that effort counted.

Grinning broadly, Rowan cast Verdant Awakening, drawing shoots of green from the cracks between the floor's stone blocks, polished smooth as river rock by hordes of tourist feet. His ivy sprouted quickly and easily, climbing into the air as if searching for a trellis, and the suit of armor clasped its gauntlets together, then beckoned Rowan through.

When Gareth tried to race after him in pursuit, the empty knight bore down on him, reaching for the scabbarded sword slung around its waist.

"Shoots from stone," it demanded, threat and a hint of exasperation coloring its rusty tone.

"Are you serious?" Gareth snapped. "Thorn already told you! Or asked you, *whatever.*"

"We have to cast, too, numbnuts," Talia muttered, gritting her teeth as she spread her hands in preparation. Though this was probably the easiest plant spell in the book, one she could certainly do—shit, even *I* could pull off Verdant Awakening, given enough time—as an Avramov, it wouldn't come as easily to her. "Welcome to the fucking competition."

"Do you seriously have to be so nasty all the time, Talia?" Gareth complained with a curled lip, affronted. "*You're* the one who's cheating, I haven't even done anything to—"

"Oh, eat my shorts, Blackmoore, why don't you."

As the two of them began casting, still sniping at each other, I sped off after Rowan, who was hurtling down a long hallway decorated with tapestries of fox hunts and medieval battles, gargoyles clinging to the interstices between the high ceiling and the walls. One of them abruptly came to life, with an awful grinding sound like a trash disposal trying to chew up a stray fork. It uttered a shrill caw, before dropping down into the hallway with a crash that seemed to shake the castle down to its fundaments, spreading its wings to block Rowan's approach.

"Feathers from clouds," it croaked. It was some kind of gryphon, falcon headed and lion flanked, a serpentine tongue flickering out of its mouth as it spoke.

Rowan's face twisted in confusion. "The hell is that one," he mumbled to himself, fisting a hand against his knotted forehead. "Feathers from clouds, feathers from clouds, come *on*, man, do the thing . . ."

My heart pounding, I waited for him to unravel this riddle—I didn't know the question/answer myself—before Gareth made it through. But before Rowan could do anything else, the Blackmoore scion rounded the corner at a dead sprint. Once he knew what he had to do, Verdant Awakening had barely taken him two minutes to cast, damn the Blackmoores and their stupid, shitty strength.

"Feathers from clouds," the gargoyle repeated, fixing Gareth with a stony glare.

I bit my tongue, hoping this one would stump him, too, but his face lit immediately. "Angel's Breath Cantrip!" he called out, with a fully unironic fist pump. "I mean, uh, wait . . . What is the Angel's Breath Cantrip?"

The gryphon nodded creakily, fluttering its wings. Gareth opened his mouth and exhaled, his breath visible, as though the hallway was much colder than it actually was—then his exhale turned into snowy white feathers, which spun lazily toward the floor.

A transmutation spell, and again, a fairly simple one; by magical logic, feathers were the same general kind of airy thing as breath, though chemistry and biology might have taken some issue with that, had anyone cared to consult either discipline. And of course Gareth knew this one right off the bat, I thought to myself in disgust. It was precisely the kind of showy illusion spell Blackmoores used all the time.

With a victorious roar that rattled the walls, dislodging a rain of stone dust from the ceiling, the gryphon dropped its wings to allow Gareth to pass, before flaring them out again to block Rowan. Just as Gareth raced onward, Talia appeared around the corner, whipping down the hall with her black braid flying behind her like a pennant.

"It's Angel's Breath," Rowan hollered over his shoulder at her, correctly assuming that the spell itself was fair game once the correct question had been spoken by one of the combatants. His face set with concentration as he opened his mouth to begin casting himself.

Leaving them to their task, I trailed after Gareth, who'd followed the Gauntlet token out into the castle courtyard, where the mandatory jousting and equestrian shows usually took place. An iridescently painted sculpture of a dragon sat coiled up in one corner, where it served as a photo op prop between jousts. It had moveable jaws, the kind you could lever up and down to make it look like it was eating your head.

But now, it came to roaring life, flapping leathery wings and exhaling controlled bouts of flame as it slouched its way toward Gareth. When it reached him, it unhinged its massive jaws—and the token flew right into its mouth, the dragon's jagged maw snapping closed over it.

"From life to nothing," it exhaled on a stream of smoke, bringing its nose close to Gareth's face once the fire had died down. Its eyes glittered like faceted jewels, and the token shone, faintly and invitingly, through the gaps between its interlocking yellowed teeth.

Like the combatants had done with the hydra so many years before, Gareth would need to pry the token out of its mouth—but unlike then, this was a challenge of wit, not of strength. He wasn't meant to be battling it.

By the time Talia and Rowan came barreling into the courtyard, Gareth had deduced what he had to do instead.

"What is the Disanimating Curse?" he called out triumphantly, a wide grin splitting his face as he lifted both hands to cast the spell that would turn the dragon back to inanimate—and allow Gareth to safely retrieve the token from its mouth.

Back in front of the castle, I clenched my fists with powerless fury; this was it, then. He was going to do it. Like always, like every damn time, the bastard was really going to win.

"Rowan," Talia called out, lightning brewing in her eyes. "On my mark! Ready, set . . . *NOW*!"

Ectoplasm burst from her hands; a coil of writhing black, winding its way around Gareth like a shroud. Before he could react, a plume of Rowan's raw magic, emerald green shading down to tender pink, twisted itself through the coil of ectoplasm, slipping into any negative space. For a moment, their life and death magics were intertwined in a floating ring, locked fist in fist like their alliance given shape.

This was it, I thought, with a rising spiral of wonder. They were really fucking doing it, just like we'd planned.

Then, with a shuddering roar like a sonic boom, their commingled magic turned into something *else*.

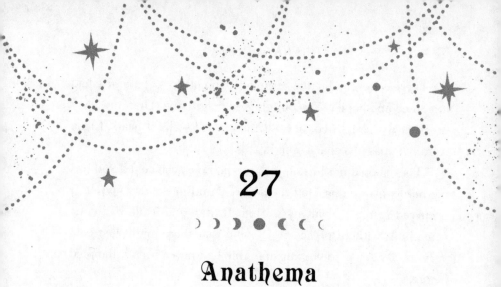

27

Anathema

J UST LIKE TALIA and I had predicted, Avramov and Thorn magics were not intended to combine. Averse as they were to each other's basic natures, they very much did *not* want to be woven into this unnatural wreath Rowan and Talia had made. But like all magic, these two raw filaments were still guided by their wielders' will—and in this instance, their wills aligned. So the two inimical strains of magic did their best to accommodate them both, transforming into something new.

What encircled Gareth now looked like I'd always imagined dark matter might look: a ring of matte black far beyond simple darkness, much blacker and deeper than even Talia's ectoplasm. Within its impenetrable folds, pinpricks of brilliant light glimmered like tiny stars. It held Gareth trapped within its center, caught helpless in its heart, canceling every spell he cast the moment it struck the barrier—every bit the antimagic forcefield Talia and I had imagined and hoped this commingled magic would become.

Back where I stood, beyond the castle's walls, I heard Elena Avramov hiss in a sharp breath.

"They should not be doing this," she said, such cold dread lining her low voice that I felt the first real inklings of fear myself. It occurred to me that at my urging, Rowan and Talia had done something without precedent . . . and that there might just be a very good reason something like this had never been attempted before.

Back in the courtyard, Gareth snarled in pure rage, the veins in his temples pounding like an impending aneurysm.

"Let . . . me . . . the fuck . . . *out*!" he bellowed, sending wild burst after burst of magic into the barrier—an uncontrolled barrage that would likely have brought the whole castle down on our heads, had the boundary not eaten it all up.

"Rowan, go," Talia forced out, both hands raised and bent back at the wrists, glistening darkness flowing like ink out of her palms. "This one's yours. If . . . if you hurry, I can hold it together by myself."

"*Hell* no," Rowan said, through gritted teeth. "I can do both. No damn way I'm letting you do this alone."

A flood of green pouring from one hand, he extended the other toward the dragon, lips forming the words of the Disanimating Curse. Sweat pearled in beads on his forehead as he fought through the spell, all the cords in his neck standing out with effort. Though all the families could animate to some degree—which meant the Animation Charm and its opposite were among the first spells baby witches learned—this was a harder spell than the other two had been, as befitted the crowning obstacle. And Rowan was casting it while he held up his end of the antimagic barrier, already a massive exertion in itself.

"You can't finish it like this, Rowan," Talia grunted, watching him struggle, her own face frighteningly pale. "Stop being a stubborn ass and just let *go*."

Rowan threw a glance over his shoulder at Gareth, who was still loosing spells left and right, shrieking with fury as each burst evanesced as soon as it struck the ring.

"He'll hurt you," Rowan said through clenched teeth, echoing my own fear. "Talia, it's not worth—"

"He won't. Just. *GO*."

She said the last with such forceful conviction that it rattled something loose in him. With a reluctant nod, Rowan let his part of the antimagic spell lapse—and with much more power abruptly available to him, he also managed to tie off the Disanimating Curse, turning the dragon from scaled, sinuous flesh to gaudily painted wood and plaster in a breath.

Knuckling sweat off his forehead, he reached up to lever open the dragon's jaws and touch the token glowing in its maw.

"Third victory goes to House Thorn!" I thundered as the glow spread through his limbs, flaring in the bright white of his sudden grin. "Houses Thorn, Blackmoore, and Avramov must now compete once more, to break the tie!"

"This is *bullshit*!" Gareth bellowed, his face turning almost maroon.

Then he thrust both hands, spitting and sparking with so much magic it distorted the air around them, right into the barrier, *wrenching* with all his strength.

Without Rowan to fortify his end, the antimagic buckled at the assault . . . then split apart, with a sound like some cosmic-sized piece of paper rending in two. Released from bondage, the bright plume of Thorn magic whipped around, searching for somewhere to spend itself, before leaping into a nearby planter—which shot up into a riot of green, bursting from a decorative shrub into something like a banyan, sprawling and leafy and many-trunked, its former container scattered around the roots in shards.

And the long filament of ectoplasm slingshotted back to its origin—burying itself fast in Talia's chest, with such force that it swept her off her feet and slammed her into the courtyard's wall.

28

))) ● (((

Then They Must Forfeit

ALIA!" I CRIED out, the Arbiter's booming octaves and my own fear turning the word into an aural cataclysm.

The very air around us seemed to tremble, until the assembled spectators clapped hands over their ears, some of them stumbling and falling to a knee. With an effort, I cut myself off, afraid I might fracture a new fault line in the ground under my feet, or set off some tectonic catastrophe beneath the town. The last thing we needed was an actual earthquake tonight.

Then I was in the courtyard in many fewer steps than it should have taken, like the puss in boots, the world blurring into streaks around me. My colossal Arbiter's form should have been too big to pass under the covered drawbridge or through the double doors, but large-scale magic like the mantle's spell did funny things to matter. I shot through the same hallways I'd seen the combatants traverse, my head just clearing the ceilings—before I tumbled out into the courtyard, where I'd seen Talia slither down the wall and collapse to the ground.

Where she now lay looking horrifyingly small, hair pooled in a black puddle around her ashen face.

Rowan was already huddled over her, his own face drawn with fear, while Gareth paced back and forth next to them with his hands clasped behind his head, muttering "fuck, fuck, *fuck*," under his breath on loop. Maybe he was sincerely frightened for her, too; but my mind leapt immediately to the less kind conclusion that he was considering any possible consequences for himself.

Rowan and Talia might have made the antimagic ring, but Gareth was the one who'd wrested it apart so hard that its shards had shattered into her.

"There you are," Rowan breathed in relief as I dropped to my knees beside him, person-sized once again. "I have no fucking clue what to do for her. She's bad, Em. Nothing's broken, or otherwise seriously damaged on a bio level, I can feel that much . . . but Emmy, look at her *eyes*."

Gently, so gently, I tipped Talia's head toward me, biting back a gasp. Her lovely eyes were open wide, but unseeing and pitch-black. No irises, no sclera, nothing clear or white showed through. Just the glistening swim of all that murk, as though she was filled to the brim with ectoplasm. The garnet at her throat shone dull and dead, not even a flicker of light still living in its facets; struck through with a starburst fracture as though it had been shattered.

For some reason this scared me most of all, my heart seizing up painfully in my chest. What happened to an Avramov, when their garnet broke?

"Is she going to be okay?" Gareth asked from behind me, voice strained. "I didn't, I really didn't mean—"

"I don't know. We need Elder Avramov," I said tightly, half mantle and half me, cutting him off. "We need—"

I heard a low whoosh, followed by the sharp rap of boot heels on stone—then Talia's mother was at my shoulder, as if she'd heard me call for her.

"Let me see her," she ordered, curls of ectoplasm still wisping around her body from whatever spell she'd used to get here so fast.

I nodded and moved aside without question; whatever this affliction was, there was nothing the mantle's magic could do for Talia now.

With grim efficiency, Elena examined her eldest daughter, running her hands over her face, throat, and chest, peering into her mouth and those unnerving blackened eyes. As she worked, more people trickled into the courtyard, holding their conversations in a low, worried murmur to keep from distracting her. The elders had all gathered, along with their immediate families; in one corner stood Igraine with Lyonesse and Merritt, Gareth's parents, his siblings Gawain and Nineve's bright blond heads bobbing nervously around them. My parents and the Thorns clustered in their own tight group nearby, with Linden and Lark at its heart, their arms around each other. And Talia's three siblings stood to their other side in a line, like ravens perching on telephone wire, close to each other but not quite touching.

All the mainline members of the four families, waiting for whatever came next.

"She's not hurt, per se," Elena finally said, looking up at me, but there was no mistaking the harshness of fear in her tone. "She's haunted. The ectoplasmic backlash of the magic hit her when it was so violently dismantled, instead of grounding itself or evanescing back through the veil—which created an opening, a connection. And now Natalia's experiencing . . . an inhabitation. Of an unusual scale."

"What does that mean?" I asked her, heart in my throat, my hands twisting into the mantle.

"It means that . . . that she's essentially become an open conduit between this side of the veil and the other," Elena said, her voice close to cracking before she gritted her teeth and, with a monumental effort, wrestled her poise back into place. "Anything can come through her—*into* her—and stay. There are quite a few shades inside her already, and if we don't act fast, there'll soon be many, many more. A legion of them."

I thought of those mournful trees in the Witch Woods, twisted around the restless spirits that inhabited them; and those trees had to house only one ghost apiece, not some horror movie horde. Fear for Talia tore through me in wracking bouts, and I was suddenly, desperately sorry that I hadn't at least tried to talk to her before the challenge. Now what if she never came back at all? How would I live with something like that?

"What do you need?" I asked Elena hoarsely, sick with fear for Talia, heart crashing against my ribs like cymbals. "What can I do?"

"We'll have to cast a banishment, here and now. The biggest that we've ever done together. It'll take all of us, down to the last Avramov." She glanced over to where her other children stood, beckoning them into motion. "Micah, Isidora—muster the family, and quick. Tell them we need them all in here, now. Adriana, kitten, you fetch henbane and nightshade for us from The Bitters, and anything else we might need."

As they rushed off to do her bidding, Igraine stepped forward a few feet, hands clasped in front of her.

"And what of the Gauntlet, Arbiter?" she said placidly, as if she was inhabiting some balmy reality completely divorced from this one. "How shall we proceed with the tiebreak challenge?"

"Igraine!" Gabrielle snapped at her, low and furious. "Mind yourself! This is *clearly* not the time."

"Of course it is," the Blackmoore elder replied, unperturbed. "What other time would there be? There's been a dreadful accident, yes, but one that, it could be argued, the combatants' own questionable strategy brought down on Scion Avramov's head."

"You mean one that *your* grandson caused!" Gabrielle retorted, her dark eyes sparkling with ire. "Own that much, at least."

"As I said, an unfortunate mishap," Igraine repeated with a magnanimous shrug. "My grandson *may* have been the catalyst, but Thorn and Avramov conduct clearly set the scene. Certainly we all saw as much. The question remains, how do we carry on? The Gauntlet rules state that the tiebreak challenge, should one become necessary, must follow on directly after the tie."

Every other head in the courtyard swiveled to me, waiting for the Arbiter to make the call. At least Gareth had the good grace to look abashed, clearly miserable at the idea of moving forward with Talia heaped on the cold stones with ghosts swimming in her eyes.

Unfortunately, I already knew from my own careful reading of the rules that Igraine was technically right; worse yet, the mantle appeared to agree with her, too. I could feel its approval emanating from within me, and the beckoning pull of the Grimoire from beyond the castle walls, where it had likely already cooked up the challenge that would break the tie.

"That's correct," I confirmed, the words curdling in my mouth even as I spoke them. "We do have to go on. Tonight."

"But the Avramovs won't have a champion!" Elena protested, one hand still on Talia's forehead, fury seething in her eyes. "I just *said* the banishment will take all of us, and it needs to happen now—which means there's no one left to take Natalia's place as alternate! How are we meant to compete if—"

"Then the Avramovs must forfeit," Igraine interrupted, as if such an injustice made all the sense in the world. A silky, malicious pleasure laced her tone, almost undetectable if you weren't listening for it as closely as I was. For all her practiced decorum, the miserable old scally was beside herself with glee. You could almost *hear* how much effort it was costing her not to grin from ear to ear. "And allow Scions Blackmoore and Thorn to carry on alone. Is that not the case, Arbiter? Rule Twenty-Two covers this exigency, I believe: protocol in the absence of a champion."

Except that there *was* a loophole here, I realized, with the sudden stirrings of excitement, the barest tickle of an idea burgeoning. The Gauntlet rules didn't specify any requirements for an alternate champion, besides the fact that one couldn't be drawn from the other competing families—which usually did mean they had to come from the same family.

But now . . .

"It does," I agreed. "Or it *would*, in the absence of a viable alternate."

Igraine's face clouded with confusion, suspicion milky in her eyes. "But there isn't one. Elder Avramov just told us as much."

I let myself sink into the mantle's elation as I rose to my feet, soaring to the Arbiter's towering height. I was so tall now that I loomed high above the courtyard, cold wind whistling around my temples, so that even the swarming host of spectators beyond the ramparts could see me easily. A goddess sprouting like a sword from Castle Camelot's campy-ass stone.

How do you like this version of Excalibur, you Blackmoore twats?

I had no real idea what the fuck I was doing, whether it would even work. But no matter what happened, I knew Talia wouldn't want me to abandon everything she, Linden, and I had fought for since the start.

For Talia's sake, I had to at least give it one good shot.

"I cede the mantle, and my authority as Arbiter of the seventh Gauntlet of the Grove, to my cousin, Delilah Harlow," I pronounced, my voice a thunderclap. "And I step in as combatant for House Avramov."

29

The Word and the Dream, the Heart and the Eye

AN ABSOLUTE SILENCE descended across Castle Camelot.

Then the Blackmoore matriarch's shrill voice pierced the quiet, Igraine being terminally incapable of calming her tits in any situation not proceeding according to her design.

"You can't *do* this!" she hissed up at me, her aquiline features thinned with outrage, like some bird of prey with its feathers ruffled. "This, this isn't just highly irregular—it's unacceptable, not to mention unlawful! The Harlows cannot compete in the Gauntlet, in *any* form!"

"Untrue," I said calmly, because by now I knew I had the right of it—the mantle magic wasn't objecting at all to my chosen course of action. Instead it pulsed inside me, steady and warm, like an internal reassurance that it still had my back. "The Harlows

have traditionally recused themselves by choice, and then historical precedent, in order to arbitrate. Now I'm ceding the mantle
and choosing to compete in Talia's stead. All very much according
to the letter of Grimoire law."

"But . . . but that's not how it's *done!*" Igraine squawked, having
run out of any objections based in fact.

"Maybe under normal circumstances, no—but under normal
circumstances, Scion Blackmoore would have been competing
against Scion Avramov herself in this tiebreak challenge," I
pointed out. "Are you really so afraid to have him face down a
Harlow instead?"

She subsided at that a little, brow furrowing; I had a point.
From her perspective, it wasn't like I was much of a threat, and
certainly less of one than Talia would have been.

Shit, from *my* perspective I wasn't a serious threat. A Harlow
witch was pretty much the weakest possible champion Talia could
have asked for as an alternate—but I was what she had, and for
her sake, I was sure as hell going to give it my all.

"Fine," Igraine acquiesced, her mouth drawing purse-string
tight. "We accept the substitution. *Against* our better judgment, let
the record show."

Rolling my eyes, I glanced over to the Thorns, more out of
respect than anything else; it wasn't like I needed their permission, any more than I'd needed Igraine's.

"Of course we do, as well," Gabrielle said, and beside her, Aspen inclined his head, a sideways smile tugging at his mouth, as
though he couldn't quite conceal his happiness at this fresh subversion. And from behind them, out of Igraine's line of vision, my
father shot me two sly thumbs-up that cheered me like not even

the mantle could have, assured me that I was doing the right thing.

Then I looked down to Elena Avramov, startled to find that she was outright smiling at me; a real smile, shockingly tender, its sweetness out of place on her gorgeous storybook villainess's face. It made her look even more painfully like Talia.

"You really do care for Natalia, don't you?" she said, as I came over to kneel by Talia one more time before I left. "How interesting."

I reached out to stroke those black drifts of hair and her clammy forehead, so unlike her normal warmth. "I really do," I said, my belly pulsing with ache. "I wish I didn't have to leave her like this."

Elena squeezed my upper arm, mouth setting firm. "My daughter's strong, and you can trust that we've got her from here. We all know how to guard against inhabitations—it's one of the very first things Avramov witches learn when they begin to wield their magic. She'll know what to do to ride the banishment out, to keep herself safe inside her mind."

"But you said there were . . . many," I said, my breath snagging in my throat. "What if she, what if . . ."

"You let *me* worry about Natalia," the elder said, squeezing me again; warm but brisk, like a fellow in arms, her shimmery jade eyes turning implacable. "While *you* go and sweep this whole damned thing in my daughter's name."

TEN MINUTES LATER, I was back outside the castle with Gareth and Rowan. I'd already handed the mantle over to Delilah, who, while struggling to contain her near rapture at this unexpected turn of events, had also been surprisingly gracious about the transfer of power.

"Thanks, Emmy," she'd murmured as I slung it over her shoulders. "I know you're not doing it for me, but . . . anyway. Still."

"You're welcome, Lilah," I'd whispered back, giving her hair a little tug; remembering that once, when we were little and before we'd chosen such diverging paths, we'd actually been friends. "Like you said—you were the one who stayed. Maybe you should have had it all along. Either way, you've got it from here."

Now she towered over us, her head blotting out the spangle of stars behind her; the ends of her long hair lifting with the wind, her warm brown eyes larger than life. The way she stood, the moon seemed to be sitting just above her brow, like an impromptu crown. A startling wash of pride engulfed me to see my exasperating cousin like this, just as beautiful and terrible as Tolkien's elven queen during her brief tenure with the infamous ring.

Somehow, it suited her.

For a moment, I felt a bitter swell of envy that I'd never wear the mantle again myself, never feel that incomparable rush of old and massive magic pounding through my veins. But I had something more important to do, and I was at least a little glad that Delilah was finally getting to live the dream. She'd probably appreciate it more than I ever could, anyway, since I had technically never even wanted it.

More fool, me.

Then the Grimoire flared blue in front of her, and I felt another hollow gut punch of loss, because I couldn't feel it; it wasn't tugging at me anymore.

"Scions Thorn, Blackmoore, and Harlow," she knelled, the air in my ears trembling with the force of her voice. Delilah's timbre was deeper than mine, and in the Arbiter's register it came across as a basso profundo that you could feel down to your bones. "The wreath awaits you, but it must be assembled. To gather up its pieces, you must find the remnants the founders left behind—Elias's word, Caelia's dream, Alastair's heart, Margarita's eye. And the soul that lies in the center of what they made together."

Hey, silver linings: at least we seemed to be done with the shitty poetry.

As she finished speaking, banners of light streamed from the Grimoire and over to the three of us, winding around our bodies—just as they had done to transport Gareth, Rowan, and Talia to their respective orchard battlegrounds.

I squeezed my eyes shut, waiting to be whisked away—but when I opened them again, I still stood exactly where I'd been; bookended by Gareth and Rowan, the ropes of light shimmering around me with pearly iridescence.

"Alastair's heart," Rowan was mumbling under his breath, musing to himself. "Could that be . . ."

He closed his eyes to complete the thought, and in the next moment he was gone. So, this *was* a portal spell, but one controllable by the bearer—which meant I was supposed to determine where I wanted it to take me, like a self-guided scavenger hunt.

"Caelia's dream!" Gareth burst out, as something dawned on him, too. Then he vanished as well, leaving me to eat their collective dust.

Every competitive instinct inside me—and I had *quite* the collection of them, to be sure—roared to kicking and screaming life. This arrangement, in which I was the last one standing ignorant, was *not* going to fly.

"Caelia's dream, Elias's word, Alastair's heart, Margarita's eye,"

I chanted to myself, palms slicking with impatience. I assumed the Grimoire didn't mean the founders' literal body parts; as far as I knew, no one was keeping Alastair's heart or Margarita's eyeballs preserved in a pickling jar—though with the Avramovs, who ever really knew for sure. But in any case, the dream and the word were abstract concepts . . .

And then, with a sudden bolt of inspiration, I knew exactly where to look first.

Tomes & Omens, I thought to myself, closing my eyes. *Tomes & Omens*. With a stomach-dropping lurch like falling in place, the world *shifted* around me—then I could smell dust and ink and dry, papery decay, a bell tinkling out warning of my arrival though there was no one else to hear it.

I opened my eyes to my father's darkened bookshop, waiting until my vision adjusted enough to let me make out the book-shelves' silhouettes before I went pelting toward the attic stairs.

"Let me be right, let me be right," I whispered to myself as I clattered up.

As soon as I flung open the door, I knew that I was; the attic glowed an unearthly, vaporous blue, the same light that always emanated from the Grimoire. I dashed toward its source, a glass display case in the Harlow section of the archive—where we kept the owl-feather quill with which Elias Harlow had written the original spellbook.

Right above the case floated three feathers, wrought of delicate blue light; perfectly rendered down to the vane, the hollow shaft, and the downy barbs. Three, one for each of the combatants to collect.

And since all of them were here, that meant I was the first to decipher this particular clue.

Grinning, I reached to pluck one of the feathers from the air. As soon as I touched it, it absorbed into my palm with a tingling buzz. Surging with triumph, I turned in a tight little circle, rotating the rest of the clues in my mind. "Caelia's dream" meant next to nothing to me, though there was the very faintest *plink* of recognition at the thought, like a drop falling from a leaky faucet several rooms over. Nagging and insistent, but not particularly enlightening.

But "Alastair's heart" brought up something more concrete—a memory of a much younger Linden in spring, leading me by the hand to the copse behind Honeycake Cottage, where she rested her palm against the trunk of a tree blooming with pale pink flowers like pastel stars.

"This was my great-great-great-great-great-grandpa Alastair's favorite tree," she'd told me, patting the bark with something between reverence and fondness. I smiled at the memory, recalling how she'd always tacked on some arbitrary number of "greats" before his name. "The first one he planted on our land. If you fall asleep under it, you'll dream of him. I always do."

As the memory faded, I closed my eyes and thought myself toward Alastair's ancient hawthorn.

When I opened them, I was standing beneath it, its branches bursting with scarlet berries like drops of heart's blood crystallized. Just below one of the lower-reaching boughs hung a single glowing blue berry, like a ghost of the others, with two frilled leaves poised daintily to either side. I reached up to pluck it, my heart sinking a little; if there was only one left, that meant both Gareth and Rowan had managed to get here before me. Rowan, because of course he would have known where to look for Alastair's heart; Gareth, because Linden had probably brought him here to introduce him to the tree, back when she still thought they were in love.

The thought of him using this ill-gotten inside information yanked brutally at my gut—yet another thing he'd stolen from Lin and turned to his advantage. But, with a fresh glow of excitement dawning inside me, I realized that I had some insider info up my own sleeve, too.

I happened to know an Avramov pretty well—and she had already shown me Margarita's "eye."

Moments later, I was in Talia's blue-tinted room, her familiar perfume coiling up my noise. The scent sparked stinging memories of us together, rising from the dark like radiant specters, our opposite-of-shadow selves shedding all that remembered heat and light. As tears prickled in my eyes, I shunted all that aside; that was for later, once this thing was done and dusted. I couldn't afford to be waylaid by emotion now.

I moved to where the scrying mirror glowed blue on its wall, two imitation garnets floating in its glass—not above it, but rather *behind* the pane, as though I'd have to reach through the glass itself to get at them. I wondered which of the other two had snagged one of the tokens already; my money was on Rowan, who also knew about the scrying mirror from our strategy sessions. But Gareth might have learned about it, too, during his dalliance with Talia.

I really had to hand it to the Grimoire, when it came to the discombobulating ingenuity of this hunt. It was much more disorienting to have us stumbling around this way, blind to who had what, rather than physically scrambling around town after one another.

"Sorry, Dread Lady," I mumbled under my breath, as I pressed my fingers to the mirror's cool surface. "Please let's not be too literal about this being your eye."

For a second, there was no give to the glass, no yield at all—then it parted coldly under my skin, like some cross between mercury and frosty Jell-O. And as I reached for one of the remaining tokens, I felt the unmistakable brush of chilly fingers over mine, like a sly little hello or even *well done* from beyond the veil. Yelping, I drew my hand back as if I'd been stung, the garnet's light dissolving into my palm.

A ghost of laughter echoed in my ears, and I thought I heard an amused whisper of "*such* beastly girls . . ." trail off at the very edges of my hearing.

Even having met the founder in the flesh—or in the spirit, as it were—once before, without Talia here as a buffer between us, it unnerved me enough that I suddenly and powerfully wanted to be gone.

I'd already figured out the last clue, the soul at the center of what the founders had made; it was Lady's Lake, it had to be. But I wanted to leave that one for last. It felt like a closing of the circle, the culmination of the challenge, like something that should necessarily be done at the very end. But Caelia's dream remained elusive, no matter how I racked my brain over what it might mean. Gareth had said *something* to me once, something quirky about his ancestor that had to do with sleep, or a pillow, or maybe a bed . . .

But whatever it was, he'd told me about it a decade ago, and now I just couldn't quite put my finger on the memory.

Goose bumps still bunching my skin, I sat on the edge of Talia's bed, dropping my head into my hands and I struggled to remember. Dream, sleep, rest, bed . . . with every passing moment in which I failed to piece it together, my panic grew. Gareth would've gotten it already; "Caelia's dream" had been the clue he muttered to himself before he vanished from Castle Camelot. And though Harlows were technically the bookish ones, the history keepers best versed in the town's secrets and lore, I knew better than to underestimate Rowan—who'd demonstrated strength, wit, and a bullish tenacity a lot like my own. If he ended up winning, I couldn't really have any problem with it. It would be, in a way, Linden's victory, too, which I could only be happy about.

But I couldn't stomach the idea of another Blackmoore Victor, yet again; especially not Gareth Blackmoore, the Prince of Bastards himself.

And more than that, now that I'd committed to being her champion, I badly wanted to win this for Talia, wanted it down to my marrow.

"Where the hell are you, Caelia's dream?" I muttered into my palms, pressing my hands into my eyes until muddy colors roiled like silt behind my lids. "And how the fuck am I supposed to find you?"

Then there was that same sudden shift of vision that had come over me the last time I'd been here, sitting with Talia on the windowsill—and I could *feel* Thistle Grove once again, as a natural extension of myself. This time it was even more shocking and inexplicable—I wasn't even the Arbiter anymore—but I could still feel everything, with barely any expended effort. Every dip and ridge of its terrain, all of its hidden nooks and crannies.

And the shape of the magic that wound like connective tissue, or a river, through it all.

I was Thistle Grove, and Thistle Grove was me—and we were, the both of us, thrumming and alive.

It had grown late in my town, already well past midnight; the tourist crowds had mostly dispersed, withdrawn to their warm beds in hotels and the many charming B and Bs. But my awareness seeped outward to find the stragglers still wandering out from bars, their heels clicking on my cobblestones, their laughter and cigarette smoke floating on my chilled air. There were the shades drifting through my haunted woods, the cats perched on fences and slinking through the streets beneath my moon, the profusion of little animals scrabbling over the velvet green expanse of my common at the center of town.

And there was the tremendous boil of magic over Castle Camelot—where, in the courtyard, the Avramovs had formed a chanting circle around Talia, who was hovering suspended with her head thrown back and mouth wide open, darkness pouring out of her on a drawn-out scream like a banshee's wail.

With an effort, I averted my awareness from that scene. I couldn't do anything to help over there, and the pain it caused to witness it interfered with my equanimity, my colossal sense of town-self.

And there was something *else* I needed to see, a smaller disturbance in the graveyard. Another patch of magical irregularity, much more benign but still distinctive.

Caelia Blackmoore's aboveground crypt in the Thistle Grove cemetery.

In an instant, I was there—standing inside the tomb, breathing in cold, stale air that had not been disturbed for centuries. There should have been nothing but darkness to see, but Caelia's crypt was aglow with blue. In the middle of the space sat an enormous bed, canopied and opulent and fit for a queen, obviously bespelled to keep away the encroaching creep of rot. I could smell the white and yellow rose petals scattered across its pillows, fresh as the day the Blackmoores who'd buried their matriarch had strewn them there.

As soon as I saw it, I finally remembered what Gareth had shared with me, on a long-ago sunny day when we lay together under one of Tintagel's many weeping willows, clouds rushing above us through its drooping leaves. Caelia Blackmoore had wanted her bed preserved in her final resting place, Gareth had said, with rose petals sprinkled over it; so her spirit always had somewhere to return to where it could dream sweetly, even after death.

It was an oddly beautiful image, the idea of Caelia's spirit settling down onto the bed, hands clasped over her chest, the ghostly skeins of her golden hair spreading over the pillow. There was something both haunting and morbidly romantic about it—just the kind of tantalizing tidbit to share with your secret Harlow girlfriend, whom you were about a month away from ditching.

Now it struck me more that the Blackmoore matriarch must have been a righteously self-indulgent hedonist who just *really* loved her bed, something I could understand on a deep level.

Unlike with the scrying mirror, there was no hint of presence here, no willful waft of Caelia herself. Just the all-encompassing silence of the crypt, along with the faint keen of the stubborn wind that wedged its way through the chinks—and the glow of the two blue roses that hovered just above the pillow, their thorns curved and petals perfectly formed.

So, Rowan hadn't been here yet, that was something—though I had no way of knowing how many of the other tokens Gareth had gathered up by now. For all I knew, he could be ahead of me;

at the lake already, maybe even back at Castle Camelot with all the tokens in hand.

I reached for one of the roses, its light filtering into my palm, the thought of the scant time I had left trickling through my head like sand through an hourglass.

Then I closed my eyes and thought myself to Lady's Lake.

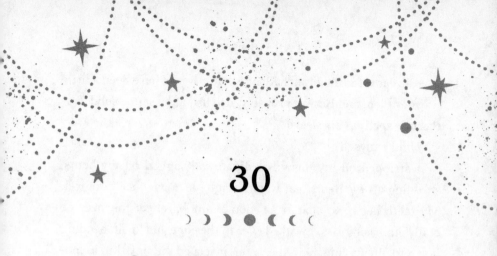

30

And the Victor Is . . .

JUST LIKE TALIA had said of me, Lady's Lake was beautiful by moonlight.

The full moon swam in the black silk of its surface, along with blurred reflections of the ice-chip stars, twinkling like sprite lights sunk below the depths. There was a hovering sense of such enormity, of a wild, vast magic, that it stripped your breath away from your lungs. This hallowed sky, and its watery twin; this jewel of a lake upon a hilltop, and the shining town down at its base, where all the magic eventually ended up like a cascade.

As above, so below. Just like all of us witches had learned since we were small.

I could see the hazy spill of blue somewhere under the water a few yards off the bank, about three or four feet down. But I'd still have to swim out to it, and then dive deep into the lake—which, by now, was bound to be blisteringly cold. Rowan had swum it once already, for the first challenge, but it would have been a little warmer then; and Rowan probably also had at least one solid exothermic spell up his sleeve.

Unlike myself.

I stripped off my duster cardigan and tugged off my boots, shedding all the items that would weigh me down once I got wet. My teeth began to chatter as soon as my bare feet touched the chilly stalks of grass. I walked over to the edge and knelt, bending down to dip my fingers in the water; it seeped into my skin in moments, and then dug down into the bone, coiling in my joints like arthritis in liquid form.

I yanked my hand back out, cursing under my breath. What the hell was I supposed to do now? It wasn't like I had time to portal to the nearest sport supply store to get myself geared up in a wet suit.

I rocked back onto my heels with my arms around my knees, seething at being foiled by something so maddeningly basic. If Gareth or Rowan appeared, I was screwed; this hurdle wouldn't hold either of them back for more than a minute at most. This was why Harlows didn't compete in the first place; like an overgrown Goldilocks, we were so magically feeble we couldn't even handle temperature extremes.

Except when it came to drinks, I thought, an unlikely idea taking slow shape in my head. Even as a child, I'd always been able to cool or heat my beverages to the perfect temperature. Obviously I couldn't extend that to the gallons upon gallons of water a lake would hold, but *what if,* instead . . .

Standing up, I summoned the Temperate Charm, the one and only little cantrip at which the Harlows truly excelled.

As magic built in my hands, warm and crackling, I ran them

slowly over my body, from the soles of my feet up to the crown of my head. Bespelling myself, so that wherever the water touched me, it would turn to a pleasantly warm bathing temperature. Then, without giving myself too much time to doubt, analyze, or overthink what I was about to do, I took a running jump into the lake, scrunching my eyes shut just before my feet struck the star-speckled black of the water's face. Bracing myself for a paralyzing gush of ice against my skin, cold pressing into my ears and nose.

Instead, I slipped under into a pool of blissful heat, lapping against me in all but the few places I hadn't been able to properly reach with my magicked hands. There was a patch of blistering cold right between my shoulder blades, and another under my left armpit where I clearly hadn't lingered long enough with the spell.

But it was nothing I couldn't handle, at least for as long as it would take to reach the sunken tokens.

I breached the water with a gasp, air icing my cheeks, then breast-stroked toward the spot where the blue glowed like a water-color wash, my unprotected back and armpit burning with chill. I couldn't even begin to think how it would have felt all over me, without the protection of the spell; my heart would probably have seized up and then given up the ghost. Despite having been born and bred in Illinois, I was decidedly *not* built for such severe cold.

Once I reached the spot, I gulped a breath and dove down hard, kicking my feet until I reached the submerged tokens—two floating thistle flowers, just like the one tattooed on my arm, little floral weapons with their bristling heads and leaves like spikes.

So, Rowan or Gareth had beaten me here, I thought with a sinking heart as I reached out to touch one. Which meant that someone else had already won—*or* that one of the other two hadn't thought to save this place for last.

As soon as my fingers closed around the thistle's stem, the portal spell yanked me back to Castle Camelot.

I materialized, gasping and dripping, exactly where I'd left—outside the castle walls with Gareth and Rowan to either side, Delilah looming above the three of us like a human skyscraper. The other two combatants wore matching stunned expressions, as though they were just as surprised as I was to find themselves back here.

"The *hell*," Gareth said with a grimace, looking around. "But I didn't—"

"Talia," I said anxiously, turning to search the crowd that was still gathered behind us for any Avramovs; I didn't see a single one. "Is she . . . are they all still in there, with her?"

"Combatants," Delilah tolled, wrenching my attention back to her. "Present your palms!"

Gareth and I held up our right hands, Rowan his left. Blue light drifted from our palms, reassembling into gathered tokens that lifted to hover in a circle above each of our heads. Craning my neck, I could see that Rowan had collected Alastair's hawthorn berry, Elias's feather, Margarita's garnet, and the Lady's Lake thistle—but not Caelia's rose. Gareth also had the berry and the garnet, as well as Caelia's rose—but he was still missing Elias's quill and the Lady's Lake thistle.

Only I had five.

Only I had them all.

My jaw fell open at the realization, just as the tokens above our heads circled one another faster and faster, until, with an explosive flash of sapphire blue, mine merged into a silver wreath, while Gareth's and Rowan's vanished into wisps.

A chorus of gasps echoed through the crowd, as the newly

minted wreath floated into Delilah's waiting palm. A smile touched her titaness's mouth, and she spread her hands ceremonially.

"Tiebreak victory," she trumpeted in clarion tones, "and victory of the seventh Gauntlet of the Grove . . . goes to House Avramov, by virtue of their Harlow champion!"

"I STILL CAN'T believe it," I said, my fingers wrapped around a mug of hot cocoa.

I sat in the living room with my parents, tucked up on the couch with my feet swaddled in a pair of my mother's fuzzy socks. Beyond the window, the sky was approaching dawn, filaments of pink and rose gold threading into the pearled gray like glinting embroidery. There had been no question of sleep once we got back from Castle Camelot, and so we'd held vigil together for Talia; the banishing had taken all night, and apparently still wasn't over. Though the Avramovs couldn't have missed Delilah's booming proclamation of my/their victory, they'd all been too wrapped up in the ritual to pay it much heed at the time. I assumed we would be the first to hear, when they were done and Talia was fully restored.

Which she *would* be, I told myself, over and over; I wasn't letting in any negativity on that front. If I'd learned anything from the Instagram witches I followed, it was the power of manifesting hope against all odds.

And when she recovered, I hoped she would still want to talk to me—because I couldn't *wait* to share with her the sweet, sweet moment in which Gareth's face had finally registered the magnitude of his crushing defeat.

"It's all so wild," I went on, taking a sip. "I mean, I shouldn't even have been able to find Caelia's rose at all. I couldn't for the life of me figure out that clue."

My father frowned, setting his mug down on the coffee table. We hadn't talked much all night, more sat together in companionable silence after we each had the obligatory tumbler of scotch to celebrate the victory I'd won for Talia.

"Then how *did* you find it?" he asked, voice brightening with interest, the inquiring scholar's mind behind his eyes firing up like an engine fueled by curiosity.

"I'm not sure," I admitted. "Thistle Grove showed me where to look, sort of. Which sounds truly nuts, now that I say it out loud, but that's what happened."

I tried to explain that multifaceted awareness, the sweeping mind meld between myself and what felt like the essence of the town.

"And it's been happening since I got back," I went on. "It's like I'm . . . merging with Thistle Grove, somehow? Which sounds downright disturbing, only there's nothing scary about it at all. I figured it had to do with the mantle magic, since that's the only thing that's changed since I came back. But then I ceded the mantle to Lilah, and it *kept* happening."

"It's not the mantle, scoot," my father said, an unfamiliar sadness creeping into the corners of his smile. "It's you. Your Harlow blood."

"My Harlow blood . . . what are you talking about?" I said, uncomprehending.

"There's a certain aspect to our history that's reserved for elders only," he said, clearing his throat. "And that's the role our family plays in this town. Elias Harlow found this place first, you know, felt its distant call all the way from Virginia. He was already here when the other three arrived, a little down the line—and they only came at all because he'd tempered the magic, enough so they could feel it, too. Made it . . . *accessible* to other witches."

Margarita's perplexing words rose like bubbles to the surface of my mind. *Dreadful bore that the man was in life, our little Grove would still have been nothing without his hand at work.*

"I still don't understand."

"Thistle Grove magic comes from the lake," he went on. "We don't know why or how, but we all know that it does. But that's in its rawest form—a white water torrent, wild and unmanageable. To most witches, trying to draw from it would be like putting your mouth to a firehose. But not to Elias. And not to us, his descendants, who share his blood. Strained through us, rendered through our witch's souls, it's a viable and potent power source for others with the gift. Like the rest of the families."

I pressed my fingers to my temples, which had begun to ache with strain. I'd never even considered the possibility that the intense way I experienced Thistle Grove magic was somehow different from how it felt to other witches. How would I even have known that it didn't feel the same to them?

"So you're saying we're like filters?" I attempted.

"Very good, yes!" he exclaimed, smiling broadly, like he might slap a gold star sticker onto my forehead if this went on. "The magic sieves through all of us, every Harlow who lives in Thistle Grove. But this rendering down we do . . . paradoxically, it makes us weaker witches than the other families. Presumably because most of our gift is preoccupied, at any given time, with filtering all that raw magic into a more manageable fuel."

Somehow this made perfect, if unfortunate, sense. We were

busy distilling down something so tremendous, so elemental, that the process of it left very little bandwidth for any *actual* spells we might want to cast. Our magical hard drives were nearly maxed out, almost no more processing power left.

The rawest of deals, just like Nana Caro had said; and this must have been exactly what she meant. *This town is in your blood,* she'd also said, *in ways you might not yet understand.*

At the time, I'd thought that she was being figurative. It made more sense now—except for one thing.

"Then why wasn't my magic stronger, instead of weaker, when I left town?" I challenged.

"Because living here has changed all of the families, altered the fundamental texture of how we work our spells," he replied, pushing his glasses up his nose with his index finger. "We're used to the lake's power now, dependent on it. It's become a part of both the town and us—the magical fuel that we instinctively reach for, that we know how to work best. Beyond its reach, our own gifts wane."

"So why couldn't I feel it before I left?" I asked. "The town, I mean. It only really started when I touched the original Grimoire."

"If you think back, you'll find it first began when you returned to town for the Gauntlet, in your formal capacity as the Harlow scion, a rising elder," my father corrected, and he was right—I remembered that raw swell of magic, so much bigger than anything I'd experienced before, that had greeted me so effusively as soon as I crossed town lines. "That would have been the beginning of the transition, from me to you."

"What *transition*?" I said, my head swimming. I hadn't slept at all, on top of being drained from my stint as Arbiter last night, and the aftermath of the adrenaline geyser that had been the tiebreak challenge. Even afraid as I still was for Talia, I was starting to flag.

"The Harlow elder serves as . . . well, think of it as an avatar of the town," he said. "While all the Harlows take part in the distillation, only one of us at a time maintains such a strong, primal communion with Thistle Grove. And now that you're back, and old enough to take it on, the communion is transitioning from me to you."

"And what if I hadn't come back? What would have happened then?"

"Then it would have shifted over to Delilah, just like the Arbiter's role."

But I had come back, just in time to ruin *all* the things for my cousin in one fell swoop.

"Why isn't any of this in the Grimoire?" I demanded, massaging my throbbing temples. This changed everything about my place here, how I thought I fit into this town. We Harlows weren't just the record keepers, after all, but something much bigger and stranger than that. And yet, I thought, with rising aggravation, I'd never even been told about any of it at all. "The Thistle Grove origin story we all get notably includes *none* of this. Why haven't I ever heard any of this before?"

If I'd known, everything might have been different. Maybe I'd never have been the kind of person Gareth could hurt as badly as he had. Maybe I'd never even have left at all, too confident in my own worth to be rattled by someone like him.

And maybe, I considered, thinking about it even deeper, this was why the Blackmoores' long reign hadn't caused the Harlows any harm. Possibly, as conduits of the magic itself, we were immune to its Gauntlet-related fluctuations, even if we didn't get to reap its benefits.

"It's a bit of a sneaky test," he admitted. "Elias thought of this role as a great privilege, an unparalleled honor. He didn't want it squandered on someone who didn't love this town enough to stay here, even without the communion serving as the ultimate prize for their fidelity. So if a Harlow heir were to leave, before the communion was passed down . . ."

"Then they never got to have it," I said flatly. "Wow. What an utter crock."

"My sentiments exactly," my mother murmured into her cup, speaking up for the first time. "*What*, James? It's the very worst sort of archaic nonsense to keep it under wraps, and it always has been. And you know it, too."

"It's *tradition*," my father argued.

"It's patriarchal codswallop," she countered, eyebrows raised over the rim of her mug as she took an emphatic sip. "And it's as though he didn't even consider the consequences for his family's standing. This town, as it is now, wouldn't even exist without the Harlows—and it would do certain other families a great deal of good to recognize as much."

"Wait, is this why we don't compete in the Gauntlet, but only arbitrate?" I asked, even more inclined to fume. "Not that we'd win as often, but still, this is a definite advantage—and we don't even get to try? Because, what, we're just supposed to settle for our *communion with the town*, as if there are no other perks to being the Victor of the Gauntlet?"

"Elias believed that being the voice, the human soul of Thistle Grove, should be more than enough for any witch," my father said, with a helpless shrug. "I imagine he didn't think longevity, good luck, or any of the rest of it really stacked up in comparison."

Unlike the other ancestors I'd been seeing in a new light, Elias Harlow was turning out to be every bit the stick in the mud that I'd thought—and not a very ambitious one, to boot. The communion with Thistle Grove was spectacular, almost unspeakably wonderful, he was right about that much; it was clear how deeply my father would miss it, once it fully passed to me. But why limit his descendants this way? Why hamstring us into being this and only this, never anything more? Who was Elias to decide that this was all any of us might ever want from our lives as witches of Thistle Grove?

I had no doubt I'd have seen and done things very differently, had I been in his shoes three hundred years ago.

But even so, this still changed things for me in a way I couldn't have anticipated.

"So, if I leave," I said dully, "I'll lose it, forever. It'll go to Delilah."

"Unfortunately, yes." My father nodded, glasses slipping down his nose. "That's about the size of it, scoot."

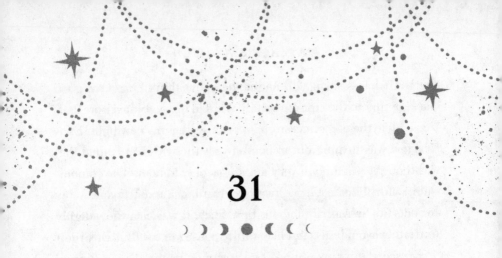

31

More Than Enough

I DIDN'T SEE TALIA again until the Blackmoores' masquerade ball on Samhain Eve, when she would be formally crowned as Victor.

I'd heard from Elena that she'd recovered well; the last of the shades haunting her had been banished with the dawn. The Avramovs had wrapped up their ghostly exorcism just about when I'd been discovering that I was now in a complicated relationship with Thistle Grove. But Talia hadn't reached out to me herself, not even to thank me for stepping in for her, or for the proxy victory I'd won. Not that I'd done it for the props, but still; it was telling. It made me think that on her end, whatever had torn between us the night of the séance was still too painful and raw to prod.

And I hadn't reached out, either. I hadn't wanted to, not until I was sure I knew what I would say to her.

In the days since the challenge, I'd spent much of my time sitting by Lady's Lake with Jasper beside me. Watching the sun wheel overhead, letting wave after wave of magic lap over me as I inhaled its incensey scent on the wind. Communing with the town below, until the soil felt as familiar as my own skin, the many breezes my own breath, the trees' slow sap like my own blood, except blood that I could actually feel as it ran through me.

Was this enough for me, I kept wondering. *Could* it be enough? And if it wasn't, and I decided not to stay; how could I ever forget how wonderful it had felt to be back, to find things both old and new to love about this town, before choosing to leave it behind all over again? But if I *did* stay, I still wouldn't get to work anything like the kind of magic the other families could make—and I knew myself well enough to know how this limitation would continue to rankle me. Especially now that I was aware of my own contribution to their strength.

And there was, of course and most of all, Talia to consider. If she hadn't changed her mind about me, after everything.

The day before the ball, I'd twitched in surprise as Delilah dropped down to sit beside me, having snuck up on ghost-quiet feet; even Jasper hadn't noticed her approach.

"It's not just *your* hill, you know," she remarked, a faint smirk tugging at her lips as she clocked my surprise. "Even if you've been bogarting it like a pro."

"Sorry," I said, huffing out a laugh. "Didn't mean to make Lady's Lake all about me. Even though, apparently, it sort of is."

My cousin tipped her head, questioning. Ostensibly I wasn't allowed to share my new status with anyone besides an elder, but honestly, fuck great-gramps Elias and all his stodgy-ass rules. Delilah was a Harlow, and if anyone deserved to know about the specifics of our tricky legacy, it was her.

This was where I could start changing the game for us, shifting the power dynamics that had always left us out.

"I *knew* it," she said when I finished giving her a recap, thumping a fist against her thigh. "I *knew* Elias wasn't just some two-bit scribe."

"And you were right. Though from where I'm sitting, he's not exactly hero-worship material, either. I'm finding myself questioning the wisdom of *many* of his calls."

She gave a vague nod, like we were going to have to agree to disagree on that front. "So, what are you going to do now?" she said, turning to look at me head-on, and to her credit, this time I couldn't detect any pressure or judgment swarming in her eyes. "Have you decided?"

"I don't know yet," I admitted, resting my chin on my knees, a faint but brisk breeze wafting over my cheeks. "I'm sorry, Lilah. I know this decision doesn't affect just me—and I also know how major it'll be for you, if I do decide to go. But there's a lot of stuff in the air, still. So many factors in play."

"Your work in the city, right?" she said, nodding sagely. "And obviously, Talia Avramov. Oh, don't look at me like that, I do have *eyes*, Emmy. And even a functional heart. It's clear she means something to you."

"She does," I murmured, my throat welling up. "And the work . . . yeah, that matters, too. So does Chicago, in the bigger picture. And then there's my parents, and Lin, that whole other side of things. The side that makes me want to stick around."

"I really do get it, you know." She shook her head, a little wry. "I know what it's like to want too many things at once. A very familiar mood, you might say."

"You should be working at Tomes, Lilah," I blurted out, with a sudden pressing urgency. "I mean it. Whether I stay or leave, you deserve to have at least that much go to you."

"I'd like that." The corners of her lips quirked up almost shyly, her glossy curls flicking in the wind. She put up a hand to comb them back from her face before meeting my eyes again. "Maybe . . . you could put in a word for me with Uncle James? He could use the help, but you know what he's like. Always saving a spot for the apple of his eye. If you really mean it, Emmy, if you're going to let me have Tomes . . . he'll need your permission. To feel like he's not stepping on your toes, giving you another reason to leave."

"Then I'll make sure he knows he has my blessing," I said, reaching for her hand on impulse. "Okay? I know I haven't exactly been generous with you in the past, and maybe . . . no, *definitely* that's my bad. But I really do want this for you."

She smiled more fully, giving my hand an answering little squeeze. We sat like that for a few minutes, hand in hand, basking in the magic gusting off the lake. Two Harlows atop their hill.

"If you do stay," Delilah said eventually, breaking our companionable silence, "can I just say I hope it's not only because of the communion? I hope you stay because you really love it here, and you can't imagine putting down roots anywhere else. Because that's what this town deserves, Emmy. And those of us who live here, too."

As LINDEN AND I stepped into Tintagel's ornate ballroom—its arched windows paned with intricate stained glass, the soaring cathedral ceiling painted with murals of heraldic beasts and mist-shrouded isles, a marble starburst mosaic flecked with gold underfoot—I didn't spot Talia in the dense crowd of revelers.

Distinctive as she was, she'd be harder to recognize tonight; falling as it always did on All Hallows Eve, the crowning gala was traditionally a masquerade.

"You ready for this, Em?" Linden asked me, her arm looped through mine. She was masked, loosely, as a marigold, in a radiant gold-shot dress with a crown of flowers on her head, her eyes hidden behind a gauzy yellow mask. It was a stunning look against the deep brown of her skin; she looked less like a flower and more like a sun.

"As I'll ever be," I said. As badly as I wanted to see Talia, the thought of it made me equally nervous. She was a tempest at even the most predictable of times, and I had no idea what to expect from her tonight. "At least they didn't skimp on the wine."

We'd managed to snag some as soon as we arrived, the wineglasses crisp and airy as wafers, almost weightless in your hand. The wine itself tasted like very expensive dried cherries soaked in milk, ridiculously balanced and smooth. Turns out, money *can* buy you some of the best things in life.

And the Blackmoores hadn't spared any expense, presumably to demonstrate how much their defeat hadn't even dinged their lofty self-regard. An extravagant buffet lined a banquet table set against one of the walls, its heaps of hors d'oeuvres, steaming roasts, and tiny frosted cakes magically replenishing. Fiery autumn leaves swirled above us in intricate patterns, like a collage in perpetual motion, and the room was lit by hundreds of hovering miniature moons moving through their phases. Whatever Blackmoore minions were tasked with maintaining such demanding spells for hours really had their work cut out for them.

But even the Blackmoores couldn't completely mask the collective drop in their morale, a subdued pall hanging over them. As far as I could tell, Gareth wasn't even here, probably licking his wounds and too embarrassed to show his face; or maybe he'd been stuck with maintaining some of the ornate spells, as a punishment for his failure. Unlikely to be true, coddled as he was, but still, I got a jolly kick out of the thought. In contrast, the Avramovs were in full raucous celebration mode, thumping one another on the shoulders, bursting into snippets of strange song, and generally having what passed for a ball with them.

Then their ranks parted to reveal Talia, who'd spotted me and Lin and had started making her way toward us.

She wore a mulberry corset in alternating panels of satin and leather, above a floor-length riot of spiky charcoal tulle, like the skirt of an extremely punked-out wedding dress. Her silver mask was engraved with scales, and a wolf's head pendant hung below her restored garnet. Her hair was half-up, thistle flowers embedded in the complicated braids that wound around her head.

She looked like a dark angel, like something that had been born in some shadow paradise. My heart swelled almost painfully to see her, the bottom of my stomach dropping out, as if I was on a too-abrupt elevator ride.

"And so the witches of the vengeance pact meet again," she said as she reached us, a cool smile curving her lips. "And victorious, no less!"

"Damn straight," Linden said, raising her glass. "Congratulations to the whole fam! And no shade from the Thorns, in case you were worried we might be holding it against you. Rowan's practically being hailed as a hero for his part in knocking the Blackmoores down a peg."

"I wasn't worried," Talia admitted. "We've never even had our turn at the helm. And besides, being salty about it would run against your wholesome grain, Angelcake."

She tilted her head to look at me, her eyes glinting lupine behind the shadows cast by the mask, and my breath snagged in my throat.

"Thank you for this boon, Harlow," she said, so formally my chest constricted. "My family is in your debt. And whatever else they may say about us, Avramovs never forget our friends."

So I was Harlow, again, and worse yet, a *friend*. You know what, I thought with a surge of determination, to hell with that.

"Then I'd like to collect right now," I said, lifting my chin, "by claiming this dance."

Talia hesitated for a moment, clearly torn; I wished her mask were a little smaller, hiding less of her face. As it was, I had no idea how to read the unyielding set of her full lips, the stern cast of her jaw. Was it just hard-shelled composure, a façade thrown up to safeguard her true feelings, or was all hope lost between us?

Then she shrugged a little, and held out her hand. "Easy enough, as return favors go. Consider it yours."

I handed my glass to Lin and took Talia's hand, a tingle rippling through me at the familiar heat of her palm as I let her draw me toward the dance floor. Compared to the gala at The Bitters, the very human string sextet in one corner was utterly conventional, playing the kind of elegant, undemanding music that let you float thoughtlessly around the floor.

"Tawny owl," she said eventually, taking in my feathered mask, the dove gray silk and crisp white lace of my dress. "Cute. And Harlow colors, this time around?"

"Let's say I'm turning over a new leaf," I said, trying to mimic her easy tone, and not let on how rattled I was by her proximity, her hand at the small of my back and her perfume stealing into my nose. "Talia, am I . . . am I allowed to ask about it? How it was with the shades?"

"Sure, why not," she said, lifting a shoulder, as if being mega-possessed was, all things considered, not *that* big of a deal. "It's not like I'm going to forget it anytime soon, whether I talk about it or not. It was . . . well, completely fucking terrible. And also phenom-enal, the most stomach-dropping thrill I've ever experienced. I thought for sure I was going to die if it went on even a minute longer, and at the same time I didn't want it to ever end. Tough to describe, if you weren't there."

I swallowed hard, unable to imagine what that must have been like for her, held suspended between such extremes as she strad-dled both sides of the veil. "I'm so sorry that happened to you."

"Well, don't be. *That* wasn't your fault," she said, as if other things indisputably *were*. "We all agreed to try. And it worked, didn't it? Because here we are. Thanks to you, we took the bas-tards down just like we set out to do. You brought it home for us, for the coven of the spurned."

Then why, I wondered miserably, wasn't I happier? I couldn't feel even a trace of that electric connection between us, as if it'd decayed to nothing and blown away, like a volatile element with a very short half-life.

But just because I couldn't feel it, that didn't mean it was gone, just that it was in hiding. And I knew a little something about that, didn't I?

"So, I'm staying," I said in a rush, before I could give myself time to second-guess what I was about to say to her. "For as long as it takes me to transcribe this wild-ass ride for posterity, at the very least. After that, I'll just have to see. But I've already let En-chantify know I'm transitioning to working remotely—and they're okay with it, as long as I still commute for a week or so of in-person meetings each month. So I'm going to sublet my Chicago place and find one here in town instead."

I could see Talia's eyebrows lift behind her mask, but she said nothing, as if I'd stunned her into silence.

"Because you were right," I added. "I *have* been hiding. I thought I could build myself into someone different, someone new . . . but it turns out maybe that's not what I want. Maybe I want to be exactly who I was supposed to be. The Harlow scion, a Thistle Grove witch. And Thistle Grove witches always come back, anytime they leave."

Her lips quirked, just slightly, before she pressed them to-gether, but that was the only sign she gave that she'd even heard me.

"And I had this . . . this maybe wild idea," I continued, faltering a little at her stonewalling. "Of brokering a partnership with the Arcane Emporium, for some sort of exclusive monthly arrange-ment for the boxes. Hopefully being the Victor will draw more foot traffic your way regardless. But with this town's history, and your whole sexy-evil-sorceress vibe, Avramovs are internet gold. And I think I could make a solid pitch to Elena, demonstrate how much inventory you could move if you worked with Enchantify."

She tilted her head to the side, thoughtfully this time. But still, not a word from her.

"Because you were also right about us," I soldiered on, though I was beginning to feel like I was maybe going to wither under this unyielding onslaught of silence. "You and me, I mean. I could very easily more-than-like you, too. And I . . . Talia, honestly, I think I already do."

Nothing but quiet scrutiny, from the darkness that hid her crystalline eyes.

"Talia, please, will you just *say* something," I begged. "I'm *dying* here."

"Why are you doing this, Emmy?" she said, low and a little hoarse, nothing at all like that controlled tone she'd been using until now. "I need to know. Because it can't be just about me—I'm not making that mistake again, especially not with you. There has to be something else here for you. Something besides us."

"That's the thing. There is," I said, my heart skipping a beat at this thaw, because here it was—she was finally giving me an opening. "Remember how I knew it was raining, before we . . . the night of the séance? Turns out it *wasn't* the mantle, after all."

I explained the communion with Thistle Grove, and the role the Harlows played in distilling the lake's magic for everyone else to use. How my intimate knowledge of the town had even helped me secure our victory for her.

"How interesting," she said once I was done, in an unwitting echo of her mother. "And you're right, it's the very pinnacle of bullshit that no one even knows the Harlows are our power plant. If it were me, I would want *everyone* to know. Shit, I'd want some kind of tithe imposed on the rest of us."

"I was thinking I'd start by including it in my Arbiter's account," I said. "So future Harlows never have to doubt their worth, their intrinsic value to this town. And that's not the only thing, either. It's . . ."

I lapsed for a moment, trying to explain what had happened to my dreams for myself, what being back in this town had done to my heart. What Delilah, in her tart, blunt way, had helped me realize.

"It's that I do love it here," I finished. "For its own sake. That it's everything I remember, but better, even more. Even if it weren't for being its voice . . . I want this to be my place again. I want this to be *my* town."

"And you really think it'll be enough for you?" she asked, and now I heard the barely restrained urgency roiling beneath the surface of her voice, the desperate, surging hope that matched my own. "Enough, forever, to make you stay?"

"More than enough," I said, my hand tightening on hers. "Especially if it means I get to be with you."

Her lips curving, she leaned in to kiss me, sending joy roaring through me like a flash fire. I wound both arms around her neck, and for a moment we just swayed together, mouth to mouth, heedless of the music, caught up in nothing but each other, fireworks exploding vast and golden in my chest.

"You were right, too, you know," she said when she drew back. "The next time you head back to Chicago, I want to come with you."

"Wait—*really*? You do?"

"Really," she assured me, with sparkling eyes and a sweet, closed-lip smile. "At the very least, I've got to experience the travesty of a fifteen-dollar cocktail for myself. I hear they're unmissable."

Before I could reply, a bright, high chiming filled the air; Delilah had stepped up to the little podium at the front of the room, the wreath glinting in her hands. The mantle wasn't on her shoulders anymore, because there was nothing left to arbitrate. The only thing left to do to close the Gauntlet was the wreathing ceremony itself.

"Don't go anywhere, Emmy Harlow," Talia ordered—and there was that smile again, that wicked marauder's grin I loved so much, sending my heart soaring in my chest. "You're going to want to see this."

"Wouldn't dream of missing it," I assured.

When she stepped up onto the podium next to Delilah, I couldn't keep a grin from stealing across my face at the thought that I was staying, and she was mine, that all of this was real. I was so beside myself with excitement, so giddy with pure thrill, that I barely heard any of my cousin's no doubt carefully rehearsed ceremonial speech.

And then Delilah was offering Talia the wreath.

"Do you accept the Victor's Wreath, Scion Avramov, and all that it entails?" she said, with a beatific little smile. Truly, my cousin *lived* for this ritualized shit.

"I do not," Talia announced, in a belling voice meant to carry through the room.

As a ripple of surprise raced through the guests, my own chest tightened with apprehension; what the hell was she doing? And why?

Then she looked directly at me, and though I still couldn't see her eyes, I swear I could *feel* the sly glint of mischief flickering in them like a pilot light.

"I cede the wreath, and all that it entails," she continued, "to my champion, Emmeline of House Harlow. The next Victor of Thistle Grove."

The low buzz of surprise blossomed into bedlam, a riot of shocked conversation that overtook the room.

"Can she even *do* that?" someone called out, and the uproar only heightened when Delilah nodded, spreading her hands to indicate her helplessness, and looking just the slightest bit annoyed that Talia was so decisively stealing the show from her.

Then Linden appeared beside me, grinning from ear to ear, her hand an insistent nudge to my lower back. "You heard your woman, didn't you? Go get that wreath, tiger."

"Did you know she was going to do this?" I demanded, my ears ringing tinny with shock, my heart pummeling my chest with such force it felt like it might jolt loose a rib.

"I didn't, but I'm not surprised . . . pure Talia power move. And what's more, she's right to do it. You earned this, Emmy. And now she's giving it to you."

With Lin's encouragement, I made my way through the crowd, barely feeling the press of people against me before they parted to make way, my face numb and thoughts spinning wild—and then a sudden, fierce spark of elation lit deep in my gut. Everything I couldn't have, all the things being a Harlow had denied me, the scars that I still bore . . . none of it mattered anymore. Because I was about to be the greatest possible Someone I could imagine. The magical Victor of this town, *and* the voice of Thistle Grove.

A new kind of history in the making, and the chance to make it my own.

My hands shook as I stepped onto the podium beside Talia, but she steadied me with an arm wound around my waist, nudging my hip with hers. Lilah looked at me like she was half happy for me, and half hated my entire guts—which, at this point, was understandable.

"Do *you*, Scion Harlow, accept the wreath and all that it entails?" she asked, with exasperated emphasis, like, *Please no one pull any further shit, this is not the day.*

"I do," I said, my voice shaking only just a little, and this time, to my utter surprise, the room exploded into applause; from the Thorns and Harlows, and even the Avramovs, once they saw their matriarch clapping for me with a knowing twinkle in her eyes. A sardonic smile hovered on her mouth, like she wasn't wholly in favor of this sudden reversal, but she certainly thought it *interesting.*

To be fair, she'd had an entire lifetime of experience at being baited and switched by Talia. She was probably the one who'd taught her how to do it at all.

In the leftmost corner of the ballroom, I finally spotted Gareth, flanked by a cluster of his cronies. He was giving me a sardonic slow clap, an expression of cultivated boredom glazing his handsome face. But his eyes flashed when our gazes met, with something like deep—and deeply grudging—respect, and he dropped his chin to give me the very tiniest of nods, like, *I see you, Emmy Harlow.*

I didn't return the nod, but I held his stare until he dropped it first, a ruddy flush blotching up his neck.

Not that I needed recognition from him, but it still rocked to know he'd never have the luxury of forgetting my face again.

Then the leaves were whirling all around me, the hovering moons waxing full all at once. The wreath settled on my head, and I was swept off the podium, crowded by a breathless crush of Harlow joy. My nana was the first to reach me, wrapping me in a ferocious hug as she declared, "You frigging *crushed* it, my Emmy . . . I'm so goddess-damned proud of you, peep!" in the kind of ringing tones that carried even across the growing clamor in the hall.

After her, my aunts Vivienne and Felicity pressed in, followed by their partners and kids, and my father's cousins—and finally, my parents, both with tears streaming down their faces from beneath their masks.

"I'm so happy for you, my love," my mother whispered into my ear, my poor father too choked up to even formulate the words, his lips trembling with emotion. "So very, very happy."

"Me too, Mom." I managed, my own cheeks wet. "This is . . . it's everything, you know? More than I could have wanted."

Then I turned to find Lin waiting for me; the friend who was as much my soul-home as this town itself. We slung arms over each other's shoulders and tilted our foreheads together, grinning into each other's giddy faces. "We did it, Lins," I whispered to her, biting my lip. "We really did, my bud," she whispered back, blinking away shining tears behind her organza mask. "We brought the damn house down, the three of us—with a little help from Row, I guess. And now you get to build us a new one."

"The highly equitable baller mansion of our dreams," I assured her. "And thank you, for loving me. Even when I didn't deserve it."

"I know you, don't I? Always figured you'd deserve it *eventually*."

She released me, scrunching her nose in a sweet goodbye and squeezing my hand one last time as she drew away, drifting back toward the Thorns. I watched her go, still biting back tears. How lucky I was to have such an enduring sanctuary in my best friend, and a second family in hers; the kind of generous people who could accept me back into their fold after years of distance and silence, as if I were truly theirs by blood.

Maybe I hadn't eaten a *totally* unreasonable amount of kittens in my former life, after all.

Then Talia was there, drawing me into the warm, perfumed haven of a hug. I flung my arms around her, squeezing back so hard she eked out a little squeak.

"Careful there, Harlow. I know I'm your forever favorite now, but don't love me to death just yet. Or I'll haunt you for an *exceedingly* long time."

"I can't believe you did this!" I said, shaking my head, still a little short of breath. "I just can't believe it."

"Oh, it's for the best." She pulled back, grinning wide and dazzling at my happiness, to sweep tears off my cheeks with her thumbs. "Let's be real, Avramovs are much more suited to subversion than governance. You'll be way fucking better at this than I would've been. And it's Samhain, right? Just think of it as both my trick and my treat."

"I . . . thank you, Talia. Thank you so, so much." I blinked back fresh tears, overwhelmed, so happy I almost couldn't stand it.

So this was what people meant, when they talked about the best night of their life. I thought you couldn't know it in the moment, that it became clear only after, viewed through the forgiving lens of hindsight. But tonight I was home, in the town that had my heart, with the wreath on my head and Talia Avramov in my arms.

And nothing else would ever come close to this.

"This is the absolute best thing," I told her, lifting a hand to cup her warm cheek. "The best gift anyone has ever given me."

"I *have* been known to be thoughtful to a fault." Her smile widened, teeth snaring her lower lip as she nuzzled into my palm. "But don't thank me just yet. I haven't even told you where we're going to celebrate."

"Well then, enlighten me, woman."

"The Wormwood Suite, back home. I've got something . . . very special in mind for us." She tangled a hand in my hair and drew me close, for a slow, lingering kiss that made me catch my breath. "I promised to show it to you, remember, way back at the gala?

And like I said, Avramovs never forget. Especially not when they're kind of in love."

"You are *such* a hopeless romantic, Talia Avramov," I told her, laughing against her lips. "Lucky for you, I'm kind of in love with you, too. And you know what else? Matching tattoos *can* be very tasteful."

"That's the spirit, Harlow," Talia whispered, drawing me back in. "Always knew you'd come around."

Acknowledgments

Every book is the culmination of a long dream—but this one was special to me, a story I've been gearing up to tell since I began writing. It was also a refuge, a safe and happy haven in a seemingly endless, terribly difficult year that robbed so many of us of so much. As such, I'll always be profoundly grateful to the many people who helped make this magical escape (and next step in my writing career) possible for me.

My agent, Taylor Haggerty, and all the other sorceresses of Root Literary: you spin dreams into books (and advances, heh), and I can't imagine navigating this journey without you. I'm especially indebted to Taylor for lending me her exceptional brain to help develop the original premise behind this book. Tay, your brainstorm emails are second to none in both inspiration and comedic gold, and it's a continuing joy and privilege to trust you with my stories.

The entire team at Berkley Books, including but not limited to: Jessica Brock, Stephanie Felty, Elisha Katz, Bridget O'Toole, Katie

ACKNOWLEDGMENTS

Anderson, and Angela Kim. You've done so much for me and this book already, and I feel so lucky to have you at my back.

My magnificent editor, Cindy Hwang, an all-around exceptional person—working with you is a dream in itself. I'm keenly aware of how few authors are lucky enough to ever get the kind of opportunity you extended to me; I'll never forget how hard you fought for me and this story. Thank you for loving and "getting" the witches of Thistle Grove every bit as much as I do, and here's to us spending lots more time with them!

My critique group buddies—Chelsea Sedoti, Adriana Mather, and Jilly Gagnon—who are always among my first readers. You're all very shiny diamonds, and I hope our Tuesdays together stretch out as close as possible to infinity.

I've been fortunate to have the kind of best friends who see you staunchly through the times when life is way weirder than fiction—you know who you are and how much I love you. (But just in case there's any confusion, you're Danea, Sharee, Claire, Jilly, Julie, Cara, and Elisar. You have seen some *things*, and I can't wait to hug you all again over gimlets.) I've also gotten to know some wonderful new friends in Chicago: Tereza, Mike, Sophia, and Olivia; Raquel, Rick, Ricky, Bella, and Micah; Nora, Mike, Bene, Myra, and Ella; and Alit, thank you for keeping my spirits up and being such generous neighborhood friends.

I owe so much to my family for each book I write, but especially this one. Thank you to my brother and parents for their enduring support; especially my mother, whose great sacrifice—though she'd *never* call it that—in taking care of my son basically night and day while I wrote this gave me the freedom to run wild.

And thanks to Caleb, who gave me and our little lion-bear Leo stability in some very turbulent times, often at great expense to himself.

I live in fear of forgetting someone crucial when writing acknowledgments; if I've managed to mess it up this time, please know that I do appreciate you, and the omission is COVID's fault and not mine.

Payback's a Witch

LANA HARPER

Questions for Discussion

1. At the very beginning of the book, when Emmy returns to Thistle Grove, she dismissively refers to the town's magical beauty as "so damn extra"—and her own magicless life in Chicago as real, the life she's chosen for herself. Do you believe Emmy's value judgments about either place? Do you think she believes them herself?

2. When she first comes home, Emmy is a little surprised by her mother's bluntness in their initial conversation. She then compares her family's arm's-length style of relating to one another to the very different bonds that exist between the Avramovs, Thorns, and Blackmoores. Which of these relationship styles reminds you the most of your own family?

3. Do you think Emmy truly comes home only because of the pull of tradition and the impressive parental guilt trip—or is the truth more complicated?

4. The families have dramatically different magical abilities: the Thorns are green-magic healers, the Blackmoores showy illusionists, the Avramovs diviners and necromancers with one foot on either side of the veil, the Harlows recordkeepers whose tea is always the perfect temperature. Whose magic would you most like to have? And least?

5. Over the course of the book, Emmy experiences a lot of guilt for the way she interacted with her best friend, Linden, and her parents after she left town. Given the circumstances, do you think Emmy did wrong by those she left behind? Would you have behaved any differently?

6. What do you think of Emmy's experience with being the Arbiter, and the magic of the mantle? Do you think you would enjoy being immersed in such intoxicating power, or does the idea make you uneasy?

7. What do you think of Elias Harlow's decision not to share with his younger descendants the magical role the Harlows play in Thistle Grove? Would you have done things differently in his shoes?

8. Would you rather be a Victor of the Gauntlet, or, like Emmy's family, the voice of Thistle Grove? How do you think Emmy will combine her two roles? How might they complement or conflict with each other?

9. All things considered, do you think Emmy's relationship with Gareth was the worst thing to happen in her life—or possibly, the best? How might her life have looked otherwise, had the romance between them never happened?

10. Why do you think Talia chose to cede her wreath to Emmy? Do you think this was the right decision on her part? How do you think Talia's mother, Elena Avramov, feels about her daughter's course of action?

11. Emmy and her cousin Delilah have a complicated relationship. Do you think one of them is more at fault than the other? Do you have any similarly fraught relationships in your life?

12. Do you think it's likely that Emmy will spend much time in Chicago in the future? How do you think she and Talia will navigate splitting their time between Thistle Grove and the city?

13. If you could visit just one of the Thistle Grove venues described in the book—consider the Honeycake Orchards, The Bitters, Castle Camelot, Lady's Lake, Tintagel, and Tomes & Omens to get you started—what would it be, and why?

There's more to come in Thistle Grove.
Keep reading for a preview of

From Bad to Cursed

by Lana Harper.
Coming soon from Jove.

1

Deviously Done

THE THING NO one tells you about summoning demons is, sometimes you have to think outside the box.

I should know; I've been calling them up into my circles since I was a kid. My mother even encouraged it, as a slightly safer alternative to a way riskier burgeoning fascination with elder gods. (PSA, if you don't want your daughter developing an interest in the gnarlier chthonic entities before she can even ride a bike, maybe don't read her Lovecraft at bedtime. Seems obvious enough, right?)

The books go on about how summonings are supposed to be these disciplined, rule-bound affairs—and most of the time, they are, if you know what's good for you. The truth is, if you take sensible precautions, it's not nearly as dangerous as people think. And *such* a rush, too; the daemonfolk are interesting as hell, pun intended. Sometimes they're inclined to share juicy secrets or ancient spells, the kind you won't find in even the oldest, dustiest grimoires. Other times they're so gorgeous it breaks your heart, or so horrifying that even a quick glimpse before you banish them is enough to leave you panting, heart battering against your ribs, blood boiling through your veins while your whole skin rolls with chills.

Shit, even when you play it safe, there's nothing quite like a demon summoning to make you feel alive.

Of course, there's always the odd time that even a pro like me fucks it up just a *wee* bit.

As usual, I'd cast my summoning circle in the warrens of basement beneath The Bitters, in a chilly, cavernous room that had started out as Elena's third wine cellar—because who gets by with just *one* these days, certainly not my mother—and now doubled as my demonic lair. No windows, musty air that smelled like centuries-old stone and aged Bordeaux, witchlight sconces flinging trembling shadows on the walls; the perfect ambiance. The summoning spell was already whipping through me like a tempest, my protective amulets glowing hot against my chest. Everything felt like it should, all systems go.

But as soon as Malachus began to coalesce, I felt a twinge of wrongness in my gut, an unsettling, instinctive awareness that something was *off.*

According to my research, Malachus was supposed to manifest as a brawny reptilian dude, macho and mindless to the max. The type of mostly harmless demon whose bark was way worse than his bite. I hadn't summoned in a while, so tonight was meant to be just a practice flex, easing myself back into the swing of things after a little break.

But the silhouette gathering in my circle, on her knees and

with her back to me, was unmistakably femme-presenting, with the kind of ridiculous waist-to-hip ratio that would've put Cardi B to shame. A swoop of hair, black and glossy as moonlit water, curled around an even darker set of wings folded neatly against her back. I could see their outline fill with a faint scrawl like one of my own croquis sketches; a vague suggestion of feathers, before they sprang into a three-dimensional profusion of lush black down. And the scent that engulfed the cellar wasn't just the usual rank whiff of sulfur and brimstone, but something sweeter, more elegant and piercing. Lily of the valley, with a subtle patchouli twist. The kind of interesting perfume that made you want to follow someone around drooling until they told you what they wore.

When she turned to look over her shoulder at me, with massive eyes the color of molten gold, my mouth went as dry as sand. I couldn't be positive, having never seen one before—they weren't exactly a dime a dozen—but for my money, this sure looked like one of the former seraphim.

A fucking fallen angel, landed in my basement.

"Oh, Hecate's chilly tits," I whispered to myself, my heart plummeting even as a rising thrill swelled inside my stomach. "This is so very deeply fucked."

From what I'd read, the fallen were ultra-wily, temperamental, and extremely powerful—exactly the kind of unpredictable dae-monfolk I do not fuck with as a general rule.

But here she was, anyway, which meant shit was about to get *extremely* outside the box.

She whipped around to face me in a single blurring motion, still kneeling, dainty little hands folded primly on her lap. Her fingers were tipped with vicious black talons, knuckles dusted with iridescent scales. She cocked her head, examining me, the tip of a forked pink tongue peeking between her lips. Then she smiled at me, wide and feral, a flash of onyx teeth with fanged canines *and* incisors.

Let me tell you, there's something viscerally unnerving about black teeth, especially ones as sharp as hers. I had a mounting suspicion that, unlike the real Malachus—wherever the hell *he* was—this chick's demonic bite might be a lot worse than her bark.

A bloom of pure dread uncurled inside my chest, shooting down into my fingertips and toes like a falling star. Alas, the thrill-chasing part of my brain that often took the wheel at times like this downright relished it. So this wasn't going to be a lesson-learned type moment, then, I noted to myself. No big surprise there; I'd never been much good at those.

"Ill tidings!" the demon said cheerfully, in a cross between a velvety purr and some gigantic gong struck directly between my ears. Gritting my teeth, I narrowly resisted clutching at my head. When it comes to demons, a show of weakness is just about the worst thing you can do. "Whom do you serve?"

The roteness of her greeting defused the tension just a hair. Demons always start with the ill tidings bit; it's what passes for good manners with them, part of some governing daemonfolk etiquette.

I drew myself up, putting on an imperious expression modeled after my mother, and doing my level best to avoid looking as rattled as I felt. When dealing with entities from the netherworld, throwing up a badass-witch front tends to be at least half the battle.

"I serve my goddess, my ancestors, and above all, myself," I replied, the traditional response of an Avramov summoner. I don't know what the Blackmoores, Thorns, or Harlows say—in the highly unlikely event that a witch from one of Thistle Grove's other magical families has ever bantered with a demon—but I'd bet my ass on some corny noise about serving the ultimate good, light conquering darkness or whatever, cue a stirring orchestral overture. Avramovs don't buy into any of that oversimplified, good-vs-evil binary crap. Like the pragmatists we are, we've always staked our claim firmly in the gray.

The problem was, this was the part where I was meant to bind this entity by her true name. Which was going to be a neat trick, considering I almost definitely didn't have the real Malachus at hand.

"And you, Malachus Azaranthinael, appear at my will and behest," I finished, crossing my fingers behind my back. Hey, worth a shot; maybe the lore was just supremely off base on how Malachus was supposed to look. "Which means you must obey . . . and begone at once!"

"A fine sentiment," the demon crooned, with another of those awful, spine-tingling smiles. In a streak of movement, she was on her feet, naked and stupidly gorgeous, a curtain of black silk hair draped over thick curves and long, smooth limbs. Her skin glowed like a paper lantern, as if lit from within. Too bad we'd started off on such a wrong foot; she probably had some killer beauty tips. "If I were, in fact, Malachus Azaranthinael."

"If you are not, why do you appear in his stead?" I demanded, trying to enforce one final shred of protocol before this already wayward train went careening completely off the rails. Demons weren't supposed to bend the rules like this; when you summon one by their true name, what you call is meant to be what you get.

"Because, as it happens, there *is* no Malachus," she said, still grinning like the void, honest-to-goddess little flames dancing in her golden eyes. Sounds like something right out of a cheesy cartoon, but it sure didn't *feel* clichéd when the abyss was staring you dead in the face. Chills crawled under my skin, crept into my knees—the type of nerve-jangling bullshit I lived for, the reason I went all in on such foolhardy antics as this in the first place. "There is, and ever was, only me . . . and the lies of Malachus I tell, to entice dim little deathspeakers like you into calling me up, unbound."

I tried not to take being called dim *too* personally, and failed.

The books do tell you that daemonfolk lie easier than they breathe. By the sound of it, this one had invented a harmless-seeming demon as bait, embedded his name into the lore for gullible assholes like me to find, and then tied his summoning to herself, like one of those fugly deepwater anglerfish that dangle a little light for their prey. Which meant that once she appeared in answer to a Malachus summons, she'd be yanked earthside without any bindings in place.

Damn, I thought, with a grudging stab of admiration, *well played*. Demons were tricksters to the bone, and she'd gotten me good, fair and square.

"Deviously done," I said, with a little dip of the head, making one last gamble. You'd be surprised how vain some of these tricky fuckers are, and how hard they fall for a little well-placed pandering. "And when they ask me into whose clever trap I stumbled, what fearsome name shall I say?"

She rolled her huge eyes, rosebud mouth pursed in exasperated disdain, like, *Nice try, witch, but maybe get up earlier in the morning next time you try to put one over on me, eh?*

"My true name is only mine to know, but you may call me . . ." she said, appearing in a shivery instant at the circle's very edge, one fine-boned foot poised above the silver line, "Davara Circle-breaker."

A tad on the nose? Perhaps. Ominous as fuck? No doubt.

In the spirit of experimentation, I raised my hands and flung a banishment charm at her, murmuring under my breath—followed by another, and another. She stayed staunchly corporeal, her inky smile only widening, her smooth form not even flickering under the assault.

"Oooh, Yaga's Baneful Banishment, how quaint!" she squealed. "I have not seen *that* one in centuries!"

She pressed against the boundary, the air around her rippling like a heat mirage. The cellar trembled with the sheer force of her assault, little shock waves radiating out from the circle as her will fought hard against the barrier of mine, testing its give. My cluster of protective amulets had already turned searing against my chest, but even my fail-safe runes were badly outclassed; they weren't going to keep me from getting soul-eaten by something of her caliber, not if she managed to break free.

I stumbled, barely keeping my feet, my heart pumping double time as uncut adrenaline crashed through my veins. If the demon got through me, she'd run roughshod all over Thistle Grove before someone else—probably my own mother, *double fuck*—managed to lock her down and banish her. Then I'd never live down the mortification of not having handled my own demonic business, not to mention whatever punishment the tribunal saw fit to impose on me.

That is, if I even lived long enough to worry about punishment.

"Not today, bitch," I muttered under my breath, thinking on my feet. "I am *not* the one for this."

I arranged my fingers into a different kind of conjuring, clouds of vaporous black seeping from my fingertips and gathering around my hands. You never really got used to the feel of ectoplasm, not even after years of handling it, its icy stickiness clinging like a noxious second skin. But my magic itself felt wild and slick, a quicksilver thread racing up my spine and churning giddy in my head.

Then came a headlong rush of ghosts, harkening to my call.

The demon blinked in confusion, as the whole host of shades that called The Bitters home began materializing around her one by one. Given that my ancestral demesne was nearly three centuries old, and impressively haunted at that, there were a *lot* of them. A mosh pit's worth of hazy gray forms, tattered and nearly translucent, trailing smudgy limbs and writhing hair.

At first, they emanated only bemused annoyance, having been rudely yanked away from whatever ghostly business they'd been minding before I called on them. Then they noticed Davara Circlebreaker, still poised at the edge of my circle, a tiny wrinkle of concern now marring her smooth brow.

Their irritable rumbling abruptly changed pitch into a disgruntled hum—which escalated very, *very* quickly into the kind of blood curdling wail you could only really describe as "eldritch."

The thing about summoning circles is, they're a one-way barrier, meant to keep things in rather than out. And the thing about ghosts of the restless dead is, they're territorial by nature, hostile to interlopers on their domain. I'd guessed that a trespasser like Davara—one that belonged in this realm even less than they did—would read as the ultimate provocation. And despite the huge power differential between a first-tier demon and a bunch of revenants, I was banking on strength in numbers, the way an angry swarm of ants can bring down an elephant.

As the throng of shades stormed Davara, a roar of pain and rage rising from the center of the circle once they'd closed in on her, I could see that I'd been right on both counts.

Then the shriek cut off abruptly in a massive flare of scarlet light, as the demon finally called it quits on this earthside outing. Apparently the prospect of munching on a witch's soul and wreaking some small-town havoc wasn't worth the trouble of getting nipped to (un)death by a rabid spectral horde.

"Woooooo!" I cheered, yanking down a victory fist as the light faded away, bright afterbursts still popping in my vision. "And that is how it's *done*, motherfuckers!"

The ghostly mob slowed in their maddened whirling, settling back to hover just above the stones. Then they turned to fix the glowing craters of their eyes on me—aka, the presumptuous scally who'd seen fit to drag them here.

"Oh, fuck me," I groaned, the garnet at my throat throbbing as I flexed my fingers. "Okay, then. Let's go."

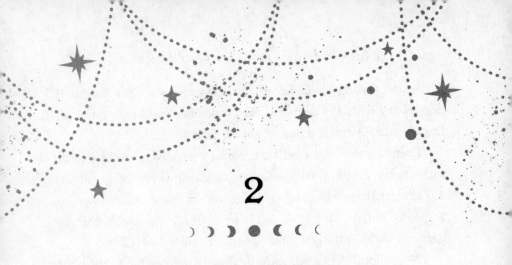

2

Not Enough Heart

I'M NOT GONNA say I agree with Aunt Elena, because that would be treacherous," Letha said, sidestepping the hairy animatronic tarantula that leapt out at her, hissing, from inside the dark passageway that led out of the teenage witch's lair. "But let's say, just as a hypothetical, if you turned *my* house into a poltergeist nest for shits and giggles? I, too, might be a little spicy with you for a while."

My cousin was referring to the lingering psychic fallout from my improvised banishment. It had taken me all night to subdue my ghost militia, and even then the fix had been only temporary; over two weeks later, we still had knives embedding themselves in the ceiling, shadowy figures hovering over you while you slept, doors slamming open and closed in a syncopated rhythm designed to drive us all mad. Not to mention the way the mirrors distorted your reflection into a Munchian horror show when you were just trying to put on some fucking mascara. You know, the kind of trippy shit that really got under your skin.

It had also scared my three cats half to death, not to mention the zebra finches, which was the part I felt the guiltiest about. Maybe it was my imagination, but even Starbuck the hedgehog seemed a little nervy.

Suffice it to say, things between me and Elena had been . . . strained, ever since.

"Just because you're turning it into a hypothetical doesn't make it any less treacherous," I informed my cousin, summoning a witchlight to hover above my palm so we didn't have to fumble through the dark. We kept the entire haunted house space—a retrofitted warehouse adjoining the Arcane Emporium, our family's occult megastore—glamoured with a fortification of the Oblivion Charm that cloaked all of Thistle Grove. Any normie visitor or member of the cast that happened to catch my spell would forget it within seconds. "Also, it wasn't for shits and giggles. I had to get rid of the demon *somehow*, didn't I? Even Elena's not such an agent of chaos that she'd be down with me unleashing an ancient big bad unto the mortal plane."

"A big bad *you* summoned in the first place, Issa," Letha pointed out with irritating logic. "For the aforementioned shits and giggles."

"Okay, fair. And I do wish Davara would've talked to me just a little before trying to bust out of the circle," I added, pouting. "I had so many pressing questions. Like, do first-tier demons naturally have such popping skin, or does she moisturize with, like, the tears of the damned or something? Do they all smell weirdly amazing, or was that just her? The kind of stuff that isn't in the books."

Letha shot me an aggrieved look. "Yeah, about all that . . . how come you didn't invite me to spot you? Davara Circlebreaker sounds like a snack. And maybe I could have helped, before things got that far out of hand."

I squeezed Letha's shoulder apologetically as we stepped into the next scene—then yanked her out of the way as a hysterical prom queen in ruffled fuchsia taffeta nearly barreled into us, fleeing a chainsaw-wielding prom king with artfully disheveled feathered hair. A cluster of real visitors—cowering by a table scattered with severed hands, corsages, and a cut-glass bowl of bubbling "poisoned" punch—shrieked with terror, then dissolved into panicky giggles.

As the prom king sprinted past us, muttering to himself, I appraised his shredded powder-blue tux and bloodstained Converse with a critical eye. Stylishly fiendish, sure; but also just kind of *dull*, in a way I couldn't quite put my finger on.

"Trust me, she was on the too-evil side of evilly hot," I assured Letha. "Even by your standards."

"Well, she might've been an edge case. And now we won't ever know, will we." Letha fixed me with a baleful side-eye, which, given how big and hooded her dark eyes were, was *extremely* baleful. "Seeing as I wasn't invited."

"I'm sorry, angel. It'd been a minute since I summoned, and . . . I don't know. I wanted to do it solo, I guess, blow off some steam. Try to get my groove back."

Letha gave a grudging nod, her cool expression thawing just a touch. She knew I'd been in an indeterminate funk lately, though she hadn't pushed me on it yet. My best friend and second cousin wasn't the cuddliest of creatures, but she *was* rock solid, the kind of unflaggingly loyal boulder of a person you always wanted at your back. You wouldn't want to find yourself downhill of Letha, because in true Sisyphean fashion, she'd roll right back down and crush you. But you could lean on her anytime you needed, rest against her with all your weight and know she'd never budge an inch.

"Okay, so you get a pass this once," she allowed. "But if I miss another demonic calamity, harsh words will be spoken. Of that you may be sure."

"Understood. So, what do you think?" I asked her, surveying the murderous prom unfolding around us. Torn banners fluttered from the exposed pipes far above, ironically wishing the class of '83 a happy life. While the prom king chased the queen around, oblivious couples covered in varying degrees of gore swayed lazily to the discordant strains of a slow, macabre cover of "Sweet Caroline." Letha's set design was impeccable as always, detail oriented and maximally creepy; my assistant director had a real eye for elevating horror ephemera into an art form. "Is it still working, six months in?"

As artistic director of the Emporium's haunted house, responsible for everything from designing costumes to hiring the cast members, this storyline was my brainchild. The basic premise was: a teenage witch just coming into her power had been spurned by the prom king/quarterback/all-purpose popular dickbag. Fueled by rage, she'd cast a bloodlust spell on the whole town that had belittled her, turning everyone into murderous fiends. Kind of *The Craft* meets *Carrie*, with a twist—and way less menstrual blood, because, ugh, no thanks.

Besides the prom, other set pieces included the teen witch's bedroom (complete with a bloody pentagram, black candles, and a human sacrifice; all the tacky accoutrements real witches never use), a classroom in which a homicidal chemistry teacher terrorized his students, a daycare full of evil munchkins running amok, and cheer practice gone heinously wrong.

"I think this one was a win," Letha replied, with a nod that rippled the slick curtain of her pink-and-purple-striped black hair. Courtesy of her Japanese mom, Letha had the kind of shining, slippery tresses I'd spent my teens chasing with too many products and an elaborate straightening regimen, before giving up the dream in my twenties. "Thematically consistent, but with enough variety to keep them on their toes. A lively palette, compelling audio, wet work decent but not overdone. A *vast* improvement over the circus of the damned, no question."

I frowned, chewing on a knuckle. "You don't think it all feels just a touch . . . uninspired?"

"Uninspired?" She glanced over at a tableau unfolding by the punch table, the teen witch cackling maniacally above a cheerleader caught in the thrashing death throes of the poison punch. "I mean, it's a little slapstick, sure, but that's part of the fun. Looks like the tourists are eating it up."

"I suppose." I nibbled on the inside of my cheek, trying to figure out what integral piece it was that I felt might be missing. "The narrative just feels a little lackluster, that's all. Like there's not enough heart."

Letha tilted her head, flicking me a bemused look. "Unless you mean that literally—which, yes, no bloody ventricles currently featuring in the program—I'm really not following, Iss. This is one of our most elaborate takes yet. And the Yelp reviews bear it out, too. Whatever we do next, we'd be smart to keep it along similar lines."

She was right; we'd noticed a significant uptick in ticket sales over the past six months, much more revenue pouring in from the haunted house than we'd seen in years. Part of it was the fact that, since Emmy Harlow had won the Victor's Wreath during the Gauntlet of the Grove last Samhain, the town's magic was no longer exclusively favoring the Blackmoores—Thistle Grove's wealthiest and most powerful magical family, and our primary competitors for immersive entertainment. As a result, the rest of us were finally getting our fair slice of the tourist pie again. And now that we were well into spring, we were considering a redesign for the upcoming Flower Moon Festival, a town celebration organized around Beltane, the pagan holiday that usually brought the most tourists we saw outside of Halloween.

I should have been stoked to launch into a revamp; there'd been a time when there was nothing I loved more than bringing a new horror story to life, especially the costumes for the cast. I used to lose myself for weeks in the design, even dreaming in fashion sketches, their flowing lines and splashes of color weaving through my delta waves as they stitched themselves into full-blown garments while I slept.

Managing the haunted house may have been my day job, but for a long time, designing those costumes had also been my joy.

Maybe the real problem wasn't that Fiendish Eighties Murder Prom didn't have enough heart; maybe the trouble was that *my* heart wasn't in it anymore. A thing I felt guilty enough about that I hadn't even mustered up the courage to share it with Letha, who knew everything else worth knowing about my life, and had since we were creepy toddlers together.

"I guess I'll have to talk it through with Elena," I said, suppressing a reflexive wince. I had a debrief and planning session scheduled with her at the Emporium right after this. To say I wasn't looking forward to a dialogue with my mother, especially in her role as Avramov matriarch, barely brushed the surface of understatement. "It's her call in the end, anyway. Maybe she'll want to keep a successful show in place for another season, make it easy on us."

Letha stopped dead, so abruptly that one of the ghastly dancing couples bumped into her. She shot them a glare so concentrated and intimidating that they hastily sidled away, discarding any budding plans of drawing her into the scene. Maybe they recognized her as one of their bosses, or maybe it was just the intense Capricorn energy Letha exuded. Despite her filigreed features and general pastel-goth aesthetic, Letha had that effect on people, like one of those gorgeous tropical frogs that actually signal their danger with pretty colors.

"What is with you, Iss?" she demanded, turning back to me. "I know you've been going through . . . *something*, for a while now. I also know you haven't wanted to talk about it, and I've been respectful of your space, like the exceptional human being I think we can agree I am. But we're just about reaching the outer limits of my patience."

"Letha, come on. It's not that serious."

"Isn't it? Because you've been shambling around like some subpar clone of your former self for months now. I mean, seriously, *you're* suddenly not feeling Fiendish Eighties Murder Prom? *You* don't want to brainstorm shiny new ways to terrorize the tourists?"

"Could it be that I'm just tired? Maybe coming down with something?"

Her eyes narrowed beneath the swooping wings of metallic pastel eyeshadow. "Isidora Avramov, I'm starting to think you've been body-snatched. Are we talking an astonishingly lame demonic passenger here? Should I be planning a prophylactic banishment just in case? Wouldn't be pretty, but I'll admit it's crossed my mind."

I chuckled despite myself at the idea of Letha attempting to spring a stealth exorcism on me, like the world's most unpleasant surprise birthday party.

"I'm still me, I swear on my witch's soul," I assured her, looping my arm through hers and tugging her gently toward the exit. "If I *wasn't* me, would I know to offer to buy you an apology Revenant 'Rita at the Shamrock Cauldron tonight, with extra pickled jalapeños?"

"Make that two 'Ritas, plus several shots of Cazadores," she muttered, reluctantly letting herself be drawn forward. "And it had all better come with a detailed walk-through of what's going on with you."

"If not tonight, then soon, promise." I gave her arm a little squeeze. "And it's really sweet, by the way, that you love me enough to throw a surprise banishment in my honor."

"Don't flatter yourself, cuz." A corner of her mouth twitched with the suggestion of a smile. "It's only because I may die of boredom if I don't get the old you back soon."

Such a liar. Beneath the flippant façade, Letha cared about her loved ones with unparalleled ferocity, even for an Avramov, and "blood is thicker than water" may as well have been our unofficial family motto. ("We neither break nor bend" being the formal creed.) I knew she'd been genuinely concerned for me, and if anything, the fact that I couldn't bring myself to open up to my own best friend and cousin about what was really going on made me feel even worse.

And even more of a traitor, to boot.

"Still," I said, letting her have this one. It was the least I owed her, what with everything I was holding back. "It's the thought that counts. And you know demonic shit has always been my love language."

Photo by Gary Alpert, Deafboyphotography

Writing as Lana Popovic, Lana is the author of four YA novels about modern-day witches and historical murderesses. Born in Serbia, she grew up in Hungary, Romania, and Bulgaria before moving to the U.S., where she studied psychology and literature at Yale University, law at Boston University, and publishing at Emerson College. She lives in Chicago with her family.

CONNECT ONLINE

LanaPopovicBooks.com
🐦 LanaPopovicLit
📷 Lanalyte

Ready to find
your next great read?

Let us help.

Visit prh.com/nextread